PRAISE FOR JULIE KAGAWA

"Kagawa knows just how to end a first volume for maximum cliff-hanger drama."
—*Booklist* on *Talon*

"A strong, promising start to the Talon Saga."
—*Publishers Weekly* on *Talon*

"Kagawa's fine storytelling elevates this novel within the crowded field of fantasy romance."
—*BookPage* on *Talon*

"Action-packed drama meets character-driven tension in this follow-up to *Talon*."
—*RT Book Reviews* on *Rogue*

"A worthwhile read for fans of *Talon* and Kagawa's other action-packed and satisfying fantasies."
—*School Library Journal* on *Rogue*

"Julie Kagawa is one killer storyteller."
—MTV's *Hollywood Crush* blog

"Kagawa has done the seemingly impossible and written a vampire book...that feels fresh in an otherwise crowded genre."
—*Kirkus Reviews* on *The Immortal Rules*

"[An] intense and thought-provoking series."
—*School Library Journal* on *The Eternity Cure*

"This is a true quest story...one that anyone looking for great action and inventive worldbuilding should be sure to check out."
—*RT Book Reviews* on *The Iron Knight*

"Kagawa pulls her readers into a unique world of make-believe with her fantastic storytelling."
—*Times Record News* on *The Iron Knight*

"Fans of Melissa Marr—and of Kagawa—will enjoy the ride, with Meghan's increased agency and growing power showing the series' maturity. Finally more than just a love triangle."
—*Kirkus Reviews* on *The Iron Queen*

"*The Iron Daughter* is a book that will keep its readers glued to the pages until the very end."
—*New York Journal of Books*

"*The Iron King* surpasses the greater majority of dark fantasies, leaving a lot for readers to look forward to.... The romance is well done and adds to the mood of fantasy."
—*Teenreads.com*

"*The Iron King* has the...enchantment, imagination and adventure of...*Alice in Wonderland*, *Narnia* and *The Lord of the Rings*, but with lots more romance."
—*Justine Magazine*

Books by Julie Kagawa
available from Harlequin TEEN

(all listed in series reading order)

The Talon Saga

Talon
Rogue
Soldier
Legion
Inferno

Blood of Eden

Dawn of Eden (prequel novella)+
The Immortal Rules
The Eternity Cure
The Forever Song

The Iron Fey series***

The Iron King*
Winter's Passage (ebook novella)**
The Iron Daughter*
The Iron Queen
Summer's Crossing (ebook novella)**
The Iron Knight
Iron's Prophecy (ebook novella)**
The Lost Prince
The Iron Traitor
The Iron Warrior

+Available in the *'Til the World Ends* anthology by Julie Kagawa,
Ann Aguirre and Karen Duvall
*Also available in *The Iron Fey Volume One* anthology
**Also available in print in *The Iron Legends* anthology
along with the exclusive *Guide to the Iron Fey*
***The Iron Fey series is also available in two boxed gift sets

LEGIN

NEW YORK TIMES BESTSELLING AUTHOR

JULIE KAGAWA

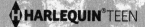

HARLEQUIN®TEEN

Recycling programs
for this product may
not exist in your area.

ISBN-13: 978-1-335-14417-1

Legion

Copyright © 2017 by Julie Kagawa

All rights reserved. Except for use in any review, the reproduction or utilization
of this work in whole or in part in any form by any electronic, mechanical or
other means, now known or hereafter invented, including xerography, photocopying
and recording, or in any information storage or retrieval system, is forbidden
without the written permission of the publisher, Harlequin Enterprises Limited,
22 Adelaide St. West, 40th Floor, Toronto, Ontario M5H 4E3, Canada.

This is a work of fiction. Names, characters, places and incidents are either the
product of the author's imagination or are used fictitiously, and any resemblance to
actual persons, living or dead, business establishments, events or locales is entirely
coincidental.

This edition published by arrangement with Harlequin Books S.A.

For questions and comments about the quality of this book, please contact us
at CustomerService@Harlequin.com.

® and TM are trademarks of Harlequin Enterprises Limited or its corporate affiliates.
Trademarks indicated with ® are registered in the United States Patent and
Trademark Office, the Canadian Intellectual Property Office and in other countries.

Printed in U.S.A.

To Tashya, Laurie and Nick, my trio of awesome.

~PART I

SACRIFICE IS NECESSARY

DANTE

She was always the favored one.

"Ember," Mr. Gordon sighed for the second time that hour. "Please pay attention. This is important. Are you listening?"

"Yes," my twin muttered, not looking up from her desk, where she was doodling cartoon figures into her textbook. "I'm listening."

Mr. Gordon frowned. "All right, then. Can you tell me what the fleshy part of a human's ear is called?"

I raised my hand. As expected, Mr. Gordon ignored me.

"Ember?" he prompted when she didn't answer. "Do you know the answer to the question?"

Ember sighed and put down her pencil. "The earlobe," she said in a voice that clearly stated, *I'm bored and I want to be somewhere else.*

"Yes." Mr. Gordon nodded. "The fleshy part of a human's ear is the earlobe. Very good, Ember. Write that down—it will be on the test tomorrow.

"All right," he continued as Ember scribbled something in her notebook. I doubted it was the answer, or anything to do with the test, so I jotted the definition down, just in case she forgot. "Next question. Human hair and fingernails are made of the same substance a dragon's claws and horns are made of. What is this substance called? Ember?"

"Um." Ember blinked. Clearly, she had no idea. "I dunno."

I started to raise my hand but stopped. There was no point.

"We discussed this yesterday," Mr. Gordon continued sternly. "All through class, we talked about the human anatomy. You should know this. A human's hair and fingernails, and a dragon's claws and horns, are all made of…?"

Come on, Ember, I thought at her. *You know this. It's in your brain, even if you were staring out the window most of class yesterday.*

Ember shrugged, slumping in her chair in a pose that said, *I don't want to be here.* Our teacher sighed and turned to me. "Dante?"

"Keratin," I answered.

He gave a brisk nod but turned back to Ember. "Yes, keratin. Your brother was paying attention," he told her, narrowing his eyes. "Why can't you do the same?"

Ember glowered. Comparing her to me was always a surefire way to make her mad. "I don't see why I have to know the difference between scales and human toenails," she muttered, crossing her arms. "Who cares what it's called? I bet the humans don't know that hair is made of kraken, either."

"Keratin," Mr. Gordon corrected, frowning back at her. "And it is *highly* important that you know what it is you are Shifting into, inside and out. If you want to mimic humans perfectly, you must know them perfectly. Even if they do not."

"I still think it's dumb," Ember mumbled, looking longingly out the window at the desert and open sky beyond the chain-link fence that surrounded the compound. Our teacher's expression darkened.

"Well, then, let's give you some motivation. If you and

Dante don't make at least ninty-five percent on your tests tomorrow, you both will be banned from the game room for a month." Ember jerked in her seat, eyes going wide with outrage, and Mr. Gordon gave her a cold smile. "*That* is how important you knowing the human anatomy is to Talon. So I would study, both of you." He waved a hand at the door. "You're dismissed."

★ ★ ★

"It's totally unfair," Ember raged as we walked across the dusty yard to our dorms. Overhead, the Nevada sun beat down on me, chasing away the chill of the air-conditioned classroom and warming my skin. *Or, should I say, my* epidermis?

I smirked at my own joke, knowing Ember wouldn't get it. And, in her current mood, she wouldn't appreciate it even if she did.

"Gordon is a bully," Ember growled, kicking a pebble with her shoe, sending it bouncing over the dusty ground. "He can't ban us from the game room for a whole month— that's completely insane. I'd go crazy—there's nothing else to *do* around here."

"Well, you could try paying attention," I suggested as we neared the long cement building at the edge of the fence. As expected, the suggestion did not go over well.

"How am I supposed to pay attention when everything is so boring?" Ember snapped, wrenching open the door. Inside, the living room was cool to the point of chilly. A pair of leather sofas sat in an L around a coffee table, and a large television hung on the opposite wall, its huge screen shiny and dark. It had over a hundred channels, everything from sci-fi to news stations to movies and sports—an attempt to keep us pacified, I suspected, though it never really worked on Ember. She would rather be outside than sitting in a room watching TV all day. The room was also spotlessly clean, despite the mess a certain sibling made of it nearly every day.

Ember stalked to one of the couches and tossed her books onto the cushions. "They never give me a break," she continued, ignoring the texts as one of them slid off the leather and fell to the floor. "They just keep pushing me—*do better, go faster, pay more attention*. Nothing I do is ever good enough." She gave me a half joking, half sour glare. "They never do that with you, Tweedledum."

"That's because I actually *pay attention*." I set my bag on the table and headed into the kitchen for something to drink. Our live-in caretaker, Mr. Stiles, was not in sight, so I figured he was either out or in his room. "They never have reason to come after me."

"Yeah, well, you don't know how lucky you are," Ember grumbled, heading down the hall to her quarters. "If you need me, I'll be in my room cramming for this stupid test tomorrow. If you hear a crash, don't panic. I've probably just smashed my head through the wall."

Right, I thought as the door to her room opened and closed with a bang. *Lucky*.

Alone in the kitchen, I poured myself a glass of orange juice and perched on the breakfast stool, brooding into the cup.

Lucky, Ember had said. Of course it would seem lucky to her. She was the favorite, the one they all paid attention to. It had always been that way. In our eleven years together, our instructors always seemed to ask her questions first, show her things first, make sure she knew what she was doing. They pushed her hard and insisted she do things right, not noticing—or seeming to care—that I already knew the answers. And when I did get them to notice, it was always to set an example for my sister. *See, Dante knows the answers. Dante already has this down.* I would kill for half the favor they showed her.

Draining the glass, I put it into the dishwasher before heading down the hall to my room. I just had to do better, I thought, resolve stealing over me. I had to work for the attention that came so easily to my sister. Ember was hotheaded and always getting into trouble; it was up to me to watch out for us both. But at the same time, if I kept working hard and excelling, eventually they would realize that I always did better than my twin. They would realize that I was the smart one; I was the one who did everything right. If Talon didn't notice what I could do, I would just *make* them see.

"Mr. Hill? The Elder Wyrm is ready for you. Please, go in."

Sitting on the couch in the cold, brightly lit lobby, I raised my head as the present caught up with me, shaking away dark thoughts and the memories of the past. I'd been thinking of Ember a lot recently, her presence weighing heavily on my mind. Guilt, perhaps, that I had failed her? That I wasn't able to keep my twin safe from her worst enemy—herself?

Standing, I nodded to the human assistant and walked toward the huge doors of Elder Wyrm's office. I couldn't think like that anymore. I wasn't eleven years old, desperate to prove I was worth something. I wasn't the pathetic, overlooked twin of the Elder Wyrm's daughter. No, I had proved myself, to all of Talon, that I was worthy of my heritage. *I* was the Elder Wyrm's right-hand man, the one she trusted with Talon's most important campaign.

And someday, if everything worked out, I would lead all of Talon. Someday, this would all be mine. I was close, so very close, to achieving what I'd set out to do all those years ago. I couldn't falter now.

The enormous wooden doors to the CEO's office loomed above me, brass handles glimmering in the light. I didn't knock or wait for the Elder Wyrm to call me in. I simply opened the doors and entered.

The Elder Wyrm was sitting at her desk, manicured nails clicking over the keyboard as her eyes scanned the computer screen. Her presence still filled the office, massive and terrifying, even though she wasn't looking at me. I walked quietly across the room and stood at the front of the desk with my hands clasped behind my back. Having an open invitation into the Elder Wyrm's office was one thing. Interrupting the Elder Wyrm, without waiting for her to acknowledge your presence, was another. I was heir to one of the largest empires in the corporate world, but she was still the CEO of Talon and the most powerful dragon in existence. Not even the son of the Elder Wyrm was exempt from protocol.

The Elder Wyrm didn't say anything or look up from her task, and I waited silently for her to finish. Finally, she clicked the mouse button, pushed the keyboard tray beneath the desktop and looked up at me. Her green-eyed gaze, identical to Ember's and my own, pierced the space between us.

"Dante." She smiled and, unlike that of many other dragons who could only imitate a smile, hers seemed genuine. Of course, that was what made her so dangerous; you never knew if what she was showing you was real or not. "Good to see you again. How was your trip back?"

"It was fine, ma'am. Thank you."

She nodded and rose, gesturing to the duo of chairs in front of the desk. I sank into one obediently and crossed my legs as the Elder Wyrm came around the desk to pin me with her stare. The weight of her gaze was suffocating, but I settled back with a calm yet expectant expression, careful not to show any fear.

"Plans are in motion," the Elder Wyrm said, and her low voice sent a shiver down my spine. "Everything is nearly in place. There is just one thing missing now. One last thing we must take care of."

My heart beat faster. I could guess what that final piece was. Of course it would be *her*. Even now, she didn't realize her importance.

"Ember Hill must be retrieved," the Elder Wyrm went on, her tone becoming frighteningly intense. The hairs on my arms rose, and something inside me shrank down in terror as the Elder Wyrm speared me with that terrible gaze. "It is imperative that she return to Talon. No more mistakes. This is what we are going to do..."

EMBER

He's gone.

I knelt in the salt, holding Garret's motionless body in my lap as the sun climbed slowly over the flats and tinged the desolate landscape the color of blood. The soldier's face was slack and pale, his skin still warm as he bled out in my arms. Around me, there were flurries of frantic movement, voices shouting, questions that might've been directed at me. But nothing seemed real. Garret was gone. I had lost him.

"Shit, he's bleeding out fast." This from Riley, kneeling on the opposite side of the soldier, holding a bloody cloth to his side. "We can't wait for an ambulance—he'll be dead in two minutes if we don't do something now."

"Here," gasped another voice behind me. Tristan St. Anthony, Garret's former partner and a soldier of St. George, dropped to his knees beside Riley. He carried a large plastic box and yanked the lid back, revealing an array of bandages, gauze and medical supplies. "I can do a transfusion right here," Tristan said, pulling a long, clear tube from the bottom of the container, "but I don't have the correct blood type. His body will reject it if it's not a match."

"What does he need?" Riley growled.

"O positive."

"Shit." Reaching into the box, Riley pulled out something that glittered metallically in the cold light. For just a second, he stared at it, as if trying to come to a decision. "I can't believe I'm doing this," he muttered, and sliced the scalpel blade across his arm, right above the bend of his elbow. Blood welled and ran down his skin, and my stomach lurched.

Tristan's eyes widened. "Are you—"

"Shut up and stick that tube in his arm before I regret this even more."

Tristan scrambled to comply. Riley stood, holding the other end of the clear plastic, shaking his head. "I fucking can't *believe* I'm doing this," he growled again, and shoved the end of the tube into his bicep.

A dark stream of red ran from his arm, twisting lazily through the plastic, inching toward the dying soldier. Fascinated, I stared at the crimson stream, heart pounding, until Riley's voice snapped me out of my numb daze.

"Don't just sit there, Firebrand! How about you start patching him up before he starts leaking *my* blood all over the ground?"

I jumped, but Tristan was already moving, pulling out disinfectant, bandages and a needle and thread with grim determination. He glanced up, dark blue eyes meeting mine, and I saw the raw emotion behind his careful soldier's mask. A lump caught in my throat, and I gently lowered Garret to the ground, then accepted the supplies thrust into my hands. For the next few minutes, we worked to keep the soldier we loved from dying on the barren flats outside Salt Lake City, while Riley loomed over us both, connected to Garret by a thin stream of red, his expression like a thundercloud.

RILEY

Whoa, getting lightheaded here.

I swayed, gritting my teeth, as a wave of dizziness washed over me, making me stagger back a step. Thankfully, Ember and St. Anthony, still bent over the soldier, didn't seem to notice. They'd patched up his many wounds, either by wrapping them in gauze or sewing them shut, and he now lay between them on the salt flats, still as death and nearly as white as the ground beneath him. I looked at Ember, at the tear tracks staining her cheeks, and wondered if she would cry for me if I ever bit the dust.

"He still alive?" I asked gruffly.

The other soldier of St. George felt his wrist, then nodded once and sat back on his heels with a sigh. "Yeah," he answered in an equally brusque voice. "For now."

"Well, that's good. I'd hate to be getting this nauseous for nothing." I watched him carefully remove the tube from the soldier's arm and tape the final wound shut. The end of the tube dropped to the ground and leaked my blood all over the salt.

"You should go," St. Anthony said in a low voice, not looking at me. "Get him out of here. Before the rest of the Order shows up."

I nodded wearily. "I'll call Wes," I told Ember. My human hacker friend waited on standby, ready to speed to our side if anything went wrong. I'd say this classified as very, very wrong. "He should be here in a few minutes."

She nodded without looking up, her attention riveted to the soldier, and I stifled the growl rumbling in my throat. Instead, I pulled my phone out of my pocket and pressed a familiar button.

"Tell me you're not dead, Riley," said the terse English voice on the other end.

I sighed. "No, Wes, I got my head blown off, and this is just my ghost speaking to you from the afterlife. What the hell do you think?"

"Well, since you're calling me, I take it things did not go as planned. Did St. George manage to get himself killed?"

I looked down at Ember and the soldier. "Maybe."

"*Maybe?* What kind of bloody answer is that? Either he's dead or he isn't."

"It's complicated." I explained the situation, and what led up to it, as briefly as I could. Wes already knew that Garret had been challenged by the Patriarch, the leader of St. George, to a duel to the death. The soldier had defeated the man, barely, and forced him to yield, ending the fight. But then he made a mistake. He'd spared his life. And while the soldier was walking away, the Patriarch had pulled a gun and shot him in the back. That move had ended *his* life, as one of his own seconds responded immediately by putting several bullets through his former Patriarch, but it came too late to help the soldier, who now lay like the dead on the salt flats outside the city.

"So much for the famed honor of St. George," I muttered into the shocked silence on the other end. "So now we need to get him, and us, out of here pronto. Think you can manage that?"

"Bloody hell, Riley." Wes sighed. "Can you not, just once, go into a situation without one of you nearly dying?" There was a pause, and I heard the growl of an engine as it rumbled to life. "I'll be there as soon as I can. Try not to let anyone else get shot, okay?"

"One more thing," I said, lowering my voice to a near whisper and turning my back on the trio kneeling in the salt. "I'm initiating Emergency Go to Ground protocol now. Send the signal through the network, to all the safe houses."

"Shit, Riley," Wes breathed. "Is it that bad?"

"The leader of St. George, their Grand Poobah himself, was just killed. Even if they don't blame us—which they *will*, you can be sure of that—things are going to get crazy from here on. I don't want any of us out in the open when the shit starts to hit the fan. No one moves or pokes a scale out the door until I say otherwise."

"Bugger all," Wes muttered, and the faint tapping of keys drifted through the phone. Even when he was on standby, Wes's laptop never left his side. "Initiating protocol...now." He sighed again, sounding weary. "Right, that's done. So now I suppose we're heading to the bugout spot to wait for the Order to flip the hell out when they hear the news."

"Get here as soon as you can, Wes."

"Joy. On my way."

I lowered the phone and glanced at St. Anthony, forcing a smirk. "I don't suppose you people brought a stretcher."

"Actually, we did." The other soldier still knelt in the salt beside Sebastian's body. His voice was grave, but a tremor went through him, barely noticeable. "The Order always comes prepared. Though we thought it would just be...one body."

A chill went through me, joining the dizziness. I lifted my gaze and looked over the huddle of people in front of me to where a still form in white lay crumpled in the salt a few yards away. Like the soldier, he was covered in blood, the back of his once-pristine uniform spattered with red from where the series of bullets had torn through his body. The Patriarch of the Order of St. George lay dead where he had fallen, the final look on his face one of disbelief and rage.

I guessed I'd be surprised, too, if I'd been shot several times in the back by one of my own soldiers. And not the one I had challenged in a fight to the death.

"Tristan St. Anthony." The new voice echoed behind us, low and frigid. I saw the human briefly close his eyes before raising his head.

"Sir."

"Get up. Step away from the dragons, now."

St. Anthony complied immediately, though his movements were stiff as he rose and stepped away from Ember and myself. His face was carefully neutral as he turned to face the man standing behind us. Martin, I remembered the Patriarch had called him—Lieutenant Martin. He wasn't a large man, or tall; he was older and had that commanding presence I'd seen in unit leaders and veteran slayers. St. Anthony stood rigid at attention, his gaze fixed straight ahead as the other regarded him with stony black eyes.

I watched intently, wondering if he was going to shoot the younger soldier right here. Execute him for killing the Patriarch, perhaps. Even though, in my mind, St. Anthony had done exactly what he was supposed to. The seconds were there to ensure the duel was fair, that no one interfered, cheated or swayed the fight in any way. Sebastian had won; the Patriarch had yielded and the duel was clearly over.

Shooting Sebastian in the back wasn't just extreme coward-ice; it marked the Patriarch, beyond any doubt, as guilty, and St. Anthony had responded as he should have. Maybe it was a knee-jerk reaction, and the realization of what he'd done was just now hitting home, but his response had prob-ably saved both their lives from two vengeful dragons blast-ing them to cinders.

But I didn't know St. George policies or politics, only that they were severe to the point of being fanatical. Maybe it didn't matter what the Patriarch had done. Maybe killing the revered leader of St. George was an immediate death sen-tence, no matter the intent behind it. It wouldn't surprise me.

By the look on St. Anthony's face, it wouldn't surprise him, either.

The officer regarded the younger man in silence for a moment, then sighed. "You did what you had to do, St. Anthony," he said in a stiff voice, making the other look up sharply. "In accordance with the rules of St. George. The Patriarch was guilty, and his actions called for imme-diate reprisal." His voice didn't quite match the look on his face, as if he would give anything to believe that it wasn't true. "You did your duty, though the council might not see it that way," he added, making St. Anthony wince. "But I will speak on your behalf and do my best to ensure you are not punished for it."

"Sir," St. Anthony breathed as, with the crunching of salt, the other officer walked up. He was older than either of them, with a white beard and a patch across one eye, and his face was twisted into an expression of hate as he glared at us.

"Know this, dragons," he snapped, his voice shaking with rage. "You might have won the day, but you have not broken us. The Order will recover, and when we do, we will not stop until Talon is destroyed. This war isn't over. Far from it. It has barely begun."

I smirked, ready to say something suitably defiant and insolent, but Ember lifted her gaze from where it had been glued to the soldier's body and glanced up at the humans.

"It doesn't have to be this way," she said in a soft, controlled voice. "Some of us want nothing to do with Talon, or the war. Some of us are just trying to survive." She looked at St. Anthony, holding his gaze. "Garret realized that. Which is why he went to you in the first place, why he risked everything to expose the Patriarch. Talon was using the Order to kill dragons that didn't fall in with the organization. St. George thinks we're all the same, but that's not true." Her voice grew a little desperate on that last word, and she dropped her gaze, staring at the soldier's body once more.

"We don't want this war," she murmured. "There's been too much killing and death already. There has to be a way for it to end."

"There is." The human's tone was flat. "It will end with the extinction of every dragon on the planet. Nothing less. Even if what you say is true, St. George will not yield. The Order will never abandon their mission to purge the threat your kind represents. If anything, this has only proved how treacherous you dragons really are. Perhaps this was Talon's plan all along—to strike a critical blow against the Order by removing the Patriarch."

"Are you really that stupid?" I asked, and all three humans glanced at me sharply. "Is the Order so blind and rigid that it won't even consider another way of thinking? Open your damn eyes, St. George. You have two dragons in front of you that hate Talon just as much as the Order. And if you believe this was some elaborate plan by the organization to off the Patriarch, you're not thinking that through. Why would Talon want to kill the Patriarch when they were pulling all the strings and had the Order right where they wanted? We—" I gestured to myself, Ember and the motionless soldier "—had to expose this alliance, or Talon would have just kept using you to wipe us off the map. Maybe you should think hard about what that means."

St. Anthony, I noted, was still watching Ember, who was kneeling by the soldier with his hand clasped tightly in her own. His eyes were conflicted, a tiny furrow creasing his brow. But then the man spoke again, his voice as hard and cold as ever.

"Take Sebastian and leave this place," he said, stepping back. "The Order will not pursue, at least not today. But there will be a reckoning, dragon. And when that happens, I suggest you stay far away, or be consumed with the rest of your kind. Martin, St. Anthony," he said, and walked toward the body of the Patriarch lying in the bloody salt a few yards away. The one called Martin followed immediately, but Tristan paused a moment, still staring at Ember before he, too, turned on a heel and marched off with his shoulders straight. Neither of them looked back.

I knelt, putting a hand on Ember's arm and leaning close. "Wes is on his way," I told her. "We'll be out of here soon."

She nodded without looking up. "Do you...do you think he'll make it?" she whispered.

I didn't want to upset her, but I didn't want to lie, either. To give her false hope. "I don't know, Firebrand," I muttered. "He's lost a lot of blood. I don't know if that bullet hit anything vital, but...he's not in a good place right now. I think you have to prepare yourself for the worst." She closed her eyes, a tear slipping down her cheek as she bowed her head. My dragon stirred, and a bitter lump caught in my throat. I remembered her words as the soldier lay dying in her arms, the whispered confession as the human slipped into unconsciousness. And I knew she would never say those words to me.

Unless he was gone.

Sickened with myself and the dark, ugly thoughts of my inner dragon, I rose and walked away to scan the barren horizon.

So. The Patriarch was dead. We'd accomplished what we'd set out to do—not *kill* the man exactly, but expose him to the rest of the Order and break up the alliance between him and Talon. The organization could no longer pull the Order's strings, because their prize puppet was out of the picture. This would throw St. George into chaos, and they would want retribution for the death of their leader, but at least they would be distracted for a while. And while they were figuring out what to do, I could move my network even deeper underground so we'd be well hidden for the inevitable retaliation.

But that still left Talon to deal with.

A chill went through me as I watched the sun creep slowly over the flats, staining the horizon red. Something was coming; I could feel it. Talon was out there, and killing the Patriarch would cause them to react, as well. Maybe that had been their plan all along. I felt like a pawn in a chess match—one who had just taken out the bishop, but then looked up and there was the queen, smiling at me from across the board.

I shook myself, frowning. I was getting paranoid. Even if Talon had expected this, our plans wouldn't have changed. We would've had to expose the Patriarch regardless, and everything would still have led to this, with the leader of the Order dead, and the soldier who'd exposed him hovering between life and death in the bloodstained salt.

I looked back at Ember and the human, huddled together on the bleak, unforgiving flats. The soldier's face was as white as the salt beneath him, half his blood, and probably a little of mine, already drying in the sun. *Try not to die, St. George,* I thought, startling myself. *Things are going to get even crazier from here, and you're not bad to have around when everything implodes. If Talon decides to come after us full scale, we'll need all the help we can get. Plus, if you die now, Ember will never be able to forget you.*

And I don't want to compete with a damned ghost for the rest of my life.

GARRET

I was flying.

The clouds stretched out below me, a rolling sea of white and gray that went on forever. Above me, the sky was a perfect, endless blue that made me dizzy to look at. I could feel the wind in my face, smelling of rain and mist, and the sun warming my back. How long had I been flying? I couldn't remember, but it felt like an eternity and a heartbeat at the same time. Why was I up here? I was... I was looking for something, I think. Or chasing something.

Or something was chasing me.

A low rumble echoed behind me. I looked back to see a wall of black clouds boiling up from the white, spreading toward me with frightening speed. Chilled, I tried to fly faster, but the sky rapidly darkened and lightning flickered around me as the storm drew closer, filling the air with the smell of ozone.

Garret.

A voice shivered across the cloudscape, soft and female, making me falter. I knew that voice. Where was she? Why couldn't I see her?

Garret, I'm here. Just hold on.

Where are you? I tried to call, but my voice had frozen inside me. At my back, the boiling wall of darkness loomed closer, streaks of lightning flashing in its depths.

How's he doing? A different voice joined the first. Low and strangely familiar, it made something inside me bristle. I couldn't remember the face, or what it had done, but a low growl rumbled through my chest before it died in my throat.

He's fighting. The female voice sounded choked, making my stomach clench, too. *His temperature is far higher than normal, and he's been delirious the past few nights. Wes thinks his body is trying to adapt to the transfusion, and that it's causing some weird side effects. But we really don't know anything.* She sniffed, and her voice went even softer. *All we can do is wait, and hope that he comes out of it.*

The other sighed. *At least he's still alive, Firebrand. I did the only thing I could think of.*

I know.

Their voices faded, swallowed by the darkness and rising wind, and a stab of desperation shot through me. *Wait*, I wanted to shout, straining to hear her voice, to follow it until I found the person on the other side. *Don't go. Don't leave me here.*

No answer except the howling of the wind and the rumble of the storm at my back. Before me, the sky continued on, forever. Rolling gray clouds with no end in sight. Behind me, the dark wall boiled steadily closer, a wave swallowing everything in its path, filling the air with the tingle of electricity.

I suddenly realized what I had to do.

I twisted around to face the oncoming storm. For a split second, hanging upside down in midair, I caught a glimpse of my shadow in the clouds below, lean and sharp, with an elongated neck and wide, sweeping wings. Then I was rushing toward the wall of darkness. The clouds filled my vision as I shot into the flickering blackness, and everything around me disappeared.

★ ★ ★

I stumbled forward, and flames surrounded me, roaring in my ears. The entire warehouse was engulfed, tongues of flame curling around the iron beams and snapping hungrily at the aisles of crates and boxes. Everywhere I looked, there was fire, screaming and crackling, tinting everything in a hellish glow, but I wasn't afraid. A nearby tower of pallets collapsed with a deafening roar, and a cloud of embers billowed into the air, swirling around me, but there was no discomfort or pain. I could feel the heat, smell the smoke and ashes settling in my lungs, but it didn't bother me at all.

Firebrand?

That same voice, low and husky, drifted from one of the aisles. *Ember,* it said again, its tone laced with worry. *You've been sitting here for eight hours. Go to sleep. Let me or Wes take watch—he's not going anywhere.*

No, said the voice that made my heart leap in my chest. *I want to be here. When he wakes up, I should be here. He was almost lucid a little while ago. I think… I think he was calling for me.*

I started toward the voice, ducking a burning beam, feeling the heat against my back and neck as I hurried forward. The voices continued, but they were fainter now, swallowed by the roar of the inferno. Overhead, a skylight exploded into shards of razor glass and rained down, pinging off the cement. Impatient, I shielded my face with a hand and jogged forward.

The Patriarch emerged from the darkness of the aisle, dressed in white and red, a sword hanging loosely at his side. Flames engulfed him, burning his uniform, clawing at his beard and leaping from his hair. His face was blackened, the skin cracked and oozing, but his blue eyes glowed in the haze and smoke, and he pointed a fire-wreathed hand in my direction.

"Traitor," he whispered. "Dragonlover. Like your parents before you. You are damned, Sebastian. Your soul has been tainted beyond all redemption, and you must be put down like the demon you are."

He took a step toward me. I raised my gun and fired point-blank at his center, and the Patriarch exploded into a cloud of swirling ashes and scattered into the smoke. But his voice continued to echo through the warehouse.

You cannot escape your destiny. Evil is in your blood, Sebastian. You will fall, and you will burn in the flames of your own making, as your parents did before you.

Lowering my arm, I strode through the ash cloud into the blackness beyond.

★ ★ ★

Sunlight blinded me. Wincing, I raised my arm, trying to see past the sudden glare. The scent of salt and sand filled my nostrils, and I heard the sound of waves, crying gulls and distant laughter. Blinking rapidly, I lowered my arm to find myself on the edge of a beach, a strip of white sand stretching out to either side and the brilliant, sparkling ocean before me.

Recognition sparked. This place felt familiar, though I couldn't remember why. Hadn't I been here before? If I had, why did the sight of the ocean fill me with both excitement and dread?

"Garret," Tristan said at my back. His voice was impatient, and I turned to face the other soldier. He wore shorts, a tank top and a slight frown as he gazed down at me. "You okay?" my partner asked. "You went all glassy-eyed for few seconds. Did you hear what I just said?"

"No," I muttered as memory came back in a rush, reminding me why we were here. Find a dragon, kill a dragon. Like we had done all those times before. So, why did this seem so dif-

ferent? I felt like I was missing something important. "Sorry," I
told Tristan, rubbing my eyes. "What was that again?"

He sighed. "I was saying the dragon is hiding right over there,
and that maybe you should go talk to it before it disappears."

He pointed. I turned, squinting against the light and the
glimmer coming off the ocean. Farther down the sand, a
group of teenagers clustered by the water's edge, laughing
and occasionally splashing each other. Between the sunlight
and the blinding glare, I couldn't see their features, just moving silhouettes against the water, sand and sky.

"I don't see a dragon," I murmured, walking forward a
few steps.

"Really?" Tristan followed, his footsteps shushing quietly through the sand. "It's standing right there, plain as day.
Maybe if you weren't so blinded by love, you'd see it for what
it really is. And then, I wouldn't have to kill you."

I turned. Tristan stood behind me, a gun held level with
my chest. His eyes were hard as they met mine and he pulled
the trigger.

There was no sound. The flash of the gun filled my vision, and I felt myself falling.

★ ★ ★

I opened my eyes.

The sky overhead was gray and dim. There were no
clouds, no glimmers of blue or sunlight through the haze.
Just a flat gray sky that seemed much closer than it should
be. I blinked a few times, and it resolved itself into a concrete ceiling with cracks running across the surface. I lay on
my back in a small, empty room, a sheet pulled up to my
chest and my hands draped over my stomach. My body felt
numb and heavy, and my head felt like it was full of cotton,

which made it very hard to think. Where was I? How did I get here? The last thing I remembered…

My mind stirred sluggishly, trying to sift through what was real and what was nightmare. What *had* happened to me? Memories rose up, familiar faces and voices, but it was difficult to separate reality from hallucination. Had I been injured? Or had I been chasing something?

Slowly, I turned my head, trying to take in my surroundings, and my pulse stuttered.

A girl slumped next to my bed, seated in a metal chair pulled close to the mattress. Her arms were folded against the sheets with her head cradled atop them, bright red hair mussed and sticking out at odd angles. Her eyes were closed, and her slim bare shoulders rose and fell with the rhythm of her breathing.

Ember. I drew in a breath, feeling the strangeness of the dreamworld dissolve as reality took its place. Suddenly, all those things—where I was, what had happened to me, how much time had passed—didn't seem important anymore. Just that she was here.

I stretched out my hand, not trusting my voice, and touched the back of her arm.

She jerked away and looked up, green eyes wide and startled. For half a heartbeat, she stared at me in confusion as her mind caught up to the present. I saw my reflection in her gaze and wanted to say something, but my voice hadn't returned quite yet.

"Garret," she breathed, her voice barely above a whisper. And then she threw herself forward, wrapping her arms around my neck in an almost painful embrace. I slid my arms around her, feeling her heartbeat against mine, her warm cheek pressed against my throat and jaw. I closed my eyes and held her, trembling, in my arms.

"Hey you," I whispered. My voice came out raspy and weak, and I swallowed some of the scratchy dryness in my throat. I became aware that I was very hot, my skin burning with fever. I could practically feel the heat radiating off me, and was thankful that only a thin sheet covered my body. "What happened?" I husked out as Ember pulled back, regarding me with shining green eyes. "Where are we?"

She gave me a solemn look. "We're in one of Riley's safe houses, an old bomb shelter he renovated from the Cold War era. We are literally underground right now. Hang on." She turned, sliding off the mattress, and reached toward a small end table beside the bed. A bowl and a wet cloth sat on one corner, a glass and a pitcher on the other. She poured the last of the pitcher's contents into the cup and turned back, cocking her head. "Can you sit up?"

Carefully, I struggled to a sitting position, feeling weak and unstable as I leaned forward, and Ember adjusted the pillows at my back. When we were done, she handed me the cup, and I forced myself to drink slowly, though the burning in my throat and deep in my chest made me want to down it in two gulps.

Putting the empty glass on the bedside table, I looked at Ember again. She ran her fingers over my forehead, brushing back my hair. Her fingers were cool and soft and left a soothing trail over my heated skin. "What do you remember?"

"I...I don't know." Everything was still fuzzy, and now the heat in my veins had become even more pronounced. I pressed a palm to my face, trying to clear my thoughts and to ease the pressure behind my eyes. "I was...fighting the Patriarch, I think," I said. "He challenged me to a duel, and I agreed to fight him. That's all I can remember."

Ember nodded. "You won," she said quietly. "You beat the Patriarch, but when the fight was over, he shot you. In the back."

A feral gleam entered her eyes, and I wondered if the Patriarch was still alive. If he had survived the vengeance of an enraged red dragon. "You nearly died," Ember went on, the murderous look fading to one of anguish. "You were bleeding out, and the only way to save your life was to perform a blood transfusion right there. There was no time to take you to a hospital. And no one else had the right blood type. So…Riley became the donor." She paused. "Riley saved your life, Garret."

For a few seconds, I didn't understand the significance, why she looked so distraught. Was she afraid that I would resent the fact that a former enemy had saved my life? Given our past, I was shocked that the rogue dragon had offered his own blood to save a soldier of St. George. Did Riley himself wish that he'd let me die? I didn't think he was that vindictive, but I *was* a rival. No longer an enemy, but a challenger in the worst way—competition for the girl beside me. If I was out of the picture, Riley would have Ember all to himself.

Then it hit me. The heat in my veins, the feeling of molten fire crawling beneath my skin. I let out a long breath.

"I have…dragon blood in me."

Ember winced. "It's been causing some complications," she said in a near whisper. "Some of it has been good—your wounds have been healing at a much faster rate than normal. But you've been delirious for the past week and a half. Until today, we didn't know if you would pull out of it." At my incredulous look, she dropped her gaze. "Wes thinks it's your body trying to compensate for the infusion of new blood, and that it should eventually adjust, but he's not certain. This has never been done before. We don't know…what the effects will be. Long term or otherwise."

Dazed, I sank back against the pillow. Riley had saved my life, and he'd done it by injecting me with dragon blood.

Was that why my heart was pumping like I'd run a marathon, even lying here on my back? My mind, already wandering and confused, began spinning in strange directions. What would this infusion do to me, inside and out? Was I in danger of dying, as the dragon blood cooked my organs from the inside? Or could it do even more outlandish things? Dragons were magical creatures; a tiny bit of ancient, supernatural power flowed through their veins. Even the Order of St. George acknowledged this. What would that do to the human body? Would I come out of this completely normal?

For a moment, I had bizarre, delirious thoughts of waking up covered in scales, or getting out of bed to find a tail coiling behind me, before I shoved them aside. That wasn't possible, I told myself, struggling to hold on to logic as it twisted and squirmed away from me. Blood couldn't do that to a person; I was in no danger of morphing into some sort of strange half dragon. The most it could do was kill me, if my body rejected the new blood and shut down organs, one by one.

Ember, I realized, was watching me carefully, waiting for my reaction. I reached for the hand lying on the mattress, and she curled her fingers around mine and held on tight, like she was afraid to let go. "It's okay," I told her, smiling as I met her gaze. "I'll deal with the complications as they come, but right now, I'll settle for still being here."

She let out a breath that was half laugh, half growl, and leaned forward, pressing her forehead to my cheek. "Dammit, Garret," she breathed in my ear. "I thought I'd lost you. Don't do that again."

"I'll try not to," I whispered back. Her skin was cool against mine, and I slid my fingers up her arms. "But will you still feel the same if I sprout wings and a tail?"

I felt her silent laughter. "Actually, that would be pretty awesome," she admitted. "Though you'd never be able to wear shorts in a public place again, so there'd be some kinks to work out."

I wanted to drag her closer, to pull her against me and listen to our hearts beat together. But my eyelids were suddenly heavy, and sleep was clawing at me, even as I struggled to stay awake. "What happened with the Order?" I asked, determined to get some sort of answer before I succumbed to exhaustion.

"We don't know," Ember said, drawing back. "After the duel, they took the Patriarch's body and left. We came straight here from Salt Lake City and haven't been up top since."

I nodded. That was smart. The Patriarch was dead. The revered leader of the Order of St. George had been slain by the enemy. Even if there was no immediate reprisal, staying off the Order's radar right now was a good idea. Still, the lack of information was worrisome. What was happening, in both St. George and Talon? We had thrown a huge wrench into the works of both organizations, and something had to come of it. Sooner or later, they were going to respond. We had to be ready when they did.

But not right now. At least, not for me. Staying conscious was becoming increasingly difficult, even though I had about a dozen more questions I wanted to ask. And something else hovered at the back of my mind, a feeling that I was forgetting something important. Something about the Order...and me. Ember must have noticed, for her cool fingers brushed my forehead again, and her lips briefly touched my temple.

"Get some sleep, soldier boy," she whispered, the relief in her voice washing over me like a wave. "You're safe here. I'll see you again when you wake up."

Lulled by that promise, I obeyed.

EMBER

I watched Garret fall asleep, relaxing into the pillows, his breaths even and slow. It was a sound, peaceful sleep this time—no jerking, mumbling or fluttering eyelids. No thrashing around in nightmare. Hopefully, the fever had broken and he was on his way to recovery, though his skin remained disturbingly hot. Hotter than any human's should have been.

But he was finally awake, and lucid, and that itself was a massive relief. Watching while he'd jerked and muttered nonsense in his sleep had been horrible. One night he'd thrashed about so violently we'd considered tying him down. I knew it was the dragon blood working its way through his system, causing fever and sickness as his body tried to adapt to or reject the infusion. I knew that without it Garret would most certainly be dead, and that Riley had saved his life with his quick thinking. But, watching him moan and thrash trying to ward away phantom enemies, hearing what was almost a *snarl* erupt from his throat one night, I couldn't help but wonder what he would be like when he finally came out of it. If he came out of it at all.

Thankfully, he had. And it didn't appear to have changed him. At least, not on the outside. What was happening *inside* him was anyone's guess; as far as any of us knew, no human had ever received a transfusion of dragon blood, so there was nothing to compare it to. I doubted Garret would sprout wings and a tail, as cool and disturbing as that might be, but I also doubted any human could get injected with the blood of a dragon and not experience side effects.

Right now, watching him sleeping peacefully for the first time in over a week was all that seemed important. He was alive, not delirious, and now I could rejoin the rest of the world. Riley, I knew, would be relieved. I'd barely seen him and Wes since our arrival, and the only times I'd left this room were the instances when I'd fallen asleep at Garret's side and Riley had carried me to my own bed. I knew he'd want to hear that Garret was awake, if for no other reason than I would stop worrying about him.

With one final look at the unconscious soldier, I tiptoed out of the room and slipped into the hallway beyond.

I nearly scraped my skull on the low, curved ceiling—again—and ducked my head with a stifled growl. The corridor was actually an enormous corrugated steel tube with rooms branching from it. A steel ladder at the far end of the tube led up to a tiny concrete hatch in the middle of nowhere, Wyoming. As fallout shelters went, it was pretty typical. Riley said he'd "stumbled onto it" many years ago and had modified it into an emergency fallback center. It was dark, it was claustrophobic, but it was, according to Riley and Wes, the most secure place we could hope for, a refuge where we could wait out the craziness up top and know that St. George wouldn't come for us all in the night.

I didn't know how much I liked the idea of waiting things out. Now that I knew Garret would be all right, sitting here doing nothing, just hoping Talon and the Order would forget about us, was sounding less like a plan and more like a stall tactic. Neither was going to forget about us. And we had worked so hard to strike a decisive blow against both organizations; breaking up the alliance between Talon and the Patriarch was a huge victory, even if it had almost cost one of us his life. To pull back and hide seemed the opposite of what we should do right now, but good luck convincing Riley of that.

The room beside Garret's, where Riley and Wes shared a bunk, was empty. So I headed to the one other place they would be, the "command room" at the other end of the tube.

Like everything in this underground facility, the command room had low ceilings, concrete walls and just enough room to move around. A square table sat in the middle of the floor, with maps and files and other documents scattered over it, and a desk with an old computer was shoved into the corner with a couple shelves. Amazingly, Wes had been able to get power running to this place. The opposite corner held a very old, yet working, television, and it was on at the moment, an overly cheerful weather reporter announcing that we were in for a soggy weekend.

As I walked into the room, I blinked in shock. Wes, unsurprisingly, sat at the computer, both his laptop and the other screen open and active. Riley stood at one end of the table with both hands on the surface, gazing down at the map spread out beneath him. He was dressed in black—black jeans, boots and shirt—and his dark hair was unkempt. I felt a stirring of heat inside me, my dragon coming to life as she always did when he was around.

But it was the third person in the room that caught my attention. She stood on the other side of the table, arms crossed, straight black hair falling to the center of her back.

"Jade?"

The slight Chinese woman, in reality a forty-foot-long Adult Eastern dragon, turned and gave me a faint smile as I stepped into the room. "Hello, Ember," she greeted me. "It's good to see you again. From what Riley has told me, I was expecting not to catch a glimpse of you for days."

"What are you doing here?"

One slender eyebrow arched. "I said I would return, did I not? When I made certain the monks were safe and had found a new temple, I promised to come back. And there is still a war to be fought." She lifted her hands slightly. "So, here I am. Though it seems I have come at a, if not bad, rather uncertain time."

"Ember." Riley rose quickly, his gold gaze meeting mine across the table. For a moment, his expression was apprehensive; I hadn't voluntarily left Garret's room since the day we'd arrived. There were only two reasons I would leave it now. "St. George?" he asked cautiously.

"He's awake," I said, making him slump, but whether it was in relief or disappointment, I wasn't sure. "The fever has broken—he was talking to me a few minutes ago. I think he's going to be okay."

"Well, that's something at least." Riley raked back his hair. "Nice to get some not horrible news for a change. If the bastard gets back on his feet soon, I could use his perspective on what the hell is going on out there with the Order."

Mention of the Order brought the current situation rushing back. I'd been so distracted by Garret, I'd nearly forgotten about it, but now it rose up again, looming and ominous. "Why?" I asked, stepping to the edge of the table. What had I missed? "What's going on? What's the Order been doing?"

He shot me a frustrated look. "Nothing," he growled, making me frown. "Not a damn thing. We haven't heard a peep from them since we left Salt Lake City. There've been no raids, no strikes, no activity at all. The Order has gone completely AWOL."

"I'm confused," I said, cocking my head. "Isn't that a good thing? We exposed the Patriarch to the rest of St. George, and Talon's hold on them is broken. They're not going after your safe houses anymore."

"Not right now." Riley crossed his arms. "But it's still too quiet. I don't trust this complete lack of response—it's not like them at all. This is probably the calm before the shitstorm."

"The Order is not the one we should be worrying about," Jade insisted, as if I hadn't said anything.

"So you keep telling me," Riley said, glaring at the Eastern dragon. "But I don't know what you expect me to do against Talon. If the organization is up to something, all the more reason to keep off their radar. We hide deep, and we hide hard. That's the only way we're going to survive."

"It is not a plan to simply hide and do nothing."

"I'm sorry—this from one of the Eastern dragons who, for hundreds of years, have done nothing but sit on their scaly butts in isolated temples while the rest of us fought the war?"

While they were talking, the news story changed to show a young reporter standing on a narrow stretch of pavement that snaked into a forest. A pair of orange and white barricades blocked the road behind her, warning lights flashing in the gray drizzle. "Authorities are still struggling to discover the reason behind the accident that caused a cargo plane full of fuel to crash into a small Arkansas town last week," the woman was saying. "As you can see, the road to the town has been blocked, and authorities have closed off the area.

Rescue crews are on the scene now and have been combing through the rubble nonstop, but so far no survivors have been found."

"When did that happen?" I asked.

Riley gave the television a cursory glance. "Couple days ago," he said in a brusque voice. "Apparently, a plane full of jet fuel took a nosedive into some hillbilly community in the mountains. Caused a spectacular explosion and wiped out the whole town, according to the news. It's been on every station for days." He shrugged. "Tragic, but not something we need to worry about."

"Correct," agreed Jade. "We should be worrying about Talon and what their plans are, now that the Order has been disrupted."

"And what is it you think we can actually do against the organization?" Riley said, turning back to her. "For that matter, what makes you think Talon is up to anything at all?"

While they were arguing, I turned my attention to the TV. The scene had changed from a map of the United States to what looked like a news conference, with a man behind a podium speaking to a handful of reporters and flashing cameras. After a moment, he stepped down, and a woman took his place behind the podium. She was tall and attractive, with jet-black hair and striking blue eyes, and for some reason, my instincts prickled when I saw her.

"Oh, bloody hell," Wes breathed from the corner.

Riley and Jade didn't hear him, or the quiet horror in his voice. Puzzled, I turned, but he wasn't looking at any of us, his attention riveted to the television in the corner. *"Shit,"* Wes swore again and glanced at Riley, still in a heated argument with Jade. "Riley, bloody shut up for a second. Look! Look who it is."

Riley craned his neck toward the TV, and his eyebrows shot up. "Miranda?" he exclaimed. "What the hell? Why is she there...?" His eyes narrowed, jaw tightening as he shook his head. "Dammit," he growled.

"What?" I asked. "What's going on? Who's Miranda?"

Riley swore again. "She an agent with the NTSB— the National Transportation Safety Board," he answered. "They're a federal agency that's called in to investigate aviation accidents across the US." He sighed, his gaze sharpening. "She's also a Chameleon, and one of Talon's best. Which means..."

"That whole story is a bloody cover-up," Wes muttered darkly. "If Talon sent a Chameleon herself to the site, they're neck-deep in whatever is going on down there."

Jade's cool gaze held Riley's across the table, and there was a warning in those dark eyes. "Talon is on the move," she said in an ominous tone. "How long can we remain ignorant? How long can we hide while they put their plans into motion, unopposed?"

"As long as it takes," Riley growled back. "Breaking up the Order is one thing. Saving hatchlings from the organization is another. Dragons who go head-to-head with Talon die, that's all there is to it. I'm the leader of this underground— it's not just my hide on the line. I have an entire network of dragons and humans to worry about, and I will not bring them under Talon's fire. No, we stay here, we hide, we let this blow over. I'm not going to put anyone in danger if I can help it."

"And what if it doesn't blow over?" I challenged. "What if it just gets worse?" I pointed at the screen. "Riley, if that's a cover-up, then Talon might have destroyed an *entire town*. That's not like them at all—they would never risk that kind of exposure unless they're planning something huge to counter it." Riley glared at me, making my dragon stir, but I held my ground. "Jade is right. Something is happening with the organization, something big. We need to know what Talon is up to before it's too late."

"Don't you start, too, Firebrand."

"They're right, mate," Wes said quietly, shocking us all speechless. We turned to him, but he was staring at the screen, his gaze dark. "Talon might've blown up a building or two in the past, but they're always careful to make it seem like an accident. This…" He shook his head at the TV. "This is a whole different animal. I've never heard of them taking out an entire town for no reason. That place is in the middle of nowhere. Unless we're missing something big, there's nothing there that Talon would want." His jaw tightened. "I don't like it, Riley. They're changing the game on us. We need to find out what the hell they're doing before it bites us all in the ass."

"*Et tu*, Wesley?" Riley growled, but before Wes could reply, he turned to me. "Hang on a second, Firebrand," he ordered. "Before you go charging off again, I think you're forgetting something." He gestured at the door. "What about the soldier? He can't come with us, not with that injury. He'll slow us down or get himself killed. Hell, he can't even stand now, much less hold a gun. How do you expect him to keep up?"

I bit my lip. He was right. Garret was in no condition to go running into yet another dangerous mission, but I also knew that we needed to find out what Talon was planning. "I… I'll stay behind," I told Riley. "I'll keep an eye on Garret while you, Jade and Wes go see what Talon is up to."

Riley snorted. "Very noble of you."

"I would come with you, Riley, you know I would," I said firmly. "I want to go, and I want to see for myself. But…" I started to rub my arms, then stopped myself. "I won't leave him behind. Not alone. And we have to figure out what Talon is doing before they surprise us with their next horrible scheme. So, the three of you go ahead. I'll stay here with Garret."

"No, you won't," Wes sighed, shocking me again. "I will." Riley turned to him, and he shrugged. "I can do just as much over the phone as in person," he said in a reasonable voice, "and you'll need someone watching the safe houses while you're gone. Let's face it, mate, she's better in a fight, and if bugger all goes down, three dragons have a better chance of making it out alive than two dragons and a human. I'll stay here, provide support and make sure St. George doesn't bleed to death and the nests don't explode. He'll be safe with me—and don't give me that look," he added as Riley raised a brow at him. "The tosser is useful—I'm not too much of a bastard to admit it. If keeping him alive means he'll kill more of St. George and Talon in the future, then by all means, I'll give him whatever he needs."

I smiled at his gruffness, seeing the flush that crept below his scruffy jawline. "Thanks, Wes."

"Yes, thank you, Wesley," Riley echoed in a mock sincere voice. "For dragging me into yet another insane scheme. I suppose if I refuse now, these two morons will go to this crash site without me." He shook his head and raised a hand before I could protest. "Fine. Great. Into the jaws of death once more—must be a Tuesday. So, now that you mutineers have decided where we're going next, why don't you tell me how long it's going to take to drive from Wyoming to Arkansas?"

Wes's fingers flew over the keyboard. "Um…about eighteen hours," he confirmed, squinting at the screen. "If you drive straight through."

Riley exhaled and shook his head in exasperated defeat. "All right," he muttered, "if we're really going to do this, let's get it over with." Straightening, he became confident again, his tone brusque and commanding. "We'll leave tomorrow. Wes, send a message to all the safe houses. Tell them—again—they are to stay put and not move unless they are one hundred percent certain Talon or St. George will kick down their door in the next twenty-four hours. I'll get things together so we can leave as soon as we can." He gave me an appraising, golden-eyed stare, and one corner of his mouth curled up. I swallowed, ignoring the slow flame coiling through my insides. "Get some rest, Firebrand," he ordered. "You've gotten only a couple hours a night this whole time, and most of that has been slumped in a chair. I know you're tired. Go to sleep."

I smirked back, ready to tell him I was fine, but then I realized he was right. I was more than tired. Between the stress of nearly losing Garret, his sickness and the constant bedside vigil, I was completely exhausted. Sleep sounded wonderful right now.

"Yeah," I agreed, drawing back. "I'll do that. Don't leave without me."

"Wouldn't dream of it."

I checked on Garret one last time before continuing to the room next door. He was still dead to the world, his breaths slow and deep. I tiptoed out to avoid waking him, walked into my own room and collapsed on my tiny cot in the corner. The lumpy, metal-framed mattress felt like heaven. I was unconscious almost before my head hit the pillow.

★ ★ ★

A knocking at my door pulled me out of a dead, dreamless sleep. Groping for my phone, I stared blearily at the glowing numbers: 6:42 a.m. Holy crap, it had been seven in the evening when I'd fallen into bed last night. I'd zonked out for nearly twelve hours.

The knocking came again, probably Riley or Jade, impatient to get on the road. Eighteen hours was a long drive down to Arkansas. I thought of Garret, and felt a stab of worry and guilt for leaving him, but he had been shot and nearly killed less than two weeks ago. He certainly couldn't come with us.

"I'm up!" I called, scrambling off the mattress. Jeez, the floor was cold. "I'm coming, just gimme a couple seconds."

I ran my fingers through my hair, smoothing it down as best I could. Yawning, I walked to the door and pulled it open.

It wasn't Riley. Or Jade.

"Hey, dragon girl," Garret said, smiling at me over the threshold. He wore jeans and a white T-shirt, and his short blond hair, clean and brushed back, glinted under the bare bulbs. His metallic-gray eyes were shining as they met mine. "You didn't think you were going to leave me behind, did you?"

GARRET

I shouldn't be up.

Not because I felt weak, or because I was still healing. I literally should not be able to stand right now, not with the injury I'd sustained. I'd nearly died; my body had suffered a massive amount of trauma that should have taken weeks, if not months, to fully heal. But last night, I'd woken up groggy and confused, and the air under the sheets had felt like a sauna. Without even thinking about it, I'd swung out of bed and slipped down the hall until I found a room with people in it. When I'd walked through the door, Wes had nearly fallen out of his chair, and Riley had uttered a very emphatic curse.

"Shit, St. George!" The rogue had given me an incredulous glare. "What the hell are you doing? You want to kill yourself? There is no way you should be up right now."

I'd tried to clear my bleary thoughts. Only then had I realized I was shirtless, and my entire chest was wrapped in bandages and gauze. "How long have I been down?"

"More than a week." Riley had stalked forward, gold eyes narrowed and appraising. "And truthfully, I have no idea how you're even standing, unless you're so delirious you don't feel anything."

Jade had appeared in the doorway, slender brows rising as

our gazes met. I'd been surprised, as well; just how much had happened while I was out? "Well," the Eastern dragon had commented in a wry voice. "According to Riley, I was not expecting to see you for quite some time. But it appears that you are not... What is the saying again? *On death's doorstep*, after all."

"Like hell he's not." It had been Wes's turn to stalk forward, yank up a chair and grab a first-aid kit from a cabinet. "Sit down, you bloody stubborn bastard, before you tear yourself open. If you die now, that damn hatchling is going to kill something."

I'd sunk wordlessly onto the chair as the hacker began cutting gauze from my back and chest. As he'd peeled back the wrappings, cool air had hit my skin, and the human had uttered a breathless curse.

"Bloody hell, are you kidding me?" I'd felt a cloth brush my skin, right over the wound, but it had barely stung. "Are you seeing this, Riley? Last week, there was a hole the size of a golf ball. Now, bloody nothing." The rag had swiped my back, a little harder this time, sending a twinge through my side. "This looks like weeks of healing, not a bloody few days. Holy shit. Holy. Shit. Do you realize what this means?"

I'd twisted in my seat, causing him to fumble with the bandages and swear. "Where's Ember?" I'd asked, looking around the room. I was still groggy, light-headed and confused. I hadn't known where we were, what had happened or why Jade was back. I'd needed answers, but first I needed to see Ember again.

"Asleep," Riley had answered. The rogue leader had stood above me with an unreadable expression on his face. "These past few days, the only times she left your room were to use the bathroom, and when I forced her to eat something," he'd gone on. "You're not going to wake her up now, St. George. She needs all the sleep she can get before we leave tomorrow."

"Leave?" I'd furrowed my brow. "Where are you going?"

He'd frowned back, and I could tell he was kicking himself for saying that, but Jade had pulled up another chair and sat down beside me, her expression somber.

"We think Talon is planning something," she'd said, and proceeded to explain everything that had happened from the time I'd been shot. She'd spoken slowly, answering any questions that I had, and when Wes was finished rebandaging my wound, I'd been almost clearheaded again.

"I'm coming with you," I'd told Riley. He'd snorted.

"Figured that's what you would say, St. George," he'd growled, and waved a hand. "Your funeral, of course. I certainly can't stop you if you want to come along, but you're going to have to keep up. That won't be a problem, will it?"

I'd risen smoothly and felt my back twinge, but it had been forgettable. I'd endured far worse, though I knew I shouldn't be this recovered. I'd seen soldiers shot in battle many, many times. I knew that one did not get up and walk around a little more than a week after the injury I had sustained. But I was not going to stay behind, not when Ember was rushing straight into danger, again.

"No," I'd told the rogue, who'd nodded briskly as if he'd expected it. "No problem at all."

★ ★ ★

Ember's mouth fell open. She stared at me in shock, her eyes huge as they scanned my face. She blinked once, as if making sure I wasn't an illusion, and then reached for me. I shivered as her fingers curled lightly around my arm.

"Garret." Her voice was breathless but worried. "How...?" She shook her head. "You shouldn't be up," she whispered. "You were *shot* just over a week ago. And not just in the leg or the arm—you nearly *died*."

"So everybody keeps telling me," I murmured back, and smiled. "I know. I know I shouldn't be here—I shouldn't even be standing for a few days at least. But…" I gave a helpless shrug. "I'm fine. Wes checked me out, both last night and this morning. The wounds are mostly healed. He said that my healing is nearly on par with a dragon's regenerative abilities, that he's never seen anything like it before in a human. I guess having dragon's blood is a blessing in disguise." Her brows lifted in amazement, and I grinned. "So you don't get to leave me behind, dragon girl. Even if I do grow wings and a tail, I'm not leaving your side. You'll just have to get used to me being—"

Ember interrupted me by lacing her fingers behind my neck, pulling me down and pressing her lips to mine. I groaned and wrapped my arms around her waist, drawing her close, feeling her heart beat against me. Heat spread through my insides, roaring in my veins, as the tension in my stomach melted away. When I was with her, everything that had happened to me—being shot, nearly dying, being infused with something I wasn't sure wouldn't eventually kill me— seemed insignificant. I would die for this girl, I realized. I would happily take a bullet for her if it meant that, today, I could hold her one last time.

When we drew back, Ember's eyes were bright, almost seeming to glow. I was wrapped in a cocoon of heat and warmth, feeling it pulse between us with every heartbeat. I wanted nothing more than to pull Ember into her empty room, lock the door and see how long it would take before the flames consumed us.

Gazing down, I stroked her cheek and offered a wry smile. "Riley is waiting for us," I murmured, and she nodded with a sigh. "He wanted me to tell you to grab your things—we head out as soon as you're ready."

Rising on her toes, she kissed me once more, long and lingering, before pulling back and stepping away. I took a furtive breath to calm the inferno within and waited outside the door while she gathered her meager belongings. Her black Viper suit was the last item to be stuffed unceremoniously into a bag before she zipped up the duffel and joined me at the door. I took the bag, shouldered the strap and together we walked down the hall to the command room.

Riley, Wes and Jade were all there, the two dragons standing around the table discussing something in quiet undertones while Wes sat at the computer, furiously typing away. As we came into the room, Jade inclined her head to me with a faint smile. I nodded back.

"There you are," Riley announced, looking at Ember. "Sure you got everything, Firebrand? It's a long way to the Ozarks, and we're not turning around this time." One corner of his mouth curled into a smirk. "We don't want to be halfway through Colorado before you realize you left your Viper suit in the bathroom."

"That was one time, Riley." Ember rolled her eyes. "And we lost fifteen minutes, tops. Let it go."

"All right," Wes interrupted, rising from the chair. "That's done. I sent the final message through the network. Everyone is on high alert, with instructions to stay put unless absolutely necessary. We're ready to move out." Since I didn't need watching anymore, Wes was coming, too.

The rogue shook his head. "Right," he said, sounding not at all thrilled with the whole idea. "Let's get this over with. Eighteen hours is a hell of a drive, so we're going to have to do it in shifts. St. George, since you're feeling so magically rested…" He tossed me a pair of keys. "You're driving first."

DANTE

Three years ago

Finals week was always hell.

"Watch it," I snapped as Ember closed the refrigerator door and nearly ran into me with the milk. "Don't you ever look before you bash into people headfirst?"

She snorted. "Jeez, grumpy much?" She sidestepped me and headed to the table. "Did something crawl up your butt in the shower?"

I yanked open the fridge door. "Sorry," I muttered, pulling out the juice. "Just tired. I was up till two last night studying."

She wrinkled her nose as I joined her at the table. "Again? You did that yesterday. And the day before. And all afternoon."

"Yes, because I want to pass," I snapped again. "Because, unlike you, I can't half-ass my way through life. Because, unlike you, everyone expects me to do better. So yes, I have to study and not spend my evenings watching TV in my room."

"Hey, jackass, I've been studying, too," Ember snarled back. "Every night, I'll have you know. So don't pull that 'I'm more persecuted than you' crap with me. If you choose to stay up all night, don't bitch at me if you're tired. It's not my fault."

I started to snarl back at her but stopped myself. She was right. We were both cranky and exhausted. The past week had been nothing but exams, studying and more exams. Not just in math, science, biology and all our academic studies; we also had daily tests measuring how "human" we could be. These were to see if we could remain under control in extreme, stressful situations, or if we'd lose it and Shift to dragon form. Yesterday, one of our "exams" had involved sitting in the middle of a circle, trying to answer calmly while everyone around us had screamed in our face or asked demanding questions. I'd kept my cool and passed easily enough, but Ember had come out of the room bristling and ready to snap at anything that touched her.

"Sorry," I offered again, and managed a half smile.

She relaxed and smiled back, mollified for now. "At least it's the last day," she said in a relieved voice. "After this, things will go back to normal."

"Yeah." I nodded. "I hope so."

"God, they'd better," Ember muttered. "If I have to endure another 'scream in your face for a half hour' exam, I'm going to bite someone's head off." She curled a lip, then took a hard bite of her cereal, crunching down with vigor. "Anyway, I have reasons to pass these stupid tests, too. Did you know that Mr. Gordon will take us to see the new horror movie if we ace the final exam?"

I smirked at her. "You *might've* mentioned that once or twice."

She ignored my sarcasm. "I'm so tired of these same stupid walls," she went on, glaring at the walls in question. "I need to get out of here, for a couple hours at least. And come on, Dante—you're excited, admit it. You've been dying to see this movie, too."

"Yes, though you know what I'm not looking forward to? Being woken up at 12:00 a.m. by *someone* sneaking into my room because she thought she heard her closet door open."

"I don't know what you're talking about," Ember answered breezily. "But you should probably leave the sleeping bag on the floor, just in case."

I shook my head, finished my glass and headed to my room for my books.

★ ★ ★

Testing was brutal. I was tired, and about an hour in, my head started to ache. But I gritted my teeth and pushed myself to finish early. Ember, shockingly, finished a few minutes after me, indicating that she *had* been studying as she'd said. I felt bad for snapping at her.

After the two-hour science test, we were ordered outside. It was midafternoon, and the sun beat down directly overhead, baking the dusty earth. A car waited for us near the gated entrance of the compound, engines humming, a man in a suit standing at the front. I was surprised, and a little wary. Testing wasn't over yet, far from it; why would they have us leave the school premises now?

The doors were opened for us by black-suited Talon employees, and we climbed in without a word, knowing questions were useless and never answered. The car pulled out of the gate, and the school soon vanished in the rear window.

As usual, it was cold in the car. A little too cold for my liking, but the tinted glass between us and the driver prevented any questions or requests to turn down the AC. Ember gazed out the window, eager to be out of the compound and away from school, no matter the situation. I was a little less enthused. Not that I wasn't happy to be outside, of course. I just didn't know what Talon had planned. Why were they taking us out of school in the middle of testing?

"Where do you think we're going?" I mused out loud, watching the desert speed by beyond the glass.

Ember shrugged. "Who cares? We're out of school and not stuck in testing for six hours. They could be taking us to the gas station and I wouldn't complain." She thought about it, then shrugged again. "Maybe they're taking us to see the movie early, because we did so well?"

I grimaced. "I highly doubt that."

Abruptly, the car made a sharp left, cruising off the narrow private road and bouncing into the desert. Startled and now even more wary, I watched the road disappear as we went deeper into the middle of nowhere.

Just as I was about to run some crazy theories by Ember, the car slowed and came to a rolling stop in a billow of dust. With a faint buzz, the glass separator rolled down a few inches, just enough for us to see the top of the driver's head over the rim.

"Get out. Both of you."

I looked out the window. There was nothing beyond the glass. No gas stations, roads, signs or cars. Nothing but desert, stretching to the horizon in every direction.

"Here?" Ember asked, echoing my confusion. "Why?"

Questions regarding orders were generally discouraged or went unanswered, so I was surprised when the driver answered. "Part of your testing," he replied brusquely. "The first to make it back passes. The other fails."

My stomach dropped, and I stared at the driver, wondering if he was serious. "What happens if we come back together?"

"Then you both fail." He made a gesture with two fingers, indicating that we leave the car. "Go."

Stunned, we slid out. As soon as the doors closed, the vehicle tore off in a cloud of dust, cruised over a sand rise and disappeared. Leaving us alone in the middle of the Mohave Desert.

Ember looked at me with defiant green eyes. "The hell? What kind of stupid test is this? The first one back passes and the other fails? Like they expect us to race each other across the desert on foot? With no phones or water or even a compass?" Glaring around, she shook her head and made a hopeless, frustrated gesture. "This is crazy. Do you even know which direction the school is?"

"Yes," I said quietly, and she blinked in surprise. "Judging from the time, and the position of the sun…" I squinted at the sky, then nodded and turned away, confident in my assessment. "The school should be…that way."

Ember sighed, crossing her arms. "Well, I'm not going to go charging off without you," she announced. "That's insane. They can suck it if they want me to pass this stupid test. We cross the finish line together, and they can just deal with two failures, right?"

For just a moment, I paused. It was likely that what Talon was really testing for was loyalty to the organization. I realized that. But if I did what Ember suggested, it would be my first real failure. I'd always passed my exams with flying colors. If I screwed up now, it would stain my perfect record.

"I don't know…" I began, but Ember tapped my arm.

"Wait a second." There was a look on her face now, the one that always worried me. The one that said she was just coming to a realization that would probably get us in trouble. "If you know where the school is, does that mean you know where the town is, too?"

I frowned. "Yes," I said slowly, gazing around. "I...think so." The nearest town was a tiny, dusty settlement with a handful of gas stations, restaurants and one very old movie theater that we'd never been to. It was thirty minutes away by car, and by my estimation, we were probably closer to the town than the school right now. "Why?"

Ember's eyes gleamed, a faint, defiant grin crossing her face. "Here's an idea," she said fiercely. "Screw their stupid test. Let's go to town instead."

I stared at her. "Skip the test? Are you crazy?"

"Why not?" Ember gestured at the terrain around us. "They dumped us here, in the middle of freaking nowhere— why shouldn't we have a little fun for once? Let's go to town and watch that movie. We can say we got horribly lost and wandered around for hours and hours. How are they gonna say otherwise?" When I still hesitated, she rolled her eyes. "Come on, Dante, we're going to fail the test anyway, you know that, right? What've we got to lose? Unless you really want to race me across the desert."

I took a breath. It was tempting. I was tired, and not just physically. I was tired of tests, tired of studying, of staying up all night only to face another grueling day of exams. And, truth be told, I was angry at Talon for giving us this impossible test, requiring the one thing I refused to do: abandon my twin.

I looked at Ember and nodded. "Yeah," I said, ignoring the brief stab of fear to the gut. "Let's do it."

★ ★ ★

It took us all afternoon to reach town, even knowing which direction we were going. The desert stretched on, eternal in its sameness. Even for two dragons who normally thrived in the heat, hours of trudging through the desert in over a hundred degree temperatures began to wear on us. By the time we saw the first of the roofs across the desert, we were hot, sweaty, thirsty and desperate to get out of the sun.

"Made it," Ember breathed, sounding triumphant. She grinned at me, eager and relieved at the same time. Her skin was slightly pink from the sun, and my own felt uncomfortably tight, making me wonder if it was possible for dragons to get sunburned. "Come on," she said, gesturing toward a distant gas station on the edge of the road. "I'm spitting sand here. Drinks first, then let's go find the theater."

My stomach danced as we approached the border of town, either in excitement, fear or a little of both. This was supremely forbidden. Cutting class, wandering into town alone, deliberately disobeying our instructors? I'd never done anything this risky before. I didn't know if I liked this feeling of nervous exhilaration and utter terror, but we couldn't turn back now.

However, as we crossed the road and headed toward the gas station, I spotted a disturbingly familiar black sedan sitting at the edge of the parking lot, and my insides gave a violent twist.

Get ahold of yourself, Dante. Not every black car is from Talon. There's no way they could know where you went—

The back door opened, and Mr. Gordon stepped out of the car, followed by two Talon agents in suits.

Ember froze. I went rigid, my mind going blank as our teacher came toward us across the lot, leaving the agents by the car. They had found us. How had they found us? Had the car turned around somehow, to make sure we were heading in the right direction? Had the driver been hiding somewhere with binoculars, watching our every move?

"Ember." Mr. Gordon's tone was impassive. He didn't sound angry, or surprised, to find us here. "Dante. Come along, it's time to go home."

Numbly, we followed him to the car. There was nothing more we could do.

The ride back was silent. I stared out the window, trying to control the sick feeling in my stomach. What would they do to us? Would this permanently stain my record with Talon? Would they decide to separate me and Ember?

I should have been afraid, and I was. I knew Talon's punishment would probably be terrible. But at the same time, the more I thought about it, the angrier I became. They were obviously watching us somehow, waiting for us to screw up. Setting us up for failure.

It wasn't fair. I thought back to all the times I had excelled, followed instructions and orders without hesitation, and my blood boiled. Hadn't I proved myself by now? Hadn't I been the model student, never questioning instructions, never complaining? Why this one pointless test that we couldn't win?

When we got back, we followed Mr. Gordon silently into one of the classrooms, where our other two trainers were waiting with displeased expressions.

"So." Mr. Gordon turned to face us as the rest of the teachers came forward. His expression was stern, disapproving. "Decided to have a little fun, did you? In the middle of your exams, no less. Would either of you care to explain what you were thinking today? And please," he added, looking at me. "Do not attempt to tell me you 'got lost.' I know that you at least, Dante, know enough to tell which direction is north.

So." He raised his eyebrows. "What were you doing in town today? Why did you ignore the test?"

"Because it was stupid," Ember growled under her breath. Mr. Gordon's eyes narrowed, and I jumped in before she made things any worse.

"I didn't understand the point of the test, sir," I said, though my own voice came out hard. "I wasn't going to leave my sister alone, in the middle of the desert. I might've known the way back, but what if Ember really did get lost? She could wander around out there for days and get hurt or dehydrated."

"That was unlikely," Mr. Gordon replied. "We were watching you both via satellite. Neither of you was in any real danger. Besides, your assessment of the exam was incorrect. We were not testing to see who could make it back first—we were testing to see if either of you would Shift into your real forms in order to make it back faster. But, as you circumvented the exam entirely, that point is moot."

Satellites. So that was how they knew. My heart sank even more. We'd never had a chance to escape. They'd known what we were doing from the very beginning.

Mr. Gordon gave me a piercing stare, seeming to read my thoughts. "Do let me make this perfectly clear, Mr. Hill," he said firmly. "We are always watching you. We are always testing you. Nothing you do goes unnoticed. Remember that, *always*."

"You were *tracking* us?" Ember was completely pissed now, and I winced. When she was this angry, there was no telling what she would say. "Well, here's a thought—maybe that's *why* we had to get out of here. Everything is work, exams and these stupid mind games. We can't ever catch a break.

Maybe if you would let up a little, we wouldn't be so desperate to leave!"

Mr. Gordon looked at me, his eyes cold. "And you, Dante? Do you feel the same?"

"I…" I hesitated, feeling all eyes on me, both human and dragon. Ember was staring at me angrily, wanting but not really expecting me to back her up. The teachers were all watching us, silently judging. Always judging. No matter what I did, how perfect I was or how much I excelled. I could never please them. And suddenly, I was angry, too.

"Yes, sir." I glared at Mr. Gordon. "From the time I got here, I've done everything you wanted. I never Shift, never ask questions, never do anything I'm not supposed to. Until now, I've aced every test you've given me, and yet I'm still being tracked? When have I given you reason not to trust me? All I've *ever* done for the past three years is excel."

The human regarded us in heavy silence for a moment, then sighed.

"Yes," he said, surprising us both. "I know we ask a lot of you. I know it seems unfair at times. But you must understand, it is for your own protection, as well as your future. We push you because it is imperative that you succeed. Because you have a destiny with Talon, and it is up to us to make certain you get there." He clasped his hands, seeming to speak more to me now, instead of my angry sibling. "You are not mere humans. You are dragons, and your future is far greater than anything a human could hope for. I know it is difficult now, but if you work hard and do exactly what Talon wants, someday you will be the ones on the other side."

The ones on the other side.

Something clicked in my head and, suddenly, everything became clear. I was a dragon, and Talon was one of the most powerful organizations in the world. If I was in Talon, I would be the one in charge. I'd be the one calling the shots. I wouldn't have to take pointless exams, listen to humans or worry that my every move was being watched. In Talon, dragons were the bosses, the presidents, the CEOs. If I was part of the organization, no one would tell me what to do ever again.

Mr. Gordon noticed my reaction and smiled. "Yes, Dante." He nodded. "Now you understand. Within the organization, you can become whatever you wish. But to get there, you must strive to become what Talon wants, even if it means putting your own desires aside for now. Remember your motto—*Ut ominous sergimous*. 'As one, we rise.' You are not merely a hatchling, you are part of something far greater than yourself. Sometimes, sacrifice is necessary."

Sacrifice is necessary.

Ember snorted, still angry and clearly unimpressed with everything. "Whatever," she muttered, crossing her arms. "I just know I'm never going to see that movie now, am I?"

Mr. Gordon was still watching me, his dark gaze assessing. His lips curled in a smug smile. "Ms. Brunner," he said, still holding my gaze. "Please call the theater and arrange a private screening for tomorrow afternoon. Tell them we will need to reserve an entire theater room for a few hours. Tell them that price is not an issue."

Ember jerked, eyes widening, and my mouth dropped open. Mr. Gordon smiled. "I think you've earned a bit of a break," our teacher said, finally glancing at Ember, who appeared stunned into speechlessness. "You are correct. It can't be training and exams every hour of every day. If you pass the final stages of your exams tomorrow, we'll all go into town to celebrate. Is that motivation enough for you, Ms. Hill?"

Ember stammered an affirmative, and Mr. Gordon nodded. But his gaze met mine over her head, and in that dark
glare, I could see the echo of his thoughts. *This is what power
is, Dante,* it said. *This is what you could have, if you do exactly what
Talon wants. At the top, no one will tell you what to do, ever again.*

At the top, you could be free.

Ember tried talking to me after we were dismissed, but I
barely heard anything she said as we walked across the dusty
yard to our rooms. My mind was spinning, and I suddenly
didn't care about the movie, or our ill-fated adventure, or
anything but the upcoming test. I knew what I had to do
now. I had a clear path, and I would not stray from it until
I reached the end, at the very top. Even though the journey
would be hard, and I would have to let some things go. It
might be painful, but in the end, it would be worth it.

Sacrifice was necessary, but I would be free.

RILEY

"Riley," said a voice out of the darkness.

I turned, shooting a bleary glance at the clock on the wall as the soldier appeared in the door frame of the cabin's tiny kitchen—4:50 a.m. Apparently, I wasn't the only early riser of the group. That, or St. George hadn't gotten much sleep, either. Yesterday had been an exhausting, mind-numbingly long day of travel, the five of us—me, Ember, Wes, St. George and the Eastern dragon—stuffed into an old black Jeep that was not designed with comfort in mind. We'd taken shifts, both in driving and getting to sit in the front passenger seat, while the rest of us huddled in the back. A couple hours from our final destination, we'd pulled into one of the many small campgrounds scattered at the base of the Ozarks and had rented a cabin for the night. It had been a relief not to have to share space in a tiny hotel room, though my mind wouldn't shut off long enough to let me sleep. Finally accepting that sleep was not an option, I'd risen and headed into the kitchen for the strongest black coffee I could make, when the soldier appeared in the doorway, wide awake, as well.

I ignored him, reaching for the coffeemaker. Well, what do you know, someone—probably St. George—had already made a pot. I poured myself a mug and took a swallow. Black and strong enough to strip paint from the wall—perfect. "What?" I mumbled.

A pause, then he took a quiet breath. "I never got the chance to thank you."

Surprised, I turned away and opened the cupboard that held the meager supplies we'd brought. "Let's not make this awkward, St. George," I muttered, pawing through cans of soup and ravioli, jerky packages and bags of candy, anything that could be heated up quickly or eaten on the road. Ugh, maybe I would just grab something later from a drivethrough. I didn't see how Ember could eat Skittles for breakfast every day. "You don't owe me anything."

"You saved my life," the soldier insisted. "You didn't have to. There was nothing anyone could have done, not with how far away we were from the city. You could've let me die."

"How much of an asshole do you think I am?" I growled, shutting the cupboard door to glare at him. "I didn't do it because I like you. I did it because it was the right thing to do. Because you're a decent shot, and you'll back us up when we need it. Because you know about the Order, how it works, what goes on in their screwed-up heads, and it's easier to stay alive when we have insider information. I did it for any number of reasons, St. George, and all of them outweighed the desire to watch you bleed out in the dirt." I narrowed my eyes, taking a sip of bitter coffee to swallow the anger. "So don't make me regret that choice with stupid questions about why I decided to save your sorry ass. Hard as it is to believe, I don't let any of my team die if I can help it. And I'd be a piss-poor leader if I let personal feelings get in the way of anything. You don't know me as well as you might think."

For some reason, that made him close his eyes in a grimace.

"Ember told me the same thing once," he said. "She was right. I didn't know anything about your kind back then. Everything the Order taught me was wrong." He drummed his fingers against his arm and glanced down the hall, where Ember, Wes and Jade still slept in quaint, woodsy rooms. "I want to know more," he said quietly. "I'm trying to understand. Even with Ember, I feel like I've barely scratched the surface."

"If only you had a dragon around to explain these things to you."

He smiled, though his expression remained shadowed and distant. "I don't want to fight you, Riley," he said after a moment, and we both knew what he was referring to. "You're not my enemy. I don't want to feel like I have to watch my back with any of my teammates. I love Ember." He said it simply, like he was telling me the weather. "And I know there's something between you and her, something...Draconic, I guess, that I might not ever understand. It's not my place to ask—she'll tell me when she's ready. But I'm here to stay. I'm not going anywhere."

I swallowed the growl and pushed Cobalt down from where he was rising up, bristling and indignant. "And you're telling me this why?"

"It needed to be said." He stared down the hall again. "We've been dancing around this for too long. I'm done hiding. I'd rather have everything out in the open. You saved my life," he continued, obnoxiously sincere and calm. "I thought I'd give you the courtesy of knowing where I stood."

Anger boiled, but I forced a smirk and pushed past him, into the living room. "Near-death experience making you sentimental, St. George?"

"Maybe." His voice remained the same. "But it doesn't change anything."

"What are you two talking about?"

Ember walked out of the hall, yawning as she came into the kitchen. Her crimson hair stuck out at every angle, and Cobalt stirred at the sight of her. With a brief smile at St. George, she walked to the coffeepot, poured the contents into a mug and padded back to join us in the living room.

"Did we wake you?" the soldier asked, ignoring, I noticed, the previous question. Ember shook her head and brought the mug to her lips.

"Couldn't sleep. Heard the two of you out here and thought I might as well get up, go over the plan or something. Ugh, that's awful." She pulled the mug away from her lips, screwing up her face, then took another sip. "I assume it hasn't changed, right? We're still keeping to the same plan?"

I sighed. "Yeah." I nodded, taking a bracing swallow myself. "Same plan. As soon as the others are up, we'll head out. We need a few things before we can pull this off."

★ ★ ★

"All right," I said, pulling to a stop on the narrow, winding road that cut through the mountain. Up ahead, a yellow barricade blocked both lanes, and a single police car sat beside it, lights flashing blue. "There's the security checkpoint." I glanced at Ember and St. George in the backseat, seeing a pair of strangers staring back. Like me, both wore black suits—or *monkey suits* as Wes so elegantly put it—and dark shades, the "few things" we had to pick up for this plan to work. I resented the fact that Wes didn't have to dress up for this stupid mission; he got to stay at the cabin. I *hated* G-man suits; the tie around my neck felt like a noose, and the jacket was tight in all the wrong places. St. George, obnoxiously, seemed perfectly at ease in a suit and tie, probably used to being in uniform, but I wanted this over and done with as soon as possible.

"Remember," I told them and the Asian dragon sitting in the passenger seat, "I'll do the talking, but if anyone asks, we're with the Department of Homeland Security. You two are assistants in training, so any questions should be directed to me or Ms. Long here."

"And what are you going to tell them?" Ember wanted to know. "You don't know any more about this Security Department than we do."

"Department of Homeland Security, Firebrand," I corrected. "And I might not be a Chameleon, but I am a master at bullshitting. Generally, I don't need to know what I'm talking about. I just have to bluster and act like the person I'm talking to is wasting my time—basically be a giant dick—and most humans will cave. If you act like you're supposed to be there, people will generally assume the same. What about you?" I asked the woman beside me. "Think you can BS your way past a guard?"

The Eastern dragon's voice was dry. "I'm sure I can come up with something."

"All right, then." I faced forward and put the car into Drive. "Let's do this."

We cruised up to the barricade, stopping as the door to the police car opened and an overweight human stepped out. I rolled down the window, watching him with as much bored disdain as I could muster as the officer strolled up to the side of our car.

"Sorry, folks," the human said, peering in at us. "The road is closed for now. You'll have to take the detour around."

I flashed the fake badge Wes had given me that morning.

"We're expected," I said in a bored, *I-can't-believe-I-have-to-deal-with-this* tone of voice.

"The DHS?" The officer pulled back, shaking his head. "Damn. I didn't realize a plane crash was such a big deal." He gave me a furtive look, lowering his voice as if there were people around to hear him. "So, what's really going on down there? You government types have been in and out for days. What, was this some kind of terrorist attack or something?"

"Sorry, but I'm not at liberty to say," I replied stiffly, dropping my arm, and the badge, from view. "And you should know better than to ask. You're lucky I don't have time to report you to your superior."

"Hey, don't get all high and mighty on me, suit." The officer stepped back with a sour look on his face. "You government hotshots think you can come through and order us around, but you're wrong. This ain't your town." But he stepped back, waving us through the barricade. "Go on. The sooner you're finished here, the sooner you can leave."

Triumphant, I rolled up the window and continued down the road, watching the flashing lights get smaller in the rearview mirror until we turned a bend and they were lost from sight.

"That was easy," Ember muttered.

I smirked. "Like I said, Firebrand. Master of BS, right here. Still, we shouldn't press our luck. Try not to talk to anyone while we're snooping around. And if you happen to see the Chameleon, let me know so we can clear out right away. The humans might not suspect anything, but she'll definitely know something's up if she sees three other dragons wandering around."

As we turned a corner, the "town" came into view, a cluster of run-down houses and trailer homes huddled between the mountains on either side of the road. *This is it?* I thought. Town *might be too strong of a word. Why the hell was Talon even here? What did they want?* I pulled off the road, parking the car in the first driveway I came to, well away from the center of town and the scattering of people wandering the street. A lot of government types, I noticed. Men and women in black suits, along with a few in uniform. Something was definitely going on.

"Everyone stay together," I warned as we exited the vehicle. "Remember, we're the Department of Homeland Security, you two are our assistants and we're here to assess the situation."

"No civilians," St. George muttered, gazing down the street. "Everyone here is an official or agent of some kind. The town is empty."

"Yeah, I noticed." I narrowed my eyes, trying to shake the unease that had settled under my skin. "Something is wrong here. This sure as hell isn't about just a plane crash. As Wes would say, I've got a bad feeling about this."

"Then it is good that we came to see what is going on," Jade put in, and if I didn't know better, I would swear there was a hint of *I told you so* in her voice. I ignored it and started walking.

As we began seeing more houses up close, I understood why there were people in suits swarming all over the damn place. And it raised the hair on the back of my neck.

The houses were all burned. Some just had a few scorch marks here and there; others were nothing but blackened shells, crumbling to ash. For more than a few, only the foundations were left, blasted cinder blocks and scorched concrete lying beneath what used to be a home. Several front yards held a colorful assortment of lawn ornaments, kids' toys, and junked cars rusting side by side. They were untouched, as was the vegetation and trees around the buildings. Only the houses were charred to nothing, as if blasted with fire from the inside.

"Jeez," Ember whispered, her eyes wide as she gazed around at the devastation. "What happened here? It looks like a bomb went off or something."

"No," I said. "A bomb wouldn't just destroy the houses and leave everything else untouched. Neither would a forest fire, or a damn crashing plane. What does it really look like happened here?"

St. George's voice was grim. "Like this place was attacked by fire-breathing dragons."

"Yeah," I muttered as a chill crept up my spine and turned the heat in my veins to ice. "Though, if Talon is behind this, I have no idea what that means. They've *never* engaged in something so blatant. The cover-up would have to be massive, and I don't see what they would gain from it. If this is Talon..." I shook my head, repressing a shiver. "Something is definitely wrong."

Voices halted us. Up ahead, a pair of humans in white coats stepped out of one of the more intact trailer homes, arguing with each other, and went hurrying away down the street. Leaving the door wide open behind them.

"Come on," Jade said. "Let us do some snooping."

We slipped into the trailer, and I was immediately struck by the smell. The faint, acrid stench of smoke lingered in the air, baked into the flimsy walls and floors. Part of the kitchen wall was gone, blackened and scorched around the edges, and it looked like the flames had spread to the living room. Tables and chairs were tipped over, broken dishes were scattered over the floor and the windows had been shattered. I wondered what had happened to the people that lived here. Had they been eating dinner, or asleep in their beds, when a dragon clawed open their door and turned the place into an inferno? Or had something else, someone else, been responsible?

"St. George," I murmured as we slowly picked our way through the rubble and charred furniture. "Is there any way the Order could have done this?"

He frowned. "It doesn't seem like them," he answered, though he sounded unsure. "They would have no reason to attack this place unless there was a dragon living here. But even then..." He gazed around the devastated living room. "They wouldn't take out the entire community. That would raise way too many questions."

"Yeah, no kidding. Which is why I'm having a really hard time believing that Talon was behind this. They're just as paranoid about discovery as the Order, if not more so. I mean, that's their entire freaking philosophy—stay hidden, blend in, don't let the humans know about dragons." I stared through the giant hole in the wall to the house across the street. Unlike this home, it had been completely devastated, burned to the ground, only a few twisted frames poking up from the ashes. "Something this huge...it flies in the face of every single thing Talon taught us since the day the organization was founded. Why would they be breaking all their rules now? It makes no sense at all." I raked a hand through my hair, shaking my head as I groped for an answer. "Maybe this wasn't Talon *or* St. George. Maybe this was a random terrorist attack, or something else entirely human."

"Riley," Ember said from the living room, her voice urgent. "Take a look at this."

I walked to where she was crouched beside an overturned

coffee table, staring at a patch of cheap carpet. The carpet was gray and thin, but when she moved the table aside, a large brown stain came to light. I winced.

"Yep, that's blood. Dammit. Well, I'd say we have a pretty good indication of what happened to the people here."

"No," Ember said, putting a hand on my arm. "That's not what I wanted to show you. Look at this."

She pointed to the coffee table, holding it on its side. It was scorched on one corner, a large black burn mark covering half the surface, but below that, raked across the wood, were four long, straight gashes.

"What do those look like?" Ember whispered, and I closed my eyes.

"Claw marks."

"Excuse me."

We turned. Two men were entering the trailer home, frowning at us as they stepped through the door.

"I'm sorry," the older one said, gazing around at us, "but this is an ongoing investigation. Who are you, and what authorization do you have to be here?"

Before I could stand up or say anything, Jade turned, flashing her badge for both men to see. "Department of Homeland Security," she said in a firm, no-nonsense voice. "We are here to assess the situation and determine whether or not we need to escalate the current threat level."

"The DHS?" The older human looked unsure. "No one said you were coming. When did—"

"Do you have evidence to support this was not a terrorist attack made on American soil?" Jade interrupted, stepping forward slightly. The man blinked.

"I… No, not really. We're still—"

"Then it is possible this was a malicious attack carried out by extremists."

"I suppose." The human sighed and looked away, flustered. "Look, we don't really know what we have yet," he admitted. "The evidence we've gathered so far has been... strange. The inspector has been trying to keep everything under wraps until we figure out what really happened here. If you want, you can check out the evidence tent at the end of the road. See the weirdness for yourself."

"Thank you," Jade said, and gave a brittle smile. "We will do that." She started to turn but paused, staring at the human as if surprised he was still there. "You may go now."

The two men retreated, practically scrambling over each other to get out of the house. They fled, slamming the door behind them, and strode away down the road without looking back. Jade, standing at the edge of the room with her arms crossed, allowed herself a triumphant smirk.

"Damn," I said as the Eastern dragon turned back. "That was impressive. I guess I'm not the only one with a master's in BS."

She smiled. "The DHS does have a public website," she said. "They list their mission statement, job offers, history, everything. When Wesley told me how we were getting onto the crash site today, I did my research. But yes." Her smile widened. "If it is necessary for our survival, I have been known to 'bullshit' with the best of them from time to time."

I snorted a laugh. "Wish you were around a couple years ago. I could've used the help. Anyway..." I glanced out the hole in the wall, down the road where the two men had disappeared. "Shall we track down this evidence tent and see if we can uncover what the hell is going on?"

The evidence tent wasn't hard to find, being a large

white structure at the edge of the road and the only building that wasn't charred, scorched or burned to the ground. Humans in suits and white coats were swarming in and out of it, but other than flashing my badge at the entrance, we didn't really get a second glance. Inside, metal shelves ran the length of one canvas wall, each of them holding boxes marked with labels in clear plastic bags. Immediately, Ember headed to the wall, her innate curiosity no doubt driving her forward, while St. George hovered at our backs, watching the crowd. Grateful that the soldier was keeping an eye out, I walked up and peeked into one box.

It held an assortment of clothing in more plastic bags. But as I looked closer, I saw that most of the garments had large brown stains soaking the fabric. Blood. And a lot of it, judging from the mangled clothes. I looked at the next box in line and saw more of the same; only this time, I could make out several long, straight tears in some of the clothes, as if made by the edge of a knife.

Or the claws of a very large reptile.

"It seems the evidence against Talon is becoming more and more damning," Jade remarked, also peering into the containers. "Between the fires, general destruction and the Talon agent on the news, it certainly seems like the organization is at least partially involved."

"I still can't believe they'd be this sloppy," I said. "They had to have known that something this big would cause a huge investigation, with everyone scrambling to figure out what the hell happened." I snorted. "Plane crash, my ass. I bet it's not even Talon that's trying to cover this up—the government has no idea what they're dealing with, so they invented a cover story to keep things quiet until they can figure it out. And since Talon has agents seeded throughout all the government agencies, they're only too happy to help."

"That might be true, but it is not the question that needs answering," Jade mused. "If the organization is involved, then the real question becomes *why*. What could they possibly hope to gain here?"

"Riley," Ember murmured in a warning voice. She pulled a bag out of a nearby crate. I looked up, and my stomach flipped.

Resting in the bag was a small, flat oval, pointed on one end and glittering a dull iron gray. Even though the color was strange, one I'd never seen before, I knew what it was instantly. We all did.

A dragon scale.

EMBER

"Give me that, Firebrand," Riley muttered, quickly stepping forward and taking the bag from my hands. It vanished into his suit pocket as he glanced around warily. "No point in giving the humans any more hints that dragons are real. Or at least that something very unnatural went down." He eyed a human wandering by who looked like a scientist, then lowered his voice again. "Regardless, I think we've seen all we need to see here."

"I agree," Jade said, nodding. "From the evidence, it is safe to assume that dragons attacked this town in their true form, and that Talon is at least partially responsible. Unfortunately, that theory creates more questions than it answers. Why would they attack this community? Especially since, as Riley pointed out, the entire point of the organization is to hide the existence of dragons from the human population. Why risk that now?"

Riley shook his head. "I have no clue, but I get the feeling we're not going to like the answer."

Abruptly, Garret stalked back, his gaze intense as he swept between us. "The woman you described is approaching this location," he said in a low voice, making Riley jerk up.

"Hell. Miranda is coming? Come on, we can't be seen by her."

We fast-walked toward the end of the room, passing more humans and looking for a way out as we went deeper into the tent. Unfortunately, there didn't seem to be a back exit, and the open room offered very few hiding spots.

"There," Riley said, nodding toward a corner of the tent that had been sectioned off. Plastic flaps hung to the floor, and the area beyond was dark. With Riley leading and Garret watching our backs, we hurried across the room and ducked through the plastic walls.

My stomach recoiled. The room beyond the flaps was dim and cold, and the sickly smell of death lingered on the air, masked by chemicals and disinfectant. A pair of stainless-steel tables stood in the center of the room, and atop the farthest counter was something long and suspiciously body shaped, covered with a sheet.

I drew in a slow breath to quiet my heartbeat and nudged Garret, who was still peering through the flaps to watch for the Chameleon. He glanced at me with a puzzled frown, but it quickly faded when he realized what I was staring at.

"There she is," Riley growled softly, not taking his eyes from the room beyond. "Hello, Miranda. What are you doing here? Covering up for the organization again?"

I tore my eyes from what was obviously a dead body and peeked through the plastic flaps again, seeing a dark-haired, smartly dressed woman enter the tent, followed by what looked like an assistant of some kind. The woman, or dragon, really, wasn't tall or intimidating—not like Lilith, who could walk into a room and freeze you in place with a glare. But everything about this woman radiated charisma, charm and confidence, much like another Chameleon I used to know.

As a certain traitorous brother entered my thoughts, I swallowed the brief pang and forced myself to concentrate on the Talon agent at the end of the other room. She spoke briskly to the assistant and pointed to several boxes along the wall. The human bobbed his head in mute agreement, and the Chameleon smiled, then spun and exited the tent as suddenly as she had appeared.

"All right," Riley mused, straightening and drawing back from the flap. "So Talon sent an agent to help with the cover-up, but also to make sure certain evidence just…disappears. Sounds like them." He nodded. "I think we're going to have to pay a visit to a certain hotel room in town."

I frowned at him. "How did you get all that? They were clear across the room."

He smirked down at me. "I was a Basilisk, Firebrand. Among my many enviable talents are picking locks, hiding in plain sight…and reading lips." His grin widened at my surprised look before he sobered and glanced through the flaps again. "Seems that our lovely Talon agent is staying at a hotel not far from here," he muttered, watching the human gather up a couple crates and leave the tent. "Those boxes of evidence are likely headed there now. If anyone knows what Talon was doing here, it will be Miranda. And if they're planning anything else like this, I'd kinda like to know when and why."

"I agree," came Garret's grave voice from behind us. I turned to find him standing next to the counter I'd pointed to earlier, only he had pulled back a corner of the sheet, revealing a truly hideous sight. The corpse lying on the table was barely recognizable as human, as shriveled and burned as it was. It looked more like a piece of charred wood than anything that had once been alive. My stomach heaved, and

I had to look away, feeling bile rise to my throat. Was that what *my* victims looked like, after I'd blasted them with dragonfire? I'd killed both Talon servants and soldiers of St. George in battle. Had they all ended up like that withered corpse? Blackened skeletons of what had once been human?

"If Talon is planning another attack," Garret continued in that same somber voice, though his steely eyes glinted in the darkness, "we need to stop it before this happens again."

★ ★ ★

We followed the Chameleon from the "crash site," tailing her white sedan until it pulled into a normal, innocuous-looking hotel, not the Ritz but not a Motel 6, either. From across the lot, we watched the Chameleon walk briskly into the hotel followed by two large men I assumed were body-guards. Left behind, her poor assistant hauled several boxes out of the trunk and staggered after them.

I looked at Riley as the human vanished through the hotel doors. "So, how are we going to do this?" I asked. "Wait to sneak in tonight?"

He shook his head. "No time for that, Firebrand. She could be leaving today and taking all the evidence with her. If we want to see what Talon is up to, we need to get in there now." He frowned and drummed his fingers on the steering wheel. "Problem is, I can take care of Miranda and get us into the room, but if she leaves any of her guards behind, that's going to make things difficult. If she comes back and finds an unconscious human lying on her floor, she's going to guess someone was there and warn the organization."

"Don't worry about that," Jade said, surprising us all. "You just concentrate on getting the Talon woman away from the vicinity and finding her room. I will take care of the guards."

He eyed her, raising a brow. "And how are you going to do that exactly? Eat them?"

"Please. I would very likely get food poisoning." She wrinkled her nose and sniffed in clear disgust. "Do not worry. As I once told our soldier friend, a *shen-lung* has her ways. You get the Talon agent out of the building and find where her room is located. Leave any guards to me."

Riley stared at her a moment longer, then shrugged. "You're awfully certain about that," he muttered, pulling his phone out of his jacket pocket. "But as we're a little short on time, I guess I'll have to trust you know what you're doing. Hang on a second." He pressed a button on his phone, then put it to his ear. "Wes. We're at the Wingate Hotel, about ten miles from the crash site. I need you to find which room Miranda's staying in." A pause, and he rolled his eyes. "Of course we're going to sneak in, what do you think?... I don't know, the Eastern dragon thinks she can get past the guards." He sighed. "Don't argue, Wes. Just do it."

A couple minutes passed, and he nodded. "Three-eighteen. Got it. I'll call you if there's trouble." He frowned. "Thank you, Wesley, your votes of confidence are always so inspiring."

"Okay," I said as Riley lowered his arm. "One problem down—we know what room she's in. How are we going to get her to leave long enough to search it?"

"Don't worry, Firebrand." Riley gave a wicked smile. "King of BS right here, remember? Watch and learn."

Pressing in a number, he held the phone to his ear and waited a few moments as it rang. "Hello, front desk?... Yes, could you please connect me to Miranda Kent's room? I believe she's staying there tonight." A pause, and he grinned. "Thank you."

I held my breath, watching Riley and counting the number of imaginary rings in my head. At three rings, he raised his head. "Ms. Kent? This is Director Smith, from the crash site? Sorry to bother you, but we recently found something of an anomaly near one of the victims, and thought you might want to see it."

As he spoke, his other hand reached into his suit pocket and pulled out the plastic bag, holding it up with narrowed eyes. "Well, we're not entirely sure. We've never seen such a thing before—it looks like some kind of reptile scale. But far bigger than any species in known existence—" He stopped, as if the voice on the other end had cut him off, and the gleam in his eyes grew brighter. "All right, then. We won't do anything until you get here. Thank you."

"Clever," Jade remarked as he lowered the phone. Riley snorted.

"I just know how Talon works, is all." He stuffed the phone and the scale into his pocket again and leaned back in smug satisfaction. "If Miranda's job is to cover this up and make all evidence of dragons disappear, something like this is going to light a fire under her tail like nothing else. She'll be desperate to get to that evidence before Talon hears about it. We should see her anytime now. Like a bat out of hell."

Less than two minutes later, the hotel doors opened and the Chameleon and a single guard strode across the lot, setting an even brisker pace toward the car, the assistant scrambling along in their wake. The woman's normally smiling face was taut as she entered the passenger side and slammed the door shut. As the guard opened the driver's side, the assistant nearly tripped over himself getting into the car. The sedan backed hastily out of the parking spot, barely missing the hood of a truck as it did, and peeled out of the lot.

Riley snickered and straightened in his seat again. "And

that," he remarked, watching the sedan turn onto the road, cutting off a van as it merged into traffic, "is how you freak out a Chameleon. But we do need to hurry, before she realizes 'Mr. Smith' is no longer at the crash site."

"One of her guards wasn't with her," Garret observed. Riley nodded.

"Yep. Which means he'll be in her room, just like I thought." He turned to Jade, who seemed perfectly calm and serene, even as my heart was pounding with nerves and anticipation. "All right, O great and mysterious *shen-lung*," he stated, and waved his hand at the hotel. "It's all yours."

Jade nodded. Taking off the suit jacket, she laid it over the back of her seat. Her heels followed, and then her earrings, being placed carefully in the cup holders as we looked on in bewilderment. "How long will you need to be in the room?" she asked, unbuttoning the cuffs of her white shirt. Riley blinked.

"Uh, not long," he said, watching her finish with the sleeves and unbutton the top. "Five minutes, at most."

The Eastern dragon nodded. "Give me ten minutes," she said, and left the car. We watched her walk barefooted across the parking lot, pulling the tie from her bun as she did, and enter the hotel through the front doors. Riley shook his head and glanced back at Garret.

"If this goes spectacularly to hell," he told him, "I'm blaming you. You realize that."

The soldier just smiled grimly.

Ten long, tense minutes later, Riley blew out an explosive breath and reached for the door handle. "Okay," he announced far too brightly. "Let's go see if our Eastern princess has managed to eat anyone."

We cautiously entered the hotel and made our way through

the long aisles toward room 318. Along the way, a maid stepped out of one of the rooms, pushing a cart, and Riley quite literally ran into it. He tumbled to the floor with a yelp, and the poor maid began a string of rapid apologies, rushing over and asking if he was all right, while Garret and I looked on in confusion. Riley, picking himself up off the floor, suddenly switched to perfect, fluent Spanish, making soothing motions with his hands and, from what I could tell, assuring her he was fine. He said something that made her laugh, and then she thanked him and walked away, pushing the cart down the hall again. I stared after her, then at the rogue, who seemed very pleased with himself.

"What the hell was that?" I demanded. "I've seen you move, and there's no way that was an accident. You ran into her on purpose, didn't you?"

Riley grinned, dusted off his pants and then held up a card between two fingers.

"I was going to say I left my key card in the room and could she please open the door for me," he admitted as we quickly moved toward the elevators. "That's always worked in the past. But I figured this might be faster."

"Risky," Garret remarked. "What if you couldn't lift it without getting caught?" Riley smirked.

"I don't get caught, St. George. Now, let's get to Miranda's room before anything else happens."

We took the elevator to the third floor and easily found room 318. The hallway was silent, and no sounds or light came from the room beyond the door. Riley cast furtive glances over his shoulder, making sure no one was around, and raised the card he took from the maid.

"All right," he said in a low voice. "Here goes. Let's see if that Eastern dragon actually did what she said she could."

He slid the key into the slot. It beeped green, and we pushed the door open.

The room beyond was empty.

Riley let out a breath, and beside me, Garret relaxed. I slumped in relief, letting muscles that had tensed up for a fight uncoil. "Okay." The rogue nodded, shutting the door behind us. "I don't know how she did it, but I'm not complaining. Let's find that evidence and see if we can discover what Talon is up to. But remember," he warned as we stepped farther inside. "Try not to disturb anything. We don't want Miranda knowing we were here. Let's find what we're looking for and get the hell out."

That sounded like a good idea. The hotel room wasn't large, and we did a sweep of the place fairly quickly. There was nothing in the main room or the bathroom, but when Riley pulled open the closet door...

"Dammit," he muttered, gazing at several cardboard boxes stacked neatly in the corner. They were taped, sealed shut, with shipping labels stuck to the sides. "Well, here's the evidence, but we can't get inside to look at it. Not without Miranda knowing we were here. Where are they sending these? I wonder." He pulled one of the boxes toward him and looked at the address on top. "NewTech," he growled, and shook his head. "Son of a bitch, there's another lab. Firebrand, grab me a piece of paper or something, would you? Looks like we to need to check this place out. Maybe Wes can find something on them."

I hurried to the desk in the corner and reached for the complimentary notepad sitting beside the phone, then hesitated. The Chameleon's laptop lay open and dark on the surface of the desk, a mug of coffee cooling beside it. As if she might have been working on something and had to rush off before she could complete it.

I reached for the touchpad and jiggled the screen to life, bringing up a page with an unsent email across the surface.

Mr. Hill, the top line read.

My stomach turned to ice. I sank into the chair, scanning the rest of the message as the cold spread to every part of my body.

I have arrived on scene, the email read. Per Talon's orders, all evidence at the "crash site" has been gathered and logged accordingly. The human officials are all too willing to accept the cover story, as they have no idea what they are dealing with. They know something unnatural happened, but so far their posited explanations range from the mundane to the absurd. I believe the organization to be in no danger of discovery. As you requested, the first boxes of evidence we have taken from the site will be sent to the specified location today. Expect their arrival in no less than twenty-four hours.

Ut ominous sergimus.

Miranda Kent.

"Ember?" Garret's voice echoed softly across the room, wrenching me out of my daze. I might've gone a little pale, because his gray eyes were worried as they met mine. "What's wrong?"

"Dante," I whispered, and both he and Riley jerked up at the name. "Dante is part of this. He's behind the cover-up. This message is to him."

Both boys came to my side immediately, peering over my shoulders at the laptop screen. "Well, shit," Riley growled in my ear. "Then we definitely need to visit this 'specified location' and see what the hell is going on."

I stared at the screen, seeing only my brother's name,

standing out from the rest. *Dante*. All the feelings I thought I'd repressed—hurt, dismay, anger, betrayal—surged up again, making my stomach turn. *Why are you involved in this? What the hell are you doing?*

The words on-screen seemed to mock me. I was vaguely aware of Riley grabbing a scrap of paper and scribbling something down. "All right, that's it," he announced, straightening quickly. "I think we've found everything we can. Let's get out of here before her guards come back."

I shook myself, following Riley to the door with Garret close at my back. Now was not the time to dwell on traitorous siblings. I would think about my brother, and his role in this whole sordid mess, later. When we were away from the hotel and shady Talon agents who could return at any moment.

But as Riley opened the door and peered out, voices echoed down the corridor, making him jerk back. Through the frame, I saw two people walking toward us down the hall. One was a large man with a thick neck and chest, one of the guards we'd seen with Miranda. The other, walking beside him, was a small, slender woman with long black hair...

...dressed only in a towel.

For a second, my brain stuttered. It was Jade, I could see that, but the woman walking toward us with the guard was as different from the poised, elegant Eastern dragon as a swan was to a chicken. Snatches of conversation drifted to us, with Jade thanking the guard for escorting her back to her room, and how silly she felt for locking herself out. Her voice was high-pitched, giggly and slightly slurred, and she swayed a bit when she walked, as if very drunk. Of course, the guard wasn't paying any attention to his surroundings, being distracted by the beautiful Asian woman in nothing but a towel. But we were still trapped. They were still coming toward us, and if we tried to leave now, the man would definitely see us.

Jade looked up, and for a moment, her eyes met mine through the crack in the door. Slowing, she reached out and snagged the guard's sleeve, tugging him to a halt in the middle of the corridor. The guard turned, frowning, as Jade rambled on, asking him questions and talking so quickly it was hard to understand her.

Now's our chance. I nudged Riley and he nodded, silently pulling open the door. But as we stepped into the hall, the guard, apologizing to Jade, started to turn back toward the room. For a second, my heart lurched, knowing he was going to see us. There was nowhere we could hide.

Jade dropped the towel.

My eyes bulged. Riley froze. The guard turned back instantly, his attention definitely not in danger of landing on us anymore. As Jade's high-pitched giggles rang out in the stunned silence, Garret, his cheeks as red as a tomato, immediately took advantage of the distraction and began walking away. I glanced at Riley, saw him staring wide-eyed at the scene in the center of the hall and punched his arm. Hard.

He jerked, giving me a sheepish grin, and we fled the floor, ducking into the elevators and out of sight.

★ ★ ★

Jade rejoined us in the parking lot fifteen minutes later, fully clothed, sliding into the passenger seat as if nothing had happened. Her serene expression remained unchanged as she shut the door and began putting on her shoes and earrings, not noticing, or choosing to ignore, the stunned silence from the rest of us.

"Well?" she said, finally turning around. "I trust you found what you were looking for, yes?" As she glanced at Riley, her lips curled in a faint, defiant smile. "Please tell me you were able to acquire what you needed from the Talon agent's room. I would hate to have given you a show for nothing."

Riley gave a bark of laughter, as if he couldn't help himself, and shook his head. "I think I've been dethroned." He chuckled as the Eastern dragon raised a brow at him. "The king of BS is dead. Long live the queen."

GARRET

"Are you bloody serious?" Wes exclaimed later that night. "You're going to try to sneak into yet *another* Talon facility? Is our life not exciting enough, or do the lot of you just have some sort of mutual death wish?"

It was late evening, and the four of us were back in the cabin, having explained to Wes what we had found at the crash site. Riley stood in the center of the living room, arms crossed, while Wes watched him from the kitchen counter. I leaned against the far wall, and Jade sat peacefully in an armchair, watching everything in silence. The only one not in attendance was Ember, who had retreated to her room as soon as we'd arrived, claiming that she had a headache and wanted to lie down. She had been quiet and withdrawn ever since we'd left the hotel, probably brooding over her brother and his involvement with Talon. I worried for her; Dante was the one person who could get under her skin and make her question everything.

Riley sighed. "It's not like it's a heavily armed secret compound, Wes," he said. "You researched it yourself. It's an office building, certainly owned by Talon, but in the middle of a city. There's not going to be guards with machine guns walking around."

"You hope," Wes shot back. "This is *Talon*. I wouldn't put anything past them, and you should know better, too, Riley. You could be walking into a death trap."

"You're the one who wanted us to uncover what Talon is up to."

"Bloody hell, I realize that! But I didn't think we were going to be waltzing into Talon itself."

"This is necessary, Wesley," Jade said in her cool, unruffled voice. "This only proves that Talon is planning something, and we must discover what that is before it is too late."

"And you know you're going to go along with it," Riley added. "So can we just skip the whining and get to the part where you actually start helping?"

"I could do that," Wes said, scowling at him. "But then, who would tell you what an absolute wanker you are?" He sighed and opened his laptop, then bent over the keys.

I rose and slipped quietly from the room toward the hallway where the bedrooms were located. Riley watched me leave over the back of Wes's stool, but he didn't say anything as I continued into the hall and walked to the door at the very end. Light glimmered through the crack at the bottom, and I tapped on the wood.

"It's open," came the muffled voice beyond the frame.

I pushed the door back with a squeak. Ember sat on her bed with her back against the headboard and one leg drawn to her chest. She had changed out of the black suit, which lay in a crumpled pile at the foot of the bed, and now wore jeans and a long-sleeved shirt, though I could still see the slick material of the Viper suit poking up through her collar. I knew she rarely went without it anymore, just in case she needed to Shift into her real form, either to escape or to attack. Her hands rested in her lap, one of them curled around an item I couldn't see.

"Hey, Garret." Green eyes rose to mine as I entered the room, and she offered a tired smile. "Shouldn't you be out there plotting our next move with Riley? Or should I say, secret agent man?" The smile widened the tiniest bit. "I meant to tell you earlier—you look good in a tie. You and Riley both. I think we should pretend to be government agents more often."

I smiled as I closed the door, though my mind wasn't on clothes right now. "Good luck with that. I think Riley changed out of his suit even before you did." Walking to the bed, I gazed down at her, feeling that odd heat start to spread through my insides. "You all right?" I asked softly.

She nodded, scooting aside to make room for me on the mattress. "Yeah," she admitted as I settled carefully beside her, leaning back against the frame. "Sorry I wasn't out there. I was…distracted."

Her arm brushed mine, and my pulse stuttered. Gently, I reached for the hand pressed against her knee and turned it over to see what she was holding. A small quartz crystal lay in her palm, glimmering softly in the light as her fingers uncurled. Ember smiled as she gazed down at it.

"Dante gave this to me," she admitted, "years ago, when we were just kids. He knew I liked shiny things. He did, too, actually. Maybe more than I did." She chuckled, though it sounded a little sad. "That's one thing the stories get right— dragons love treasure. We each had our own little hoard that we hid from each other. I knew he wanted to keep this." She tilted her palm so that the crystal gleamed under the lamps. "But he gave it me instead. It's the only thing from Crescent Beach I've been able to take with me." She wrinkled her nose. "Well, besides the damn Viper suit. Everything else I've lost or had to give up, but I still have this."

Her eyes were shadowed. Reaching down, I took her hand, curling my fingers over hers. "I'm sorry," I murmured. "I know you miss him."

"What is he doing, Garret?" Ember whispered, closing her eyes. "I keep going over that email in my mind, from every possible angle, and coming to the same conclusion. I thought I knew him. I thought Talon was just deceiving him, lying to him like they do to everyone else. I was sure that if Dante really understood what they were about, what they really did, he would never have stayed with them. But..." She opened her eyes, and her expression was tortured, making my insides knot. "If he was involved with the cover-up, then he knew what was going on, what Talon was doing. He knew that they...killed everyone there, massacred an entire community like it was nothing." She curled her fingers around the quartz again, making a fist. "What's happened to you, Dante?" she whispered, and her voice was almost accusing. "How could you have been a part of that? Dammit, if I ever see you again, what am I supposed to do now?"

"Ember." Reaching out, I gently pulled her against me, wrapping my arms around her. She was quiet, curled up against my side, the hand that clutched the quartz trapped between us.

"I thought I could save him," she whispered at last. "I wanted, so badly, for him to be with us. I thought that if I could just make him see what Talon is really like..." She trailed off, pressing her face to my chest, making my heart thump in my ears. I said nothing, just holding her, feeling the heat pulse between us, until she let out a ragged sigh and drew back. "I guess I was fooling myself," she went on, her voice harder now. "He's one of them now. I think I've always known, especially after what happened in Vegas. Dante has always been one hundred percent Talon. I just didn't want to believe it."

"Don't give up just yet," I told her, running a thumb over her cheek, making her blink at me. "I know it feels like he's betrayed you, and now it's us against him and Talon. But you can't lose faith that, someday, you'll be able to make him see the truth. That he'll realize what he's doing, what the organization is really about, and he'll leave. Turn his back on the entire thing."

"I don't know, Garret." Ember half closed her eyes, circling my wrist with her fingers. "How long can I keep hoping? How long can I afford to believe that he'll somehow just abandon everything Talon has taught him?" She sighed, running her palm down my arm, making my skin tingle. "I know how stubborn Dante is. And now, he's further within the organization than ever before." She shook her head. "I don't know him anymore, Garret. Even if I could get to him, could I ever change his mind?"

"You changed mine."

She opened her eyes and peeked up. I gave a half smile. "It's because of you that I'm here," I told her. "That I'm fighting Talon and St. George, and trying to save the rogues. I want to make up for my past, but it's more than that." I took her hand, holding her gaze. "Ember, because of you, I have to believe that I can get through to Tristan. And Martin, and the entire Order of St. George. To convince them that we've been mistaken this whole time, that some dragons aren't soulless killers that deserve death. I think we have a chance to someday end this war, and to stop the fighting for good. To finally have peace." I pressed a palm to her cheek. "I believe that…because I met you."

She blinked rapidly. I ran my fingers gently through her hair, brushing it back. "So don't underestimate yourself, Ember," I murmured. "If you can convince a soldier of St. George to completely abandon the Order and start fighting for dragons instead, there's nothing you can't do."

Rising to her knees, she laced her arms behind my neck, leaned forward and kissed me. I sighed and slid my palms up her back, pulling her close. Her lips were gentle but insistent, and I parted my own slightly, feeling my blood heat as her tongue teased mine. A fire seemed to ignite in the pit of my stomach, crawling up toward my heart, which thumped faster in response.

Ember drew back and sighed, resting her forehead against mine. "Thank you," she said as I drew in a cooling breath. "You have no idea how glad I am...that you're here." Her fingers traced my neck as she sat up, making me shiver. "Sometimes, I think you're the only thing keeping me sane."

"I doubt it, dragon girl," I replied, offering a wry smile as she cocked her head. "I doubt you need me for anything, but..." Reaching up, I stroked her cheek. "I'm glad I'm here, too."

She gazed down at me, eyes shining emerald, her fingertips brushing the side of my face. "I love you, Garret," she said softly, making my heart turn over. I hoped... I thought I'd heard those words before, on the salt flats of Utah right before I'd slipped into darkness. But that had been a hazy dream; this was real. "You know that, right? I was afraid I'd never get the chance to say it, and I should have told you a long time ago."

"I love you, too," I whispered back. "For the rest of my life. However long that is." It was amazing sometimes, how quickly she could make me forget. Forget the war, and the

Order, Talon, everything. Outside this room, Riley and Wes plotted how we were going to sneak into another Talon facility; the organization was up to something big, and I had no idea what was going on in my own body. If I should be worried about the constant sensation of molten fire in my veins. But, much like in Crescent Beach, nothing seemed quite as urgent when Ember was this close. I could let go of the perfect soldier's discipline and be myself, the Garret I'd had no idea existed before I met her. And I could say things I never would have considered a year ago.

I met those emerald eyes and gave a rueful smile. "We might not have a lot of time," I said quietly, and ran my hands up her arms. "But however long we have, I'm not going anywhere. I'm yours, dragon girl. I always have been."

Her eyes went a little glassy, and she kissed me again. I leaned back against the headboard and closed my eyes, feeling the inferno flare between us once more. It flickered and pulsed, like my blood was boiling on the inside, and Ember was the fire that ignited it. But rather than wanting it to stop, it pushed me to continue, to drag the girl closer until nothing separated us. Until the flames rippling under my skin burst free and surrounded us, burning but not consuming. Ember's fingers dug into my shirt, the echo of a growl rumbling in her chest, and I felt something inside me respond.

A crash from the living room made us freeze. Both our hearts were pounding wildly, and the tiny space between us almost shimmered with heat as we listened to the muffled voices through the wall, ready to rush out if there was trouble. But after a moment, it appeared that nothing was wrong; someone had just dropped a mug on the hard wooden floor. Wes was applauding someone—probably Riley—who growled at him to shut up. Ember gave a small smile and drew back.

"I wish we could stay here," she said, her voice a little breathless. "But I guess we should head out and see what the others are planning, huh? Before Riley comes banging on the door." She winced. "Or…through it."

I echoed her wince. I wanted to stay here, too, but angry dragons in log cabins seemed like a bad idea. "You ready for this?" I asked, and she nodded.

"Yeah," she sighed, sliding off the bed. "Back into Talon. Back into heavily-armed facilities crawling with security guards and people shooting at us if we're caught. With no real idea of what we're *actually* looking for. What's one more crazy suicide mission, right?" She grinned at me and held out a hand to pull me to my feet. "We lead an exciting life, huh?"

"Yes, we do," I agreed, lacing our fingers together as we headed for the door. Riley might see us and be angry, but I wasn't going to hide what I felt any longer. "And I have a feeling it's going to get more exciting from here on out."

When we reentered the living room, a man stood just inside the front door. He was bald, wearing orange robes, and he was talking to Jade in low, furtive Mandarin, while Riley and Wes hovered close by and watched warily.

"What's going on?" Ember asked as we swept inside.

"No clue," Riley muttered. "This person showed up a few minutes ago, banging on the door with an 'urgent message' for Jade." He shrugged. "I'm guessing a temple is in danger or a group of monks need her help with St. George."

"No." Jade turned to us, her eyes grave. "Worse, I'm afraid. I am needed elsewhere. I will depart tonight."

"Again?" Riley frowned. "Can't these monks do anything themselves?"

"It is not the monks," Jade said. "I have been called home, to China. A summons has been issued, the first one in over two thousand years." She looked away, her eyes distant and troubled. "The *shen-lung* are gathering. I must go."

"You're not coming back this time, are you?" I said. It was a heavy blow. Jade was not only a powerful, dependable ally; I had come to see her as a friend, as well. The Eastern dragon paused as she glanced at me, her eyes troubled.

"I do not know," she replied. "Perhaps. I know that our work here, against Talon, is of utmost importance. But this cannot be ignored. My people are a solitary race. A gathering is called only in the most dire circumstances, when the fate of our very existence hangs in the balance. I suspect that the upheaval within the Order and Talon's move to destroy my kin are at the heart of it. If they have called a summoning, then I must be there."

Riley shook his head. "Well, if you have to go, we can't stop you," he said. "Lousy timing, though. We could've really used your help inside Talon. But if this summoning thing is that important…"

"It is. And I am sorry I cannot go with you to Talon. But my duty to my people comes first."

"Keep in touch," I told her as Riley crossed his arms. "At least give us a call when you know what's going on."

"I will." Jade took a step back, toward the door. "If I can, I will return as soon as I am able. That is a promise from a *shen-lung*." She turned to the monk and said something in Mandarin; he bowed deeply and walked out the door. "Good fortune to you all," the Eastern dragon said, and gave me a slight bow before turning to follow the human out the door. "Hopefully we will meet again."

EMBER

I hated long stakeouts.

I wasn't going to complain. Sitting on the top floor of a parking garage, peering at a building across the street through a pair of binoculars, was better than fleeing through twisty aisles while being shot at by human maniacs. And it was certainly better than sitting alone in a hotel room, waiting for something to happen or for someone to return. But after a few hours of nothing—seeing the same building, same street, same everything—I began to get restless. I wanted to get out and *do* something. Not something frivolous; I knew what was at stake. I knew I couldn't be distracted from our mission. But I wasn't good at sitting still for long periods of time without getting incredibly bored.

"What are we looking for again?" I asked Riley, who sat next to me in the driver's seat with the windows half-way down, also peering through a pair of binoculars. Wes perched in the back with his laptop open, of course, and Garret had been sent to scout the other side of the building. I'd wanted to go with him, but Riley wouldn't let me, saying that I was way too recognizable by Talon to casually stroll around the building, where any guard or security camera could pick me out of a crowd. Garret, while he wasn't exactly unknown to Talon, was less familiar, and could blend into the throngs of humanity wandering the streets. He was also better at spotting undercover guards, cameras, concealed weapons and other threats. So he was down at street level, doing the soldier thing, while I sat up here with Riley and Wes and watched the office building, not really knowing what I was looking for.

Riley sighed and lowered the binoculars. "This is just surveillance, Firebrand," he explained, giving me a sideways look. "We don't want to go charging in half-assed, without knowing what we're up against. I want to know when the security shifts change. I want to know where their guard posts and cameras are located. I want to know if anyone I recognize is working here now, because they're sure to recognize me, as well. This is Talon." He raised the binoculars again, peering down at the huge glass doors across the street. "I'm not leaving anything to chance if I can help it. Wes? Has St. George placed the camera? Do you have a visual of the other side yet?"

"Hold your bloody horses, I'm working on it."

The side door opened, and Garret slid into the back, hoodie and dark glasses making him appear like a stranger for a moment. "There's an entrance to an underground garage on the other side," he announced, brushing back the hood and stripping off the shades. "But it's guarded, not open to the public. I put the camera under a bench across the street from the garage entrance. So we should be able to see who's going in and out."

"All right, then," Wes muttered, typing something on his laptop. "And...there we go. Huh, well not bad, St. George. I can see every bastard coming and going, down to the license plate numbers. *And* it's not in a planter box where all I see are leaves."

"*One* time, I did that," Riley growled.

"There was also that instance when a dog peed all over the camera because you stuck it on a hydrant."

"Shut up and watch your computer."

I gave Garret a smile and turned back to the window, raising the binoculars. Below, the streets and sidewalks bustled with people like every other city. Cars and humans cruised blissfully past the office building, unaware of its true nature. Unaware that, right above their heads, their movements were being watched by a pair of dragons and a modern-day knight.

A black sedan with tinted windows pulled in front of the building and stopped at the curb. The front passenger door opened, and a large man in a suit and shades stepped out, looking distinctly bodyguard-esque. I was about to prod Riley, to see if he recognized whatever Talon hotshot was about to leave the car, when the bodyguard reached out and opened the passenger door.

And Dante stepped out of the vehicle.

I gasped, and for a moment, the world lurched to a stop. I hadn't seen my twin since that fateful night I'd fled Crescent Beach, when Dante had sent Lilith after me and Riley. The night he'd betrayed us to Talon. I remembered him in shorts and a T-shirt, with a baseball cap perched atop his head and a backpack slung over one shoulder.

He looked different now, in an expensive black suit and tie, his previously longish red hair cut short. He looked poised and important and busy as he stepped onto the sidewalk, talking into his phone and ignoring everything around him. He looked...like a true Talon executive.

My heart ached, and I swallowed hard, watching as my brother hung up the phone and slipped it into his jacket pocket. I'd been secretly hoping Dante was unhappy in Talon,

that he had realized his mistake and was regretting everything that had happened. But seeing him like this, watching
him straighten his tie, gaze imperiously down the street and
head briskly toward the office building...it was like he had
stepped into the role he was destined for.

"Well, well," Riley growled beside me, and I heard the
anger in his voice as he peered through his own binoculars.
"Look who showed up. The little snitch himself."

"Dante is here?" Garret echoed as the lump in my throat
grew bigger. He leaned forward, gazing through the windshield at the street as my brother and his bodyguards walked
up the steps and vanished through the glass doors. "Why do
you think he's come?"

"Who knows," Riley muttered. "But I'm guessing it has
something to do with that evidence. If he was involved with
what happened at the crash site, maybe he wants to see it
for himself."

My hands were shaking as I lowered the binoculars, but
I wasn't sure which emotion it was attached to. Grief, rage,
excitement? Something else? All three? "I have to see him,"
I said quietly, making both Riley and Garret glance at me.
"I have to talk to him before he goes back to Talon. This
might be my only chance."

"Ember..." Riley began, his voice a warning. I turned on
him with a growl.

"It's Dante, Riley," I said, narrowing my eyes. "I don't care
that he's part of Talon now. He's still my brother."

"Dammit, Firebrand, you know what he's like," Riley
snarled back, gesturing down at the street. "You know we
can't trust him. Brother or not, he sold us out to Talon. Hell,
he sent a Viper to *kill you*. Remember that? Remember Faith,
and Mist? That was all Dante, Ember. Family doesn't matter

to him anymore. After everything he put us through, you should know that by now."

"I know," I said in the most reasonable voice I could manage, though it was hard not to snarl back at him. Frustration and anger boiled, made worse by the dragon and the sudden heat erupting inside me, but I kept my words calm. "I know I can't trust him. I know he'll sell us out to Talon again." I gazed down at the office building, at the doors my twin had vanished through, and clenched my jaw. "I want him to confirm it. I want to look him in the eye and ask why he would give the order to have his own sister killed because she wouldn't conform to Talon." My voice trembled a bit on the last sentence, and I took a breath to steady it. "I want to ask why he chose the organization over me. And I want to see his face when he answers."

Garret placed a hand on my arm and squeezed gently before turning to Riley. "If Dante was involved with what happened at the crash site, then he'll likely know what Talon is up to," he said calmly. "If we want answers, he might be the best one to ask."

"If we can even get to him," Riley muttered, crossing his arms. "And that he'll actually talk when we do." He gave me an exasperated look. "If he's as stubborn as his sister, I foresee all kinds of problems."

"Also, not to be the voice of reason or anything," Wes broke in, "but this *is* a Talon facility. You're not going to just stroll in the front doors and say, *'Hello, we're your most wanted dragons and we've wandered right into your office. Cooperate with us please.'* I say 'you' and not 'me,' because there's no way you're getting me anywhere near that building. I will stay up here with the sane people, thank you very much. Which, I think, is just down to me, at this point."

I narrowed my eyes at the rogue. "You know I'm going to see him, Riley, with or without you."

"Shit, yes, I know." Riley sighed, raking a hand through his hair. "I just want you to be very sure, Firebrand. Dante is part of Talon. I don't want you going down there thinking you can convince him to leave. He's dangerous, because he's your brother and you're not seeing him as the enemy. But he *is*, do you understand? He is just as dangerous as Lilith or Faith, maybe even more so. A Viper will kill you without blinking an eye, but you at least know where you stand with them. Chameleons, though, are masters of manipulation and lies. They'll tell you exactly what you want to hear, and they'll screw you over while smiling at you all the while." He shook his head in disgust, giving me a piercing glare. "So, you can't trust anything he says, Ember. No matter how much you want to believe it. He'll try to get us to lower our guard, to relax around him, and then he'll sell us out to Talon at the first opportunity."

"I know," I said, though my chest squeezed tight at Riley's words.

"Repeat it back to me, Ember. Just so I know you get it."

"I can't trust him," I echoed bitterly. "Dante is part of Talon and will betray us all if we give him the chance. Satisfied?"

"Wish I wasn't." Riley exhaled and peered down at the building again. For a few moments, he stared out the window, eyes narrowed, mouth drawn into a thin line. I saw the echo of Cobalt in his profile, a phantom blue dragon with sweeping black horns and bright golden eyes, and felt a flicker of heat pulse through my veins. "All right," the rogue muttered at last. "This is what we're going to do."

DANTE

"Welcome, Mr. Hill," the man in the business suit greeted me as we came through the front doors. "We cannot express what a pleasure it is that you are here. How was your flight?"

"Fine," I returned shortly. Then, in an attempt not to let my mood get the better of me, I added, "Mostly uneventful, thank you."

"Good to hear, Mr. Hill," the human continued, and began rambling about how truly privileged they were that I had arrived, how they hoped this office was doing wonderful things for the organization, and other useless compliments that were mostly lip service. As if I couldn't smell the fear that radiated from the human like body odor. How he was trying so hard to appear normal and conversational, when he knew exactly what was happening.

"Have the packages arrived?" I asked when there was a break in the stream of endless chatter and adulation. The human bobbed his head as we stepped into a narrow elevator, squeezing into the center of the floor. My two guards loomed over us, silent and menacing, and the human eyed them nervously as the elevator climbed toward the higher floors.

"Yes, Mr. Hill. All arrived safely this morning." The man

pulled a handkerchief out of his jacket pocket and dotted his balding head with it. "And the boxes you requested were delivered to conference room C for your inspection. We're headed there now."

"Good."

The elevator stopped on the eleventh floor and opened with a ding. I followed my bodyguards out and immediately turned, pressing my palm into the doors to stop them from closing. The human blinked at me across the threshold.

"I can find my own way from here," I told him. "Thank you for your assistance, but I'm sure you're busy enough without having to escort me around the building. We'll be fine." He hesitated, and I gave a wry smile. "I'm actually fairly adept at finding my way around Talon offices. It's no trouble at all. You can return to your work."

The blood drained from the human's face in relief. "Of course, sir," he almost-whispered. "Right away. If you need anything, please don't hesitate to call."

"I won't. Thank you."

I stepped back, and the doors slid shut, taking the human from my sight. I turned and made my way down the nearly empty halls, passing a few humans in business attire, until I found conference room C.

"Wait here," I told my guards at the door. "I don't want to be disturbed." They nodded mutely before placing themselves on either side of the frame, hands clasped in front of them, and proceeded to look stern and intimidating. Opening the door, I stepped inside and closed it behind me.

Silence descended. The room was dim and cool, with stark white walls and no windows to the outside world. A long table surrounded by black leather chairs sat in the center of the carpet, and a single rectangular box had been placed atop it.

For a moment, I didn't move, staring at the box sitting inconspicuously on the tabletop. It was unmarked and unremarkable. The first of several boxes that would stop here before continuing their journey to the Vault. I knew it had been packaged with utmost care, so that no sloppy mistake would reveal their contents. No one from the human world could guess what lay inside.

My stomach churned, and I shook myself angrily. *Stop it, Dante*, I told myself. *You're being ridiculous. There is nothing to fear.*

Setting my jaw, I walked across the room to the table. A box cutter lay on one of the packages; I snatched it up and, without hesitation, slashed the blade down the center of the cardboard. Within the box was another, even smaller box, and I cut that one open, too.

As I pulled back the flaps, the smell of smoke and charred things wafted up, making my stomach turn again. The container was filled with clothes, sealed in plastic and neatly labeled, but the stench of smoke still clung to everything. The fabric was burned, singed and in tatters, but I knew that wasn't enough reason for it to have been taken from the scene. Setting the bags on the table, I examined them carefully and finally saw why these pieces of clothing had been removed.

Not only were they singed, but several of them had been ripped apart. A few had puncture holes left from pointed fangs and talons, the fabric around the holes stained dark with blood. Evidence that not only had these clothes, and whoever had been wearing them, been burned, they had been savaged, as well.

Torn apart by dragons. My dragons. The vessels I sent to destroy the town.

I stared at the ravaged piles of fabric, forcing myself to acknowledge what had happened. Massive death and destruction, blood and pain and fear, by my hand. I hadn't set the fires or torn into those humans myself, but I had given the order. The vessels were my tools, as surely as a gun or a blade, and I had used them for slaughter.

Sacrifice is necessary.

I knew that was true. I knew everything we did was for the good of our race. And the vessels were our most powerful force to date in the war with St. George. With them, we could finally start to turn the tide, strike a real blow against our ancient enemies. Numbers had always been our weakness, not enough bodies to fight back against the Order, and every loss we took was devastating to our entire race. The vessels would change that. Without them, we would still be heavily outnumbered and outgunned. Without them, St. George would still be pushing us toward extinction.

But there was a difference between sending the vessels into war with genocidal, highly trained soldiers who hated our kind and normal, everyday humans who didn't even know about dragons. And there was a large distinction between attacking heavily armed and armored humans and those sleeping peacefully in their beds. That community hadn't stood a chance. They hadn't even known what hit them before they were dead.

What will Ember think of this? What will she think of you?

I smiled grimly. I knew what Ember would think. She would be horrified, appalled. She would call me all kinds of terrible names. And she would be right. I had chosen this course, for the good of our race and our people. She would never believe it, but I was still doing this for her. For all of us.

And though I would never admit it out loud, I was doing it for myself. I was almost there. I was closer to my goal than ever before, but I wasn't there yet. *Just one more step*, I told myself. One more step to the top, and the thing I desired most.

Freedom.

Silently, I made note of everything in the box, recording it all carefully onto my tablet. More would be arriving soon—more containers full of burned clothes, blood, ashes and death. I would inspect them, as well, before they made their final journey to the Vault, but I had seen all I needed. Now I had to wait and trust the Elder Wyrm, as I always had. We would make our race powerful again. Together, we would not only bring our species back from the edge of extinction, we would make certain neither St. George nor any other humans ever threatened our survival again.

By any means necessary.

★ ★ ★

The rest of the day passed in a blur of cataloging, meetings, phone calls and more meetings. I deliberately kept busy, using work as a shield against my own thoughts. The only annoying thing was the aura of fear and tension that continued to linger throughout the day, putting everyone around me on edge. Still, I remained past business hours, staying at my desk when most other employees had gone home. By the time I made the final call to Talon HQ and hung up the phone, the sun had set and the offices were empty.

With a sigh, I leaned back in my chair and looked at the clock on the wall, both relieved and dreading that the day was almost done. My two bodyguards hovered close, silent and protective, even though there was no one else around. I spared them a glance and frowned slightly, realizing I didn't even know their names.

"Time to go, sir?" one of them asked.

I let out a long breath and stood, rubbing tired eyes. "Yes," I answered simply. "Call for the car. Tell it to wait for us in the parking garage."

"Of course, sir."

We walked back through the empty building, down silent, deserted hallways, and took the elevator. The doors opened into the underground garage, mostly empty but for a few cars still parked in their reserved spaces. I spotted our vehicle and began a brisk walk toward it. Shadows closed around us, and my shoes knocked quietly against the concrete, echoing the sudden thud of my heart.

I held my breath, but we reached the car without incident, making me slump with relief. One bodyguard opened the passenger side door, and I slid into the backseat as the door closed behind me.

"Hello, Dante."

My heart stood still. Ember sat across from me, her eyes glowing a hard green in the shadows of the car. As I stiffened, the locks slammed into place with a loud click, and my sibling raised a black handgun and pointed it at my face.

PART II

The Wyrm Turns

DANTE

"Ember, when did your parents die, and what was the cause of death?"

I could feel Ember's impatience from the other side of the seat, in the way she reluctantly tore herself from the window, in the annoyed look she shot our escort, Mr. Ramsey. Even with my headphones on, I knew what she was thinking. She was dying to get out, practically bursting at the seams with eagerness.

"Ember, did you hear me? Answer the question, please."

Ember sighed. "Joseph and Kate Hill were killed in a car accident when we were seven years old," she said, sounding like she was reciting a line from a play. I suppressed a wince at how stiff and flat her voice was, but Mr. Ramsey didn't seem to notice.

"Go on."

"They were going to see a Broadway musical, *West Side Story*, and were struck by a drunk driver on the way home," Ember continued in that same bored monotone. "My brother and I went to live with our grandparents, until Grandpa Bill developed lung cancer and could no longer take care of us." She kept talking, but her gaze strayed out the window again, at the ocean just beyond the glass. I knew it was killing her, being this close, yet not able to touch it.

Hang in there, sis. We're almost there.

"Dante." Mr. Ramsey's attention shifted to me, as I'd known it would. "What is your real objective while in Crescent Beach?"

I pulled the buds out of my ear and hit Pause on my iPhone to give the human my full attention. Ember might be so distracted that she could barely think, but I hadn't forgotten the real reason we were here. "Observe and blend in," I answered calmly. "Learn how to engage with humans, how to *be* human. Assimilate into their social structure and make them believe we are one of them."

Ember rolled her eyes, mocking my perfect dedication as she usually did. I gave a small shrug. I didn't mind; one of us had to keep us grounded.

The rest of the ride passed in silence, and we were soon pulling into a small subdivision of neat white villas and tidy yards. I watched the houses roll by, seeing the many humans walking, jogging or riding their bikes down the sidewalk. They looked so…carefree, I thought. Carefree and ignorant. Completely unaware that two dragons were watching them from the backseat of a car.

Ember was going to love it here.

We pulled into the driveway of one of the many villas along the road, and after a brief introduction to our guardians, Mr. Ramsey left, and our appointed "aunt" showed us to our rooms.

After closing the door, I set my suitcase on the bed and gazed around, taking everything in. This was it. Assimilation had officially begun. From here on out, everything I'd learned, all my training, would come into play. When Talon called for me at the end of the summer, I would be ready for whatever they required of me.

If I could keep my reckless, impulsive twin from doing anything crazy.

Easier said than done, Dante.

Quickly, I changed, then headed toward Ember's room, knowing she would be leaving the house as soon as she could. I hadn't even knocked on her door when it swung open and my twin slammed into me from the other side.

"Oof." I staggered back, wincing. "Ow. Well, I was going to ask if you wanted to go check out the beach—" *...together. Where I can keep an eye on you, make sure you don't Shift and fly off into the sunset, or lose your temper around a human and char them to ash...* "—but it looks like you beat me to it."

Ember grinned, that same wicked, defiant grin she'd challenged me with when we'd still competed with each other in everything. Not realizing she was always the favored one, and that I competed because winning was the only way I could make them see me. "Race you to the water," she challenged.

"Come on, sis. We're not in training any—" But she was already past me, flying down the stairs, and I scrambled to catch up.

Later, after dunking each other in the ocean and getting it out of our systems, Ember and I wandered down the beach, checking out our new home. Ember seemed especially fascinated by the surfers farther out in deep water, gliding down the waves on their colorful boards, and that was mildly concerning, knowing she would want to try it sometime. Swimming was one lesson we hadn't gotten a lot of in the Mohave Desert. As we continued down the strip, Ember's eyes were huge, looking at everything, but I was searching for something specific.

I found it a couple minutes later—a group of human teens, playing volleyball in the sand. I observed them carefully as we approached; most of them were attractive—for humans—athletic, obviously well-off.

Perfect.

I nudged Ember's shoulder. "Come on," I said, and began walking toward the group. She followed hesitantly, frowning.

"Um. What are we doing?"

I gave her a wink. "Fitting in."

"What, right now?" She eyed the humans. "I mean, you're just going to walk up to a bunch of mortals and talk to them? What are you going to say?"

I grinned at her and ambled toward the net. My sister, who had never backed down a day in her life, was shy. "I figured I'd start with 'hi.'"

Warily, she followed. As if on cue, one of the human's dove wildly for the ball and sent it bouncing right for me. Instinctively, I caught it, and five pairs of eyes turned in my direction.

"Hey." I looked at one of the girls and offered my most charming smile, the one that could make my teachers believe whatever I wanted. "Need a couple extra players?"

The girl nearly fell over from staring at me, but one of the guys gave me a shrug. "Sure, dude." He was, I noticed, looking at Ember even as he spoke to me. "The more, the merrier. Come on in and pick a side."

I smiled and joined them, even as I bit down a snort. *Too easy.*

★ ★ ★

Lexi and Calvin were pretty cool for humans, despite Calvin's promise that he would teach Ember to surf when she asked about it. And Lexi talked…a lot. Even more than Ember, which was saying something.

And then, I saw him.

We were hanging out at the Smoothie Hut, a place that sold what our teachers referred to as "junk food," when a weird shiver went up my spine. I turned from Calvin and gazed at the parking lot, just as a guy pulled up on a motorcycle and stared at us for a few seconds. He wore a leather jacket, and his black hair was messy and windblown. He met my stare, and one corner of his mouth curled up in a smirk, even as his eyes glinted yellow. Definitely not human.

Another dragon.

A *rogue.*

I didn't know how I knew he was a rogue. Maybe because no dragon from Talon would randomly show up in a place where there were already two hatchlings. Maybe it was his eyes, gleaming and dangerous, or that defiant smirk that said he knew exactly what we were...and pitied us for it.

"Gorgeous Biker Boy." Lexi sighed in response to something Ember said.

I felt a kick to my shins from below and jumped. Ember was giving me a worried look, and I realized that I'd been staring back at the rogue, the echo of a growl rumbling in my chest.

What are you doing, Dante? Get ahold of yourself.

Quickly, I excused the both of us, saying that our guardians wanted us home early tonight. I expected Ember to protest, but she only nodded and followed me back down the beach. When we were out of sight of the two humans, however, she jogged up and lightly smacked my arm.

"Hey," she demanded. "What's with you? You nearly went psychopathic lizard on me, right in front of two very normal humans. What's the deal?"

"I know," I rasped. "I'm sorry. It's just..." I raked a hand through my hair, still keyed up. "Do you know what that was, in the parking lot just now?"

"You mean the other dragon? Yeah, I kinda noticed."

"Ember." I gave her a solemn look, willing her to understand. "That wasn't anyone from Talon. That was a rogue. I'd bet my life on it."

She blinked at me. I saw nervousness and alarm cross her face at the realization, but also something that raised the hairs on my neck. Curiosity. And…anticipation. The rogue intrigued her. And that, more than anything, made me realize I had to act. Before my twin did something unforgivable, something Talon could not overlook, and ruined the future for us both.

★ ★ ★

Back in my room, I turned on my computer and went into my email account. The cursor blinked in the address bar, waiting, as I sat there, trying to decide what to do. Finally, I put my fingers on the keys and typed in the one address I was supposed to use only in an emergency. The one my teachers had given me, and only me, because they knew I would inform Talon if anything was amiss in the area. Because they knew I would take my mission seriously.

Even if it meant we might be pulled out.

I hesitated a moment more, typed Rogue in Crescent Beach into the subject line, then began composing a brief, to-the-point message. I didn't know what this meant for us once Talon received the information. I knew what would happen to the rogue, and I wasn't sure I wanted to be in town when the Vipers came for him. I did know this was my duty, not only to Talon but to my sister. I would protect her, and our future with the organization, from any and all threats.

Even if the greatest threat was from Ember herself.

EMBER

Dante froze, his eyes going wide as he stared at me. As soon as the door closed and the locks engaged, a shout came through the tinted windows as something slammed into his bodyguard outside. Dante jumped, his attention going to the window, where Garret had just hit the guard from behind. There were brief scuffles on both sides of the car as Riley emerged from the darkness and tackled the second guard, making the vehicle rock as the dragon slammed into it. It didn't last long; we had the element of surprise on our side, and the guards had been caught with their figurative pants down. After a few more grunts, shouts and bodies being slammed into metal and glass, the fight was over, and silence descended once more.

Dante slowly turned back to me as Garret and Riley dragged the bodies into the darkness. His eyes glinted angrily as he faced me down over the gun barrel. "Ember," he said, his voice calm. "How did you get in here?"

"Wasn't hard." I was relieved when my voice came out mostly steady. "We saw you arrive this morning and made note of the car's license plate. When the car came back a few minutes ago, I knew you were coming down. This place only has one security guard." I jerked my head toward the garage entrance, though I kept the gun trained on Dante. "Once we got past him, the rest was easy."

"I see." His voice was hostile. It made a knot form in my stomach, and at the same time, anger flooded my veins. He had no right to be angry, not with the crap he'd put us through. "So, what are you going to do with me, Ember?" he went on. "Kill me? Are you going to shoot your own brother, right here?"

"Maybe I will," I shot back, and raised the pistol, making him tense. "You certainly had no qualms about giving the order to take *me* out."

"What are you talking about?"

"Come on." I sneered, angry that he would lie, that he would try to play it off. "Mist and Faith? The whole debacle in Vegas? That setup was all you, Dante—you told me that yourself. You admitted that you were the one to send them after me."

"Yes, I did." Dante's eyes narrowed. "To bring you back to Talon. They never had orders to take you out. I wouldn't do that to you."

He's lying. Faith told you she had orders to kill, and those orders came from Dante. But my resolve wavered. I didn't want to believe my brother would actually try to kill me.

"Ember." Abruptly, Dante closed his eyes, shaking his head. "This isn't...how I wanted our reunion to go," he almost-whispered. "I don't want to fight you, sis. I never did." Opening his eyes, he gave me a sad, almost pleading look. "I just want you to come home."

"Talon isn't my home," I said softly. "Not anymore."

The locks released, and the front passenger door clicked as someone opened it from the outside and slid into the seat. "The famous Dante Hill," Riley stated, giving him a slightly dangerous smile as the door closed behind him. A pistol appeared in his other hand, casually resting against the seats as he draped an elbow over the chair backs. "You've caused me quite a bit of trouble these past few weeks."

Dante stared at him, and for a moment, his eyes glittered with pure, unbridled loathing. A chill went through me, but then Dante smiled, and all emotions vanished behind a civil mask as he nodded at the other dragon.

"Not quite as famous as you, Mr. Cobalt," Dante replied in a voice of chilly politeness. And suddenly, he wasn't Dante anymore but a Chameleon, the kind Riley had warned me about. The sick feeling in my gut spread to my whole body as I realized I didn't recognize him now. That brief glimpse of my brother, the twin who'd looked out for me my whole life, had vanished, leaving only the Chameleon behind. The thing Talon had turned him into. Settling comfortably against the cushions, as if this was a perfectly normal meeting, he crossed his legs and smiled. "Where are my guards and my driver, if you don't mind my asking?"

"Taking a nap."

"And will they wake up again?"

"I don't think they're the ones you need to worry about right now," Riley said as a shadow emerged from beside the car. Garret leaned against the front door and crossed his arms, doing the whole on-watch thing. "But if you're asking if I killed them...no, I didn't. I'm not quite the monster Talon would have you believe." His smirk widened. "Actually, I find that kind of ironic, considering the circumstances."

"I'm afraid I don't know what you mean."

"I'm sure you don't."

Dante shook his head. "Well, this is getting us nowhere." He turned away from Riley, as if dismissing him, and looked at me. "You obviously went through a lot to get to me, so I assume you want something. What can I do for you?"

I swallowed. "The town in Arkansas," I began. "We know Talon was involved, and we know that story about the plane crash is a cover-up. We also know that the evidence collected at the site was sent here, to you." No change in Dante's expression; he regarded me with a practiced blank, pleasant expression that gave no hint to his thoughts or feelings. "Why did Talon attack that community?" I asked in a harder voice. "Why did they kill all those people? What are they planning now?"

"Ember," Dante said in a reasonable tone, "listen to yourself. I don't know where you got your information, but you've obviously jumped to the wrong conclusion. You're accusing Talon of murdering an entire town, dozens of people, when for centuries, everything we have done has been to remain hidden and avoid detection. Why would we risk that kind of discovery?" He laced his fingers together on his knee, giving me a slight frown. "I assume you witnessed Miranda on the news. She was only there to make certain the humans would not discover our existence. It's a standard precaution."

"But why would she need to be there at all?" I demanded. "Why would Talon need to cover something up, if they weren't involved?"

"There was a Talon agent on the plane that crashed," Dante explained calmly. "The plane was one of ours, and it was carrying jet fuel to one of Talon's bases on the eastern coast. Sadly, the agent on board was killed in the explosion with the rest of the community, but we still needed to send Miranda to investigate and remove any evidence that could point back to us. Again, standard precaution. Talon is protecting its interests and covering the truth of our existence, as they have always done."

I hesitated. His explanation sounded perfectly reasonable, though I knew I shouldn't believe him.

Dante's serene expression didn't change. "Think about it, Ember," he continued. "Our agents are stretched thin as it is. We don't have the numbers for the type of operation you're talking about, even if we wanted to expose ourselves like that. What you saw was Talon trying to cover its tracks, and the evidence was sent here, to me, before it goes on to the Vault."

"Well," Riley broke in. "Wouldn't I feel silly...if that wasn't the biggest line of bullshit I've ever heard." He leveled the pistol at Dante's face. "Did you forget who you were talking to, *hatchling*? I was a Basilisk, remember? I know what's left behind after a large explosion." He narrowed his eyes, staring Dante down. "We went to that site. There was no plane. No debris. No crash. Nothing exploded in that town, but things did mysteriously catch fire. And, funniest thing, there were these odd gouges in the floors that looked exactly like dragon claws. So cut the crap. I've heard your shit before, and you're not fooling anyone."

Dante regarded the rogue with a patient, almost amused look that suggested Riley was being unreasonable, but didn't dispute his claims. He *was* lying, I realized. He had just lied right to my face, and I'd considered believing him. Angry now, I clenched a fist on my leg. Dante was a Chameleon, I reminded myself. I couldn't trust anything he said.

"Stop lying to us," I growled. "What really happened there, Dante? We know Talon is planning something, and you're a part of it. What's going on?"

"Even if I did know," Dante answered coolly, "what makes you think I would tell you anything?"

"Because if you don't," Riley said in a tone of dark warning, "we're going for a little ride. We're going to spend some quality time together, the four of us, and you're not going back to Talon until you tell us what we want to know. How long it takes doesn't matter. I can be very patient." Riley smiled, raising the gun very slightly off the chair back. "So decide, Chameleon. You can tell us now, or later. Your choice."

Dante paled. Just a little; he hid it well, but his skin turned ashen all the same. "Look, I *don't know* what happened at the crash site," he insisted. "The evidence and the reports came in late this afternoon, but I haven't had the chance to look at them yet."

"And where are these reports?" Riley asked.

"Back in my office." Dante crossed his arms. "But you'll never get there, not without tripping the alarms or running into security. If you try to force your way in, you'll have the police swarming this place in a matter of minutes."

Riley was silent for a long moment. I could see him thinking, see the indecision in his eyes as he struggled with what to do next. Finally, he opened his door, slammed it behind him and stalked around to our side. Wrenching open the passenger side, he pointed his weapon at Dante. "Get out."

Stone faced, Dante complied. Quickly, I opened my own door and scrambled out, while Garret watched the proceedings warily, a hand on his own weapon. "What are we doing, Riley?" I asked, coming around to their side. Dante stared at me, his gaze shadowed and dark, making my insides twist.

"We're going inside," Riley said. "And Dante here is going to escort us."

My stomach dropped. "Inside? But this is a Talon office. Guards, security, alarms, traps—isn't that what you told me? Why are we going to risk going in?"

"What else are we going to do, Firebrand?" Riley gave me a weary look. "We've come all this way. Everything we've done until now will be for nothing if we don't figure this out. Yeah, I know, it's Talon. It'll be a risk either way, but at least if we have the boss with us, no one will try anything. Isn't that right, *Mr. Hill*?"

Riley turned, giving Dante a dangerous grin. "I'm sure you know your way around the office and past the security," he said as Dante stiffened. "So this is how it's going to work. You're going to get us through the doors, past the cameras and all the alarms. If we run into anyone, you're going to convince them that absolutely nothing is wrong, or you'll be down one less employee." His eyes narrowed, his voice turning cold and hard. "If the police or anyone from Talon shows up, I have no problem using you as a hostage. Or a meat shield. You get me, Chameleon?"

Dante glared at him, then gave a tight nod.

"Good." Riley gestured him forward with his gun. "After you, then."

We started across the parking garage, Dante leading, Riley close at his back. Garret and I trailed close behind. I saw a pair of legs behind a pillar—Dante's guards, I guessed—but beyond them and us, the garage was empty. The office building, too, seemed unnaturally dark and still. Dante let us in through the garage door, using a key card to get in, and said nothing as he led us to an elevator at the end of the hall. A uniformed guard sitting behind a desk straightened quickly as we approached. I saw Riley tense, his hand straying toward the gun hidden beneath his shirt, but Dante strode up without hesitation.

"Good evening, sir." The guard gave Dante a pleasant smile, then eyed the rest of us over his shoulder. "Everything all right?"

Dante nodded. "Just giving some friends a tour of the building," he said, sounding perfectly at ease. I held my breath, knowing how we must look: a trio of vagrant-looking young people trailing another teen in a very expensive suit. But the man behind the desk immediately nodded.

"Of course, sir. I'll let security know."

He waved us through. We passed the desk and entered the elevator at the end of the hall.

When the elevator doors closed, Riley suddenly pushed Dante into the wall, the gun beneath his chin. "That," he growled as I flinched at his brutality, "was entirely too easy. No one in Talon lets three strangers waltz in off the street. What are you playing at, Chameleon?"

"Who do you think you're dealing with?" Dante's voice was equally as hard, and he glared back at Riley with cold green eyes. "Some low-level computer monkey? I *own* this place. Everyone here answers to me."

Stunned, I stared at him. I'd always known Dante was ambitious. He had rarely talked about his plans for when he finally got into Talon, but I knew he had them. But an executive? A corporate partner? How had he risen so far in such a short time? He was sixteen, same as me. Either his Chameleon talents were nothing short of miraculous, or there was something else going on.

Either way, I didn't like it. And neither did either of the boys. Garret's posture was tense, his eyes shifting between Dante and the glowing numbers above the door, climbing steadily upward. Riley, still pinning Dante against the wall, gave a grim smile.

"Just remember, Mr. Hill," he warned, pressing the gun to his chest. "I expect you to get us in with no problems. Any alarms 'mysteriously' go off, or if we run into any trouble, I'm putting a hole through you first."

I clenched my jaw at Riley's threat but didn't say anything. Dante wasn't our friend, I reminded myself. He was a Chameleon. I couldn't think of him as my brother right now, though it still made me slightly ill, seeing him like this. I wished it could be different, but Dante didn't seem inclined to leave Talon, no matter what I said to convince him otherwise.

The elevator stopped, and as the doors slid open, we all tensed, half expecting a line of guards on the other side, taking aim with their guns. The dark, empty corridor that greeted us didn't make me any less nervous. Dante stepped forward, but Riley reached out and grabbed his shoulder, pressing the gun into his ribs.

"Slowly," he growled. "Don't get too far, Chameleon. Like you said, you're just giving us a tour."

"Yes," Dante said in a tight voice. "And they're certainly not going to expect anything if I go creeping through the halls with you, hostage-style."

Riley chuckled darkly and released him. "Just remember, I can shoot faster than you can run. Let's go."

We entered the floor. Past the elevators was an open floor of cubicles and desks, all empty and dark except for the flicker of computer screens. Dante led us across the room, our shoes clicking against the tile, and down another corridor with individual offices lining the hall. These, too, sat vacant and still, large glass windows showing off the night sky and the blinking cityscape below.

"I don't like this," I whispered to Garret. "It's too empty. I thought Talon would have more security, or alarms, or something. This is too easy."

"Agreed," was the low reply. "Stay on your guard."

"My office is through here," Dante explained as we reached a door in the middle of the hall. "The reports are logged into my computer. One moment while I unlock the door." He slid his card into a key slot, then pushed the door back to reveal an empty, darkened room.

Riley gestured at him with his gun. "After you."

As we stepped through the door together, Dante turned, as if to throw the light switch. Suddenly his arm shot out, something small cupped in his palm, striking Riley in the ribs. There was an electric flash of white, the buzz of static, and Riley snarled, jerking as if he'd been stung.

The lights came on, revealing half a dozen armed, armored humans in the room, pointing their guns right at us.

RILEY

Well, shit. We'd walked nose-first into a trap.

Still reeling from being tased, I didn't move fast enough, and Dante slipped out of reach. He was smiling as he backed toward the desk and the trio of guards standing there with their guns aimed at my middle. St. George already had his weapon out, pointed back at them, but it was too late.

Dammit! This was bad. I'd known the devious little bastard had been up to something, but it was worse than I'd thought. This was more than bad luck or bad timing, and it wasn't coincidence that everything—Miranda, the evidence, and Dante—had pointed us here. I knew a setup when I saw one. We'd been played.

"Did you really think we had no idea you were coming?" Dante asked, a pleased smile curling his lips as he confirmed my suspicions. He met my glare and shook his head. "Did you really believe your presence went unnoticed at the crash site? Why do you think Miranda was on television to begin with? Because we knew you would recognize her, and if you did, you would come snooping around. We had her giving 'press interviews' on every news station for three days straight, to make sure you saw her." He circled the desk and stood behind it, two guards flanking him like attack dogs.

"The evidence would lead you here, as we knew it would, and everything else just fell into place." That arrogant smile turned sharp as he gazed at me, eyes glittering with hatred. "I will admit, I'm going to enjoy watching you die, Cobalt. For everything you've done, all the grief you've caused me, and Talon, I hope it's painful. A quick death is more than you deserve."

I smiled coldly back. "You think you can take me down, *hatchling*? Do your worst."

"Dante." Ember stepped forward, prompting half the guards to level their guns at her. The heat inside flared as Cobalt surged up, making my skin feel tight. Ember ignored the guards and their weapons, keeping her gaze on Dante. "Don't do this," she pleaded. "Please. You can still walk away. Look at what Talon is doing. They destroyed an entire town, killed every human there. That can't be what you wanted. My brother was never a killer."

"You don't know me anymore, Ember." Dante's voice was weary. "You don't know what I've done, what I'm willing to sacrifice, for our race. I know what Talon is planning. It's far too late for me to go back." He raised his chin, his voice becoming defiant. "*I* gave the order to wipe out that town. No witnesses, no survivors. And I would do it again, if that's what Talon wanted."

Dammit. I spared a glance at the soldier as they were talking. He was tense, pistol drawn and ready, his body coiled to spring into action. He caught my gaze and gave a tiny nod. I returned my attention to the twins as the air in my lungs started to boil.

"You gave the order," Ember repeated softly. "But...why? How could you do that?"

"You don't understand now," Dante said. "But you will.

Once you come back with me, you'll understand everything, I promise." His voice softened, turning almost gentle. "We belong with Talon, Ember. It's our destiny. Once you come back, you'll see why." His attention shifted to the guards standing around the room. "Bring me the girl," he ordered, taking a step back. "Kill the rest."

I exploded into Cobalt, surging up with a roar as the guards opened fire. Bullets tore past me, a couple sparking off my chest plates and several punching through my wing membranes. I sent a cone of fire at the nearest guard, and he reeled back, blazing like a torch. At the same time, Ember pounced on another, changing into a dragon midlunge, and St. George closed with a third, grabbing his weapon arm and forcing the muzzle away. Two pistol shots rang out, and the guard crumpled to the ground.

Growling, I turned on the last two guards, who had converged behind the desk and were raising their weapons to fire. Dante was nowhere to be seen, but the open door behind them told me where he'd escaped to.

"Dante!"

With a snarl, Ember reared back and sent a fireball at the desk, where it exploded in a burst of light and heat, causing the guards to reel away and crumple to the floor. Without hesitation, she leaped over the desk and bounded through the door after her twin.

"Dammit, Firebrand. Wait!" With a curse, I followed her, St. George right behind me. The door opened into a narrow hallway, and I hurried to keep up with the red dragon, my talons clicking against the tile.

We burst through the final door into a room much different than the one we'd just left. The ceiling was vast and soaring. A mezzanine ran the length of the opposite wall, a veranda stretching corner to corner twenty or so feet over-head. Directly below the railing, an elevator door slid shut, indicating where the little snitch had disappeared to, but getting to him might be challenging.

At least a dozen humans stood in the shadows of the mezzanine, staring at us as we came in. They were armed with pistols, all pointed in our direction, and wore identical gray uniforms, but that wasn't what made my skin crawl. There was something else, something…wrong about them. I just couldn't put my finger on it.

It hit me, and a jolt of shock zipped up my spine. The bastards weren't just wearing identical clothing; they looked *exactly* the same. They had the same shaved heads, the same faces and blank, empty eyes. They gazed at us, two dragons and an armed human, with absolutely no emotion. No surprise, fear, wonder or anything.

"What in the world…?" Ember growled, stopping as we faced the line of identical humans. "What *is* this?"

"Ember!"

Dante appeared on the mezzanine, a pair of creepy twin humans flanking him, and gazed down at us imperiously. "I was hoping it wouldn't come to this," he said as Ember tensed at the sight of him. "I've sealed this floor," he added, making *me* tense. "None of you are getting out. Ember, I'll give you one last chance to surrender without violence. Return to Talon, and I swear you won't be punished. We can be together again, as it should be. But if you stay with that rogue, I can't protect you from what's to come. Please." He gripped the railing, his gaze only for the red dragon. "Come back to Talon with me," he said, his voice quietly desperate. "You don't know what's coming, and if you're on the other side when it hits…" He shook his head. "You'll be swallowed whole with everyone else."

"What's coming, Dante?" Ember called as something cold settled in my gut, making me shiver. "What is Talon planning?"

"I can't tell you that," was the answer. "Not here. Once you return to the organization, though, you'll understand everything."

"And what about Riley and Garret?"

Even from here, I saw the gleam of hatred as the other hatchling looked at me. "Cobalt is the most wanted criminal in the organization," he said, venom dripping from his words. "And the other is a soldier of St. George. I cannot imagine how you think Talon would spare either of them.

"But," he added before either Ember or I could speak. He took a deep breath, letting it out slowly, and looked at Ember once more. "If you promise to come back with me tonight," he said in a grave voice, "they can go. They can walk out of this building at least. I can't promise anything beyond that."

"Don't strain yourself, Chameleon," I sneered, unable to simply stand there and take his insults. "What would Talon say, if they discovered you let the infamous Cobalt slip right through your slimy fingers?"

"They wouldn't be happy," Dante replied, not to me but to Ember. "But bringing you home is more important. Nothing matters more than that." A pause, and then he added, in an even softer voice, "I miss you, sis. I want things to be like they were before. You don't know…you have no idea how important you are. Not just to me, but to all of Talon. It's not my place to explain it, but you and I are special, and not just because we're siblings. Come back with me, and you can see for yourself."

"Dante," Ember said in a strangled voice. She had crouched down, tail and wings pressed tight to her body, and was trembling. "I don't—"

"You don't belong with them," Dante insisted. "You belong with Talon. It can be how it was before. We can be a family again."

"I..." Ember hesitated a heartbeat more, then raised her head, glaring at her brother. "No," she said in a firm, clear voice. "I have a family. Right here. You and I are siblings, but the brother I knew wouldn't slaughter a whole town of humans just for the good of our race. You've changed, Dante. You're not my brother anymore. And if you want to kill Riley, or Garret, or anyone I care about, you'll have to fight me, too."

For a moment, the Chameleon stared at her, disbelieving. Then his eyes glowed with anger, and he took a step back.

"If that's your decision." His voice had gone cold and slimy again, and he raised a hand, sweeping it over the humans below. "Then you leave me no choice. You will see the power of Talon, and why our enemies stand no chance against us. Vessels!" he called, and the row of identical humans raised their heads. "Initiate!"

The humans started to change. To *Shift*. Almost as one, they swelled, stretching and growing as wings tore through their backs and scales covered their bodies. In the space of a heartbeat, over a dozen identical, metallic-gray dragons stood where a human mob had been moments before.

My spines bristled as I stumbled back a step. *What the hell?* This was even worse than the humans. They were all dragons—hatchlings, judging by their relatively small size—but they stared at us with that same blank, emotionless gaze that made my insides recoil.

Soulless. The word popped into my head, and I shivered. *They look soulless, completely empty. There's nothing behind their gazes, nothing at all. They look like machines. Like fucking robots.*

"Dante..." Ember's voice was a horrified whisper, as well, as she cringed back from the row of blank-eyed dragons. "What is this? What have you done?"

"This is the future," Dante said, raising both arms as if to embrace them. "This is what's going to save us from extinction. Don't you see what they represent, Ember? This is our hope. We can finally turn the tide against the Order."

"You've created soldiers." This was from St. George, the first thing he'd said in a while, and he sounded just as quietly horrified as the rest of us. "These have been bred for war and nothing else." He narrowed his eyes at Dante. "How many has Talon created?"

"More than enough," Dante said. He smiled coldly as the clones continued to watch us with empty pale eyes. "Enough for our race to crush our enemies. Enough for dragons to return from the brink of extinction and never to be forced back. Not by St. George. Not by anyone."

"This is wrong, Dante," Ember said, gazing up at him. "Can't you see what Talon is doing? Don't you know what this means?"

"Yes," Dante replied. "It means Talon will save our race, that St. George will fall, and *you* will return to the organization with me tonight. Whether you want to or not. Vessels!" he called, and the dragons straightened to attention. "Attack! Kill the male dragon and the human, but leave the female alive. Restrain her if you have to, but bring her to me!"

As one, the line of dragons surged forward. There were no snarls, no roars or bellows or shrieking battle cries. They were as silent as death as they came at us, a terrifying gray tide.

I snarled my own battle cry, but before I could move, St. George stepped forward with a sharp, "Look away!" and hurled something into the room. A small, round object sailed through the air and landed in front of the approaching clones. They slowed, blinking at the object, just as I realized what it was and quickly turned my head.

The flashbang exploded in a brilliant burst of light, flaring white through my closed lids, and the shock wave knocked me back a step. Now the clones screamed, hissing with alarm and fury, making my blood chill, but for a split second, they were frozen in shock.

"Run!" I snarled to the others, and we fled, bounding back into the corridor. Gunshots echoed behind us as St. George fired shots into the stunned clones before he slammed the door and hurried after us.

"Where are we going?" Ember called as we entered the room where Dante had sprung his first trap. The humans were still sprawled motionless on the floor, but the room had changed. Steel walls covered the windows to the outside, blocking any escape by flying through the glass. I snarled a curse and looked around for another way out, but there were only the two doors into the room, the one we first came in with Dante, and the one that led back toward the army of clones.

St. George slammed the door to the hall and turned to Ember, beckoning her to the still-smoldering desk in the corner. "Ember, can you shove that against the door?"

The red dragon nodded, bounded to the desk and slammed her horns against the side. I hurried to join her, and the heavy piece of furniture groaned as we pushed it across the floor and shoved it in front of the door. Not that it would do much good against a fire-breathing dragon, even a small one, but it might slow them down a few seconds.

"What now?" Ember panted as we backed off, just as a heavy thud echoed from the hall beyond, and the door rattled on its hinges. I winced.

"We have to find a way off this floor," I growled, glancing at the barricaded windows. Dammit, the slimy little bastard sure had screwed us over royally. If I knew Talon at all, every window and exit to the outside would be similarly blocked, but we had to try. "All the exits will be sealed off," I said. "But if we can get to another floor, we might have a chance. They can't have sealed the whole building." *I hope.*

The door rattled again, and a trio of claws curled around the edge, raking gouges across the wood. A pale, slitted eye glared at me through the crack, making my blood run cold.

"Come on," St. George said, and we fled the room, heading back the way we came in. We passed more rooms in the same state; steel curtains covered the windows, preventing not only an easy way out but blocking all views from the outside, as well. Bursting into another room, I muttered a curse, gazing around frantically. This one was a "cubicle hell" open floor, with desks and computers sectioned off into identical workstations that covered the room like a maze. On the opposite wall, a glowing exit sign beckoned enticingly, and I bounded in that direction.

We came to the fire escape at the end of the hall, but of course the metal door was firmly locked. St. George slammed his shoulder into it a couple times, to no avail.

"Stand back, St. George," I growled after a few moments of watching the human slam into the barrier. "Let's see how well it holds up to dragon claws."

"Riley!" Ember gasped. I turned to see a dozen pale, shining eyes floating in the dark, moving toward us through the cubicle maze. St. George fired off several rounds, and though I heard bullets striking scales and horns alike, none of the clones made a sound as they advanced. If they could feel pain, they didn't show it.

"The elevator shafts!" Ember hissed as we scrambled away from the exit, trying to lose the clones in the labyrinth. "Even if Dante cut the power, we can climb down the cables."

"Good thinking, Firebrand," I whispered, ducking around cubicles. "Let's hope your brother hadn't thought the same." All around us, I heard the click of talons over tile, the flutter of wings and the hiss of tails as they brushed against walls and corners. The clone things had spread out and were combing the floor for us. And though I'd done this thing before with both Talon and the Order, it was a surreal feeling, being hunted by your own kind. I wondered how nasty these things were in a fight, because I had the sinking suspicion that we were going to find out sooner or later.

"Elevators!" Ember whispered, coming to a stop at the edge of the cubicle.

They sat against the far wall, out in the open, of course. I stifled a groan and peeked out of cover, seeing a long gray tail slink around a cubicle, disturbingly close.

"We'll have to make a run for it," I whispered, pulling back. "St. George, once we reach the elevators, I'll have to Shift back, so I'll need that change of clothes quick. I won't be able to climb elevator shafts in dragon form, and I'd rather not do it naked."

The soldier nodded and unshouldered the backpack. "I'd rather you not do it naked, either," he muttered.

I ignored that. "Ready?" I asked, but at that moment, something lean and scaly leaped atop the cubicle wall. It spotted us and gave a hiss of discovery, baring its fangs, and I winced. "Go!"

We ran for the elevators, hearing the rest of the clone dragons give chase from wherever they were in the room. I didn't dare look back to see how many were coming, or how close they were. St. George reached the elevators first and slammed his shoulder into the doors, prying them open. I had just enough time to see the metal box through the widening crack before something slammed into me from the side and knocked me off my feet.

Snarling, I rolled to my back, lashing out with my hind claws as my attacker pounced, making no noise as its jaws went for my throat. My back legs caught it in the armored stomach, stopping the lethal fangs from snapping in my face.

I shoved it off and lunged to my feet as another clone hit me from behind. This time, I felt claws score my back and sides as curved talons ripped through my scales and sank into the flesh beneath.

With a roar, I spun, trying to dislodge the thing that clung to me like a leech, seeing the rest of the pack closing in. Gunshots rang out behind me, and one of the clones staggered and went down. But that didn't stop the rest of them, and I snarled in both fury and frustration, trying to loosen the dragon's death grip on my back.

Ember hit us hard, striking the clone full-on with her horns, knocking him away. Spreading her wings, she stepped in front of me and let out a roar that shook the walls, and amazingly, the clones hesitated.

"Riley!" St. George snapped as the dragons blinked and surged forward again. Ember and I scrambled for the elevators as the soldier pried the doors open and disappeared through the crack.

"Get the hatch open!" he told me as we squeezed into the small metal box. It was a tight fit; two dragons and a soldier definitely wouldn't have fit, but thankfully Ember had already changed back into human form, her black Viper suit covering her body like paint. Unfortunately, that left her virtually defenseless against the mob of dragons on the other side of the doors. A clone followed us, sticking its head through the crack, baring its fangs. St. George bashed it in the side of the head with his pistol, rocking its head to the side, and it retreated with a hiss. Gritting my teeth, I reared onto my hind legs, ignoring the stab of pain that went through my side, and pushed against the square hatch on the ceiling. It was sealed, or stuck, because it didn't move. I shoved on it harder, and it rattled, raining dust into my eyes. It still didn't open.

A flurry of gunshots echoed inside the elevator box, making my ears ring. The clones had crowded the opening, eyes and teeth shining as they surged against the doors, and were starting to push through. They flinched away from the bullets as St. George continued to fire, but there were so many, and they would soon force their way inside.

With a snarl, I rammed my horns into the metal hatch as hard as I could, and the trapdoor finally flew open. "Ember!" I called, dropping back to the floor. She glanced up, and I positioned myself so she could use me as a stepstool. "Go!"

The girl darted from behind the soldier, took two steps and launched herself off my shoulder, reaching for the open hatch. Her arms hooked the edge of the opening, and she slid through as gracefully as any gymnast.

"St. George!" I snapped, but the soldier was already moving, dodging a dragon's talons as he hurried to my side and leaped for the top of the elevator. I whispered a curse, watching his legs vanish through the opening—too small for me to go through in my present form. I was going to have to Shift.

Sorry, Firebrand, I thought, and forced myself back to human form. *There's no time for modesty now. You're just going to have to deal for a few minutes.*

A clone wriggled its way into the box and snarled at me just as I sprang for the trapdoor. Scrambling onto the roof, I caught a split-second glimpse of the elevator filled with hissing, pale-eyed dragons before St. George slammed the hatch door shut and locked it.

I collapsed on the roof for a second, panting. My side throbbed. Nothing felt broken, but blood was seeping down my skin and dripping to the metal in small puddles. The gashes I'd taken along my back and ribs burned like someone had poured acid in them.

"Are you all right?" Ember hovered a few steps away in her black Viper suit. Though her voice was concerned, her face was as red as a beet in the darkness, and she didn't look directly at me. Any other time, it would've been adorable. "You're bleeding pretty bad."

"I'm fine," I gritted out, heaving myself upright. "A few holes in my hide aren't going to kill me."

"Can you climb?" St. George asked. He had already yanked open the backpack and was pulling out a change of clothes. His demeanor was calm and practical; we had to climb down the elevator cables to get to the bottom floor, and then we had to get out of the building and escape into the city. All of which would be difficult to do in the nude.

Dammit, I really need to think about stealing a Viper suit one day.

A thud echoed below us, and the hatch door rattled. "Don't think I have much of a choice," I said, and snatched the articles of clothing the soldier tossed at me. "You two, get going. I'll be right behind you."

"Riley..." Ember began.

"No arguments, Firebrand. Unless, of course, you want to see me run naked through the streets."

That got her moving. With one last worried look, she turned and made the short leap onto the rusty service ladder against the wall. St. George watched her descend until the top of her head vanished from sight, then turned to me.

"Hurry," he said calmly. "I'll cover you."

I scowled at him as I yanked on the pair of jeans. "I'm fine, St. George. You don't have to stay here and babysit—"

The elevator hatch burst open, and a scaly gray head lunged out, hissing. I jumped, and St. George instantly raised his weapon and shot it twice in the head and neck. It screeched and dropped away, and the soldier lowered the pistol, backing away with a steely expression. "That's it, I'm out," he announced as clones began clawing their way through the opening, hissing and snarling. "Move!"

I went, leaping from the roof and grabbing the rungs as I came down, wincing as my back and ribs protested the sudden stop. I shimmied down a few feet and felt the ladder shake as the soldier landed on it, as well. The elevator shaft echoed with the snarls and hisses of the dragons above us, but either they were unable to climb down after us, or Shifting into human form to pursue hadn't occurred to them yet.

Though that did give me a rather morbid realization.

"You know," I panted, seeing Ember below me, moving swiftly down the rungs, "those things *are* dragons. If they wanted to kill us, what's to stop them from filling this entire shaft with fire and burning us to a crisp while we're human?"

"Not helpful, Riley!" came Ember's voice from somewhere below.

"They don't want to kill us," St. George replied. "At least, not all of us. They want Ember alive, to take back to Talon. That's what Dante said."

"Yeah, well, good luck with that," Ember said defiantly, her feet thumping on the rungs as she climbed down the shaft. "I can't believe Dante would set us up like this…again." She sighed. "Dammit, who am I kidding?" she whispered, her voice nearly inaudible in the darkness. "If Dante knew we were coming here, he'd know I would want to talk to him. He made sure that I would see him, just to lure us in here. So this…this is my fault."

"Stop it, Firebrand," I growled down at her. "We all agreed to do this. We all wanted to know what Talon was up to, if they were planning anything shady. I think we sure as hell got our answer." A shriek rang out somewhere overhead, and I shivered. "So now the question becomes, what can Talon do with an army of soulless clone dragons, and what's that going to mean for the rest of us?"

"Nothing good," St. George muttered above me. I couldn't argue with him there.

We continued down the shaft in silence until we reached the last floor. Swinging myself onto the ledge between the drop-off and elevator doors, my legs nearly buckled and I staggered. Ember quickly grabbed my arm, pulling me back from the edge.

"We need to bandage those," she whispered, her gaze going to my shirt, where I could feel the bloody fabric sticking to my skin.

"Let's get out of here first," I muttered back as St. George joined us on the ledge, also giving me a concerned look. I stepped away from them and wedged my fingers into the crack between the elevator doors. "We'll call Wes, get back to the safe house and then decide if we need to build a giant underground shelter to wait out the next fifty years while Talon unleashes the dragon apocalypse. St. George, grab the other door, would you?"

He did, and together we pried them open, though I had to bite my lip to stifle a grunt of pain as we slid them back. The soldier leaned out and peered into the darkness beyond. "I don't see anyone," he murmured. "Looks clear."

Silently, we slid out of the elevator and crept down the hall, which opened up into a spacious lobby with high ceilings, a large front desk and a few chairs and sofas placed strategically over the floor. To the right, an escalator led up to a second-floor balcony that overlooked the lobby, and straight ahead, maybe fifty feet away, were the front doors that represented freedom.

"Almost there," Ember whispered, and bounded forward.

We sprinted for the doors, but before we were halfway across the floor, Dante's voice cracked like a whip in the silence.

"Ember! Stop!"

I looked back, and my heart sank.

The lobby behind us was full of dragons. Not just a dozen or so; a massive flood of iron-gray clones crept from the shadows along the walls, hissing as they came into the light. They slithered over the tables and sofas, leaped atop the welcome desk on the back wall, crowded forward in a mass of scales, wings and teeth. More identical humans appeared on the balcony overhead, raised their assault rifles and pointed them down at us. Standing between them, glaring down at us in triumph, was Dante.

We hit the front doors, Ember slamming her body into them with a crash, but they held. I reached them and drove my foot into the barrier between us and freedom, but they didn't even shake. *Sealed*, I realized, staring at the thick metal barriers in dismay. Nothing short of an explosive or a speeding dump truck was getting through them tonight.

I slumped and slowly turned to face the army at our backs. *End of the line, Riley.* I was wounded, St. George was out of ammo and we were backed into a corner with a sea of dragons closing in from all sides. *Wes*, I thought, *I'm glad you're not here. Sorry to bail on you like this, but take care of my underground for me.*

I took a deep breath, glanced at St. George and smirked. "You take the hundred on the left, I take the hundred on the right?"

He gave me the grim smile of someone who was prepared to go down fighting. "Meet you on the other side."

"No!" Ember cried, her voice ringing through the lobby, and lunged forward.

EMBER

I stepped forward, putting myself between the clones, Garret and Riley. Instantly, the dragons tensed, muscles coiling to spring at me. Ignoring them, I raised my head, seeking the lone figure on the balcony.

"Call them off, Dante! Tell them to stand down. I want to talk to you!"

"Hold," Dante barked, his voice barely audible over the hissing of the clones. They froze immediately, becoming as still and silent as rocks. But they were still just a lunge away from us, a chilling, unmoving wave, blank eyes glittering in the darkness. I took a deep breath and stepped forward, glaring up at my twin. "I have a proposal for you."

"Ember." Garret's voice echoed at my back, soft and wary, making my stomach tighten. He could guess what I was about to do. "Don't."

Ignoring him, I closed my eyes, gathering my resolve, then looked up at my brother again. "Let them go," I said firmly. "You win, Dante, but I'm setting the terms now. No one dies, that's my proposal. You want me to come back to Talon?" I gestured behind me. "Swear to me that you'll let them live, and I'll go with you tonight."

"Ember!" Riley snarled, and I spun on him, furious.

"Let me do this, Riley," I snapped, desperate to convince him. "We can't win this one. Even if we fight, they're just going to kill you and take me back, anyway. At least this way, I'll know you're alive. You and Garret both. Please." My gaze went to the soldier, standing rigidly beside him. "Don't fight them," I whispered, lowering my voice so only Garret and Riley could hear. "Don't throw your life away. There's too much at stake now. Look around you." I made a tiny gesture at the army of dragons at my back. "Someone has to fight this. Someone has to warn the rest of our world what Talon has done. The underground, St. George, everyone will be affected. Who knows how many of these things Talon has?"

Garret came forward. His expression was tormented as he stared at me, but he didn't argue. He knew, just as I did, that we couldn't win. "And what about you?"

"I'll be all right," I whispered. "They're not going to kill me, not with all the trouble they've gone through to take me alive. I don't know why they want me so badly, but if I have to go back, I'm damn sure going to get something out of it." Stepping close, I put a hand on his cheek, gazing into his eyes. "I can't watch you die," I whispered. "Not when there's something I can do to stop it. At least, this way, you'll still be free.

"If Talon wants me to come back," I continued, raising my voice again, making certain Dante could hear every word, "they're going to let you go. If not, if they try to kill you here, I swear I will fight this army till my last breath, and I will take down as many dragons as I can. They're going to have to kill me to get me to stop." I turned then, facing my brother, who still watched imperiously from the balcony. "I'll come back with you," I said. "But only if you let Garret and

Riley go. That's my bargain, Dante. Either we all leave this room alive and unharmed, or none of us do."

Dante was silent a moment, considering. Around us, the clones were also motionless, waiting. I could feel Garret and Riley at my back, tense and ready to explode into action, but I couldn't look at either of them. I knew they would fight without hesitation. Even vastly outnumbered and outgunned, I knew they would struggle as long as they were still breathing, and they would die bravely defending what they loved. But they would still die. We couldn't stand against Talon's new army, this mass of chilling dragon clones who stared at us with eyes like empty mirrors. Even if I went back to Talon, if Riley and Garret were still alive, there was hope.

"Very well." Dante's voice drifted down from the balcony. "If that is what it takes to get you to come back, Ember, then you have a deal. I promise I won't kill them."

"That's not good enough." An annoyed look crossed his face, and I narrowed my eyes. "They walk out, right now, before I go anywhere with you. I want to see them go. And I swear, Dante, if I surrender and you double-cross me, you will never get my cooperation. I'll fight you and Talon every step of the way, for the rest of my life, until you kill me."

"I know you will," Dante replied, frowning. "I know you're stubborn enough to do it. And I don't want that, Ember. Believe what you want, but hurting you is the last thing I set out to do." He sighed, running a hand over his head. "All right," he finally said. "You have a deal, Ember. The soldier and the rogue can leave, and I won't try to stop them."

I crossed my arms. "Prove it," I ordered, making his jaw tighten. "I'm not taking a step until I know you're serious. Open this door, right now, and let them go."

Dante's eyes flashed green with anger, but he turned and pulled out his phone, tapping the screen several times. A moment later, there was a beep behind us, and the metal barrier in front of the door slid up.

Raising his head, Dante addressed the army of dragons below him. "Vessels!" he called. "Stand down! Now!"

The horde of dragons rippled back, sinking to their haunches or bellies, but still watching us with flat, silvery eyes. They didn't move, but their bodies were like tightly coiled springs, ready to attack with a word.

I caught Riley's gaze, watching me from against the door frame. He was breathing hard, one side of his shirt stained dark red. I could see Cobalt just below the surface, wanting to burst out and fling himself at his enemies, numbers and consequences be damned. But there was also weary resignation in his eyes; he knew there were too many to fight, that we would die if we made our final stand here. I could tell he was thinking about his hatchlings, his network and his underground, because they were never far from his mind.

I swallowed hard and peeked back at Garret. He stared down at me, his gaze intense, metallic eyes stony with determination. "Ember," he whispered, and his voice was anguished. I put a hand on his chest.

"Go, soldier boy," I told him. "Get out of here. You know we can't win this one. Walk out, and live to fight another day."

Footsteps thumped behind us. A pair of guards approached, weapons raised menacingly, to flank me on either side. Garret retreated a few steps, backing up until he stood with Riley, the open door at their backs. Riley pushed himself off the frame, his gaze dangerous as he met my eyes.

"We'll find you," he promised, his eyes glowing as he

took one step back, toward the open door. "We'll get you out again, I swear it."

"I know," I whispered, memorizing their faces before I jerked my head at the door. "Go. Get the hell out of here before Dante changes his mind. Go!"

Their jaws tightened, and they went, both of them, slipping through the door and out of sight. Not two seconds after they cleared the frame, the metal barrier slid back with a clang, cutting us off from each other and trapping me in the room with the clones.

I swallowed the terror threatening to overwhelm me and turned to face Dante, alone.

The soldiers closed in. One of them took my arms and slapped a pair of thick metal cuffs around my wrists. They were heavier than normal handcuffs, solid bands of steel nearly two inches wide. I didn't know what good they would do if I decided to turn into a dragon, but my stomach dropped all the same.

Without speaking, the guards motioned me forward. I spared a last look at the door Garret and Riley had gone through, hoping they were running as fast as they could from this place, before taking a deep breath and stepping into the dark.

Back to Talon. Like a delinquent runaway, only I knew my punishment would be far worse than anything the humans could think of. What *would* Talon do to me? I wondered. Lock me up for the rest of my life? That seemed rather pointless, considering all the trouble they went through to find me. Would they torture me for information about Riley's network and Garret's knowledge of St. George? Or—and my stomach heaved at this thought—would they ship me off to *the facility*, where I would become a breeder like the rest of Talon's disgraced female dragons?

Garret and Riley are free, I told myself as my stomach threatened to crawl up my throat. *That's all that matters. They're alive, and as long as they're out there, they'll be fighting to get me away from Talon. I just have to endure until then, and not give Talon anything they want.*

Shaking, I followed my captors single file through the room, passing dozens of metallic-gray dragons who watched me with pale, empty eyes. The guards led me into an elevator, which opened up onto the balcony overlooking the main floor. From up here, the sea of clones looked even more ominous, a glittering mass of scales, horns and wings. Dante stood with his back to me and both hands on the railing, gazing out over the clones. He glanced at me over his shoulder as I approached with the guards. "I didn't want it to be like this, Ember," he said as they drew me to a stop a few feet away. "I didn't want to use force. Once we get back to Talon, you'll see what we're really trying to do."

I raised my cuffed hands. "Seems pretty obvious to me."

His face tightened, but he didn't order them removed. "You're a danger to yourself, Ember," he said, turning from the railing. "I want to trust you, but you've been with that rogue too long, listening to his lies. Please understand, this isn't forever. But until we return to the organization, I can't take any chances. I'm sorry."

He raised his hand, gesturing someone forward. A woman stepped out from the shadows, not a clone but a human in a white lab suit. The suit itself made me nervous, but the syringe glittering in one gloved hand made me even more jumpy.

"What is that?" I growled as she stepped toward me, smiling in a way that I guessed was supposed to be calming, but it just made me want to bite her.

"Dractylpromazine," Dante answered. "A mild sedative. It won't hurt you. It will just make it impossible to Shift for the next few hours. Hold her still."

The guards took my arms, immobilizing me as the woman stepped up and smoothly sunk the needle into my skin. I clenched my jaw at the stinging pain, remembering what Riley had told me about the drug, which was *not* a "mild sedative" but a very powerful tranquilizer that worked on our dragon half. Talon had developed it to further control and threaten the dragons in the organization, because not being able to Shift was one of the most frightening things that could happen to us. Almost immediately after the needle was removed, I began to feel drowsy, my limbs heavy and unresponsive. I shook my head, fighting to stay alert as Dante watched me with somber green eyes. I curled a lip at him.

"I suppose Talon told you that drugging your sister was necessary, as well," I said scathingly.

"No." Dante's brow furrowed. "But I know you, Ember. I know how you'll react, and I can't risk anything happening to you. Even if I have to prevent you from hurting yourself." His words sent a chill through me as I realized what he meant, that he was about to do something I wouldn't like. Dante gave the human in the lab coat a quick glance. "Has the drug taken effect?" he asked.

"Yes, sir. It should be at full strength now."

"Good." He turned from me, pulling out his phone and placing it to his ear. "Squad two," he said quietly. "Initiate. Take the rogue and the human. Alive."

"What?" I snarled and lunged forward, but the guards grabbed my arms, holding me back. Instinctively, I tried to

Shift, but there was no response from the dragon, making me furious and terrified all at once. "Dante, you lying, two-faced bastard!" I raged, struggling against my captors. "You said you would let them go."

"I did not. I said I would let them *live*." Dante's expression was hard as he watched me, knowing I had tried to change just then. "Cobalt is the worst traitor Talon has seen in centuries," he went on. "I will not return to the organization having let him slip through my fingers." He shook his head. "No, I will keep my word and not kill him as I originally planned, but you all will be returning to Talon tonight." His eyes narrowed, and he gave a small, chilling smile. "The Elder Wyrm is expecting us."

PART III

Fang and Fire

RILEY

I groaned and opened my eyes. Then immediately wished
I hadn't.

"Shit," I growled, pressing a hand to my forehead. My
skull throbbed, probably from the whack I'd taken, courtesy
of a rifle butt to the side of the head. The motion also revealed another fun discovery: thick metal cuffs were locked
around my wrists, heavy-duty manacles made for gorillas
and Frankenstein's monster. Blearily, I lowered my arms,
waiting for the cobwebs in my brain to clear out. How I
got here was kind of fuzzy. I remembered being surrounded
by an army of robot-like dragons, feeling utterly helpless as
Ember bargained with her slimy brother for all our lives. I
remembered the look on her face as she watched us leave,
unable to stop her, or save her, knowing there was no way
in hell that Talon would just let me go.

Turns out I was right. The soldier and I hadn't gone a hundred yards when a squad of a dozen armed clones appeared
from nowhere, surrounding us. While half of them pointed
assault rifles at our faces, one pair had dragged me forward
and shoved me against a brick wall. I was already injured,
furious at the betrayal, and didn't exactly appreciate being
manhandled by two soulless humans, so I might've snarled

and elbowed one in the face as hard as I could. Which might not have been the brightest of ideas, as the other had instantly responded by clocking me in the temple with the butt of his gun. That was the last thing I remembered.

"You awake?" came a familiar voice in the corner.

"Yeah," I muttered, raising my head to peer at my surroundings. Unsurprisingly, I was sitting on the floor of a small, dark cell. The walls were made of steel, there were no windows and the heavy, barred door at the front looked like it could stop a charging buffalo. A pair of cots were set into one wall, bunk-bed-style, but both were empty. St. George sat against the opposite wall watching me, manacled hands resting on his knees.

"How long was I out?" I rasped.

"Hard to tell. At least a few hours, and most of that was the drive. We haven't been in here very long." His gaze narrowed. "They stuck you with a needle while you were unconscious," he told me, making my stomach churn. "I'm guessing it's something that prevents you from Shifting."

"Dractylpromazine." I exhaled and leaned my head against the wall. "Yeah, I'll be stuck in human form for several hours at least. And they'll probably keep dosing me with that crap to keep it that way. Or at least until they have no interest in keeping us alive anymore." On impulse, I gingerly pulled up my shirt—hard to accomplish in shackles—to reveal strips of gauze and bandages wrapped around my ribs. "Oh, well, look at that. The bastards want me alive and healthy for a little while longer at least. Can't have me dying on the interrogation table, I guess." I lowered the fabric, grimacing. "Where's Ember?"

"I haven't seen her," the soldier said darkly. "We weren't

in the same vehicle. And they blindfolded me when they brought us in, so I'm not even sure where 'here' is."

"Well…" I craned my head to look up at the ceiling. "I'd say we're underground, though I have no idea where. Could be in a city, could be out in the wilderness, but deep enough that no one outside of Talon knows we're here. The organization likes to do their dirty business where no one can see it."

St. George glanced at the barred door and the guards flanking either side. "Why haven't they killed us yet?" he muttered, his eyes dark. "If they can't get what they want from us, why are they keeping us alive? We know too much. We've seen that dragon army." He turned, frowning in my direction. "They don't need us. Talon has been hunting you for years, and I'm still a soldier of St. George in their eyes. Dante would've killed us if Ember hadn't stepped in. What are they waiting for?"

"That's easy," I said. "It's not about us, St. George. We're leverage. To get Ember to do what they want. You saw what happened with that twin of hers." His eyes widened, then hardened in fury. I gave a tired nod. "Our lives aren't important. For some reason, it's always been about her. As long as we're alive, she's not going to do anything that will put us in danger. If she doesn't cooperate with them, they'll threaten to kill us, or torture us, or something equally awful and blackmail-ish. That's how Talon works. And of course Ember, being Ember, will do whatever they say, to save our lives."

St. George clenched his fists. "We have to get out of here," he said in a low voice. "You've escaped Talon before, right?"

"Yeah, but I wasn't exactly in the middle of an armed Talon facility," I answered. "They know who we are, and they're not taking any chances. Maybe if I could somehow get to a computer and contact Wes…but I wouldn't expect him to storm this place to rescue us. And I sure as hell wouldn't want any of the hatchlings to try it. Best I could do is warn him about Talon's new clone minions and tell him to keep the underground as safe as he can." I sighed, shaking my head. "There's also another reason for Talon to keep us alive. One that's probably not going to be pleasant for either of us."

"They want information," St. George muttered.

I nodded. "Yeah. And you can guess how they're going to try to extract it. From both of us."

"I've been trained to withstand torture," the soldier said in a calm voice. He glanced at me again, his expression grim. "I won't betray your network."

"Appreciate it, St. George," I said, more grateful than I'd realized. "But I don't think we're going to have much of a choice, in the end. Not if we're stuck here for a while. Talon always gets what they want, eventually."

The creak of the door interrupted us. St. George stood quickly, but I stayed where I was, watching as the heavy iron barrier groaned and swung back, revealing four emotionless, identical humans with large guns. I smirked at them from against the wall.

"Hey, guys. I'd get up, but, uh…my head kinda hurts. You understand, right?"

The clones didn't answer. As one, they stepped aside, parting like elevator doors, and a smaller figure walked through the gap to stand in the frame. St. George tensed, and I stiffened as two bright, crystal-blue eyes met mine across the room.

"Hello, Cobalt," Mist said, smiling. "Ready for round two?"

EMBER

I paced the floor of my room, unable to sit still. It was a fairly standard bedroom, with a twin bed in the corner, a desk and a bookshelf, a separate bathroom, even a television on the wall. Nicely furnished, for a prison cell. There were no windows, of course, and I knew the heavy metal door would be locked, even without turning the handle. And the large, two-way mirror on the wall wasn't fooling anyone. At least the cuffs were gone, and it had been a few hours, so the Dractylpromazine might've worn off.

The door beeped, making me jerk my head toward it, and a few seconds later a human clone opened it and stepped aside as Dante came into the room. I clenched my fists, fighting the urge to fly across the floor and grab my twin by his two-timing neck. His clone bodyguards made that impossible, however, even if I was able to turn into a dragon. Besides, I had bigger questions I wanted answers to.

"Where are Garret and Riley?" I demanded as soon as Dante stepped through the frame. His brow furrowed before smoothing out again.

"Alive," was the cool, infuriating answer. "And they'll remain that way...as long as you cooperate."

"You're a real piece of work, Dante," I snarled. "Do you

even hear yourself? What kind of soulless bastard makes threats like that?"

Dante stared at me, expressionless, before turning to his guards. "Leave us," he ordered quietly. "Lock the door and stand guard, but don't return until I call for you. Go."

Without hesitation, the clones turned and left the room. The door clicked shut, and my brother turned back to me. "All right, Ember," Dante said, walking forward with his arms slightly raised. "Here I am. No guards, no one to stop you. Do your worst—"

I punched him in the jaw as hard as I could, landing a solid right hook across his chin. He staggered back and nearly fell, one hand going to his face. For a few seconds, he stood braced against the wall, cradling his jaw in stunned silence. Finally, he straightened and pulled his hand down to gaze at the blood on his fingertips before turning to me.

"Feel better?"

"No," I whispered as my eyes started to burn. "Damn you, Dante! How could you turn on me like this? You were my best friend—we used to do everything together. And now look at you." I stepped back, shaking my head. "You're one of *them*."

"I turned on *you*?" Dante sounded genuinely shocked. "You're the one who left. Ran off with that traitor and went rogue. You walked out, not me. I've done nothing but try to bring you back to Talon."

"Against my will."

"If I didn't bring you home, they were going to kill you."

"Hello, doesn't that bother you?" I cried, throwing up my arms. "If I didn't do what they wanted, they would kill me. If dragons don't conform to Talon, they get Vipers sent after them. How is that freedom? How is that for the good of our race?"

"It's for our survival," Dante answered stonily. "We can't have everything we want, not if we're going to exist in this world. If you haven't noticed, there's a war out there. We're being pushed toward extinction, Ember. Sometimes, sacrifices have to be made. Dragons who break away from Talon are a danger to us all."

"How do you know?" I challenged. "You haven't even met any rogues besides me. All you know is what Talon preaches at you." He gave me an exasperated look, as if *I* were the unreasonable one, and it made me want to pull my hair out. "Dammit, open your eyes, Dante. Talon doesn't have our best interests at heart. They're not who they say they are."

"Ugh, we're having the same argument we had in Crescent Beach," Dante said, making a hopeless gesture. "And nothing has changed. Look, sis, just…come with me, all right?" His expression became hopeful, pleading. "There's someone you have to meet. When you do, you'll see why we belong with Talon. You'll see why we're special." He took a step back, holding out a hand. "No more arguing. Just come with me. Please."

"Do I have a choice?"

I thought that might irritate him, but he only shook his head. "No," he murmured, almost sadly. "You don't." He took a short breath, as if he were nervous on my behalf. "The Elder Wyrm has called for you, Ember. It's time you met the leader of Talon, face-to-face."

The elevator came to a stop, and the doors slid open.

Dante stepped out, followed by his bodyguards, and glanced back at me. "Come on, sis," he urged as I hung back in the box. The elevator had opened onto a short hall with a pair of massive wooden doors at the end. "We're expected. You don't want to keep the Elder Wyrm waiting."

I took a furtive breath and stepped through the frame to join Dante in the hallway. Another pair of guards stood at the entrance, and they gave Dante short nods as they pulled back the doors. I followed my brother into a massive office, stark and cold for all its elegance, everything colored in black, white and gray. A chill hung in the air that had nothing to do with the air-conditioning, and I shivered.

The desk was empty, but a figure stood at the windows, gazing out on the city below. When she turned, it was like watching a giant—a mountain—turn to stare at you, crushing you under the weight of its gaze. The breath left my lungs in a rush, and I suddenly couldn't move, frozen like a mouse under the stare of the most powerful dragon in the world.

"Ember Hill." The Elder Wyrm smiled, and it was somehow even more terrifying than if she'd roared and spit fire at me. "We meet at last."

"Nothing to say?" the Elder Wyrm asked after a moment of silence as I tried to convince myself not to cringe in terror. My hands were shaking, my eyes fixed to a spot on the carpet, unwilling to stare directly at the woman in front of me. The Elder Wyrm's voice was quietly amused as I stood there, trembling. "Your brother says you are opinionated and quite verbose, especially when it comes to my organization. Well, speak, then, Ember Hill. Do not fear—there will be no repercussions for speaking your mind. I simply wish to know your thoughts."

I had to force myself to breathe. *In and out, Ember, in and out. She's not going to kill you, at least not yet.* "I don't…really know why I'm here," I managed.

The Elder Wyrm gave me a puzzled look, raising her brows. I swallowed the fear screaming at me to be silent, and continued. "I mean, I don't know what you think you're going to convince me of," I went on. "You went through a lot of trouble to bring me back, so you must want something from me. But I've seen what Talon does, both to the humans and our own kind. And I know you're hoping that I'll just fall in line like everyone else, but...I'm not going to change."

"That is where you are mistaken, I'm afraid."

I stared at her, heart pounding. Her voice was calm, certain. As if she had complete confidence in what she was saying. The Elder Wyrm smiled again, those hard green eyes appraising me like a sculptor would a block of marble, seeing how he would have to break it down to achieve the final masterpiece.

"You don't know who you are, Ember Hill," the Elder Wyrm stated. "You have no idea why you are so important to Talon. You must have wondered why we would go through all this trouble to bring you back, instead of simply letting Lilith deal with you. To 'correct her mistake,' as she wanted."

A shiver went through me at the mention of my old trainer. "I thought it was because of Dante," I said, deliberately not looking at my brother, who still stood motionless behind the Elder Wyrm with his hands clasped in front of him.

The Elder Wyrm chuckled. "Dante has no sway over the organization. Not yet. Soon, perhaps." She spared him a brief glance over her shoulder, a chilling glint of satisfaction in her eyes. Dante gazed straight ahead, statue-like, as the Elder Wyrm turned back to me. "Which is why you are so important to Talon, Ember," she continued. "You and your brother both. You see, twenty years ago, I made a decision. This organization, this empire, has been my whole life. I have watched it grow, flourish, even in the face of St. George and everything they do to rip it apart. For hundreds of years, I have guided Talon, and I have watched our numbers grow from a mere dozen dragons to the global power we are now. And yet, it is not enough. I have seen nations rise and fall, lived through countless wars, watched the birth of many new and wonderful things. I have built this empire from nothing, and I intend for it to endure until the end of time. But I know I cannot live forever."

The Elder Wyrm turned from me to stare out the window again. Her expression, reflected in the glass, was solemn. "Twenty years ago," she continued, her voice becoming distant, "I decided I needed an heir. I built Talon from nothing—I refused to leave it in the hands of a stranger. Even the best-intentioned dragons would not concede to my wishes. They would try to make Talon their own. They would change everything and destroy my vision in the process. I did not want to leave my company to someone not of my blood."

My heart had started pounding again as I realized where this was going. *You'll understand soon,* Dante had whispered to me, right before we came here. *You'll see why we're special.*

I clenched my fists. *No,* I thought, disbelieving. *It can't be true.* The Elder Wyrm turned from the window, her eyes piercing as they stared at me.

"So you see, Ember," she said. "You are more important to Talon than you know. You and your brother were destined from the beginning. You are my blood, the true heirs of the organization, and I need you to continue my work after I am gone. Dante has already accepted his role." She gestured to my brother, though her gaze stayed on me. "It is time to stop playing these foolish games and take your place in Talon, where you belong."

I swallowed hard, still staggered from the revelation. I was the daughter of the Elder Wyrm, the most powerful dragon in the world. The heir to Talon, and everything it offered.

"I told you, sis." Dante's voice was low, triumphant. "This is where we belong. Think of what we could do together." He stepped forward, smiling in a way I'd never seen before, chilling and intense. "You always wanted a family," he said. "But you've always had one right here. And now, we can be the most powerful family in the world."

For just a moment, I hesitated. The organization was right at my fingertips. Talon could be mine in the future; what could I do with that much power?

My stomach turned, and I staggered away from him. "No," I whispered, shaking my head. "I don't want this. I won't be a part of Talon, whether it's at the bottom or the top. All the power in the world isn't worth what I would have to pay."

"What are you talking about?" Dante glared at me, anger and disbelief written across his face. "Ember, you don't get it, do you? No one will challenge us at the top. We can finally be free. True freedom, without having to run from anything. Isn't that what you've always wanted?"

"At what price?" I snapped back at him. "What will I have to do, to stay at the top? Massacre another town? Slaughter a group of hatchlings in cold blood?" I shook my head, feeling my stomach roil. "There was a time when you wouldn't even *think* of doing that. And now you'll commit whatever atrocity they want."

"Enough, both of you." The Elder Wyrm's expression was calm as she raised her hand, and two guards stepped forward to flank me. Dante fell silent, stepping back to glower at me, as the Elder Wyrm shook her head. "Well, I am disappointed that you feel that way," she said as the guards took my arms. "But no matter. There are other avenues for negotiation that we haven't explored. I'm sure we can find something we agree on."

"Don't waste your time," I told her. "I won't be a part of this, of whatever you're planning. I'd rather die than be enslaved to Talon forever."

"Such dramatics." The Elder Wyrm smiled in a way that chilled my blood. My legs shook, and I had to fight to remain upright, to not sink to the floor under the weight of her stare. "And you have much to learn in the way of business. You see, everything has a price. Even the most stubborn, passionate souls have a breaking point. And we have millennia of experience in finding that one thing someone can't live without." She gestured, and as the guards turned me away, her final words became an echo of dread in my ears. "Make no mistake. You *will* serve Talon, one way or another. We just have to find that breaking point."

DANTE

I watched as the guards led Ember away, a furious, roaring buzz in my ears. Had she really just done that? Stood before the Elder Wyrm, the oldest, most powerful dragon in the world, and *defied* her? Told her flat out that she wouldn't cooperate? That she wouldn't take her destined place in Talon, because the rogue had showed her differently?

Dammit, Ember. I clenched my fists. How could she be so pointlessly stubborn? She was the Elder Wyrm's *heir*. We both were. I'd really believed that, once she knew who she was, she would realize the enormous potential staring her in the face. Together, we could change Talon and the whole world, but she didn't see that. She saw only what *she* wanted, what Cobalt had told her. He had blinded her with his lies, turned her against me. Everything she'd done, everything that had come between us, began the moment she had met the rogue in Crescent Beach.

"Well," the Elder Wyrm mused as the doors to the office closed once more. Her voice wasn't angry or surprised or remotely disturbed. "That could have gone better."

I took a breath to calm the fear and anger roiling within. My sister refused to bend. What would happen to her now? You did not defy the Elder Wyrm without consequences. I desperately wanted to ask, but at the same time, I knew that would be a breach of protocol. The Elder Wyrm was not to be questioned. Her word was law. If she thought you needed to know something, she would tell you.

"Dante," the Elder Wyrm said, making everything inside me go still. I turned out of habit, the calm, blank mask hiding the turmoil within. The CEO of Talon wasn't looking at me, however. She was still gazing at the door through which Ember had disappeared.

"You will leave tomorrow," she said, and my stomach dropped to my toes. "Go to our main laboratory and prepare the vessels and their handlers for the upcoming mission. The first stage of the plan is nearly upon us. I want you to lead it."

"Of course," I said, though my voice came out a little choked. "Right away. But…"

The *but* was out of my mouth before I could stop it, and I winced. It was a tremendous honor to be chosen for this assignment. This was the most important task I had ever been given, the first step in finally ending the war with St. George, and the Elder Wyrm was entrusting it to me. I knew I should be grateful, excited, terrified. But if I left now, would I ever see my sister alive again?

The Elder Wyrm turned then, raising an elegant silver eyebrow. "But?" she repeated, her voice lethally soft. I shivered, but there was no going back now.

"What of Ember?" I asked, almost dreading the answer. "I mean…what does Talon plan to do with her, now that she refuses to cooperate?"

"You needn't worry, Dante." The Elder Wyrm gave a faint smile, not fooled in the slightest. "She may be uncooperative now, but we have ways of making even the most stubborn see reason. Often, all it takes is time. Now that she is here, back where she belongs, I am positive that she will come to accept her place in Talon." She met my eyes, solemn and terrifying, and I instantly dropped my gaze. "Rest assured. I have no intention of killing your sister. You have my word on that. Now, go." She turned and walked back to her desk, brusque and businesslike again. "You are no longer needed here. Ember is home, and now we must turn our sights to the future." The Elder Wyrm sat down and folded her hands on the surface of the desk, her eyes piercing. "Our greatest moment is at hand, Dante," she said, her voice sending shivers up my spine. "All the pieces are in place, poised for that final move. The final checkmate. And you are the one who will bring it to pass. I await word of your success."

I left the Elder Wyrm's office, feeling torn in several directions at once. Of course I had to obey the Elder Wyrm. There was no doubt in my mind. Once the leader of Talon gave you an order, you had to carry it through. And this was our most important project to date. Our entire future hung in the balance. I knew it was a great honor, being chosen to carry it out.

But at the same time, I was loath to leave. Ember was finally home. I wanted to talk to her, if not to convince her to join us, then to attempt to understand why she was being so stubborn. How could she not see the huge potential staring her in the face? We were the offspring of the Elder Wyrm. Why couldn't she think about what we could do together, once we both ruled Talon?

I needed someone to keep an eye on her while I was gone, to make sure she was all right, and that she wouldn't somehow sneak off again. The guards were competent, I supposed, but they didn't have a vested interest in my sister. And Ember, as I'd seen time and time again, was just stubborn and crafty enough to be dangerous. Even if she couldn't Shift, she might be too much for them to handle. I didn't trust any of the humans in this place to keep my sister safe, to be competent enough to deal with her.

But...there *was* someone who could.

Making my decision, I headed for the elevator.

GARRET

"Well," Riley sighed at my back, "today is going to be loads of fun. Ready for this, St. George?"

"Don't have much of a choice, do I?" I muttered, mentally steeling myself for what I knew was coming. I sat in a chair with my hands cuffed behind the metal back, a spotlight shining in my face. To my left sat a table laid out with instruments and needles that glinted under the light; it wasn't hard to guess what they would be used for.

Behind me, Riley snorted. "Try not to scream like a little girl *too* much," he said. "My perception of you isn't that great to begin with."

The door opened, and a girl entered the room, followed by two men in white suits. Riley turned his head, and I felt his smirk even without seeing it.

"Mist," he drawled. "We just keep meeting like this. What's the matter, didn't get enough of me last time?"

The girl ignored him, but the men picked up a pair of syringes from the table, walked over and smoothly sank the needle into my neck. It burned as it entered my skin, and I clenched my jaw. Some sort of truth serum, if I had to guess. That would make resisting difficult, but I could not break and tell them what they wanted to know. Too many people depended on us. If Talon discovered them, they would all be in danger. Everyone I knew—Wes, Jade, Tristan, all the dragons in Riley's underground—Talon wouldn't spare any of them. And somewhere in this place, maybe close by, Ember was being held against her will.

Ember, I thought, and closed my eyes. *Where are you? Are you going through the same hell we are?* The thought of her strapped to a chair with a spotlight in her eyes, being prodded and tortured for information, was more painful than anything they could do to me. *I'll find you, somehow, I promise. Please, hang on.*

"Are we ready?" Mist's soft, cool voice made my heart pound, and I took a furtive breath, cementing my determination. *I'm ready*, I told myself, opening my eyes. *Let's get this over with.*

"I'm surprised Talon let you do this again, Mist," Riley said behind me. "It went so well for you last time. Though I am a little hurt. I thought we had something special." His voice, though starting to slur, was heavy with sarcasm. He shifted in his chair, jerking his head back toward me. "But I don't know why you decided to drag this poor bastard into it. If you think you're going to get more out of him because he's human, you're sadly mistaken. You think I'd share my network secrets with a weak-willed mortal?" Riley sneered, his tone cutting. "You're wasting your breath. He doesn't know anything."

Why are you protecting me? I wondered, but then I realized. *No, he's trying to protect his underground. He doesn't think I can take this, that I might talk.*

Mist walked around to observe me with appraising blue eyes. I met her stare, careful to give nothing away. To not let on that my eyelids were growing heavy, and the room was starting to ripple at the edges. "Or perhaps the opposite is true," she said, watching my face intently. "Perhaps, against all your better judgment, you have let a soldier of St. George into your inner sanctum, and now he knows far too much. About you, and your underground, and all of Talon." Her eyes narrowed, shrewd and calculating. "There are rumors that the Patriarch, the leader of the Order, is deceased. And that a single soldier was able to defeat him." My gut knotted, but I kept my expression vacant. Mist raised an eyebrow and smiled. "I think there is more to this human than you're letting on, Cobalt. And you are trying to protect both him and what he knows."

"Hey." The sneer in Riley's voice sounded completely legitimate. "If you want to browbeat the kid until he wets himself and confesses that he still sucks his thumb at night, you go right ahead. I'll be happy to share the attention."

"No matter. You will both talk soon enough." The faint smile lingered on the girl's face as she walked back to the table. "Leave us," she told the two men, who straightened quickly. "You're not needed. I'll take it from here."

They nodded, but before they could go, the door swung open again, and a figure walked into the room. This time, it was Mist who straightened quickly. "Mr. Hill," she exclaimed as Dante walked across the floor to stand before us. "I wasn't expecting you."

DANTE

"Do we need to stop the procedure?" Mist asked as I walked into the room. A few feet from her, Cobalt and the soldier of St. George sat back-to-back, hands cuffed behind them, a spotlight shining into their faces. I would admit, I felt a flicker of both relief and vindictive satisfaction to see Cobalt like that; Talon's most infamous criminal would finally be brought to justice. And I was the one who had captured him.

"No, Miss Anderson," I said. "I apologize for the interruption, but there is something I need you to do for me."

"Come to finally take your shots, Dante?" the rogue asked, his expression twisted into a smirk. "It's a lot easier to be brave when the guy can't hit you back."

"I am not here for you, traitor," I said calmly, refusing to glance at him. "You are no longer of any consequence. Miss Anderson, if you would please come with me. I need to speak to you in private."

Her brow furrowed. "But what of the prisoners?" she asked. "I have orders to question both Cobalt and the soldier, and the truth serum should be taking effect now."

"Don't worry, Miss Anderson." I spared a quick glance at the rogue, keeping my voice professional, not letting the satisfaction leak into my tone. "I've assigned someone to take over. They should be here any moment now."

A flicker of emotion went through her cold blue eyes. Was it worry? Irritation? Defiance? I wasn't sure, for it was gone in the space of a blink. "Of course, sir," Mist said, coolly polite as always. "If that is what you desire."

"Dante," the soldier of St. George called before we could step out. I gave him a look of amused surprise. I expected Cobalt to throw out a few parting insults, but the human, from the little I remembered of him in Crescent Beach, had always seemed reserved. Of course, he was still a soldier of St. George, a human who hated our kind and who, very likely, had been in Crescent Beach to kill us both. "Where is Ember?" the soldier asked. "Is she all right? What have you done to her?"

"I'm afraid you don't get to know that, St. George," I stated, though the genuine concern in his voice surprised me. "I am certainly not going to share my sister's whereabouts with you. Ember is too important to Talon to risk. Rest assured, she is safe, and she is out of your reach. Neither of you will ever see her again."

The door opened again, and another dragon stepped through, a young adult with slicked-back hair and beady black eyes. Mist saw him, and a fleeting look of disgust crossed her face before it was neutral once more.

"Mr. Luther will take over the interrogation," I said, nodding to the other Basilisk. "I understand he has a knack for this type of procedure, so you needn't worry about your orders, Miss Anderson. They have been taken care of."

Luther glanced at the prisoners, then back at Mist, smiling. "Have the subjects been prepared?" he asked in a thin, high-pitched voice.

"Yes," Mist replied with cool disdain. "They've been given the truth serum, though I must warn you. I've dealt with Cobalt before—he is highly resistant to questioning, even if he has been drugged. I think you're going to find this task challenging."

"Oh, don't worry, Miss Anderson," Luther said, rubbing his hands together. "I enjoy a challenge. And forgive me for saying so, but you are far too nice for this. If the drugs won't do it, there are other ways of making them talk."

Mist's gaze hardened at the other dragon's words, but she simply nodded. "Of course," she replied, gesturing toward the prisoners with a distinct *have at it* motion. "They're all yours."

"Well," I said, a strange sense of guilt stealing over me. This was Cobalt, I reminded myself. The rogue who had stolen Ember away and turned her against me. He was getting exactly what he deserved for all the trouble he'd caused Talon and myself. "We'll leave you to it, Mr. Luther. Miss Anderson, if you would come with me, please."

She followed me out of the room, down several hallways where guards and humans in white coats nodded to us respectfully, until we stepped into the elevator and the doors closed behind us.

"I suppose you are going to inform me why you pulled me away from my job, Mr. Hill?" Mist asked as the box began to ascend.

"I am."

"And I suppose the reason could not wait until after I had completed my interrogation of Cobalt and the soldier?"

"No." I gave her a hard look. Mist had never openly challenged me. Though I had often caught hints of skepticism or disapproval whenever we spoke, she had always been coolly professional. Now she seemed almost irritated that I had stopped her from questioning the rogue and the soldier. I remembered that Cobalt had bested her before, in a very similar situation. Mist had tried to get information out of him and had not only failed to do so but had let him escape in the process. I knew she had returned to the organization and had been reassigned; I didn't know if she had been disgraced by her failure, or if Talon had blamed the rogue.

Maybe her attitude was about revenge, I mused. Or, perhaps, her wish to redeem herself for that past failure. In any case, it didn't matter. I needed her for something else.

"I'm leaving today," I told her. "By order of the Elder Wyrm. My car is on its way now. But, before I go, I need you to do something for me, Mist."

She raised an elegant silver eyebrow. "And what is that, Mr. Hill?" she asked coolly.

"I want you to keep an eye on Ember," I said, making her blink. "Make sure nothing happens to her, and that she doesn't try to escape." I paused, then shook my head. "Actually, I'm sure she'll try. But make sure she doesn't succeed. I need to know she'll be safe, and there's no one else I trust to do this. You don't need to guard her door 24/7, just know where she is and what she's doing. I'll feel a lot better about leaving if I know you are looking out for her."

"I see." Mist's voice was flat. "And if Ms. Hill does get into some kind of trouble, what am I supposed to do?"

"Stop her," I said. "However you can, without doing permanent harm. And inform me right away. Just remember, Ember is very important to the Elder Wyrm. Stop her from doing anything foolish—but if she comes to any harm, I'm not the one you need to worry about."

The Basilisk sighed. "As you wish, Mr. Hill. I will keep

an eye on your sister for you, and inform you if anything is amiss. Is there anything else you need me to do?"

"One more thing," I said as the elevator stopped and the doors opened. "The Elder Wyrm has decreed that we do not need Cobalt or the soldier anymore. When Luther is finished with the interrogation, no matter the outcome, kill them both."

EMBER

The door to my room clicked and swung open.

I looked up warily from the bed as three armed guards entered the room flanking a human in a white coat. Dante was not among them this time.

"Where are Garret and Riley?" I asked, sliding off the bed. I didn't know how long it had been since I'd seen the rogue and the soldier, and my worry for them was a constant gnawing ache in my stomach. I knew Talon would never let me see them, and it was driving me insane. "I don't need to know exactly where they are," I told the human. "Just tell me if they're all right."

"They're alive," the human said in a slightly threatening voice. "And they will continue to remain so, as long—"

"As I cooperate. Yeah, you've told me that before. I get it."

His lips thinned. "Hold her still," he told the guards, who walked forward and took my arms. The scientist reached into his coat pocket and pulled out a syringe, the needle glinting ominously under the lights, and my heart sank.

Another dose of Dractylpromazine. Fear and despair rose up, threatening to crush me. I forced them down. How were we going to get out of this? I'd been racking my brain to come up with an escape plan that didn't leave one or more of us dead, but it seemed that Talon had countered our every move. I thought about attacking and fighting my way out. But I couldn't Shift yet, and I had no doubt that Talon would happily kill Riley and Garret if they felt they no longer needed them. And Talon was counting on that. They knew I wouldn't risk the lives of the rogue and the soldier. My attachments, as Lilith would say, were my greatest weakness.

Garret, I thought, swallowing the tightness in my throat. *Riley. I hope you're all right.* Where were they now? What was happening to them? Imagining the awful things Talon might do to the infamous rogue and the soldier of St. George made my stomach hurt. *Hang in there, both of you; we'll find a way out of here, somehow.*

The needle slid into my skin, a brief stab of pain followed by a feeling of drowsiness. Briefly, I wondered where Dante was, and the Elder Wyrm. And which of them was responsible for what was happening now.

"Take her to lab station two," I heard the human say as the world started to go dark. "And for God's sake, be careful. We don't want her damaged before she reaches the Elder Wyrm."

That was the last thing I heard.

★ ★ ★

I flinched and opened my eyes.

I was lying on my back, gazing up at a sterile white ceiling. My head spun. There was a weird, bitter chemical taste in my mouth, and the light overhead was hazy. I blinked several times, clearing my vision, and my blood turned to ice.

The Elder Wyrm loomed above me, regarding me impassively, though her massive presence filled the entire chamber. I jerked and realized I couldn't move; my wrists and ankles had been tied down with leather cuffs, and there were straps across my waist and chest, holding me immobile. Instinctively, I tried to Shift, to break free of the restraints, but my dragon wouldn't respond at all. Panicked, I thrashed against the bindings, feeling the enormous power of the Elder Wyrm pressing down on me from all sides.

"It's easier if you don't resist," the Elder Wyrm said. Panting, I glared up at her, and she gazed back. "Stop fighting. It is useless. You cannot Shift. There are a half-dozen vessels guarding this room, and only a select few know where you are. I would rather not have to sedate you, but I will not risk you injuring yourself. Calm down, before I have someone do it for you."

"What do you want with me?" I growled.

The Elder Wyrm regarded me another moment. A chilling smile crossed her face, making me shrink down in terror.

"Everything."

"I…won't talk," I said, though my heart was pounding and my breath was coming in short gasps. Riley had said Talon had no problem torturing people for information. If you had something they wanted, they wouldn't stop until they acquired it, by whatever means necessary. Apparently, not even the daughter of the Elder Wyrm was exempt.

"Talk?" the Elder Wyrm repeated, and raised a brow. "You think you are here to be interrogated," she mused, and gave a soft chuckle. "No, Ember Hill. You have no information that I want. I don't care about Cobalt's network of traitors and runaways. The secrets of St. George mean nothing to me. I am not even concerned about the Eastern dragon that followed you over from China. Soon, none of that will matter."

"Why am I here, then?"

"You have no idea what you really are," the Elder Wyrm went on. "Or why you are special. To the dragons of Talon, you are my daughter, the heir to the empire along with

Dante. They don't know your true purpose—none of them have figured it out, not even your very clever brother. You see, Ember…" She smiled again, no less frightening than before. "Dante is the backup plan. You were always the chosen one."

"I don't understand," I whispered, heart pounding as she drew closer, looming over me. "Dante and I were raised together, and he's always been loyal to Talon." A thought came to me then, making my breath catch. "So, that story you told us in your office…was any of it true? Is Dante related to me at all? Are we even siblings?" The sudden realization that Dante might not be my brother, after all, hit me like a punch in the stomach. Even with all our differences, the times he'd betrayed me, stabbed me in the back and sided with Talon, he was still my twin. To think that he might be just some stranger, some random dragon that had been raised alongside me…it seemed wrong. Like my brother *had* died, after all.

"You don't understand." The Elder Wyrm shook her head. "Dante is of my blood," she continued, making me slump in relief. "As are you. Though not in the way you would expect. As far as Talon is concerned, you and Dante are my offspring. The blood of the Elder Wyrm—that is all that matters. *How* you were created is something only a few know."

I stared at her, the world spinning around me as I finally got it. "We…we're clones," I whispered. "Dante and I…we're like the vessels, or whatever you call them."

"No," said the Elder Wyrm firmly. "You are not like the vessels. The vessels were created to be mindless, programmed to obey commands and little else. They are a perfect army, but they exist to serve a single purpose. They have no individuality, no thoughts of their own. You, however…" Her gaze roamed my body, as if seeing what lay beneath the sheets, scrutinizing it. It made my skin crawl. "You and your brother were engineered for perfection. You might have begun life in a vat, but I wanted you and Dante to develop normally. To reach your full potential. You were genetically constructed to be superior, but I needed your growth to be natural, untampered with. That was essential."

"Why?"

For a moment, in that tiny room, the Elder Wyrm just stared at me, her eyes distant and dark. In that gaze, I felt the weight of a thousand years, someone who had watched worlds rise and fall, who had seen so much death, atrocity, chaos and evil that nothing affected her anymore.

"I am old," the Elder Wyrm said, and her voice seemed to echo all around me. "Older than you know. Older than any living creature on this planet. I have spent the past few centuries building this empire from nothing, and it has become exactly what I envisioned. But there is still so much to do, and I haven't much time left. Even dragons cannot live forever."

"So, that's why you need us," I guessed. "You wanted an heir to take over Talon. Someone who would share your ideals and do exactly what you wanted."

"Not...exactly." The Elder Wyrm stepped forward, her eyes glowing green in the shadows, making me want to sink into the mattress. "That is what the rest of Talon thinks. They know I would never leave my organization in the hands of just any dragon, even one that is loyal to the organization. An older dragon would ignore my wishes and attempt to make Talon their own, to tear down my ideals and replace them with their own desires, and I have worked too hard to relinquish that control. I wanted someone of my blood, someone I could shape, and mold, who would continue my work should I fall. Dante is exactly what I need in an heir.

I have no doubt he will do exactly as I wish and honor my will, if I am ever gone. But that is not why I created you.

"You are the perfect replica of me," the Elder Wyrm went on. "We share the same blood, the same DNA, but it is more than that. You were specifically engineered to house my memories, my essence, if you will." In the shadow cast by the overhead lights, her eyes glinted. "You are *my* vessel, Ember Hill," she told me. "The envelope of my soul. Once I am 'programmed' into your brain, I will live for another thousand years. I have not come this far, and built so much, to abandon it to something as trivial as death."

"But…" I was having trouble breathing; this felt like a nightmare. A paralyzing, horrific nightmare, something that couldn't be real. "What about the other vessels?" I asked, my voice coming out small and desperate. "Can't you use one of them?"

"No. The vessels were created for one purpose only, and that is war. Because their growth rate was so rapidly accelerated, their brains did not develop fully. They are able to accept simple programming. Anything more complex, and there are…complications." The Elder Wyrm made a vague, disgusted gesture. "For a time, we experimented with implanting the memories of a runaway hatchling or rogue into a vessel. But something always happened—the vessels went mad or became catatonic, and we would have to destroy them and the donor dragon." She said this calmly, like she was discussing a TV sitcom, not casually admitting the experimental mind rape and murder of numerous dragons.

"The vessels are unsuitable for memory transfer," the Elder Wyrm continued. "They excel at what they were bred for, which is obeying orders and dying for our cause. But they cannot imprint memories or personality. For my objective to work, I needed a daughter, someone who shared my blood and my DNA. Who had the chance to grow up, to learn and develop normally, even as she rebelled against everything we stand for." One elegant white hand rose to frame my face. Her nails lightly scraped my cheek before I flinched away. The Elder Wyrm smiled. "You will be my vessel, Ember Hill," she said, and though her touch was light, her eyes were cold. As if she was inspecting an outfit for flaws. "My new body, in which I will live forever."

"But…" I scrambled for a response, a way out, anything to stop this horrific reality from going forward. "You don't know if this procedure will work, you just said so yourself. The vessels can't imprint memories or personality. What if you get into my head and we both go nuts?"

"Oh, my dear." The Elder Wyrm chuckled again and shook her head. "What makes you think you and Dante are the only children I created?"

My heart seemed to stop. "But you said—"

"I said the *vessels* are unsuited for memory transfer. Of course I would not risk myself if the procedure had not been perfected." The Elder Wyrm shook her head at me, smiling. "You are not the first daughter of mine, Ember Hill. Nor the second, nor the third. You are simply the oldest. There were others, many others, before you. The first experiments were quite dismal—many were lost to madness, deformities or other failures. But we kept trying, knowing that with every clone we put down, we learned something new. We learned that the brain must have the chance to fully develop, to experience memory, emotion, personality and all the things that cannot be artificially emulated. So you see, daughter…" The Elder Wyrm smiled her coldest, most terrifying smile yet. "The secret of immortality is within my grasp, and it will be mine alone."

"And...what happened to all the other clones?" I whispered. My sisters, the siblings I had never known. The Elder Wyrm's terrifying expression didn't change.

"They were destroyed."

Straightening, she took a step back. "Unfortunately, before my memories can be implanted, we will have to remove yours," she said. "Two personalities in one mind will certainly cause complications. I will no doubt have my hands full trying to adjust to my new body without having to fight your presence for control. Better that no trace of your personality remains when I settle in."

Horror threatened to choke me. "You can't do that," I whispered.

"Of course we can," the Elder Wyrm said. "Humans have been doing similar things for years, even without old magic. Brainwashing, hypnotism, forced amnesia...the mind is a curious thing." She stepped back, watching as I forced myself to breathe, to not panic, though I felt that, if I opened my mouth, I would start screaming and not be able to stop. "Sacrifice has always been necessary for the survival of our race, Ember," the Elder Wyrm said. "I know it means little now, but this will ensure that Talon never falls, and dragons are one step closer to ruling the world, as it should be."

"Why now?" I asked desperately. "If this was what you were planning all along, why the charade? What was all that about having me take my place in Talon with Dante?"

"That was for Dante's benefit," the Elder Wyrm replied. "He is still disturbingly loyal to you and would not take the truth of your creation well. I allowed him to think he could save you, because a willing heir is much easier to work with.

Which is why I sent him away for a time. I knew you would never agree to conform to Talon. From what I have seen and heard, you have been corrupted thoroughly by Cobalt. There are ways to get you to do what we want, of course, ways to leverage your cooperation. For instance, it is hard to be willful when your friends are screaming in pain on the other side of the glass."

I closed my eyes, feeling my stomach turn inside out with the realization. I'd never had a chance here. Talon knew exactly what to do to get me to cooperate. If I saw Garret and Riley in pain, if the choice was between killing for Talon and letting either of them die… I would probably agree to whatever they wanted.

"But that is unnecessary," the Elder Wyrm went on. "Your cooperation is not needed, Ember Hill. The timing is perfect. I have my army. I have my heir. Everything is in place. The only thing I require now is immortality."

A human in a white coat appeared, his head bowed in respect as he approached the Elder Wyrm. "Ma'am? We're ready to begin."

"Excellent." The Elder Wyrm's predatory stare settled on the human. "And you are certain the procedure will be complete before the night of Fang and Fire?"

"Yes, ma'am."

The Elder Wyrm gave a brusque nod, and the scientist walked to the head of the gurney and grasped the sides. "I'm afraid this is the last time we will see each other," she said as he began pulling me away. "Apparently, the process of removing your memories is an involved procedure and will take time to fully complete. If you accept the process and do not fight it, it will be much easier for you." She gave me an amused look as the scientist paused at a door, pulling it open. "Of course, I realize that would be like telling a fish not to swim. You do remind me of myself when I was your age, though that was a long, long time ago. I've almost forgotten what it was like, to be young." Her smile widened, becoming almost wistful. "I must admit, I am looking forward to having another thousand years."

Then the gurney was pushed through the frame, the door closed behind us and the Elder Wyrm was gone.

As the gurney rolled forward, I thrashed against the restraints, trying desperately to Shift, to summon the strength to ignore whatever drugs they'd stuck me with. But I felt nothing but a cold sluggishness within, and despair settled heavily in my chest, joining the anger and fear. A man waited in the room beyond, another scientist type in a long white lab coat, smiling at me as I was rolled forward. "Ah, here she is," he exclaimed, peering at me through his glasses. "Ember Hill, what a pleasure it is to meet you. You must be terribly excited—after sixteen years, your true purpose is finally being fulfilled. To be the Elder Wyrm's chosen vessel, what a tremendous honor."

"Yeah, I don't really see it like that," I growled at him. He chuckled.

"Nonsense. This is what you were created for. Just think, if immortality can actually be achieved, what will that mean for both dragons and the entire human race? I, for one, am eager to see all my hard work finally come to fruition. Now then, let's get a look at you." The scientist pulled the stethoscope from around his neck and put it to my chest. "Hmm, heartbeat is abnormally fast," he muttered, and I glared at him.

"Oh, really? I wonder why that is." My voice shook, and I had to force myself to breathe calmly. "You're just brainwashing and turning me into a zombie so that the Elder Wyrm can move into my head. Nothing evil there."

"Brainwashing? Oh, no, no, no. This is nothing so crude." The scientist put the stethoscope back around his neck and smiled at me fondly. "Brainwashing involves high levels of trauma, either physical or mental, to break down a subject's personality, beliefs and sense of self so that they can be replaced with a new set of ideals. The process can take months, or longer, and the subject still retains who he is at his core. His memories have not been erased, merely suppressed." He paused as two other scientists converged on me, tightening straps, pulling my eyelids down to shine a light into them, swabbing my skin with something that stung my nostrils. "What *we* are going to do is a complete mind wipe," he went on when there was a lull in the ministrations. "We are going to extract your memories and all the emotion, knowledge and skills attached to them, so that your brain will be fully receptive to new memory, skills and personality. Think of it as erasing your computer's hard drive, removing all files and data, destroying any harmful information or viruses it might've picked up and completely starting over."

"And…what will happen to *me*?" I asked. I tried, once more, to Shift, to burst into my true form and burn my way out of this laboratory of horrors, but the dragon refused to stir. The scientist continued to smile and speak casually, as if he was explaining to a child why the needle wouldn't hurt.

"Well, for the procedure at least, your memory will be electronically stored," he replied, nodding to something off to the side of the gurney. I craned my neck around to see what looked like a large computer bank, with several men in white coats hovering around the screens. "We've had fairly good success with saving individual memories," the scientist went on, "though eventually they do break down and are lost. But, ultimately, it will be up to the Elder Wyrm to decide what to do with yours. If she wants to keep you for later use or erase you completely."

"So, you're saying that *me* as an individual, everything that makes me who I am, will be destroyed. Gone forever." The human regarded me serenely but didn't answer, and my heart fluttered around my ribs like a panicked bird. I bared my teeth at him. "I hope you know that's essentially murder. Isn't there some sort of oath that condemns that? Do no harm? Don't play God? Any of this ringing a bell?"

"Oh, my dear, I'm not a doctor. I'm a scientist." The two other men returned and began sticking electrodes to my forehead, neck and arms, while the scientist watched them. "And even if I were, the Hippocratic oath only applies to humans. 'I will remember that I remain a member of society, with special obligations to all my fellow human beings, those sound of mind and body as well as the infirm.' If we are going to quote passages at each other."

He gave me a thin smile as his helpers finished their task and walked away, leaving me with about a dozen wires connecting my skull to the computer bank. "But you are a dragon," the scientist continued. "In the decades I have spent among your kind, I have seen and come to accept certain things. You are not like us. Your minds are more like a computer than anything else—logical and calculating, capable of retaining massive amounts of information, able to recall the smallest fact across hundreds of years. You are truly a remarkable race, I will admit. But you are not human. And even if the Elder Wyrm was not expecting me to complete this procedure, I have worked on this project for too many years to stop now. Now, at last, we will see if immortality is really possible."

Another scientist approached and handed him the first needle and syringe. "Well, we are almost ready to begin," the head scientist stated, pressing the syringe so that a few drops of clear liquid squirted out the top. He nodded in satisfaction and looked down at me again. "I don't know about you, but I am quite excited. Aren't you just a little pleased to know you will be contributing to such a massive breakthrough? Just think of what this will mean for your entire race."

"Fuck you," I snarled, the most elegant thing I could come up with at the moment. He chuckled, shaking his head.

"Well, I would say that such language is unwarranted, but in a few hours it's not going to matter." He raised the needle. "This will put your brain into a relaxed state, which will make it easier for us to extract your memories. It shouldn't take long, but you might experience some mild to severe hallucinations as the drug takes effect. Are you ready?" He lowered the needle toward my arm. "Any last words?"

I was shaking violently, but forced my voice to be even. "I think I'm going to stick with my original thought of 'fuck you.'"

"Hmm, not the most original, but if that is what you feel..." He slid the needle into my arm and injected the contents. "Farewell, Ember Hill," he said as he stepped back. "I hope you go gently into that good night. If all goes well, the next time we speak, I will be addressing the Elder Wyrm."

Garret, I thought as the ceiling started to sway. *Riley. I'm sorry. Wherever you are, I hope you can get out of here. Escape, and live to fight Talon another day. You'll just have to do it without me.*

RILEY

"Well," St. George muttered beside me, "that could have gone worse, I suppose."

I cracked open one puffy eye to glare at him, trying to focus through the throbbing in my skull. And ribs. And face. The soldier lay on his back, much like I was doing, and looked nearly as awful as I felt. *Nearly*, because the interrogator's questions had been directed mostly at me. Though St. George hadn't escaped unscathed, either. He had, I would grudgingly admit, held up like a trooper, refusing to break even through the worst of it. Luther was not the most subtle of interrogators, preferring the "answer my question or my minions will punch you in the face" technique, rather than the mind games I knew Mist was capable of. And it had been a *long* session, at least several hours. It was probably the middle of the night or very early morning, though it was impossible to tell time in this place. The only good part was watching that little bastard's face when he realized we weren't going to give him what he wanted. "How, exactly?" I croaked.

"At least they didn't kill us."

"Not certain if that's a good thing right now, St. George," I replied. "That just means they can do this again in a few hours." Gingerly, I attempted to sit up. Pain ricocheted through my body, and I grimaced. "Ow. Okay, that's a cracked rib. Maybe a couple cracked ribs. Bastards." I slumped against the wall, breathing slowly and waiting for the stabbing sensation to fade. A few feet away, the soldier still lay on his back, gazing at the ceiling.

"They're going to kill us, aren't they?"

I let out a slow breath. "Yeah," I muttered, feeling something dark and cold settle over me. "Maybe not at the same time—they'll still need one of us to use as leverage against Ember. But...yeah, they're going to kill us."

St. George nodded slowly, as if he'd already expected it. Slumping against the wall, I let my head fall back, regret and failure turning sourly in my stomach. I thought of Wes, my hatchlings, my underground. Who would protect them, now that I was gone? Wes was competent and the smartest human I'd ever met, but he didn't have the survival skills needed to keep everyone safe. I wished I could have prepared them better.

And I wished I could've seen Ember, one last time.

"How long?" St. George asked, his own voice contemplative. As if he, too, was thinking of everything he regretted, everything he wished he could have done. I shook my head.

"Probably not long. I imagine they'll want at least one more interrogation session. With the right drugs this time."

St. George raised his head, frowning.

"Right drugs? What are you talking about?"

"You've never been under the effects of a truth serum, have you?" I asked, and he shook his head. "I have. With Mist actually." I leaned my head against the wall, remembering that night in Vegas and the first interrogation with the other Basilisk. Even with my training, resolve and determination not to talk, I'd almost given up my underground. The various drugs the Talon scientists had created specifically for use against our kind were nasty and extremely potent; the organization had a long history of getting what they wanted, no matter what.

"I don't know what she stuck us with at the beginning of the session," I went on, hearing the soldier struggle upright, "but it wasn't sodium thiopental, or their version of truth serum. We'd both be babbling like a pair of drunken idiots if it was."

"So, she lied." He settled against the wall next to me, his voice tight as he leaned carefully into the metal. In my peripheral vision, I could see a trickle of dried blood running down his temple, a dark bruise beginning to form above one eye. From the way my whole face was throbbing, I knew I looked just as rough. "Or made a mistake."

"Mist doesn't make mistakes." I shifted to a more comfortable position, one that didn't put pressure on my injured ribs. "She's a Basilisk. We're trained to remember the tiniest detail, no matter how insignificant, because our lives may depend on it. And you didn't spend much time with her, but from what I saw…" I shook my head. "She's good. Much too good to forget something as important as dosing your interrogation victims with the right drug."

He eyed me from against the wall. "If she was that good, how did you escape the first time?"

"I said she was good." Despite the hopeless situation, I grinned, which turned out to be rather painful as my cut lip tore open again. "But I'm better."

"Well, nice to see that my abilities weren't completely written off."

I looked up. Mist stood in front of the cell door, arms crossed as she peered through the bars at us. Her blue eyes raked over us both, assessing, before she smirked. "Luther certainly did a number on you both, didn't he?" she observed. "Unfortunate that had to happen, but from the hissy fit he was throwing when he left this morning, I'm guessing you didn't tell him anything."

I threw back my own smirk. "Is that why you're here, Mist? Come to finish the job? You think you can do better?" She probably could. Dragon constitution or no, I ached. My head hurt, my face felt swollen to twice its size and moving the wrong way sent a sharp twinge through my ribs. The thought of yet another "interrogation" session made my gut curl with dread.

I just wanted to lie down on the nice, cold floor and let my bruises start to heal. But showing weakness like that to a Basilisk, who was trained to spot and exploit the tiniest flaws and weak points, was a huge mistake. Even if she was going to kill us afterward. So I rose, ignoring the pain in my side, and walked to the front of the cell, staring at her through the bars. She gazed coolly back, unconcerned, and I narrowed my eyes.

"What's your game?" I asked. "I know you didn't give us the wrong drug by accident." I curled my lip into a smile. "Or was that the plan? You knew Luther would be taking over the interrogation, and you didn't want *him* to be the one to make us talk. That honor would be all yours."

"You do have a very high opinion of yourself, don't you?" Mist gave me a look that was both subtly amused and disgusted at the same time. "I wasn't expecting Dante to show up, or for Luther to take over," she admitted. "As for what I stuck you with, it was estazolam."

I frowned. "Estazolam? But that's—"

"A mild sedative. That made you feel slightly drowsy."

Mist made a vague gesture toward my face. "I had to drug you with something to make it seem like a standard interrogation, in case anyone was watching. In fact, I was about to share that bit of information with you in the interrogation room when Dante came in and interrupted us."

"Why would you do that?" St. George asked, echoing my confusion. He hadn't moved from where he sat against the wall, and I didn't blame him. He was, after all, just a human. A tough human, granted, but not quite as resistant to pain and injury as a dragon.

Mist sighed.

"I would think it was obvious," she said, and before I could reply that no, it really was not, she added, "I'm here to help you escape, of course. But we'll have to move fast. There's not a lot of time."

In the moment of stunned silence that followed, my heart gave a violent leap. *Escape.* I had nearly given up hope a few minutes ago. I'd known that no one would be coming for us. There was no way out of Talon. I'd expected another interrogation session or two and then, when they'd gotten everything they could from me and the soldier, they would kill us both. That was how Talon worked. Even if they were keeping us alive to ensure Ember's cooperation, as soon as they got what they wanted, they would get rid of us. We were disposable. Unimportant.

But if Mist was offering to help us escape...

Ruthlessly, I stifled those thoughts, refusing to believe. This was Mist, the Basilisk who, not three months ago, had lured me into trusting her only to betray that trust. She hadn't given any indication of wanting to go rogue before; in her own words that night: *I am what Talon requires. The organi-*

zation entrusted me with this task, and I will not fail them. She wouldn't throw everything away to go rogue now.

"Oh, of course, why didn't I get that?" I said, sneering at the pale-haired girl on the other side of the bars. "Because that makes perfect sense—the loyal Talon employee helping their most infamous criminal escape the organization, betraying everything in the process." I shook my head. "You, going rogue? Why in the world would you think I'd believe that?"

Mist's placid expression didn't change. "*You* did."

"I had my reasons."

"And I have mine." Her eyes narrowed. "Do you think you're the only one with secrets, Cobalt? Do you think you're the only dragon who feels trapped by the organization? Who has his own agendas, not just Talon's?"

This was a completely different attitude than the one I had encountered before. And I trusted this change of heart as much as I trusted a live viper. "Why would you help us?" I demanded. "A couple months ago, you were trying your damnedest to expose my network, and kill me in the process. What changed?"

"I had a job to do then," Mist answered, unrepentant. "Just like I have a job to do now." Her eyes flicked back to me and narrowed. "Make no mistake, Cobalt, it wasn't my call to help you tonight. I'm just following orders."

"Whose?" I asked, incredulous.

The hint of a smile crossed the girl's face. "My employer would rather remain anonymous," she said. "For safety. I'm sure you understand." She glanced back at me, the amusement fading as a shadow of impatience crossed her face. "We don't have much time," she said in a low voice. "I can get you out of here, on one condition."

Aha, there it was. I knew she wouldn't do this out of the

goodness of her heart. "Let me guess," I said. "You need our help."

"I don't need *you*," Mist answered. "I need that hacker friend of yours."

"What do you want with Wes?" I growled.

Mist sighed. "There's a sensitive file my employer wants me to steal," she explained. "But it's too heavily encrypted for me to find by myself. And as I assume your human hacker friend wouldn't trust a word I say, I figure he needs to hear it from you." She glanced at the door, as if making sure no one was coming in, before continuing in a lower voice. "This is the deal, Cobalt—I get you to that computer, you contact your computer genius and help me steal the information I need. Tonight. Then we leave the premises before Talon realizes what's happened."

"Just me? What about St. George?"

She gave the human a dubious look. "I doubt he can even stand, much less walk. Luther's 'techniques' are intended for dragons, after all." The girl shook her head, frowning. "There's no time to wait for him to heal. We have to…"

She trailed off, a look of mild shock crossing her face. I glanced over my shoulder, just as St. George rose and walked calmly to the front of the cell. His jaw was set, tight with suppressed pain, but there were no obvious signs of injury, not even a limp, as he drew close to the bars.

"Don't worry about me," he told the Basilisk in an even voice. "I'm fine. I'll keep up."

Mist appraised him. It was clear she was surprised to see him on his feet and was observing him carefully to see if he was as hale and healthy as he claimed. To be honest, I was a little surprised, too. The human was tough, but not *dragon* tough. Unless there was something I was missing. Something...

Oh, crap. Dazed, I stared at the soldier as my brain finally put the pieces together. This wasn't the first time the human had healed abnormally fast, not the first time he could stand when it should've been impossible. *Is that the reason he isn't dead now? What kind of freak did I create?*

I kept these thoughts to myself. Now was not the time to dwell on anything but escaping this god-awful hellhole. Mist continued to appraise the soldier, unaware of my sudden realization. St. George gazed back calmly, and she shrugged.

"If you can keep up, human, I'm not going to stop you." Her gaze narrowed. "But if you fall behind, don't expect me to stop. My mission is to retrieve that file—nothing else matters."

"And you would trust us to help you?" I asked. "Just like that?"

"Why wouldn't I? It's not like you can report me to Talon, not unless you wish to be caught again. Of course, you can try to overpower me and escape by yourselves..." Her lip curled, as if she found that thought amusing. "But since I am aware that your last dose of Dractylpromazine wasn't even an hour ago, and I can still Shift without fail, that seems imprudent. The far wiser course would be to do what I ask. So..." She stared me down. "Do we have a deal?"

To my surprise, it was the soldier who answered.

"No," he said quietly. Mist blinked at him in shock. "Not without Ember," he went on as I kicked myself for not thinking of her sooner. "I'm not leaving her here. You want our help," he said, glancing at me, "you get her out, too."

"That might be impossible," Mist replied, sounding annoyed. "She was taken to the private lab early this morning.

I have no idea what they're going to do to her, but only a few scientists and a handful of guards are allowed past those doors. Trying to rescue one more person could put us, and the mission, in jeopardy. Freeing the two of you is going to be difficult enough. We can't risk it."

"Sorry, Mist." I crossed my arms. "But I'm going to agree with my soldier friend. Ember comes, too, or no deal."

Her lips thinned, as if our insistence on rescuing Ember was throwing a wrench into her plans. "You would throw away your one chance of escaping Talon?" she asked. "They're planning to kill you both tomorrow, you know. If you stay here, you're going to die."

"And you'll never get what you need," I told her, and the soldier nodded. I was playing hardball, but neither of us was bluffing. I would not leave Ember behind. I would rather stay and let Talon kill me than have Ember think I abandoned her. I knew St. George felt the same. "You get her out," I said, "and we'll help you in return. If not, we all die and you fail your mission. But we're not leaving without her."

The girl closed her eyes. Apparently, she had not expected this. "Very well," she said. "She'll be on the last floor. Once we get the information I need, I'll take you down to the lab, and we can try to rescue her, as well. That's the best I can offer."

"Ah, sorry." I shook my head. "We get Ember out first, *then* we'll help you get what you need."

She raised a brow. "You are awfully demanding for being on the wrong side of the bars," she mused. "And what do we do with her once we find her? Waltz back through the building with the most recognizable dragon in Talon? What if she's drugged or incapacitated in some way? How are we going to get to the information while dragging her along?"

"I'm sure you can find a way," I said, but Mist's eyes hardened.

"No." She shook her head, crossing her arms. "I'm not going to risk it. I need whatever is on that computer, and getting to it will be dangerous enough without trying to sneak Ember Hill through the building. Once we rescue her, we'll have a limited amount of time to get out before Talon's entire security force comes after us. There'll be no time for anything else."

"What if we split up?" St. George suggested. "I can go after Ember while you and Riley go after the file."

"You'd need a key card and a code to access the elevators," Mist replied. "And there will be numerous guards and security cameras along the way. If you're with me, I can get you to the lab with minimal problems. If you're by yourself, the second anyone sees you, our plan falls apart." She set her jaw, her voice nonnegotiable. "Information first, then the girl. I am not budging on this."

"Really?" I gave a dangerous smile. "So we help you out and then you'll do the same, huh? And what's to stop you from stabbing us in the back as soon as you get what you need?"

"Absolutely nothing," Mist said, holding my gaze. "But you're going to trust me, Cobalt. Because this is your only way out, and you know it. Because if you die here, your underground is as good as gone. Talon will wipe them off the map, and now they have both the numbers and the resources to do it. They're planning something huge, something that will change both our worlds forever, and you need to know what it is just as much as I do."

Dammit. She was right, and she knew she was right. "All right," I growled. If the choice was either die in a Talon cell or die trying to get us all out of Talon, I'd go for the one that gave us a chance, miniscule as it was. "This is getting us no-where. We can either stand around threatening each other, or we can just get on with it. So, how were you planning to get us out of here?" I asked Mist. "We can't exactly open the door and stroll down the hall in plain sight."

Mist gave that faint, mysterious smile. "Actually," she said, holding up a key, "that is precisely what we're going to do."

EMBER

"She's nearly ready."

The voice echoed around me, hollow and cold. I spun, peering at my surroundings in confusion. I stood in the center of a vast, rocky plain that stretched on until it met the sky. Behind me, a chain-link fence encircled a cluster of familiar gray and white buildings. Seeing them made my stomach flip-flop with nerves. My old school, in the middle of the Great Basin. But...why was I here now?

"Excellent," said another voice, seeming to echo out of the sky. "Then prepare the procedure. The drug will bring her most vivid memories to the surface first so they can be removed. Once they are gone, we'll have to dig deeper, but this is a good place to start."

I frowned, gazing around for the people the voices belonged to, but other than the silhouette of a buzzard soaring overhead, I was alone. A moment later, I couldn't remember what had been said. A warm breeze ruffled the scrub around me as I gazed through the fence at the buildings that were as familiar to me as the back of my hand. I had spent so much time here, very nearly my whole life. But that didn't explain why I had come back.

"Ember," said another voice, closer than the last and much

younger. It sounded alarmed. I looked up and saw two small figures a few yards away. They were about six or seven, with the same bright red hair and green eyes. I gasped as I realized where I was, recognizing this moment in time.

"Ember!" young Dante said again, louder this time. A lump rose to my throat as I watched him, solemn even at six years old. His red hair was shaggy and hung in his eyes as he stepped forward. "Come on, sis. Don't poke it, you'll make it mad. Let's go back."

The little girl with the red ponytail ignored him. Crouched on the balls of her feet, her attention was riveted on what lay before her. A fat brown snake with vivid diamond markings down its back sat tightly coiled in the sand, head pulled into an S while its tail rattled threateningly.

My stomach tightened. Curious and unafraid, tiny Ember ignored her brother's repeated warnings and prodded the serpent with a twig. The snake reared back, its warning rattle growing louder, faster, but the girl didn't back off.

"Ember!" Dante said, and bent down, grabbing her by her shoulders. At the same time, the snake lunged, a blinding streak of tan across the desert floor. Dante cried out, falling to his side, and tiny Ember gasped.

"Dante!" she cried, instantly forgetting about the snake, which slithered off and vanished under a bush. Dante lay on his side, cradling his arm and making soft whimpering sounds. I knew he was trying not to cry out, to be brave so that his little sister wouldn't be afraid. Blood oozed from two rather large puncture marks in his skin, and the lump in my throat grew even bigger. I hadn't realized how much the bite had hurt him until now.

"Dante," tiny Ember said again, her eyes huge and frightened now. "I'm sorry! I'm so sorry! I didn't mean for it to bite you."

"It's...okay," Dante panted. "It doesn't hurt that much, Ember, really." He was lying; it was easy to see he was in horrible pain, but the younger version of me relaxed. She believed her twin so easily, and it made my throat tighten.

"Besides," Dante went on, attempting a smile, "I'd rather the snake bit me and not you. That's what brothers are for, twin brothers especially."

I bit my lip, my eyes prickling at the corners as tiny Ember sniffed and scrubbed a dirty hand across her eyes.

"Stupid," she remarked. "Now I have to tell Mr. Gordon that a snake bit you, and he's going to blame me as usual."

Dante winced. "You can tell him...that I was poking the snake if you want," he said, his voice tight with pain. "Or that we were wandering around outside and I tripped over it." But Ember shook her head.

"No," she said firmly. "It really is my fault this time. The snake would've bitten me if you hadn't been here." She gazed at her brother in complete adoration before she sighed and rose to her feet. "Besides, he wouldn't believe me, anyway," she said as she dusted off her jeans, then extended a hand to Dante. "You *never* get into trouble."

Dante took her arm and let her pull him upright, clenching his jaw. "Because I don't go *looking* for it," he said in a voice much too wry for a six-year-old. Tiny Ember shrugged, apparently not getting the sarcasm.

"Ember and Dante Hill!"

I turned. A man was striding across the yard on the other side of the fence, a human in a collared shirt and khakis, looking stern as he stalked forward, eyes furious. But when he reached the gate and yanked it open, taking a breath to shout something, he disappeared. Vanished like the image on the television screen when you flipped it off. I blinked, then turned to whatever he'd been about to yell at.

There was nothing. Empty desert greeted me as I looked back, a barren landscape stretching on to the horizon. I frowned and turned in a slow circle, trying to determine where I was, but there was nothing but sand, rock and emptiness as far as I could see. I shivered and rubbed my arm, staring at a spot in the dust, certain *something* had been there a moment ago. Something…important, but I couldn't remember what it was.

Then the desert twisted, flickered like a bad signal feed, and everything went white.

GARRET

I walked behind Riley, my wrists bound with metal cuffs, following Mist as she led us down a narrow white corridor. A pair of identical, blank-faced guards hovered at my shoulder, their footsteps sounding in unison and echoing down the hall. Mist walked in front of us all with her head high and her gaze straight ahead. A few men in white coats passed us, but they averted their eyes or ducked into other rooms or hallways as we approached. They were humans working in a Talon building, and here, dragons were the masters.

I breathed a furtive sigh, trying to ignore the pain in my side, the puffiness of my eyes and lip. I ached, but it was bearable. Far more than I knew it should be. And Mist's plan of getting us through the building, daring as it was, seemed to be working. When she'd handed us a pair of manacles through the cell bars and told us to put them on, we'd both hesitated, making her sigh.

"Don't be ridiculous," she'd said in an overly reasonable voice. "If we're going to walk down the halls in plain sight, we have to make it seem realistic. I can bluff my way through a lot, but it still has to *look* like you're my captives. I'll release you when the time comes, don't worry." Riley had still looked dubious, and she'd shot him a glare. "If my plan was to lead you into a trap, it would be rather silly for me to open the prison cell, *where you were already trapped*, and let you out, wouldn't it?"

Riley had grunted. "Fair point," he'd muttered, and snapped the cuffs around his wrists, rolling his eyes. "So, it's the classic 'prisoner transfer' ruse, huh? Never gets old."

"What if we run into Dante?" I'd asked. Mist's eyes had glittered with more than casual suspicion, maybe even fear, as she'd met my gaze. I was a human and a soldier of St. George, I'd reminded myself. In her eyes, I was the enemy, perhaps even more than Riley himself. "He'll certainly recognize us and want to know where we're headed."

"That would be true," Mist had answered coolly, "if he were here." She'd waited until I had locked the shackles around my wrists before unlocking the cell door. "Fortunately for us," she'd continued, pulling the door back with a screech, "Mr. Hill had to take his leave this morning. That will make things easier, though we still have to be very, very careful. We don't want word to reach the Elder Wyrm's office."

Riley's face had turned the color of glue. "Wait," he'd gasped, staring at her. "Did you just say the *Elder Wyrm* is here? Right now? In this building?"

Mist had nodded, and he'd staggered back a pace. "Shit. You couldn't have mentioned that earlier? Holy Mother of all that is holy...*why*? What's here that would bring the Elder Wyrm out of..."

He'd stopped, his face going even paler, and I'd guessed the reason at about the same time.

"Ember," I'd muttered as he'd given me a dark, slightly glazed look. "That has to be why Dante was so eager to bring her back, why there was an army of dragons at that site. The

Elder Wyrm must have sent him in person, and it has something to do with Ember."

"Now you see why we have to do this quickly," Mist had said, her cool voice tinged with fear. "If the Elder Wyrm discovers my betrayal, none of us are leaving this place alive." She'd glared at us again. "So, the two of you follow my lead and do *exactly* what I say. No heroics. We might get out of here in one piece."

She'd walked to the door of the prison block and pushed it open. A pair of guards, the same dragon clones that had ambushed us that night with Dante, had entered the room, and Riley had stiffened.

"Don't worry." Mist had turned and smirked at him, as if she'd known what he was thinking. "The vessels have been trained for obedience and to follow the commands of certain dragons in this location. I happen to be one of them. They don't disobey orders, they don't talk back and they don't ask questions. We're going to walk through the building in plain sight, and no one will stop us."

She'd given an order, and the clones had surrounded us, staring straight ahead as they'd moved into position. Riley had snorted, his expression curling with disgust. "Take a good look, St. George," he'd muttered. "This is what Talon wants us to be. Soulless, mindless and obedient. I wouldn't be surprised if the Elder Wyrm wants to get rid of us all and replace us with these things."

Mist had opened the door again and peered down the hall. "We're clear," she'd said quietly, and glanced back at us. "Stay close, keep your heads down and don't say anything unless I tell you to." She'd straightened and taken a furtive breath, as if steeling herself. "All right, let's go."

I'm coming, Ember, I'd thought as we moved out, the clones flanking us and Mist in the lead. *Wherever you are, just hang on a little longer.*

We'd walked out of the room into a narrow cement corridor, which had turned into the long, well-lit hallway we were walking through now, with white tile floors and doors lining either side. A few humans in long white coats or business suits wandered the floors but, much as Mist had said, kept their heads down and paid us no attention when we walked past with the clones.

"Miss Anderson?"

A thin man stepped into the hallway, his black eyes narrowing as he stopped us in the corridor. With a chill, I realized it was the dragon that had interrogated Riley and me last night. I saw Riley's shoulders tense, saw the muscles in his arms tighten as he clenched his fists, and hoped he wouldn't do anything rash. The Basilisk gave us a wary look, then turned to Mist with a frown.

"Where are you going with the prisoners?" he asked, his sibilant voice grating in my ears. The same smooth, hissing voice that had informed us, again and again, that it would be better if we just told him what he wanted. "I was going to interrogate them again in a few hours." He eyed us with a hungry smile. "Perhaps this time, a more delicate approach is required. We will see if a scalpel and a pair of pliers can encourage them to talk."

Riley smirked. "Maybe you should try that on yourself, Luther," he said mockingly. "It would certainly be an improvement."

The other Basilisk turned on him, eyes narrowing to black slits, but Mist broke in before he could say anything.

"You had your chance, Luther," she said, disdain coloring her voice. "Mr. Hill was not pleased with the results of your interrogation and has put me back on assignment. Your skills are no longer required."

Luther bared his teeth with a hiss, making me tense. For a split second, I could see his other form, a thin black dragon with mottled green wings, looming over the girl. A chill raced up my back, even as the blood in my veins boiled. The image had been so real; I had never seen anything like that before.

Mist faced the furious Basilisk and didn't back down. "If you are displeased, take it up with Mr. Hill," she said. "Or, better yet, you could go straight to the top. I am sure the Elder Wyrm will be very interested to learn of your failure."

The blood instantly drained from his face. "N-no," he stammered, backing away. "That's not necessary." He gave us one last glare, eyes gleaming, before turning an oily smile on Mist. "Well, good luck, Miss Anderson," he said, his tone oozing. "Perhaps your techniques will succeed where mine did not, but if you need any help, or expertise, you have only to call."

"Thank you," Mist said icily. "I'll keep that in mind."

Luther nodded, gave us one last smile and continued down the hall. Mist watched him until he turned a corner and was out of sight, then glared at Riley.

"If you don't want us to be discovered, Cobalt, perhaps you shouldn't antagonize everyone we come across."

Riley grinned. "Worried, *Miss Anderson?*" he replied. "I thought you wanted this to be realistic. It would have been more suspicious if I just took the slimy bastard's insults and didn't say anything."

Mist shook her head. But she didn't say anything else as she led us down the corridor again, moving a little faster now, until we came to the elevators near the end of the hall.

"Get in," she ordered as the doors opened. We did, and the clones followed, flanking us inside the box. Mist pressed a button, the doors slid shut and the elevator began to ascend.

Mist motioned briskly to Riley and inserted a key into the cuffs at his wrists. "I have your phone, Cobalt," she said as the shackles were removed. "When we get to where we're going, I need you to contact your hacker friend and explain the situation. I hope he's as good as everyone seems to believe. From here on out, we have to move as fast as we can."

"What are we looking for, anyway?" Riley asked.

Mist hesitated, then turned to me. "I'm not entirely certain," she admitted, unlocking my restraints. "But that computer is supposed to hold the plans for…something big. Something that has to do with the vessels, and what the Elder Wyrm intends to do with them. There have been rumors circling about something called the Night of Fang and Fire, which I admit sounds cheesy but is troubling all the same. My employer would like to know exactly what this Night of Fang and Fire is."

Riley and I shared a glance. The Night of Fang and Fire? It certainly sounded like we should be worried about it. At the same time, it made me desperate to get to Ember. To get us all out of here and find someplace safe before the world exploded in a hellstorm of dragonfire.

The elevator stopped, and the doors slid open to reveal an office-type floor, though the hallways were dark and looked deserted. The only lights came from the glow of screen savers through open office doors.

"Stay here," Mist told the clones, who didn't so much as blink at her. "Guard the elevator until we return." To us, she jerked her head down the hall. "The room isn't far. Let's go."

Following her lead, we hurried down the corridor, turned

a corner and paused at a plain office door with narrow floor-to-ceiling windows on either side. Mist produced a key card from a cord attached to her belt and slid it into a slot reader near the handle. The door beeped once, and we slipped inside.

A large desk with a single computer sat in the center of the room, and Mist quickly shut the inner window blinds before turning to us. "Here," she said, tossing Riley a phone. "Call your friend. I figure we have a couple minutes before night security comes by, so make it quick."

I carefully pulled down the blinds a crack and peered into the darkened hall, watching for moving shadows or flashlight beams, while Riley spoke urgently into his phone.

"Wes." His voice was a raspy whisper. "It's me... No, I'm not dead, obviously... Yeah, we were caught by Talon." He winced. "Ow. Dammit, will you calm down? We're fine, no one is dead yet." He frowned, and his voice became a growl. "Look, just shut up and listen, all right? I don't have a lot of time."

A thin white beam flashed down the hall before a shadow turned a corner and came toward our room. I motioned to the others to be silent and pressed back against the door. Riley and Mist ducked behind the desk, Riley hiding the phone in his jacket to snuff out the light, and we held our breath as a human passed in front of the windows. His shadow slid over the blinds, and his footsteps knocked against the tile floor as he went by, not slowing, and faded away into the dark.

I slumped in relief as the other two popped out from behind the desk, Riley snarling quietly into his phone again.

"That's what I said. I need you to hack into Talon's computers and..." He paused, frowning. "Dammit, Wes. What do you want me to... Hang on." He pressed a button on the phone and placed it on the desk. "All right," he whispered, sliding into the desk chair. "What do you need on our end?"

"Bloody hell, Riley," came Wes's voice over the speakerphone, sounding harried. "All right, listen. First, you'll have to open the browser and go to this IP address. That will download an exploit that will grant me access to—"

"On a time limit, Wesley," Riley growled. "Don't need an explanation, just give me the damn address."

"Right. Hang on, then." He rattled off a list of numbers, and for a moment, the sound of tapping keys filled the silence of the room. I turned back to the window and peered through the blinds, searching for the guard. On the phone, Wes and Riley muttered back and forth for a few tense moments before Wes gave a triumphant grunt.

"I'm in. Found the file." He paused a moment, his next words begrudgingly impressed and eager at the same time. "Well, that *is* a nasty encryption, isn't it? I've just the thing for you."

A flashlight beam cut through the hall again, and I motioned everyone to get down. We dove behind cover and held our breath as the guard passed by once more, but this time stopped to shine his flashlight through the cracks in the blinds. I flattened myself to the wall, holding my breath, until the light dropped from the window and the guard moved on once more.

Riley sat up, hissing into the phone. "Wes!"

"Hold your bloody horses. These things take time."

"We're sitting in the middle of a *Talon* office building, surrounded by people who want to beat the crap out of us, then kill us. We don't have time."

"Got it!" Wes's voice rang with triumph. "I'm in. There,

your damn file is unlocked. So, what's so bloody important that you had to…oh…"

His words trailed off. Riley scrambled upright and slid into the chair with Mist right behind him, leaning over his shoulder. Both peered at the screen for a moment, their faces glowing blue-white in the darkness.

"Holy shit." The rogue's voice sent shivers down my back, and I turned from the window. Riley leaned back in the seat, shaking his head, his face full of horror. "St. George, you need to see this, now."

I hurried around the desk and bent next to Riley to peer at the screen. After a few seconds of scanning the words on the computer, a chill crept up my spine as I realized what I was looking at.

It was a list…of Order chapterhouses around the world. The main headquarters in London was at the top, but below it were several more chapters throughout the United Kingdom, France, the United States and several other countries. Even more troubling, it listed the amount of security the bases had, the approximate number of soldiers, the exit and entry points and the time zone of every chapterhouse around the world.

And at the very top of the list, a timer, counting down the hours.

I looked at Riley, who drew in a long breath. "Do you know what this is, St. George?" he asked, his voice subdued.

I nodded. There were other things it could be, harmless, less sinister things. Talon could simply be keeping an eye on the Order, making sure their enemies would not attack and take them by surprise. There were other reasons this file would exist. But I was a soldier, and I knew where the signs were pointing. Talon had an army now. And St. George had always stood in their way.

"It's a battle plan," I said.

"My God," Mist breathed, her blue eyes wide as she scanned the list. "The Night of Fang and Fire...they're planning to attack the Order. All the chapterhouses, in one night." She looked up at me, horrified and amazed. "They're planning to destroy the Order of St. George in one fell swoop."

Riley made a strangled noise. "Not only the Order," he whispered in a voice of quiet rage. "Look at this."

Below the St. George chapterhouses was another list of locations, all through the United States. These I didn't recognize, but Riley swore heavily and shook his head. "Those are my safe houses," he growled. "Most of them, anyway. Some aren't in use anymore, but still." He ran a hand down his face and snatched the phone from where it sat on the desk. "Wes," he growled, shoving away from the computer. "Did you hear all that? Recall the safe houses right now, all of them... Yes, all of them! Get everyone out of the open before this goes down... Don't worry about us, we'll be there as soon as we can... Dammit, Wes, don't argue with me, just do it!" He yanked the phone from his ear and glanced back at me. "When is this supposed to happen?" he snapped.

I looked at the top of the screen. "In three days," I said numbly. Three days before Talon unleashed destruction upon St. George and the rogues. Three days to try to find a way to stop it. If they could be stopped.

But first...

I looked at Mist. "Get us to Ember," I told her. "Right now."

RILEY

The trip to the final lab was mostly a blur. Mist herded us
back into the elevator and used her key card to gain access
to the lowest floor, where, she explained, Ember was being
held. She told me a few other things, about security and the
layout of the floor, but I was finding it difficult to concentrate. I was desperate to get to Ember, desperate to find my
Sallith'tahn and life-mate, but I was still reeling from what
we'd just uncovered. The Night of Fang and Fire. In one
imminent, terrible night, Talon was going to attack not only
the Order of St. George, but every safe house, nest and rogue
dragon they could find, with the intent of destroying Talon's
enemies once and for all. And, from everything I'd seen, they
finally had the numbers to do it.

The Order of St. George was going to fall. After hundreds
of years of hunting us toward extinction, killing and slaugh-
tering without regret, the genocidal maniacs were finally getting what they deserved. Talon would sweep through with
their army of clones, dragons they had bred for destruction,
and wipe St. George off the map.

And that, in the most ironic twist of fate I'd ever encountered, terrified me.

I felt no sympathy for the Order. Present company excluded, I hated St. George and every fanatical, trigger-happy individual in it. I had lost friends, colleagues and hatchlings to their endless war, and there had been countless nights where I struggled to keep my underground safe and my hatchlings off their sights.

But I didn't want them wiped out. I didn't want them gone. Because I knew that, without the Order of St. George, there would be no one left who could challenge Talon. They balanced each other, kept the other in check. The reason we had to hide, the reason Talon was so leery of discovery, was plain and simple—because they were afraid of the Order. Because they knew what the Order represented: humanity's fear of the unknown and what they would do if they found out dragons were real.

Without St. George, that balance would tip. Without the Order, there would be nothing to stop Talon and the Elder Wyrm from achieving what they'd wanted from the start. Complete and utter dominion. How they would accomplish that I wasn't entirely sure, but destroying an entire organization of professional dragonslayers seemed like a good first step.

I didn't know how we were going to survive the coming storm. I didn't know what the world would be like in the future, a future where Talon had no opposition and no one to stop their plans, whatever they were. I did know that I was going to rescue Ember, recall all my safe houses and then find the deepest, darkest hole where we could hide and wait this out. And hope that, when the dust settled and we reemerged, the world would still be intact and not burned to a crisp.

I spared a glance at the soldier. He stood next to me with a gun held loosely at his side, staring at the elevator doors.

His face was stony, his eyes flat and dangerous. Most likely, he was thinking of the Order and what he could do to save them. Or perhaps he was thinking of Ember. I did know one thing: we were done with Talon. If anyone got in our way right now, they wouldn't live long enough to regret it.

"This is it," Mist said quietly as the elevator came to a halt on the very bottom floor. "Beyond this hall is the lab where we will find Ms. Hill. It will be guarded, so be prepared. We might have to fight our way through."

I glanced at the clones beside me. "What about your two puppet dragons?"

"They will follow orders," Mist said. "Because I will be the one giving them. But the security guards on this floor are human and will attempt to stop us when we approach. We need to silence them quickly before they sound the alarm. If they do alert the rest of the building, we're as good as dead. Are you ready?"

"Yes." St. George stepped forward, his expression hard. I glanced at his face and realized that whatever stood between him and Ember was probably going to die. "Let's go."

EMBER

We need to speed up the process.

Lowering my arm, I gazed around, shivering as the disembodied voice echoed from a cloudless sky. I stood at the edge of a sandy beach, white cliffs looming behind me, a red sun sinking into the waves and sparkling off the water.

Is that wise? Her mind is already under a lot of stress. We could do irreversible damage to her psyche if we go much faster.

As long as her memories are extracted, it won't matter if her psyche is damaged. But the Elder Wyrm wants this done today. Dig deeper.

Anger and horror stabbed at me, and I turned in a circle, trying to pinpoint the voices that faded into the wind. *Stop it*, I tried telling them, though my voice was frozen inside me. *Whatever you're doing, whatever this is, please stop.*

More voices caught my attention. I turned, discovering that the beach wasn't empty. A few yards away, a group of six—three boys and three girls—clustered together at the water's edge. I looked closer, squinting against the sun, and my heart jumped as I recognized them all. Lexi, Kristin…and I…stood talking to a trio of older college guys whose names I had mostly forgotten. One of them—Colin, I abruptly remembered—kept trying to put his arm around me, and I kept squirming away.

I drew in a slow breath as the memory became clear. *This*

is Lone Rock Cove, I realized. *And it's…*that *evening.* My heart turned over. *The day I met…*

I looked over, and Garret Xavier Sebastian walked past me, striding toward the group at the water's edge.

Dread bloomed in my stomach. I was suddenly terrified, filled with a horror and desperation I'd never felt before, though I didn't even know why. I only knew I had to stop this, keep him from reaching the group and setting those chain of events into motion.

Wait! I lunged after him, reaching for his arm. *Garret, wait!*

My fingers passed right through his body, and he continued toward the group in the distance, followed by Tristan. *No*, I thought in despair, hurrying after them. *Garret, stop. Don't go.*

Her mind is retreating. She's struggling to hold on to that memory. Increase the dosage and the current, now.

Sir, the procedure is at near max. Any more and we're pushing the limits of what she can take.

Do it. This is a linchpin memory. Something significant happened to her on this day, that's why she's fighting so hard to keep it. Once we remove it, the others will become much easier to…what? Who are you? How the hell did you—no, stop!

Thunder boomed overhead, and everything fractured.

GARRET

"Ember!"

I leaped across the room, past the bodies of the two guards, shot dead before they knew what was happening. Four men in white coats cringed away from me, but I ignored them. My body ached, protesting the movements, but I barely felt the pain. My whole attention was riveted to the scene in the middle of the room.

Ember lay strapped to a gurney in the center of the floor, wires and electrodes connecting her to a large computer in the corner. Her eyes were closed and her skin was nearly white as I rushed to her side. Heat blazed through my veins, turning the air in my lungs hot as I yanked the wires from her face and neck and began unbuckling the straps tying her to the bed.

"Stop!" One of the scientists came forward, hand outstretched, glaring at me. "Don't touch that!" he ordered as I contemplated putting a bullet through his shiny skull. "You have no idea what you're doing—"

With a growl, Riley shoved his gun into the man's forehead, his eyes dangerous. "Keep talking," he snarled as all color drained from the human's face. "Give me a reason to blow your brain through the back of your skull."

The scientist froze. From the corner of my eye, I saw Mist direct her two clones to guard the doors before motioning the remaining scientists against the wall. The men obeyed, holding up their hands. They didn't look like they would try to stop us, which was good, as my entire focus was getting Ember out of here.

The last of the straps were removed, and I gathered her in my arms, lifting her shoulders off the mattress. "Ember," I murmured, and pressed a palm to her cheek. It was cold, ashen, and my heart gave a violent lurch. I felt for a pulse, nearly collapsing with relief as I felt the faint flutter of life beneath my fingers. Whatever had happened to her, whatever horrible things they had put her through, at least she was alive. "Hey," I tried again, shaking her gently, desperate for her to open her eyes. "Ember, wake up. Can you hear me?"

There was no answer. The girl remained limp and unresponsive in my arms, and my desperation grew. "Ember..."

Against the wall, the lead scientist shook his head. "She can't hear you," he said, making Riley turn on him with a growl. "I doubt she can hear anything now, and don't snarl at me, dragon. I'm not the one responsible for this." He glared at Riley and myself, his thin face taut with anger. "You fools don't know what you have done," he snapped. "This was a delicate procedure, and you've gone and blundered into it without knowing what was at stake. You can't just yank the plug without risking permanent damage to the subject's mind."

"What were you doing to her?" Riley asked in a hard, dangerous voice.

"I don't think I can tell you that."

"No?" Riley pressed the muzzle of the gun harder to the

man's forehead, his eyes glowing yellow in the brightly lit room. "Then I guess we don't need you, do we?"

"All right, all right!" The scientist held up his hands. "I'll tell you, for all the good it will do now." He leaned back from the gun and ran a hand over his face, seemingly unaware that the rogue was fighting hard not to Shift and tear him into tiny pieces. The Dractylpromazine was starting to wear off, because the flicker of a dark blue dragon suddenly overlapped with Riley for the barest of seconds, gold eyes blazing in fury as they glared at the scientist. Who, dangerously for him, didn't notice.

"Ms. Hill was…is…the Elder Wyrm's vessel," the human went on. "That is why she is so important to the organization. As one who shares her blood and DNA, she was genetically engineered to house the memories and consciousness of Talon's CEO."

"Wait, *what*?" Riley gaped at the scientist. "Shares her blood? Are you telling me that Ember is—"

"The daughter of the Elder Wyrm, yes." The scientist nodded and glanced at Ember, not seeing Riley's pale face, the shock filling his eyes. "She and her brother are the heirs to Talon, though it was always the Elder Wyrm's intention to raise a daughter for the sole purpose of extending her own life. We were extracting Ms. Hill's memories so that the Elder Wyrm's presence could take over her mind without opposition." He frowned then, shaking his head, and glared back at the rogue. "Of course, now that you and your friends have quite literally pulled the plug on this fragile operation, there is no telling what state of mind she will be in when she revives. If she wakes up at all."

Horror flooded me. I looked down at Ember's body, willing her to wake up, to open her eyes. She lay like a doll in my arms, her head lolled back and her hands limp at her sides. With shaking arms, I gathered her close, pressing my forehead to hers, praying my thoughts would reach her.

Wake up, Ember, I thought, fighting the despair clawing at my insides. *You're too strong to let this beat you. Come back to me, dragon girl.*

Ember didn't respond.

EMBER

I raised my head, and found myself alone. The beach was gone. The ocean was gone. I was in the middle of a black void, darkness surrounding me like a vacuum. It wasn't nighttime; there were no shadows clinging to the ground or hanging in the air. There was no ground. No sky. Just...blackness.

"Where am I?" I whispered.

A soft growl echoed out of the darkness. "I think the better question," something said behind me, "would be *who*. Also, what the hell?"

Spinning around, I came face-to-face with a dragon. With...myself.

★ ★ ★

The human gaped at me, green eyes widening. She looked like a startled deer in headlights, dazed and frightened. Like prey. I saw my own reflection in her eyes, my wings partially open, my neck raised to gaze down at her. It was a strange sensation; I'd only seen myself, my true self, maybe once or twice. The human face I saw much more often, gazing back at me from mirrors and shiny surfaces, the girl who had become the real me.

"What...the hell?" she stammered, taking a step back. "What is this? What's going on?"

I snorted. I had been awake for only a little while, and even now, I felt groggy and disoriented. Every time they stuck me with one of those damned needles, I blacked out and didn't know anything for a time. "I have no idea," I told the girl—*me*, I supposed. Other me. The one who cried and loved and followed emotion rather than instinct. The one who insisted we love a human, instead of our *Sallith'tahn*. I curled a lip at her. "I've been asleep. You're the one who has been awake through all of this. You tell me."

Other me shook her head. "This has to be a nightmare," she muttered, putting a hand to her face. "It can't really be happening. I can't be standing here, having a conversation with *myself*."

"Why not?"

"Because...it's impossible!" She ran the palm down her face, her eyes a little glassy. "I'm dreaming," she muttered again. "That's all. You're a nightmare, a figment of my imagination. I just have to wake up."

I growled, the sound vibrating through the void around us. "From where I'm standing, *you're* the hallucination," I told her through bared teeth, and she flinched back. "I've always been here. From the beginning. You're the human part that won't accept who we are." She shook her head, denying it, and my anger flared. "If anything, *I'm* the real one. And maybe if I get rid of you, everything will be as it should."

I backed away as the dragon stalked forward, eyes blazing against the void. Okay, maybe this wasn't a hallucination. And even if it was, being attacked and torn apart by my dragon, quite literally *myself*, would probably screw up my head pretty bad.

"Stop it," I told her, forcing myself to stand my ground. "This is crazy. We can't fight each other."

Dragon me stopped, but didn't look convinced. "We've been fighting each other for a long time, didn't you know that?" she hissed. When I gave her a puzzled look, she actually sneered. "Don't act dumb. You know what I'm talking about. Ever since you met that boy, that human, all you've been doing is fighting me. We're not human, and he won't be around forever. Cobalt is your life-mate, our *Sallith'tahn*. Why do you keep denying who we are?"

"I love Garret," I told her firmly, realizing what this was about. "And I don't want my choices to be defined by instinct. You keep pushing me at Cobalt, but it's not going to change what I feel for Garret. I can't choose who I love, anymore than I can choose the *Sallith'tahn*." She watched me with blank dragon eyes, and I gave a bitter smile. "But I don't know why I'm telling you this—love is a human thing. I wouldn't expect you to understand."

Dragon me snorted again, sounding indignant. "What the hell gave you that idea?" she demanded.

★ ★ ★

The girl glanced at me sharply, a look of confusion crossing her face. "What are you talking about?"

With a gusty sigh, I sat down, folding my wings to my back as the flames within flickered and died. I supposed it was time to stop denying it. "Cobalt is our *Sallith'tahn*," I told her simply. "I don't have to do any pushing. You feel the pull toward him just as much as I do." I paused, waiting for her to deny it, knowing she wouldn't. She couldn't. "So why do you think I feel any different toward the human?"

She stared at me, an expression of shock crossing her face as she realized. "You love Garret, too," she finally whispered.

I didn't answer, feeling the truth burn its way into my heart as surely as the hottest flame. Yes, I did. I loved the soldier, the dragonslayer, the *human*, with a fierceness I'd never experienced before. Emotion wasn't just for my other half, I could admit that now. But still, it was Cobalt who called to me, who brought the flames within to life, who made me feel like a *dragon*. Who understood flying and hoarding and breathing fire, things that only a dragon got. Without him, I sometimes felt that I—this side of me, anyway—would shrivel up and disappear, leaving only the human half behind.

After a long silence that throbbed like a heartbeat through the empty void, human Ember threw up her hands. "So... why are we fighting each other?" she asked despairingly. "If we both feel the same, why is this happening?"

I closed my eyes, feeling we were both rushing toward a final, inevitable conclusion. "I think," I said slowly, "you just answered your own question."

★　★　★

I drew in a breath as the dragon's words sank in. "We... keep fighting each other," I said, and the familiar green eyes opened to stare at me. "That's why we're split like this, why I feel like I'm two separate creatures sometimes. But we're not. We're not dragon *and* human. We're the same. Two sides of the same coin. We've just been struggling against the other for so long, trying to resist our instincts, because we didn't understand."

Dragon me curled her tail around her legs, her voice full of weary resignation. "So, what do we do now?"

"I think we have to stop fighting each other."

She cocked her head in a surreally familiar way. "That sounds a little too easy."

"I don't think so." I looked at her, really looked at her, seeing—for the first time—myself. Not my dragon side, not my baser instincts, but me. And I realized what I—*we*—had to do.

I smiled sadly, wishing I could have figured this out a lot sooner. "Riley is our *Sallith'tahn*," I murmured, nodding. "That's just how it is, and I have to accept that." The dragon was watching intently, green gaze solemn in the darkness. "But instinct doesn't have to define me," I whispered firmly. "It doesn't have to control my life. I don't have to suppress it, or try to fight it. It's not a choice between what I want to be more, dragon or human." I closed my eyes, feeling something inside me unravel, a knot coiling free. "I'm a dragon," I said firmly. "That's all. Not a dragon that can love, or a dragon that has to fight to be more human. I'm both...and neither. I'm just me."

Just me.

I opened my eyes.

His face swam above me, metallic-gray eyes bright with fear and anguish as they came into focus. I felt his arm around my shoulders, and one calloused hand pressed to my cheek, trembling slightly. I felt him freeze as I opened my eyes, heard the ragged intake of breath as our gazes met.

"Ember." He blew out a shaky breath and pulled me to him, pressing his forehead to mine. I wrapped my arms around his neck, feeling the strength of his arms holding me close, one hand tangled in my hair. "Are you all right?" he whispered.

"I..." My head felt strange, like it was stuffed with cot-

ton and floating several inches above my neck. I couldn't remember how I got here; it felt like there were dark blotches
on my brain, smudging out the memories. "I don't know," I
admitted, looking up at Garret. "What happened?"

"Save it for another time." A cool, impatient voice interrupted us. "We have to leave this place, now. Before the
Elder Wyrm realizes what is happening."

Garret and I drew back, and my eyes widened at the girl
on the other side of the room. "Mist?" I exclaimed as the
dragonell gave me an exasperated look. "What are you doing
here?"

"It's all right, Firebrand." Against the far wall, Riley
smiled at me, looking relieved, as well. Though he held a
gun pointed at the face of an angry-looking scientist. "She's
on our side, at least for now." He gave her a look of begrudg-
ing respect. "I don't know what her real motivation is, but
she got us here. We wouldn't have made it this far without
her help."

"Can we please save the speculation for later?" Mist
snapped. "We still have to make it to the ground floor and
get off the premises. And this little side trip has significantly
delayed the escape plan." She glanced at the scientists, her
face darkening. "We should kill them, to make sure they
don't sound the alarm when we leave."

"No." Quickly, I slid off the gurney and leaned on Garret
as my legs shook and the room swayed. His arms wrapped
around my waist, holding me steady. I could feel his heartbeat through his shirt, feel the warmth pulsing from his skin
as I looked at Mist. "No killing," I told her. "Not in cold
blood. Find another way."

The other dragon gave me an exasperated look and glanced
at Riley. "I'm so glad we stayed behind to rescue her," she

said acidly. Frowning, she turned to the two vessels and pointed at the scientists. "Stay here. Guard the humans. If they step away from the wall, kill them."

The clones moved forward obediently, herding the scientists into the corner and keeping their guns trained on them. The lead scientist glared at us as he was backed against the wall.

"You'll never get out," he said. "There are a dozen cameras between here and the ground floor. Not to mention the vessels, the guards and the rest of the security. All that has to happen is for one camera to spot you, one alarm to sound. Even with this traitor with you, you'll never make it out alive."

"You know, we could always kill you right now," Riley growled, turning on the scientist and raising the gun back to his face. The human cringed away, futilely covering his head, as if that would stop a bullet, and Riley gave a grim smile. "Fortunately for you, everyone here is going to be a bit distracted in a few seconds. Mist?" He glanced at the second Basilisk, an evil smile crossing his face as he pulled out a phone. "Wes is in."

"Then let's get out of here."

"Roger that. Wes…" Riley put the phone to his ear, narrowing his eyes. "Now."

RILEY

For a second, nothing happened. The scientist glared at me, tense and apprehensive, waiting.

Then a ringing alarm blared into the silence, making everyone start. The lead scientist jumped the highest of all and gazed around wildly as the shrill ringing continued to sound. I grinned at him smugly.

Hacked the fire alarm and disabled the cameras—nice job, Wes. Hopefully that will be enough of a distraction for us to sneak out unnoticed. I glanced at my companions and jerked my head at the door. "Time to go! Let's get out of here."

We ran, leaving the room and sprinting down the hallway to the elevators. The alarm was still blaring nonstop, and if I knew Wes, he'd probably called the fire department, too. Mist reached the doors at the end of the hall first and growled a curse.

"Elevators are down. We'll have to take the stairs. This way!"

We followed her up the stairwell, our pounding footsteps echoing up the shaft as we climbed. Three flights later, we burst onto the ground floor and gazed around warily. From what I had pieced together, this was a private office campus, with buildings up top to act as a front, hiding the very secret, high-tech laboratories beneath. This floor was dark and empty, though the alarm still blared through the corridors, making my ears ring. It looked like most of the employees had already fled the building.

Abruptly, the fire alarm ceased, and silence throbbed in my ears.

"That's not good," Mist whispered, and started down a corridor that cut through various offices. No one appeared at the end of the hall, no footsteps echoed in pursuit, but my skin crawled in the sudden, disturbing stillness. "Come on," she beckoned. "We'll go through the loading dock where the trucks make the deliveries. No point in risking the main doors."

Everything was quiet as we slipped through the offices, following Mist down several hallways until she opened a door that led into what looked like a storage space. The floors were cement, and boxes of varying size were stacked along the walls and in neat aisles down the center.

"Almost there," I heard Mist say under her breath. As if she, too, was counting the steps to freedom. We trailed her along a wall of boxes, rounded the corner and froze.

A thin man stood before a line of guards, their assault rifles pointed in our direction. More than a dozen cold, silvery eyes stared at us across the cement floor as the row of vessels took aim, their faces blank. Behind them and the smiling form of Luther the Basilisk, the doors of the loading dock beckoned, tantalizingly close. But they might as well have been a million miles away.

"Well, well," Luther said, his sibilant voice oozing with triumph. "And what have we here? Miss Anderson, haven't you been the sneaky, sneaky agent. Going rogue? Helping Cobalt escape? I wouldn't have expected it of you."

Footsteps shuffled behind us, and another line of vessels stepped from behind a tower of boxes and hemmed us in.

Luther's smile was cold as he stared at me. "You thought I wouldn't guess what was happening when the fire alarm sounded?" he asked. "When the security systems were abruptly jammed? I asked myself…if you—or *any* Basilisk," he added, looking at Mist, "were to stage some kind of daring, miraculous escape, where would you most likely go? It was a gamble, between here and the sewer tunnels, but…" He raised his hands, as if to embrace us. "Here you are."

Dammit. I shot a desperate look around the room, wondering if there was a way out of this. If there was, I didn't see it. The soldier had his gun drawn, but by the grim look on his face, he knew he was going to die, as well.

"Miss Hill," Luther said, his gaze shifting to Ember. "If you would kindly step away now. I would not want for you to accidentally come under fire. We will be returning to the Elder Wyrm presently, right after we destroy the traitors."

Ember bared her teeth at him. "You want them, you'll have to kill me, too."

"Don't be foolish, girl." The Basilisk frowned. "They're going to die one way or another, and you will be taken back to the Elder Wyrm where you belong. No need to make this harder on yourself."

Ember stood her ground, though I saw her hands tremble before they clenched at her sides. My throat ached for her. The rest of us would die quickly, but she would be taken away, her memories extracted and probably destroyed. So that the ancient leader of Talon could achieve immortality.

The Elder Wyrm's vessel. My stomach dropped, and I closed my eyes, realizing how we could get out of this. It was a gamble, and Ember might hate me—hell, she might kick my ass later—but there was nothing else I could think of.

I'm sorry, Firebrand, I thought, pulling out my pistol. *I hope you can forgive me for this.*

"Very well," Luther said when Ember didn't move. "Then I suppose we will do this the hard way. Vessels," he ordered, his voice reverberating through the walls. "Kill them. All except Ember Hill. Destroy the rest and bring her to me."

I surged up, snaked one arm around Ember's waist from behind and pressed the muzzle of my gun below her chin.

She stiffened, and so did the Basilisk, his dark eyes widening as he realized what was happening. "Stop!" he called sharply, and the vessels froze, their gun barrels pointed right at us. Panting, I glared at Luther over Ember's shoulder, trying to calm the fear sweeping through me. I could feel Ember's taut body against mine, the tension and shock lining her muscles, and hoped she would not try to struggle or throw me off. *Trust me, Ember,* I thought, willing her to understand. *I'm trying to save us all. Don't explode on me.*

"Here's what's going to happen, Luther," I said, locking eyes with the Basilisk. "You're going to let us go. You're going to let me and everyone else walk out of here, unmolested, or—" I prodded Ember's jaw with the barrel of the pistol "—you can kiss the Elder Wyrm's daughter goodbye."

Luther stared at me, his expression stony, and my heart pounded. I had to play this just right. For all his creepiness, Luther wasn't stupid. If he called my bluff, we were done. The only reason this insane gambit might work was that I knew the one thing that terrified Luther, terrified all of us. The Elder Wyrm. I had to make him believe I wasn't bluffing. I wasn't Riley; I was Cobalt, the criminal leader of the rogue underground, and I had no issues sacrificing another dragon if it meant saving my own hide.

"You really expect me to believe that?" The Basilisk gave

an oily smile, making my stomach drop. "You really expect me to stand here and believe that you would shoot one of your friends in cold blood, to save yourself? No, agent." He shook his head. "The Cobalt I've seen, the Cobalt I have studied over the years, is not that ruthless."

"Yeah?" Ignoring my fear, I flashed the Basilisk the meanest, nastiest smirk I was capable of and shoved the gun farther into Ember's skin. She gasped, tensing in my arms, and Luther's eyes narrowed. "Can you really afford to take that gamble?" I asked, holding his gaze. "What would happen if the daughter of the Elder Wyrm is killed while you were trying to prevent our escape? It certainly wouldn't just be your job on the line."

Luther didn't answer, but I caught the flicker of raw fear that went through his eyes, and knew I had struck a chord. The rest of my party hadn't moved. I could see the soldier in my peripheral vision; he had lowered his gun, but he still watched me with a hard look, one hand clenched at his side. I couldn't see Mist; I just knew she was somewhere behind us, watching this morbid drama play out.

I kept my attention on the Basilisk, knowing he was wavering. "If you think I'm bluffing, you're sadly mistaken," I lied, and gestured to the vessels surrounding us. "I know when I'm beat. And the way I see it, I'm already dead. But you know what I have no problem with? Taking you down with me. And hey..." My thumb reached up and pulled back the hammer with an ominous, metallic click. "If I have to die, I'd rather give her a clean death, right now, then let the Elder Wyrm win. But it's your move, Luther. What's it gonna be?"

Luther glared at me, fear and hate warring in his eyes. But after a long moment, his shoulders slumped and he stepped away, barking an order to the clones. The vessels straightened, lowering their guns in perfect unison, and the Basilisk jerked his head at the door.

"Go," he snarled. "But this isn't over. There is nowhere in the world you can hide. Nowhere for you and your little underground of traitors to be safe. We will find you, and we will purge your stain from the face of the earth. You're only delaying the inevitable."

I would've said something snarky, but at the moment I was too relieved. Still keeping my arms around Ember, and the gun pressed below her chin, I jerked my head at the rest of them, and we began walking toward the metal doors.

"Don't follow us," I told the Basilisk as we passed. "If I even suspect we're being tailed, or that a Viper is out there waiting to snipe us in the head, I will have no problem pulling the trigger. We walk away clean, and no one in the organization tries to follow until we are completely gone."

Luther gave me a flat stare, but nodded tightly. St. George threw open the metal door, and I dragged Ember through the frame, out of the building and into the sunlight.

Mist and the soldier followed at my heels. Through the door lay a flat, empty parking lot, surrounded by lawn, trees and concrete. In the distance, past another set of buildings, I could see the tree line that marked the security fence, but I had no idea how we were going to get to it.

"Mist," I growled, glancing at the silver-haired Basilisk at my shoulder. "Where to now?" I felt highly exposed, knowing that just a few yards away, the most powerful dragon in the world was watching us through a pair of thin glass doors. "How do we get out of here? And I hope you had a better plan than 'on foot.'"

"Give it a second," Mist said, gazing around the lot. "He knew the plan was set into motion. He should be…there."

A car suddenly streaked around a corner and skidded to a halt a few feet away. Mist sprang forward, wrenched open the door and motioned us inside. Still holding Ember, I pulled her into the backseat, the soldier right behind us, as Mist slammed the door and lunged into the front. I held my breath, waiting for gunshots, for a snarling Viper to land on the windshield and fill the car with fire. But nothing happened except the tires squealing as the car tore across the lot, through the open security gate and into the city streets.

★ ★ ★

Holy shit. We'd escaped. We'd actually escaped from Talon.

Cobalt, you are the officially luckiest son of a bitch in the history of SOBs. Wait until Wes finds out; this will go down in dragon history. If Talon doesn't kill you in the next five minutes. I looked down at my "hostage" and winced. *Or Ember. Or St. George for that matter.*

"Um, Riley?" Ember's voice, though not exactly furious, was not happy. "Are you going to let me go soon?"

"Sorry, Firebrand." I eased the gun away from her throat, but didn't loosen my grip around her. "Not yet. Not until I'm positive we're clear of Talon. I wouldn't put it past the Elder Wyrm to be keeping tabs on us right now, trying to see where we go. Once we're out of the city and I'm sure Talon isn't following us, we can drop the farce. And you can punch me out then, if you like."

She sighed. "No," she muttered, finally relaxing against me. "Once I got past the shock and the 'what the hell are you doing,' I realized you were trying to save us. We wouldn't have made it out if you hadn't done that. Though you did freak me out for a second there, Riley." A shiver went through her, making my stomach twist. "You sounded entirely serious. *I* almost believed you."

I closed my eyes. "I would have never done it, Firebrand," I whispered. "That whole time, I was terrified Luther would call my bluff. I had to make it sound as convincing as I could, because there was no way I could even think about pulling that trigger."

"I know," Ember murmured back. "And I knew, deep down, that you wouldn't. Even...even if I am the Elder Wyrm's vessel, and she just wants me to extend her own life. And it might've been better for everyone if you did." She gave another violent shudder before taking a deep breath, seeming to brush it off. "But we're out," she breathed. "We made it out, all of us. Your stupid bluff actually worked, and that's why I'm not going to punch you in the face when we get out of this."

"I might," said the soldier in a low voice.

I glanced at him, and the hairs on my arm rose. His jaw was set, his eyes angry as he met my gaze. His pupils had contracted until they were razor-thin slits against the gray of his irises. And for one crazy, surreal moment, it didn't feel like I was staring into the face of an angry human. It felt like I was staring down a rival drake, and he was seconds away from snarling the ancient challenge and lunging at me with fangs bared.

But then he blinked, and his eyes went normal again. I ignored the possessive anger in my gut and gave him a weary smile. "Well, you're welcome to try, St. George," I said. "But I'm not extending the same offer. You want to kick my ass, you'll have to do it the old-fashioned way."

"Perhaps if we can stay on target," came an exasperated voice from the front, and Mist peered back at us. Her eyes glimmered blue in the fading light. Beside her in the driver's seat, a man in a dark suit gazed straight ahead, silently ignoring the three dragons and the soldier of St. George surrounding him. I wondered who he was, if he was employed by Talon and if he was now royally screwed for helping us escape.

"We need a place to hide," Mist said, gazing at me. "One where Talon can't track us down. From what we saw, all of your safe houses have been compromised. I have a place we can go—my employer set it up in case it came to this."

"No," I said, and she blinked at me. "Sorry, Mist, but trusting you to get us out is one thing. Trusting some mysterious Talon employer to provide us with a safe house is a little out of my comfort zone. The fewer people who know where we are, the better."

"You don't have any more safe houses," Mist said. "Talon found them all."

"Not all of them." I went over Talon's list in my mind, making sure this final sanctuary wasn't among the targets. "I have one last place we can go."

Mist regarded me a moment longer, then shrugged. "I'd argue that you are being paranoid, but it would be a waste of effort. And I suppose it doesn't matter where we go, as long as it's safe."

"Yeah," I muttered as the sense of foreboding descended on me once more. I wasn't sure any of us would be safe, ever again. *Call Wes*, I thought, planning our next move. *Contact all my safe houses. Gather every rogue, hatchling and human friend I have and take them to the deepest, darkest, most impenetrable hole I can find.* The storm was coming, looming on the horizon, and if any of us were caught in the open when it hit, no one would survive. I just hoped that, when the initial fury had passed and we poked our heads out again, the world would still be there, and not burned to ashes by dragonfire.

EMBER

"You will be my vessel, Ember Hill," the Elder Wyrm whispered, her eyes glowing emerald as she loomed above me. "My new body, in which I will live forever."

"No," I snarled, fighting against the straps. "Get away from me! I won't forget him. I won't forget any of them."

"Stop fighting, sis," Dante murmured, walking around the gurney. He gave me an exasperated look and shook his head. "Why are you resisting? This is where you belong. This is your destiny."

"Dante," I pleaded, gazing up at him. He stared down with impassive green eyes. "Help me. You don't know what she's planning. What she really wants to do. Please." I gave him a desperate look. "You're my brother. Don't let her destroy us all."

Dante smiled. "I'll save you, Ember," he whispered, and climbed onto the gurney, resting cold hands on my shoulders. Chilled, I stared into the face of my twin and saw his eyes had turned a pale, silvery white. "I'll save you," he whispered again, digging curved nails into my flesh. Blood welled and ran down my arms, and Dante's nostrils flared. "Don't worry, sis. Dragons will never have to live in fear again. I'll save us all."

His body exploded, becoming long and sleek, iron scales ripping through his business suit, dark wings flaring behind him. Baring bloody fangs, the vessel drew back with a piercing shriek and went for my face.

★ ★ ★

I jerked awake, heart pounding against my ribs, a cold sweat covering my face and neck as the snarling face of my brother faded from my mind. Shaking, I sank back against the pillows, gazing around the room and trying to remember what had happened.

After escaping Talon, we'd driven through the night, setting a frantic, nonstop pace as we strove to outrun the organization and whatever agents they were sure to send after us. At the next town, we'd ditched our driver, Mist's contact, who'd told us he would return to his employer now that we were away from Talon. Though we still hadn't known who this mysterious employer was, no one had really cared at that point. We were out of Talon; that was all that mattered. After dropping the driver off at a bus stop, Riley had taken over, heading west into the setting sun.

"Where are we going?" Garret had asked, peering out the front window at the road stretching out before us.

"Somewhere safe," Riley had answered, his voice short. "Somewhere I can gather all my rogues together so we can avoid the shitstorm that's coming. We only have three days to make sure everyone is out of the open when that Night of Fang and Fire hits."

I'd blinked. That had been news to me. "The Night of Fang and Fire?" I'd asked, and Riley had cursed.

"Dammit, that's right. You weren't with us when we hacked those files. Wanna give her the short version, St. George?"

"Talon is going to attack," Garret had told me, his voice grim. "They plan to hit all the Order chapterhouses in one night, as well as all of Riley's safe houses. They're going to use the clones to wipe out their enemies in one fell swoop."

Horror had flooded me. "Oh, God," I'd whispered. "That's what Dante was talking about. His plan...when he said we wouldn't survive what was coming." I'd remembered the genuine fear in his eyes when I refused to cooperate with the Elder Wyrm, his desperate insistence that I give in, and my rage had boiled. He'd known. He'd known what would happen that whole time. And, sickening as it was, he was probably in charge of it. "What are we going to do?" I'd asked.

"I told you," Riley had said gravely. "We're getting the hell out of the way. We're calling the underground back, making sure everyone is accounted for, and then we're going to hide as deep and hard as we can while we wait for this hurricane to blow over."

"What about the Order?" Garret had asked.

"What *about* the Order?" Riley had snapped in return. "They know how to kill dragons, they'll be fine. Let them deal with it themselves."

"If Talon takes them by surprise, when they're outnumbered and they don't know what's coming, they won't stand a chance," Garret had insisted. "They've lost their Patriarch. The leadership is probably fractured and the council is scrambling for control. The Order is in chaos—no one will be ready to deal with an army of dragon clones. We have to contact them, let them know what Talon is planning."

"What?" Riley had glared at him in the rearview mirror. "I'm sorry, are we talking about the same Order? The one whose leader shot you in the back a few weeks ago? Who threatened they would see our kind extinct, even after everything we did to break them away from Talon? Who would kill us all as soon as they see us, because they still haven't learned there is a difference between rogues and Talon?

No." He'd shaken his head. "I'm done with the Order. They wouldn't listen to us, anyway. My responsibility is to my underground and my hatchlings, nothing else. I won't put them in danger, and I'm not going to lose them to Talon. The dragonslayers will have to get by without us." Garret had started to protest, and Riley's voice had become a snarl. "We are not contacting the Order, St. George. End of story."

The soldier had backed off, falling silent, but his set jaw and the dark look in his eyes had told me that that wasn't going to be the end of it.

We'd driven on through the night. Exhausted, I'd dozed on Garret's shoulder, and he'd leaned back, drawing me into his arms. The mood of the car had been somber; everyone had seemed a bit shell-shocked. We'd known we had to talk, discuss what we had learned and plan what we were going to do next. But my brain had been fried, overloaded with the barrage of what we'd been through. I'd felt numb, and that apathy had been comforting. As had been the feel of Garret's arms around me, reminding me that I was safe. That I wasn't strapped to a table with a bunch of blank-eyed scientists poking and prodding me like I was a lab rat. I hadn't wanted to remember the terror and helplessness I'd felt when the Elder Wyrm had told me I was simply a vessel, a body grown in a lab for the purpose of extending her life. I hadn't wanted to think of the scientists messing around in my brain, or what memories they had taken before Garret and Riley showed up. Right then, I hadn't wanted to remember anything.

When the car finally had shuddered to a halt in the early hours of dawn, I'd looked up, surprised. In front of us had sat a large but rather run-down-looking farmhouse, with a sagging wraparound porch and a blue tiled roof. An old barn had squatted off to the side, all color leeched from the boards until they were a dull, uniform gray. Hills and fields had surrounded us and had done so for the past thirty minutes as the car had rattled and bounced its way down a narrow dirt road that had finally run out at the steps of this place.

"Where are we?" Mist had asked from the passenger seat.

"My last safe house," Riley had muttered, turning off the headlights. Gazing up at the sagging building, he'd sighed. "No one knows about it—I've never used it before. In case the worst happened and my network was exposed, I wanted a safe place to hide everyone. This is my last-ditch, shit-has-hit-the-fan fallback point. There's a couple hundred acres of nothing in every direction. No one is going to find us here."

He'd opened the door and stepped out, and the rest of us had followed, our feet raising tiny dust clouds as we'd stepped onto the driveway. It had been quiet out here; there'd been no horns, no sounds of traffic, no people hurrying down sidewalks. Nothing but the cicadas and a lone bird could be heard for miles.

Footsteps had echoed from the house, and a woman had walked onto the porch, squinting over the railings as she'd peered down at us. She'd been lanky and rawboned, her brown-gray hair pulled tightly behind her, and she'd looked like she'd spent most of her time out in the sun. She'd stepped to the edge of the porch and crossed her bony arms, shaking her head at Riley.

"Well, well. Never thought I'd see you again, lizard. It's been a while."

Riley had given her a tired grin. "Hey, Jess. Yeah, it has. What's it been, six, seven years since I was here last?"

"Try eleven."

"Ah. Well, you haven't aged a bit."

"Insufferable lizard." The woman had dropped her arms

and beckoned us inside. "Come on in, everyone. There's plenty of rooms, and I'll see if I can find some bedding for y'all." She'd paused as we'd started forward, her gaze seeking Riley again. "Can I assume, since you and your friends have shown up out of nowhere, that *it* has finally happened?"

"It?" I'd looked at Riley, confused. He'd grimaced.

"Yeah. Sorry, Jess." He'd offered the woman a grim, apologetic smile. "Wes has already given the signal for the safe houses to clear out. The first of the hatchlings should be arriving soon."

"How many dragons are we talking about?"

"If everyone gets here?" Riley had scratched the back of his head. "Seventeen."

She'd sighed. "Then I'm going to need a lot more bedding."

★ ★ ★

I didn't remember much after that, just accepting an armful of clothes and sheets from the lanky woman and being directed upstairs to a small, cozy room with two twin beds. I'd paused long enough to strip out of the thin white hospital gown I'd still been wearing from the lab and pull on the oversize T-shirt before collapsing onto one of the mattresses. I'd been out almost before my head hit the pillow, but being unconscious hadn't stopped the dreams. Dreams of Dante, and the Elder Wyrm, and Talon looming over us all, ready to strike. And myself, strapped to a table, waiting for the Elder Wyrm to move into my body.

Shivering now, I pulled the covers around myself and sat there for a moment, waiting for the fear to die down, for the faint, nagging sense of horror and despair to fade away. I was the Elder Wyrm's vessel. A *thing*, created in a lab, just like the clones. And those memories the scientists had taken—had

I lost anything important? I didn't think I had—I still remembered Garret, Riley, Dante, Crescent Beach, the rogues,
Talon and St. George—but if I *had* lost anything, I wouldn't
even know what it was.

My stomach roiled. I felt dirty suddenly. As if those scientists were still in my brain somewhere, poking around. Seeing things they had no business seeing, secrets and memories
that were mine alone.

I needed a shower. Something to wash the clinging taint
of the scientists, the lab and the Elder Wyrm from my skin.
The bathroom, I remembered, was down the hall, past several bedrooms like this one: small and quaint, with wooden
floors and checkered blue-and-white curtains. It was quite
bare, only holding a dresser and a pair of beds, as if it hadn't
been lived in for a long while. If ever.

Throwing back the covers, I rose and found a set of clothes
on the dresser, trying not to grimace as I pulled them on.
The flowery, yellow-and-green sundress wasn't something I'd
normally wear, but it would have to do. Everything I owned,
the very clothes on my back, had been taken away by Talon.

Including my Viper suit.

"Dammit," I sighed, feeling a brief, unreasonable stab of
loss. Not the worst thing Talon had taken from me by any
means, but it was a blow nonetheless. The Viper suit had been
the last thing I'd owned that was *mine.* Now I had nothing.

No, that's not true, I told myself. *You still have your memories…most of them, anyway. All your skills, everything you've
learned, the friendships and connections you've made in the past
sixteen years. Talon tried to take those, as well, remember? They
truly tried to take* everything. *If Garret and Riley hadn't gotten
there in time, there'd be nothing left but a body. An empty vessel,
just like the clones.*

"Perspective check, Ember," I told myself softly. I was still alive, with most of my memories intact. Riley and Garret were all right, and somehow, impossibly, we had all escaped from Talon. We were safe.

For the moment.

I shivered again. Riley's warning came back to me, dark whispers of the storm on the horizon. Talon was coming. The Night of Fang and Fire, the final purge to completely destroy the Order of St. George, Riley's underground and all of Talon's enemies, was drawing close. Garret was right; we couldn't sit here, doing nothing, waiting for Talon to appear on our doorstep. We had to do *something*.

Abandoning my plans for a shower, I opened the door, stepped into the hall...

...and walked right into Garret.

He grunted as I gave a small yelp of surprise and staggered back, rubbing the bridge of my nose. "Garret. Sorry, I didn't see you." He stared at me solemnly over the threshold, and I cocked my head with a frown. "Why are you lurking outside my door?"

"I was waiting for you." He gave me a concerned look, as if that should be obvious. "Are you all right?"

I swallowed, feeling abruptly self-conscious under that metallic gaze. "Yeah," I answered, turning away to walk back into the room. "I'm fine." *Fine as anyone can be when they discover that they're really a clone created in a lab to house the memories of the Elder Wyrm.* "Where's Riley?" I asked, hearing Garret enter the room and close the door behind him. "Did Wes ever get here? What are we planning to do now—"

Garret's arms closed around me from behind, pulling me against him. My heart jumped, and my stomach flip-flopped, as the soldier leaned in, pressing his forehead to my neck.

"Garret?"

"Sorry," he muttered, and his voice was choked. "Just give me a second." He shuddered, and his arms tightened around me. "I almost lost you yesterday," he whispered. "It didn't really hit me until later, but we almost didn't make it. If Mist hadn't gotten us out when she did, if she had waited any longer…"

I reached up and squeezed his arm, trying not to imagine what would've happened if the procedure had gone as planned. "I'm okay," I whispered. "It's over now."

He shook his head. "When I saw you strapped to that table," he muttered, "and that scientist told us what they were doing, it took everything I had not to kill him and every human in that room. If they had succeeded, if they had really taken all your memories so that the Elder Wyrm could move into your body…" His hands, pressed against my stomach, became fists. "It would've killed me," he murmured. "To know that you're alive, but you're not…*you* anymore—I can't think of anything that would be worse."

I swallowed. "And you don't care that I'm just a vessel?" I asked hesitantly. "A thing created in a lab?"

"Ember." Garret released me and gently turned me to face him. His gaze was intense, worried, but not angry or repulsed. "Do you care that my parents were part of Talon?" he asked, making me frown. "That they were servants of the organization, working for the Elder Wyrm?"

"No." I shook my head. "Of course I don't."

"Why not?"

"Well, because that doesn't reflect on *you*, Garret. You're not responsible for what your parents did in the past… Oh."

He raised an eyebrow, knowing I had just proven his point. "But that's different," I argued. "You had normal parents.

You weren't created in a laboratory, like some creepy Frankenstein monster."

Garret stepped closer, his gaze holding mine. "If I was, would you think any less of me?"

"I... No."

"And what if I wasn't entirely human anymore? What if I had some sort of strange blood that turned me into something unnatural? Would that affect anything between us?"

I sighed. "No, and I'm starting to realize how unnatural our relationship really is."

He chuckled, looking thoughtful. "*Vessel* is a good term," he said softly as I blinked in confusion. "I get now why they're called that."

"Really? I don't."

He sobered. "The Order believes that our bodies are just shells, containers for the soul. It's what's inside that's important— our memories, our consciousness, what makes us who we are. That's what I was afraid of losing, Ember. You, not your body. Outer appearances aren't important. Though you are beautiful, you know that, right?" I think I blushed, and he smiled, leaning closer. "I didn't fall in love with how you looked," he murmured as his hand rose, gently brushing my cheek. "I fell in love with *you*."

My eyes watered, and everything inside me melted into molten goo. "You are getting entirely too good at making a dragon cry," I said, and kissed him.

His arms slid around me, drawing me close as a soft exhale escaped him. I closed my eyes, letting the horror, stress and fear of the past few days fade away, momentarily forgotten. Garret's kisses were gentle, unhurried, though they were laced with passion and relief. Heat flickered between us, and for the very first time, there were no feelings of reluctance.

No anger, disgust or snarling protests from the dragon. No confusion or doubt. Just acceptance. And something so powerful it felt like my insides were going to erupt into flame and consume me from within.

I am in love with this human, I thought, and it felt completely right.

The soft creak of the door opening interrupted us. We pulled back as a girl entered the room with an armful of sheets and blankets.

She jumped when she saw us, her eyes widening. I gasped in surprise. "Nettle?" I exclaimed as the other hatchling gaped at me. Dark and willowy, her dreadlocks bristling atop her head like spines, she looked unchanged from the day I'd met her in Crescent Beach. "What are you doing here?"

"Um, duh. Emergency recall signal." Apparently, Nettle could recover quickly enough for a smart comeback. "Every nest and safe house in the system has been ordered to clear out and come here. Remy and I just arrived a few minutes ago, and there's a whole heap of hatchlings wandering around downstairs. Where have *you* been?"

"Sleeping," I muttered as Garret gave a quiet chuckle and released me. "Besides, that's not what I meant. Why are you *here*?" I gestured around us. "In my room?"

"Because all the other rooms have been taken." Nettle looked annoyed at having to explain this. "And everyone has to double up. Your room was the last one to go." She glanced at Garret and arched an eyebrow. "Sorry, I didn't realize you were *busy*. Do you two need a moment?"

I frowned, but Garret touched the back of my arm before I could say anything. "No, it's all right," he stated. "Riley wanted us to find him as soon as Ember woke up. And Wes arrived a couple hours ago. We should go see what they're planning."

"Oh," I said. "Right." Back to reality. Much as I wanted to close the door and have Garret all to myself, we couldn't relax. Talon was still out there. The Night of Fang and Fire was still coming. If I knew Riley, he was doing everything he could to prepare and hunker down. "Any idea where they are?"

"Riley is outside somewhere," Nettle answered, moving to the twin bed opposite mine and tossing her sheets to the mattress. "I heard Remy say he's in the tornado shelter out back. I guess he's expecting a storm or something."

Oh, you could say that. "Come on," I told Garret. "We need to find him. I'm sure he's come up with some sort of plan by now."

Garret nodded, and we walked out of the room and down the hall, where a cacophony of voices had replaced the previous silence of the farmhouse. They grew louder as we walked downstairs, and my eyes widened in astonishment.

The living room and kitchen were filled with dragons. Hatchling dragons, all of them; teens and young adults lounged on the sofas and chairs and were seated on stools along the counter. Most of them sat clustered together, talking in furtive voices. A few had sought out isolated corners to sit by themselves, watching the other dragons with wary eyes. There were two adult humans in the room who seemed to be watching over the group, along with one older dragon that, if not a Juvenile, was pretty darn close.

For a moment, I could only stare. There were more hatchlings in this one room than I had ever seen in my life. All of them rogues who had rejected Talon, who had seen through the organization's lies and wanted to live free. And that made me both very happy and very, very nervous. I suddenly understood why Riley kept his network so scattered and isolated from each other, and why there were only a couple dragons per safe house. If St. George was to kick in the door and storm the room right now, there would be a *lot* of dead dragons before the fight was over.

"Pretty amazing, isn't it?" Garret murmured beside me, apparently thinking the same. "So this is Riley's underground. I've never seen so many rogues in one place. If the Order ever saw this…" He shook his head. "Let's hope that *never* happens."

We wove through the living room toward the front door. I spotted Remy sitting in an armchair, surrounded by a group of older teens, and waved. But the usually cheerful hatchling didn't smile back and quickly averted his eyes as we passed. I wondered what *that* meant but had no time to dwell on it as Garret pushed open the screen door and we stepped onto the porch.

"Okay," I said, gazing around. It was quieter out here than in the farmhouse. A warm breeze tugged at my hair, swirling the leaves into tiny dust devils in the yard. I was struck again by the lack of noise; it reminded me of my old school in the middle of the desert where Dante and I had grown up. Though the scenery was more interesting at least.

A chill ran up my back. I could remember the school—the cluster of long cement buildings in the center of an eternal wasteland. I remembered my brother and myself growing up: the isolation, the long hours of study, the endless boredom. But…there were blanks in my memory, places in time that skipped, entire interactions and scenes I was missing. How much had been taken from me? Weeks of memories?

Years?

I shuddered and pushed those thoughts away. My brain was still too fractured to deal with them now. Later, when everything died down and I had a chance to think, I'd try to piece together what was gone and what I remembered. "All right," I said, turning to Garret. "So, now we need to find a tornado shelter. Any idea where that would be? Maybe around the back of the house?"

"Wait." Garret stepped close and took my hand. "Before we look for Riley," he said, "I need to talk to you about something. In private."

GARRET

Ember stopped and looked at me. "Is something wrong?"

"No," I answered. "Well, maybe."

"Maybe?"

I grimaced and took a step backward, pulling her with me. "Come on," I said, glancing through the front window at the crowded living room full of dragons. "Not here. I don't want anyone else to hear this."

Looking puzzled and wary, she followed me down the steps and across the yard, toward the faded, sagging barn at the edge of the field. Bypassing the barn doors, I led her around the side of the structure, out of sight of the farmhouse. "Okay." Ember turned to me, bemused. "This is kind of mysterious—"

Her words were cut off as I stepped forward and kissed her, pressing her into the wall. The action startled her, and in truth, it surprised me, too. I hadn't been planning it; this was not my sole purpose of bringing her back here. But the opportunity was there, and I discovered I didn't want to let her go just yet. She gave a startled gasp, her hands going to my shoulders before she slid them around my neck and kissed me back.

"Sorry." Pulling away, I offered a rueful smile. "Couldn't

help myself. We sort of got interrupted, and with how crowded everything is now, I figured I would take advantage of the quiet." *Plus, we might not have much time left.*

"What's gotten into you, soldier boy?" Ember ran her fingers down the side of my face, and I closed my eyes. "Not that I mind, but this isn't like you."

I sobered. "Talon is coming," I said, destroying the tranquility with that one simple statement. Her smile faded, her eyes turning grim and dark. "We don't know how big that clone army is, but we do know that they plan to attack soon. Riley was right to call everyone here—his safe houses were on Talon's strike list, and he needs to take care of his underground. I get that. But…the Order is in danger, too. If Talon hits them now, when they're disorganized and still reeling from the Patriarch's death, they could very well wipe them out. Or cripple them so badly they'll never recover." I paused, measuring my next words, wondering how she would take it, then sighed. "I have to warn them."

"Warn them? How?" She stared at me for only a moment before she got it, and her eyes narrowed in alarm. "You're leaving, aren't you?"

"I won't ask you to come." I turned away, gazing back toward the farmhouse. "Your place is here, with Riley and the other rogues. You should be with your own, especially now. But… I have to go, Ember. I don't agree with St. George or what they do anymore, but I can't let them be wiped out." I thought of Tristan, of Lieutenant Martin, and the soldiers I had grown up with. "The Order was my home, and there are still good people there. I have to try to warn them."

I felt her presence behind me. "I know. I figured you would try to contact the Order sooner or later, no matter what Riley said." Stepping close, she took my hand, weaving her fingers through mine. "But you're crazy if you think I'm going to let you go alone."

Relief spread through me, which surprised me a little. I hadn't realized how much I'd wanted her to come, to choose me, until now. But at the same time, I didn't want to take her from her own kind unless she was absolutely certain. This was still St. George, the enemy of all dragons, and the war was far from over. "Are you sure?" I asked, turning back to her. "I don't know if they'll listen to me. I'm still the most hated person in the Order right now, and their views on dragons haven't changed. It will be dangerous, Ember. They'll probably try to kill us both."

"I know." She stepped closer, looping her arms around my neck. "And yes, I'm sure. You said so yourself—someone has to take that first step. Someone has to start trusting the other side, or this war will never be over." Green eyes peered up at me, confident and unafraid, as I slid my arms around her. "We'll change things, soldier boy, one step at a time."

The crunch of approaching footsteps caught my attention. I released Ember and turned just as a trio of teens came around the corner of the barn. They were all hatchling dragons, but at least one of them, the boy out front, was bigger and older than me. He had spiky black hair and dark eyes, and I realized that these were the dragons that had been talking to Remy earlier in the living room. Their postures were stiff, their faces hard, making me tense. I'd seen those looks before, indignant and challenging—they were looking for trouble, and I could guess who their target was.

"Can we help you?" Ember asked in a cool voice.

They ignored her, turning to glare at me with dark, hate-filled eyes. "Hey, human," the oldest dragon spat, confirming my suspicion. "Heard an interesting story about you today.

Someone said that you're really a soldier of St. George. Is that true?"

"Who told you that?" Ember demanded.

"The scrawny kid. What was his name again?" The teen shrugged. "He came with the black dragon."

Ember let out an exasperated sigh. "Dammit, Remy," she muttered. "You and your big mouth. Stop spreading rumors already."

"So, is he right?" one of the other teens demanded, glaring at me. "Were you really a dragonkiller?"

"Yes," I said simply, and their expressions darkened. One of them curled a lip with a low growl, clenching his fists. The lead dragon didn't move, but his pupils turned slitted and reptilian. "I'm not with the Order anymore," I went on, knowing these three wouldn't care. They would see only what I had been—a former dragonslayer of St. George, their greatest enemy. Nothing I said would convince them otherwise, but I still had to try. "I left that life, and St. George, behind. I'm not here to fight you."

As expected, they didn't back off, and the lead dragon took a menacing step forward, his pupils still razor-sharp. I saw the tension in his arms and shoulders and knew he was gearing up for a fight. "Murdering bastard," he growled.

"Hey," Ember snapped, and stepped forward, bristling, as well. "Didn't you hear what he said? He's not part of the Order anymore. He's on our side, so you three can just back the hell off."

"Fuck that." The leader hadn't taken his gaze from me the whole time. He took another step, and this time the others followed, crowding forward. "I had a friend once, St. George," the lead dragon said icily. "Another hatchling Cobalt freed from Talon. We were living in a safe house up north, minding our own business, not bothering no one. Until the night St. George kicked down the door."

I repressed a sigh, knowing it had to be something like that, that the now familiar story would always come back to haunt me. And nothing I could say would make it right or better. I might not have been on that raid, but I'd been on many like it. And depending on how long ago it was, I couldn't be certain I *hadn't* been on that strike, that I hadn't participated in what was coming next.

"I got out," the dragon continued, "but my friend was shot dead in front of me. Four soldiers gunned him down while he was lying on the floor, begging them to stop. A kid who hadn't hurt anyone his entire life." The teen's eyes glimmered, nostrils flaring, like he was drawing in a breath to unleash a gout of flame. "So wha'd'ya have to say to that, St. George?"

"Nothing," I said wearily. I could apologize, but it would hold no weight. It would not erase the crimes of my past, the blood on my hands or the hatred in the eyes of the dragons before me. They were not here for apologies or to be reasoned with. They wanted vengeance on St. George, to strike back against the Order that had persecuted them for years, and I was the perfect candidate.

"That's what I thought," the lead dragon growled, and drew back a fist. "Fucking bastard. This is for Isaac."

Ember's menacing growl cut through the air, making him pause. The girl hadn't moved, but her eyes glowed ominously, her pupils razor-thin against the green. "One more step, and you'll have to fight us both," she warned.

"Ember," I said quietly. "Don't." She glared at me, angry and defiant, and I shook my head. "Don't defend me," I told her. I'd known this could happen if anyone found out what I'd been.

Stepping forward, I faced the three enraged dragons and steeled myself for the barrage. "Take your shots," I told them. "Let's get this over with."

They started toward me, fists raised, just as there was a ripple of power, and a wall of scales, wings and snarling red dragon lunged between us. I stepped back, and my attackers drew up short as Ember lowered her head, opened her wings and rumbled a growl that made the air tremble.

"I said, *no*," the red dragon snarled. "I don't care what Garret says, I'm not going to stand here and watch you three pound on him just because he'll let you. You want him, you'll have to go through me."

"What the hell?" The leader sounded outraged. "You're defending him? The stinking soldier of St. George? What kind of traitor dragon are you?"

"Yes, I'm defending him!" Ember exploded. Her tail lashed, smacking the barn wall with a hollow bang. "I'm defending him because he is not your enemy. Because all he has done from the moment he left the Order is try to help rogues and other dragons. Because it doesn't matter what he tells you, you've already made up your minds not to listen." Tongues of fire snapped along her fangs, flickering brightly in the shade as the red dragon gave a furious snarl. "This is why the war never ends," she raged. "Because we refuse to let go of the past. Because we're too damn stubborn to sit down and actually talk to each other."

"*Talk?*" The lead dragon sneered, glaring at me over Ember's spines. "What's there to talk about? He's a fucking dragon-killer."

All three teens' attention was focused on Ember now, so

they didn't see Riley melt out from behind the corner and stride up behind them, his expression dangerous. Without a word, the rogue leader calmly hooked the neck of the teen leader's shirt, yanked him back and threw him face-first into the barn wall. The teen bounced off the planks, reeled back and collapsed to the ground as the other two yelped and skittered away, eyes wide.

Groaning, the stunned teen rolled over and looked up to see Riley standing over him, smiling grimly. "Kain," Riley said in a perfectly conversational voice. "What the hell do you think you're doing?"

"Cobalt! Nothing, I..." Kain staggered upright, rubbing his jaw, then turned to point at me. "He's a soldier of St. George! Did you know that? Did you know he's a dragon-killer?"

"Of course I did, moron," Riley growled, narrowing his eyes. "Considering I *brought* him here, did you think I had no idea? Yeah, he used to be part of St. George. He's also fighting for us now, and he has a lot of info on the Order that I thought would be useful in, oh, I don't know, protecting brats like you from St. George. I brought him here because I was looking at the bigger picture, and I thought everyone else could see it, too." His eyes narrowed. "But it seems that my network is nothing but a bunch of hotheaded thugs who want to pick a fight."

Kain shrank back, looking cowed, but still glaring at me with a mixture of fear and hate. "St. George killed Isaac."

"We've *all* lost someone, hatchling," Riley interrupted with a growl. "There's not one of us who hasn't been affected by the war. We've all been shot at. We've all seen friends die." His voice softened a bit, his eyes going dark. "I remember that day. I remember getting the call from your guardian. I was going to move you and Isaac to another safe house because there were rumors of St. George activity in the area. But I waited too long and didn't make the call in time. If you want to blame anyone for that, blame me."

Kain glowered, looking sullen, and Riley sighed, running a hand through his hair. "I'm not here to argue with you," he said. "I'll make this perfectly clear once, after that I'll get really annoyed. There is to be no fighting with *anyone* on this property. Human, dragon, soldier, rabid bull, I don't care. This happens again, the next one you'll be fighting is me. You got that?"

"Yeah," Kain mumbled, looking at the ground. "I got it."

Riley gave a short nod. "Then get out of here, all three of you. Save the fighting for when Talon or the Order storms the property. Move." They scrambled off, heading back toward the farmhouse. Riley shook his head.

"Idiot hatchlings," he muttered, crossing his arms. "Looks like I'm going to have to have a talk with everyone about what is and isn't allowed around here. Though you would think 'no Shifting, no flying, no beating the crap out of anyone' would be common sense by now." He glanced at Ember, still in dragon form, and raised an eyebrow. "I'm including you in that statement, Firebrand."

She snorted and raised her chin. "Not sorry."

"Color me shocked."

I took a quiet breath. "Thanks," I said, making them finally turn to look at me. "But you didn't need to do that. Either of you. I could've handled it."

"They were assholes." The red dragon's gaze narrowed, scrutinizing. "And three on one is not cool, in any world." She thumped her tail against the ground. "Besides," she continued, still glaring at me, "I know you, Garret. Would you have even fought back?"

I shrugged. "I know how to take a hit without being seriously injured. If I fought back, they might've Shifted, and then the potential for serious harm would be almost unavoidable. And I didn't want you to have to deal with that." I gave her a wry smile. "If I'm going to get beat up, I'd rather three humans do it than three dragons."

"Don't be so fucking noble, St. George," Riley said. "It makes *me* want to punch your lights out."

"Yeah, well…" Ember curled a lip, showing a flash of fangs. "I wasn't about to stand there and let them attack you. In *either* form. Anyway, there was more to this than just stopping a fight." She glanced at Riley, defiant. "Two dragons just stood up for a soldier of the Order—how often do you think that has happened? If we're going to send a message, it has to be for everyone touched by the war. We have to show that dragons and St. George can actually get along, that they don't have to fight each other." She looked at me then, emerald gaze intense. "I'm ready to try. To show the Order who we really are, face-to-face."

"What?" Riley straightened, his gaze turning suspicious and wary. "Hold on. Who's going to face the Order?" he asked, a thread of warning in his voice.

I sighed; no trying to hide it now. Though he had to find out sooner or later. "We are." I gestured to Ember and myself. "St. George needs to know about the threat that's coming for them. Ember and I are going to meet with the Order and warn them about the clones. Before it's too late for us all."

RILEY

"Are you *crazy*?"

That was my second response. I didn't voice my first, which went along the lines of *Fuck that*. Ember glared at me, ready for a fight, and St. George looked grim but determined.

"So, how long have you been planning this, St. George?" I glared at the soldier, who met my gaze calmly. "I seem to remember specifically saying we weren't going to try to warn the Order. But you were going to ignore that no matter what I said, weren't you? When did you contact them?"

"Last night." The soldier's answer was unrepentant. "I sent a message to Tristan, no one else."

"Uh-huh." I looked at the red dragon now, matching her glare. "And when were you two going to let me in on your little scheme?" I asked her. "Or was the idea to sneak off without saying anything and leave the rest of us high and dry?"

"You know we wouldn't do that, Riley," Ember returned hotly, her spines bristling. "After everything we've been through, you should know us better by now. Do you really not trust us at all?"

"Dammit, that's not it, Ember." I groaned, raking a hand over my scalp in frustration. "It's not that I don't trust you.

Or St. George, as much as it pains me to say it. It's just that I can't go with you this time." I glanced back at the farmhouse. "My first responsibility is to my underground, especially now that Talon is coming for us. I can't leave them alone, even for a day or two."

She sobered. "I know, Riley."

"No, you don't." I whirled on her and she took a step back. "You might have forgotten we're supposed to be *Sallith'tahn*, Ember, but I haven't. I've been as fucking patient and understanding as I can. I haven't said anything about you and St. George, I haven't gotten in your way and I've tried very hard not to notice whenever you two go sneaking off alone." I didn't glance at the soldier as I said this, but I could sense the brittle unease surrounding all three of us. "I've kept my promise," I told her softly. "I'm trying to be all right with this, but you're asking me to let you go into St. George territory, alone. I have to choose between the safety of my life-mate and the safety of my underground—do you realize what a sucky choice that is?"

"Life-mate," the soldier said quietly, as if something had just clicked in his head. "*Sallith'tahn* is…life-mate, in Draconic?"

I blinked at Ember. "You didn't tell him?"

We both stared at the red dragon. For a moment, Ember seemed frozen, trapped. She gazed past us with glassy green eyes, wings and muscles quivering, as if she couldn't decide whether to stay or flee.

Then she relaxed. Closing her eyes, she took a deep breath, and two thin wisps of smoke curled from her nostrils as she exhaled. When her lids opened, her eyes were dark, shadowed, but there was a steely resolve in her expression that made my heart beat faster.

"Garret." Her voice was calm, serious. St. George watched her, his expression shut into that blank soldier's mask I'd seen before. "I have to talk to Riley for a minute. It won't take long. Don't leave without me, all right?"

The soldier gave a stiff nod. He turned away, walked around the barn wall and disappeared. Ember let out a gusty sigh and bowed her head.

"I'm sorry," she whispered, almost too soft to be heard. And I didn't know if it was directed at me, St. George or us both.

Raising her head, she gazed at me with shining green eyes, setting my blood on fire. "We need to talk, Riley."

"Yeah," I agreed, crossing my arms. "We do."

"Not here." Ember raised her head and looked around, as if suddenly realizing how out in the open we were. Granted, we were in the middle of nowhere; it wasn't like a family in a minivan would come cruising around the bend and spot us. But it made me nervous all the same. "Can we find a place that's more private?"

"Just Shift back, Firebrand. No need to stay scaly to talk, right?"

"I…can't." Ember looked momentarily embarrassed. If she hadn't already been in dragon form, I suspected she would've turned as red as her scales. "They took my Viper suit while I was in Talon, so…"

I tried very hard not to grin and say the first thing that came to mind, which might've resulted in a blast of flame to my face. "What about inside the barn?" I asked instead. "No one will see us there, right?"

She nodded, and I led her into the barn, sliding open the heavy wooden door and waiting for the red dragon to pad inside. The interior of the building was spacious and cool, with high rafters and several stalls that were probably used for animals once. Thankfully, the stalls were empty now, as having a large, scaly predator waltzing in would not have gone over well. Bars of sunlight slanted through the wooden planks, gleaming along Ember's scales as she stalked to the middle of the barn and turned to face me.

"All right," I said, walking up to her. "We're alone. Start talking, Firebrand."

She shook her head. "I need you to do something for me first, Riley."

"What's that?"

"I need you to Shift. Right here."

Surprised, I frowned at her. "Why?"

"Because I…I need to say this to Cobalt. That's the other reason I asked to go into the barn. I want us both to be ourselves, with no interruptions. Please."

I sighed. "All right," I said, even as Cobalt surged up with excitement. "If that's what you want. Though I do have to point out, a barn full of dry straw might not be the best place for this. Let's try to remember that everything here is very flammable."

I stripped out of my shirt, tossing it to one of the hay bales, feeling cool air hit my bare skin. As I started unbuckling my belt, Ember turned away, hiding her head under her wing. I smiled at her bashfulness.

"Still hanging on to that human modesty, Firebrand?" I asked as my jeans joined the T-shirt on the hay bale. "You can look, you know. I don't mind."

Her tail thumped the ground, and she didn't peek up from the curtain of her wing. "Will you just hurry up and Shift?" she growled. I might have teased her some more, but the sudden desire to be in my real form was too great to ignore.

I relaxed, and Cobalt reared up with a growl of impatience, bursting through my skin. Wings and tail uncurled, feeling like they'd been crushed and flattened for far too long, and the rush of fire through my veins made the air around me shimmer with heat. Settling on all fours, talons digging into the soft wood, I raised my head and looked for Ember.

Ember met my gaze, eyes dilating as we stared at each other, both in our real forms at last. The heat in my veins didn't die down but flared higher, consuming and powerful. Everything faded away, until she was the only thing I could see. I was filled with the urge to lope forward, cover the space between us in a few strides and pounce on the red dragon, driving us both to the ground. Where wings and tails and breath would intertwine in the hay, and our combined heat would rise up and spread through our veins until it consumed us both.

Swallowing a growl, I controlled my basest instincts and stalked forward, forcing myself to move slowly and not bound over the straw to get to her. "All right," I said when I was about a lunge away. "Here we are. What was so important that you needed to tell me like this?"

"Cobalt." She paused, as if gathering her courage. For a moment, I sensed a terrible struggle within; her talons sank into the floor planks as if she were teetering on the edge of something huge and had to force herself to go on. "I need you…to let me go."

I snorted. "I've never been able to stop you, Firebrand," I told her. "I knew St. George would probably try to warn the Order sooner or later. I just wish you weren't going with him."

"No." Her voice was a whisper. "That's not what I meant." She looked away, her eyes distant and shadowed. "I wasn't talking about what happened with me and Garret today. It's more than that. I mean…" She hesitated, not meeting my gaze, then took a deep breath. "Cobalt, I don't want you to wait for me any longer. I don't… I don't want to be your *Sallith'tahn*."

For a moment, the world seemed to stop. I stared at her, the last statement echoing all the way to my soul. "What?" I finally asked, and my voice sounded hollow in my ears. Ember closed her eyes.

"We were wrong," she said, and though the words trembled, her expression was firm. Her eyes opened, piercing and intense, gazing up at me. "Talon was wrong. Dragons *can* love. We are quite capable of every emotion the organization has tried to stomp out. But Talon has told us we can't feel human emotion for so long it's become truth. And we've become sort of fractured because of it.

"I love Garret," Ember said quietly. With a start, I realized I had never heard those words from her in dragon form. "I know we're supposed to be life-mates, Cobalt, and I'm so sorry, but I don't…" She faltered again, looking at the ground. "I don't…"

"You don't love me," I finished for her, and she flinched as if I'd struck a physical blow. "I never asked you to, Ember."

"I know," she murmured. "But we can't move on, any of us, with the *Sallith'tahn* hanging over our heads. I need you to let me go, Cobalt. I don't want you to be waiting for Garret to die so we can be together. That's not fair, to you or to me."

"I'm a dragon, Firebrand," I said flatly, trying not to let the anguish I was feeling bubble to the surface. "A human lifespan is nothing. I can be patient."

She shook her head. "I don't want you to," she said, a little more forcefully. "I don't want to be with someone because of instinct."

I growled, feeling desperation rise up to swirl with the despair. "You said dragons can love like humans, that it's a part of us. Well, so is the *Sallith'tahn*. If you deny it, you're denying a part of who you are."

"Cobalt." Ember stepped forward, coming very close. I looked down and saw my reflection in her brilliant green eyes, felt the heat pulsing between us. She held my gaze a moment, then asked, very softly, "Do you love me?"

"I…" Taken aback, I staggered away from her, mind spinning. She waited, her gaze never leaving mine. "That's not something you can just drop on me, Firebrand."

"I know." Ember's voice was gentle. "But…I need more than the *Sallith'tahn*, Cobalt. If I have to choose between instinct and love, I'm going to go with love. That's my choice, and I can't be with someone who can't return my feelings. So, I have to know. For both our sakes. Do you love me?"

"I…I…don't know," I stammered. "That's not something I have much experience with, Ember. Hell, I spent my whole life thinking that dragons *can't* feel that human crap. That it wasn't something we could do." I sighed, putting a talon over my eyes, resisting the urge to dig my claws into my skull. "I don't know what you want from me," I growled. "I would give you everything, but I don't know if I can… feel that way." Raising my head, I glared at her. "Just because you say dragons can love doesn't mean I know what the fuck it's supposed to feel like. Is wanting to be with you not enough? Is accepting you as my *Sallith'tahn*, the dragon I'm supposed to be with for the rest of my life, different than the human's idea of love? I don't know. Hell, maybe this is love, after all. Maybe…" I faltered and had to sit down for a moment. "Maybe I do."

Ember squeezed her eyes shut. "When you're sure," she whispered, her voice strangely thick, like she was holding back tears, "when you figure it out, come find me again. But for now, please accept that I love Garret, and I don't want the *Sallith'tahn* coming between us." Opening her eyes, she met my gaze without hesitation or doubt. "I want you to move on, Riley," she said. "Find someone else who is worthy of you. Who can give you their whole heart. You deserve it. And I…can't give you that. I'm sorry."

Numb, I took a step back. I thought I would be furious, maybe homicidal. I thought I would want to find a certain human, blast him to cinders and scatter his remains across a hundred acres of nothing. I thought I might want to snarl profanities at Ember, the soldier and the whole damn world. But right then, I just felt hollow. Empty. Like someone had carved a hole in my stomach and there was nothing left but a vast, yawning pit.

Ember, watching me closely, swallowed hard at my silence. "Riley…"

"Is that all?" My voice came out flat, and she winced. "Are we done here?"

Ember bowed her head. "Yeah," she whispered. "I guess we are."

Spinning around, I strode back to where I'd left my clothes on the hay bales by the door. Not caring what Ember thought at the moment, I Shifted to human form and began pulling them on, feeling the dragon's sorrowful gaze on my back. And though the vindictive side of me rejoiced at her grief, wanting her to feel the same pain, I knew I couldn't leave it like this. If she went into St. George territory with the soldier and never returned, the guilt would kill me.

After drawing my shirt over my head, I paused, then addressed her over my shoulder, not quite able to look her in the eye. "Be careful out there," I told her softly. "I know you can handle yourself, and you don't need me, but this is still St. George we're talking about. Come back safe, Ember."

"I will."

There was more I wanted to say, questions I wanted to ask, arguments and protests wanting to burst forth, but it didn't seem to matter now. I stepped through the frame into the late-afternoon sun and closed the door behind me, hearing the hollow thump echo all the way to my soul.

I've lost her.

I slumped against the wall, feeling numb inside and out. Ember was gone. She had truly chosen the soldier, to the point that even the life-mate bond meant nothing to her. How she could resist the pull of the *Sallith'tahn* was a mystery; I had no idea how she could just ignore that instinctive knowledge that we were supposed to be together.

But she had. And she'd made it perfectly clear where we stood now. Just being with the soldier wasn't enough, it seemed. She wanted to sever the *Sallith'tahn* completely. I was willing to wait for her, to let her be human until she realized how very short their lives truly were, but even that wasn't enough.

Move on, she'd told me. As if I could. As if this wouldn't consume me from the inside, tear me to pieces little by little every time I saw her.

No. With a mental shake, I pushed myself off the door, hardening my emotions. I couldn't fall apart now. Over a dozen hatchling dragons still waited for me beyond the yard.

Trusting me to keep them safe from the massive storm brewing on the horizon. Talon was coming for us. I had lost my *Sallith'tahn*, but I was still the leader of this resistance, still responsible for dozens of innocent lives. I wouldn't fail them.

So be it.

Goodbye, Ember. I stepped away from the barn and forced myself to move, to walk toward the farmhouse without looking back. *Maybe someday, when this war is over and the soldier is gone, you'll look to me again. And maybe...I can learn to love like a human, as well. But not now.* Raising my head, I walked a little faster. *I've been distracted for too long. Talon is coming. I have to look out for my own now, and make sure that, whatever the organization throws at us, we're still alive at the end of it.*

EMBER

In the cool darkness of the barn, I listened to Riley walk away. Listened to his footsteps fade into silence and curled my talons into the wood to stop myself from going after him.

I staggered across the floor to sink down in the corner, curl into a ball and put my head under my wing, shutting out the world as the realization stabbed me like a knife.

Cobalt is gone.

I started to shake. Hot tears welled in my eyes, spilling over to run down my scales, and I let them come. I didn't regret my decision. It had to be done; Riley deserved to be with someone who could give themselves to him completely, who wasn't in love with someone else. And I couldn't truly be with Garret until this *Sallith'tahn* issue was finally put to rest. I knew I had done the right thing, for all of us.

But I could still feel the awful ache of loss inside, a gnawing emptiness that hollowed me out, making me feel empty and cold. I loved Garret with everything I had, but I couldn't deny that it was Cobalt who made my dragon side stir and come to life. He understood me in a way a human never could. He shared my love of flying, my fascination with shiny things and the heat surging within that sometimes felt like it could consume me. Things only a dragon could comprehend.

And now, he was gone. I had let him go, so we both could be free. But that didn't mean it hadn't killed me to do it. To see the look on his face, stunned and devastated, when I said I didn't want to be his *Sallith'tahn* any longer. It had taken everything I had to keep talking, to force myself to say those words. A few minutes of falling apart where no one could see it didn't seem like too much to ask.

After several minutes, I heard the barn door open and close, and quiet footsteps, not Riley's, rustled across the straw. Instinctively, I curled even more tightly around myself, pressing tail and wings close to my body. I didn't know if I could face *him* right now, either. I hadn't told him about the *Sallith'tahn*, what it meant, why Cobalt was supposed to be my life-mate. I'd meant to, of course. There just hadn't been a good time.

"Ember." His voice was calm, but it still made me wince. His footsteps stopped right beside me, close enough to touch. "I brought you a change of clothes."

Warmth fluttered through my stomach. Even angry, he was still thinking of me, knowing I didn't have my Viper suit anymore. Or maybe he just wanted to get on the road as soon as possible, and I was slowing him down. Either way, I needed to Shift, but I wasn't going to do it with Garret standing there.

"That's fine," I said from beneath my wing. "Just leave them on the ground. I'll change back in a minute and meet you outside."

I waited for his footsteps to walk away, but he didn't move. "Are you all right?" he asked, surprising me. It wasn't a routine question; he seemed genuinely concerned. Or maybe I was just hoping he was.

"Yeah," I mumbled. "I'm okay." *I just drove off my*

Sallith'tahn, my life-mate. Cobalt might never speak to me again. And I don't know how angry you are with me for not telling you. "I'm sorry, Garret," I said, grateful of the wing barrier between us, flimsy as it was. I didn't want to see his eyes and whatever anger, disgust or sorrow lay within. "I meant to tell you earlier, and I know it's an awful way to hear it now but…" I took a quick breath. "There's this thing called the *Sallith'tahn*. It's the Draconic word for life-mate, though you already know that." Garret didn't say anything, and I didn't dare peek up to see what he was thinking. "It's not something we choose, or initiate ourselves," I went on. "It just happens. But when a dragon finds its *Sallith'tahn*, they're supposed to be together for life. Or that's how it always was, before Talon, anyway.

"But," I went on quickly, "I don't want to be with someone because instinct says I should. I want to choose who I want to be with. And I…I don't love Riley." For some reason, my voice broke, and fresh tears trickled down my scales at that statement, but I forced myself to say it. To really acknowledge the truth, to myself as much as anyone else. Riley was a fellow dragon, a best friend and my *Sallith'tahn*. We would always be connected, and I would always consider him one of the most important people in my life. But I didn't love him. Not like I loved Garret.

"So," I finished. "That's the *Sallith'tahn*. That's the thing between me and Cobalt. What I've been feeling…ever since I met him, really. It's messed all of us up for a long time, but I finally told Riley…that I wanted to be with you." Still no answer from the human above me, and I closed my eyes. "I love you, Garret," I whispered, clenching my talons in the straw, "but I don't know if the *Sallith'tahn* will ever go away. If it doesn't, I might always feel that connection toward Cobalt. I don't know if you can accept that, but…it had to be said. I don't want any more secrets between us."

There was a moment of hesitation, and I wondered if he was going to walk away. If this life-mate thing was too weird for him to handle.

With a rustle of straw, the soldier knelt at my side. His hand came to rest lightly on my shoulder, sending a ripple of current through my whole body. "Is that why you're hiding from me?" he asked in a soft voice.

"I'm not hiding," I answered, still not uncurling.

He tapped a finger gently against my wing. "So, you're telling me that you're a dragon, and you might feel dragony things from time to time."

I lifted my wing a bit and peeked up at him. He gazed back, not quite smiling, but there were no hints of anger, disgust or jealousy on his face. Hope fluttered, and I uncurled a little more, folding my wing to my back again. "So, you're okay with this?"

"I wouldn't say I'm *happy* about it," Garret answered calmly. His fingers gently traced a wingtip, making me shiver. "But I knew there was something between you and Riley that I didn't understand. Something only another dragon would get. I'd already accepted that when I made my decision to stay." His gaze rose to mine, and a resigned smile finally tugged at his lips. "You can't be completely in love with a dragon and expect anything to be normal."

The heaviness weighing me down vanished, and warmth spread through my whole body. I sat up, and Garret put a hand on my neck, his gaze never leaving mine. "I'm here, Ember," he said. "Dragon or human, it doesn't matter to me. Whatever form you're in, and whatever comes of it, I'm not going anywhere."

"Dammit, Garret." My eyes watered again, and I blinked hard. "Don't say things like that when I can't kiss you without biting your lips off."

This time, his smile seemed to banish the shadows from the barn. He rose, brushing straw from his jeans, and I stood, as well. Things were far from okay, and the situation with Cobalt was an open wound on my heart, but he was free. And Garret had chosen to stay. Maybe now the three of us could finally move forward. And hope that time would heal the terrible scars we gave each other.

"Tristan has a place for us to meet," Garret said, returning to the task at hand. "It's halfway between here and my old chapterhouse, not too far, but we'll have to move fast. Are you ready to go?"

I nodded. "I'll meet you outside."

DANTE

"Hello, Mr. Hill. We've been expecting you."

A table of about fifteen dragons looked up at me as I entered the room. All older than me. All important. Some I recognized instantly. Mr. Roth, the Chief Basilisk, Mace, Lilith. Dr. Olsen and his team were present, as well, and the scientist bowed his head as I passed, approaching the table.

Fifteen sets of ancient dragon eyes watched as I took my place beside Mr. Roth. A few weeks ago, I would have been nervous, maybe even terrified, to be facing this many older dragons on my own. But that was before I knew who I was. Before I had the power of the Elder Wyrm herself at my disposal. I was not just some nameless hatchling; I was the heir to Talon, the son of the most powerful dragon in the world. No one here would dare challenge me.

Excitement and elation fluttered within. I was close. So close to finally achieving my dream. Just one more step to the top, and freedom. Everything I wanted was almost in my grasp. There was just one last thing I had to accomplish.

An old dragon rose from his seat, scarred and grizzled with a glass eye that glinted in the dim light overhead. "The Night of Fang and Fire is nearly upon us," he said in a low, gravelly voice. "It is time to strike the final blow against Talon's enemies and wipe them out for good. Commanders..." He gazed around the table. "You know why you are here. Are there any final questions before we begin?"

"Sir." I rose from my seat. "If I may?"

"Mr. Hill." The old dragon blinked his one good eye and stared at me. Clearly, he was surprised, and maybe a little annoyed, to have his meeting interrupted. But he only bowed his head and motioned for me to go on.

"I have a request, sir," I said calmly. "If the targets have not already been determined, I would like to be in charge of leading the attack against the Order's Western chapterhouse in the United States."

"The Western chapterhouse," the dragon repeated. "I don't see why not, but is there a particular reason you want that target, Mr. Hill?"

"Yes," I replied simply. "There is." He waited for me to go on and, when I didn't, gave a quiet huff.

"Such as?"

"My reasons are my own, sir," I said as politely as I could. He grunted, obviously not pleased but not wanting to argue with me, as I'd suspected. "But this chapterhouse has given me, and Talon, a lot of grief in the past. Suffice to say, I want to make certain it's destroyed."

GARRET

"Ember." I reached over and gently shook the girl beside me. "We're here."

She stirred and sat up in the passenger seat, taking a moment to scan her surroundings. It had been a long drive from the lone farmhouse in the middle of nowhere, and the scenery had certainly changed. Now large buildings, intersections and traffic replaced endless fields and open sky, unusual for the farmlands of Idaho but not for a city like Reno, Nevada. It was late evening, and the sun had nearly set behind the distant looming mountains. Headlights lit the roads and streets, horns blared and swarms of people meandered down the sidewalks.

I repressed a sigh. Another large, crowded city. I missed the brief respite of the farm; despite the many noisy teen dragons sharing the house, you could still walk outside and hear nothing but birds, insects and the wind in the trees. It reminded me of my old chapterhouse, isolated deep in the Mohave Desert, a sanctuary from the rest of the world.

"What time is it?" Ember asked, turning back to me.

"Eighteen forty-five," I answered, and at her slightly bewildered look, added, "Quarter to seven."

She nodded and gazed through the windshield at the restaurant on the edge of the parking lot. "He's meeting us at seven-thirty, right?"

"Yes," I answered. "Though knowing Tristan, he's probably already here." I'd contacted my former partner almost immediately after arriving at the farmhouse, though I hadn't known whether I'd hear from him again. After what had happened with the Patriarch, I wouldn't blame him if he wanted nothing to do with me. Once I'd sent the message, I'd wondered if Tristan himself was all right. I might have defeated the Patriarch in battle and destabilized St. George, but from what I'd heard from Ember, it was Tristan himself who had shot and killed the leader of the Order. He wouldn't be punished for it; I knew that at least. The Patriarch had broken the rules of the duel, confirming his guilt, and Tristan had acted accordingly. But it was still a heavy weight to bear, executing the man the Order revered above all others.

To my surprise, he'd responded within minutes, insisting we meet face-to-face. Reno was a good halfway point, and an unassuming restaurant, surrounded by witnesses, was a good spot for both of us to know we weren't being set up. We were still enemies, on opposite sides of the war, and I couldn't drop my guard.

Ember checked the pistol strapped to her waist, pulled her shirt down to conceal the holster and glanced at me. "Ready?"

I nodded. "Stay alert," I told her. "I know you're aware of what we're up against, but Tristan is still part of the Order. We can't expect him not to turn on us."

We walked across the parking lot together and ducked into the restaurant. Inside, the hostess smiled brightly as we approached, not noticing the way we both scanned the room, searching for enemies.

"Good evening," she greeted us as we stepped up to the podium. "Two?"

I shook my head. "We're supposed to be meeting someone here," I told her. "St. Anthony?"

"Ah, yes. He told us you were coming. Right this way, please."

She led us to a corner booth, gesturing to the seats with a bright, "Enjoy your meal," before walking away. I continued to stand, feeling Ember go rigid beside me. For the man in the booth, gazing calmly up at us with his hands folded on the table, was not Tristan.

"Hello, Sebastian," Lieutenant Gabriel Martin said, and indicated the seat across from him. "Please, sit down."

I didn't. I tensed and quickly glanced around the room for anyone who could be a soldier of St. George. Lieutenant Martin sighed.

"Relax, Sebastian. I'm alone. There's no one here but me, and no one in the Order knows where I've gone. Now, please…" He gestured to the booth again, giving me a tight smile. "Sit down. You and your dragon are in no danger, at least not today."

Warily, we did as he asked, sliding into the seat across from him. "Where's Tristan?" I asked, and his face darkened.

"Back at the barracks. He won't be joining us." Martin paused as a waitress arrived to take our drink order. After she left, he took a sip of his water and continued in a grim voice. "Sebastian, you should know that after the incident with the Patriarch, St. Anthony was taken into custody. He admitted to meeting with you outside of St. George and to conspiring against the Patriarch, both treasonous offenses as I'm sure you know. There were some in the Order who called for his execution for the part he played in aiding you that night."

My stomach dropped. I knew Tristan had taken a huge risk in helping us, that St. George could see him as a cocon-spirator of the whole event. I'd hoped his actions would be overlooked in the general chaos; the last thing I'd wanted was for my former partner to be punished, too.

"Fortunately," Martin went on, "or unfortunately, de-pending on how you look at it, the Order is in a bit of up-heaval at the moment. With all the disorder and confusion, no one has gotten around to organizing a trial. Or, at least, they have bigger issues to worry about. And I have no in-tention of reminding them anytime soon.

"But," he went on as I relaxed a bit, "when the duel ended and you vanished with those dragons, I suspected we hadn't heard the last from you, Sebastian. And I knew if you were to contact the Order again, it would be through St. An-thony. I've taken it upon myself to keep him under constant surveillance, so that when you resurfaced, I would know."

"Then it was you who answered me yesterday," I said. "You set up this meeting, not Tristan."

"That I did."

"Why?"

Martin didn't answer right away. He stared down at the table with his fingers steepled in front of him, his eyes dark.

"You're an agent of change, Sebastian," he said at last. "For good or ill, events happen around you that no one can predict. It's been that way since you first came to the Acad-emy. Before that, even. Since the day Lucas found you in the Talon compound and took you in as a soldier for the Order. I've watched you through the years, and I've seen it happen time and time again. Whenever something impor-tant happens, something that could shake the very founda-tions of everything we know, you are always in the middle of it. Now the Patriarch is dead, the Order is in turmoil and Talon grows ever stronger because of it." He glanced at Ember, sitting silently beside me, and his jaw tightened. "I should kill you, Sebastian," he went on, making me cringe inside. "For turning your back on the Order and everything it stands for. You betrayed your brothers, and you betrayed me. But worst of all…" His eyes narrowed. "You betrayed Lucas, the man who saved you, who brought you to us and taught you everything you know. He would be ashamed if he could see you now."

I kept the pain from my face, but if he'd stabbed me with a knife, I doubted it would have hurt as much as those words did right then. I thought of my mentor, remembering his words, the way he'd always pushed me to do better, to try harder. To be the best. The perfect soldier. Lucas Benedict would accept nothing less. After he'd been killed in battle, I'd thrown myself into training with a single-minded determination to become that perfect soldier. If it was Benedict sitting across from me now, and not Gabriel Martin, would my mission be the same? Would *I* still be the same?

"But," Martin went on with a sigh, "you were also the one who discovered the truth. You brought this conspiracy to light, you and your dragons. And regardless of what St. George believes, you risked much to bring it to the Order's attention. I will not forgive what you've done, but it would be foolish of me not to hear you out." His voice turned cold and hard, and his eyes glinted as he spared the girl beside me a glare of loathing. "Even if I must sit down to dinner with a demon."

Ember's lips thinned, but she didn't say anything. She knew nothing she said would change Martin's disposition toward her. She was a dragon, and so, in his eyes, she was a monster.

But he didn't know her at all. He'd never seen her bravery, her kindness and determination. He'd never seen her risk her life for someone, be it human or dragon, because all life was precious to her. He didn't know how much she hated the endless fighting and killing and longed for the day when the war would be over. Even with Ember sitting right across from him, all he saw was a dragon.

But he was still here, talking to us. Sitting across from his sworn enemy and having a conversation, instead of trying to slaughter it outright. It was a start, I thought. We wouldn't be able to end the war overnight, but at least it was a step in the right direction.

"So." Martin folded his hands before him again. "Talk, Sebastian. You risked contact with St. Anthony for a reason. I assume it was for something important." His expression darkened. "Though, I will warn you both, I'm not sure what you think the Order can do, now that that the Patriarch is gone."

"Why?" asked Ember, the first thing she'd said since meeting Martin. He gave her a hard look, but answered calmly.

"When Sebastian exposed the Patriarch's involvement with Talon, it threw the Order into chaos. His death has fractured it even more. There is a divide within St. George, between those who accept that the Patriarch was working with the dragons, and those who believe he was set up. Chapterhouses have called their soldiers back and are operating independently from each other. Everyone is outraged, but no one knows what to do or who to trust." Martin's gaze narrowed. "It's quite the mess you left us, Sebastian," he said. "So I hope that, whatever news you're about to tell me, you don't expect the Order to respond in haste. Or at all."

Ember released a slow breath. "Talon was expecting this,"

she said, her voice full of quiet horror. "They were probably planning to expose the Patriarch themselves, and we just hurried things along."

I was thinking the same, and the sick feeling in my gut grew stronger. With the Order so fractured and disorganized, it was the perfect time for an attack. Unintentional or not, we might have given Talon the exact opening they needed. Martin's jaw tightened, his gaze sharp as it flicked between us.

"I assume this is about Talon, then." It wasn't a question.

I nodded. "Sir," I said, looking up at him. "You have to contact the Order. We came here with a warning—Talon is going to attack St. George. We don't know when, but it's going to be very soon."

Martin straightened. "An attack?" he said. "On St. George soil? Where is it taking place?" he asked, leaning forward. "Which chapterhouse?"

"All of them," Ember said, making his brows rise. "Every chapterhouse, every Order sanctuary around the world, is going to be hit on the same night. At the same time."

"That's impossible," Martin said flatly. "Talon doesn't have the numbers for that kind of operation. Especially since we've taken out more dragons in the past three years than we ever have before."

"Most of those dragons weren't part of Talon," I said, feeling the anger rise up from the girl beside me. "They were rogues, deserters who left the organization and went into hiding. Or dragons who never belonged to Talon at all. All you've been doing is taking out Talon's enemies, the dragons they've wanted out of the way."

"Regardless." Martin leaned back, seemingly unconcerned. "It doesn't matter if these 'rogues' were part of the organi-

zation or not. Talon still does not have the manpower for a
full-scale assault on the Order."

"They do now," Ember broke in. "They have an army of
dragons. And if you don't take this seriously, they're going
to hit St. George when no one is prepared for it, and they're
going to wipe you out."

He gave her a long, scrutinizing look. "And how would
this be a bad thing for you, dragon?" he asked in a quiet
voice. "Sebastian I can understand. He has been twisted and
corrupted by the enemy, but in his heart, the loyalty to the
cause and his former brothers in St. George cannot be erased
so quickly. But you…" His voice turned cold. "You are a
dragon, and we are at war. If the Order falls, your kind will
be free to do what you wish. Talon will win. Why would you
try to prevent the complete destruction of your enemies?"

"Because some of us don't want that," Ember said firmly.
"I swear, you Order types only hear what you want to hear.
Will you please just *listen* to what I'm saying? I am telling
you that I'm not a part of Talon. I don't want any more killing. I have no desire or intention to enslave anyone or take
over the world. But if you don't warn the rest of the Order
about this attack, Talon will kill you all. And that would be
disastrous for everyone, my kind included."

"So you say." Martin still didn't sound convinced. "That
does not tell me how Talon has acquired an army large
enough to take out the Order in one night."

"Talon is cloning dragons," I said flatly. "That's how
they've acquired their army—they've grown them from the
blood and DNA of other dragons. Numbers don't matter
anymore, because they can just make more of them."

For the first time, Martin seemed taken aback. His skin
paled, and he stared at me with a mix of disbelief and hor-

ror. "Cloning dragons?" he repeated. "Are you very sure about this?"

I nodded. "We've seen them firsthand. They're not like the others. These dragons have been bred for war and fighting and nothing else. They're not meant to be human, or to blend in with the rest of the population. They're throwaway soldiers that don't care if they live or die."

"How many?"

"We don't know exactly," Ember replied. "But we can assume it's enough to take on St. George. Especially now that the Order is so disjointed." She shivered a little, her voice turning grave. "You've never seen dragons like this—they've been programmed by the Talon scientists for obedience, and now they're like machines. No fear, no self-preservation instinct. They won't break or run away, even if most of them are slaughtered—they'll just keep coming until whatever they're sent to kill is completely destroyed."

"So you have to warn the rest of the Order," I repeated. "Warn them that Talon is getting ready to attack, and they need to prepare themselves for a full-scale invasion. This assault is supposed to be soon, in a day or two at most. The chapterhouses can't stand alone—they're going to need support from the rest of St. George if they want to survive."

Martin's face was pale now, and he nodded. "I'll try, Sebastian," he said. "I'll make it my top priority to warn the rest of the Order." His brow furrowed, and he shook his head. "But because of the infighting, and because the chapterhouses are operating individually now, it's become difficult to send such a widespread message. Even if I can, I'm not certain they will listen. If the warning comes from me, it will be subject to immediate suspicion."

"You?" asked Ember. "Why?"

"Because of my association with Sebastian and my role in the fate of the Patriarch," Martin replied. "I spoke for Sebastian at the assembly. I urged the officers to listen to what he had to say. I chose to believe a traitor and dragon convert over my own Patriarch. And I was one of the seconds at the duel. I watched St. Anthony execute the leader of St. George and did nothing to stop it." His eyes darkened, a flicker of emotion crossing his face, too fast to distinguish. "Because of this, there are those within the Order who believe I am just as guilty as Sebastian. As such, they will question my motives. They will want to know where I received my information, and if it becomes known that I met with Sebastian and one of his dragon comrades, they will certainly call for a trial, if not my execution."

"But you're warning them about an attack from Talon," Ember said, aghast. "Why should it matter where the information came from? The Order should be pulling together to defend themselves, not fighting about who met with whom."

I sighed. "Because St. George doesn't trust anything that comes from Talon," I said, and Martin nodded. "Because all dragons are the same to them, and anything that comes from Talon is tainted, corrupted or a trap. They'll never believe that a dragon, or anyone who sympathizes with them, wants to help the Order of St. George."

"Some might believe," Martin said slowly. "If they're warned about an impending attack from Talon, some in the Order might take the necessary steps to defend their chapterhouse. But as a whole, it will take a miracle to pull St. George together now. I only hope we can survive the coming assault." That stark black gaze met mine, his expression grim. "Is that all you wished to tell me, Sebastian?"

"Yes," I answered numbly. There were other things I

wanted to know, about St. George, and Martin, and my former brothers. But this was not the time for questions, for Martin to explain. "That was all, sir."

Martin nodded and rose. "Then if you'll excuse me," he said, tossing a bill to the table and stepping away. "I must return to the Order. There is a message that needs to be sent tonight. Sebastian…" He gave me a brief, unreadable look. "I don't know why you betrayed us," he said, "or why you choose to stay with the lizards, but it appears you are still an important player in this struggle, no matter which side you are on. You affect the events around you, whether you mean to or not." His gaze sharpened. "I wonder if you know what it is you are truly fighting for."

I held his gaze. "I know what I'm fighting for, sir," I said quietly. "I know which side I'm on, and it's not for Talon or St. George. It's for change. We've been at war for so long we can't see the truth that's right in front of us." I felt Ember's eyes on me, as well, and deliberately reached over, placing a hand atop hers. "They don't have to be our enemies. If the Order would give them a chance, and not see them as demons, maybe this fighting can finally come to an end."

Martin didn't say anything. He stood there, brow furrowed, as if fighting a silent battle within. Finally, he exhaled, and his shoulders slumped, his next words barely audible.

"Come back with me, Sebastian."

I started, gazing at him in shock. "What?"

"I want you with us," Martin continued. "Back at the base. You're a damn fine soldier, even if you're not fighting on our side. And you know these—" he paused; I suspected he was going to say *things* but changed his mind at the last minute "—dragons better than anyone else. I want you to explain what is happening to the rest of the troops, give them the full story, so they really know what's coming."

"They won't believe me, sir. They're likely to shoot me on sight if I came back."

"No, they won't," Martin replied. "I'll be there. They don't have to believe—they just have to follow orders. But I want you to explain it, Sebastian. You know the dragons. Your presence will give us a better chance in combating them. And the men know you. As a traitor, yes, but there isn't a trooper there who hasn't heard of the Perfect Soldier. If you are with us, I feel we stand more of a chance against Talon."

I sat motionless, a heavy weight seeming to settle over me. After Benedict died when I was just eleven, Martin had taken me under his wing. He hadn't been the mentor Benedict had, but he had made sure I was excelling, doing my best at the Academy. I hadn't seen him much while I was at school, but whenever our paths had crossed, he'd made certain to talk to me for a few minutes, inquiring about my classes and training, making sure I had everything I needed. He had been another solid, commanding presence in my life at St. George, another reason I pushed myself so hard to become the best. His disappointment in me, in what I had become, was a constant ache that gnawed at me from the inside. But knowing what was coming, that this might be the last time I would see him, was even worse.

I knew I should help my former brothers. I wanted to stand with them again—not to eliminate dragons, but to defend my old home from the army that would tear it apart. Martin, Tristan, all the soldiers I had grown up with…it made me sick, knowing they might die. Martin was right; I was still loyal, if not to St. George's ideals, then to the people who had been my family once. They didn't know what was coming. I didn't want to abandon them to Talon and its soulless dragon army.

But I had another family now. Another group who had my loyalty and my friendship, and one girl in particular who had more than that. Much as I wanted to accept Martin's offer, to return to St. George as a voice for dragonkind, there was no way I would leave Ember behind.

"I'm sorry, sir," I murmured, and Martin's jaw tightened. "But I can't go back with you. The Order isn't the only one Talon intends to wipe out. My place is here."

Martin's voice was cold. "With the dragons."

"Yes."

"I see." Martin drew back, his posture stiff as he prepared to leave. "If that's your decision, then goodbye, Sebastian."

"Lieutenant," Ember said before he could spin on a heel and stride away. "Wait. Just a moment, please."

Puzzled, I turned to her. She wasn't looking at either of us but stared at her hands on the tabletop, her eyes dark and conflicted. Concerned, I brushed her leg, which made her close her eyes. "Ember? Are you all right?"

"Garret…" She took a quiet breath, opened her eyes and turned to face me. There was something new in her gaze now, a somber determination that almost overshadowed the fear and reluctance. "You should go with him," she said, making my stomach drop. "Go back to the Order and tell them about us, about the rogues and the dragons outside of Talon. They'll listen to you."

"No." Desperation flickered, and I shook my head. "What about Riley and everyone else? Talon is coming for them, too."

"We'll join you," Ember replied firmly. "I'll go back and convince Riley that we need to face Talon together. All of us. Rogues and St. George alike, fighting as one. It's the only way we can stand against that army."

Ember gripped my arm, her gaze intense. "So you have to go back and tell them we're coming, Garret. Make sure they know we're there to help. And I'll try to gather as many on our side as I can. Provided St. George doesn't kill us on the spot." She looked up at Martin. "If a group of dragons arrives at the gates of the Western chapterhouse to join you in fighting off Talon, can you promise your soldiers won't shoot them full of holes as soon as they see them?"

Martin looked stunned. "Dragons helping the Order?" he repeated, as if the very idea was impossible. "It would never stand. The rest of St. George——"

"Is going to be attacked by Talon soon," Ember interrupted. "Along with every dragon not aligned with the organization. We're not helping you—we're joining forces so that both our sides aren't completely wiped out." She shook her head. "Don't tell me you don't need our help. You're alone, Lieutenant. St. George has been broken. You need allies, otherwise Talon is going to win."

"Ember..." I began, and she turned on me, her gaze intent.

"No, Garret," she said firmly. "We have to do this. We can't hide anymore. Talon is just going to keep coming. If they destroy the Order, the rest of us will be next."

"I know," I said, taking her hand. "I'm not arguing. I'll go back to St. George, and I'll tell them everything I know. Everything I've learned while I've been with you and the rogues. And hopefully, they'll listen to me this time. But..." I trapped her hand in both of mine, gazing into her eyes. "I don't know if you can get Riley to agree. Think of what you're asking him to do. If our plan is to fight that army, not all of us are going to make it, Ember. Some of us are going to be killed. You have to accept that." Her face tightened, and I squeezed her hand. "You can be sure Riley knows that. And you've seen how protective he is when it comes to his underground. What if you can't convince him to let the hatchlings fight? We can't force any of them into battle, and they've all been hunted by St. George, or have seen friends die. Like Kain. What if they refuse to help the Order?"

"Then I'll come alone," Ember replied. "And I'll help you fight. I'm not leaving you, Garret." She held my gaze, green eyes flashing. "I won't let you face Talon without me. Even if no one else comes, you'll have at least one dragon fighting at your side, I promise."

Martin cleared his throat, sounding uncomfortable. "If we're going to leave, Sebastian, we should go now," he said. "It seems as though there is not much time, and we have a lot of work to do."

"Yes, sir," I answered automatically, but when he stepped away, added, "I just need a moment."

He frowned and seemed about to say something, perhaps to reprimand a soldier for contradicting his officer, something I had never done while I was in St. George, only to remember that I wasn't one of his any longer. "Very well," he said, nodding. "I'll be outside."

With one final glance at Ember, he spun on a heel and strode away. I waited until he was truly out of sight before turning to the dragon beside me.

She gave me a sad smile. "Well, that certainly didn't go how we expected, did it?"

I shook my head. "I was hoping we would leave together for once."

"I know." With a sigh, she leaned against me, resting her head on my shoulder. "We can't seem to catch a break, can we? Since the moment we met, it seems that all we've done is been forced apart for one reason or another. It would be nice to have one uninterrupted block of time together, like normal people."

"We're not exactly normal, are we?"

"No," she whispered back, and turned her face into my shoulder, closing her eyes. "I hate to do this, Garret," she murmured. "Every time we leave, I'm terrified that I might not ever see you again. What if I don't make it back in time? What if the Night of Fang and Fire comes tonight, and by the time we get there, the Order has been completely destroyed?" She paused, her next words barely audible. "I just figured out this whole being-in-love thing," she murmured into my shirt, making my heart turn over. "I can't lose you now."

"We're soldiers," I told her softly. "It doesn't matter which side we're on. As long as the war continues, we have to fight. Or watch everything around us burn." She pressed closer, the heat of her body pulsing against my side as I reached down and took her hand. "Someday," I murmured, lacing our fingers together. "Someday the war will end, and the fighting will stop. That's why we're doing this. To make St. George understand that not all dragons are monsters. They're starting to listen, Ember. A year ago, even a month ago, Martin would never have considered meeting with a dragon and an ex-soldier like this. We're changing things." I gently squeezed her hand. "*You're* changing things. Just by being here, being willing to talk to St. George, you're challenging everything they know." *Like you did with me.*

"What about Talon?" Ember wondered darkly. "And the Elder Wyrm? The Order believes dragons are ruthless creatures who want to take over the world. She's certainly not doing anything to change their minds. And after they see the clones…" She shivered. "No one can look at those things and *not* think 'soulless monster.'"

I winced. She was right; seeing that army of vicious, mindless dragon clones would not help our cause to convince St. George that the creatures they were fighting didn't deserve to die. "One step at a time," I muttered. "We'll take care of the Order first, and then we'll worry about Talon."

She nodded, falling silent. And for a few heartbeats, we sat quietly against each other, lost in our own dark thoughts, yet unwilling to move. Realizing this could be the last time we saw each other. Again. As Ember had said, it seemed that we were forever being forced apart, by the war, by our enemies, even by each other. Reluctance battled a weary sense of resignation. It would always be like this, I realized. Fearing for each other's lives, knowing that each moment together could be our final one.

"You have to go, don't you?" Ember murmured at last. I nodded.

"Yeah," I husked out, reluctant to pull away, knowing I had to. "Martin is waiting for me. He'll be impatient to get back." Back to St. George. Back to the Order and the brothers I had betrayed. If I didn't know Martin so well, I might think he was setting me up, attempting to trap me behind enemy lines. But Gabriel Martin, in all the time I had known him, had always been a man of his word, even when it came to his enemies. I wondered what the other soldiers would say, how they would react, when I came through those gates. Not as a prisoner or a hostage, but as a soldier once more. One who was loyal to dragons.

I guessed I would find out soon enough.

"If Riley doesn't come," I told Ember, "if he decides not

to risk his underground, tell him I understand. And...tell him thank you. He'll know what for."

"I will." Ember drew back, blinking rapidly. "And we'll see each other again," she said, her eyes shadowed but determined. "I'll be there soon, with or without a rogue army." She pressed a hand to my cheek, her gaze fierce, as if she was memorizing my face. "Just promise me you'll stay alive until I can get there, soldier boy. If I'm going to die fighting Talon, I'm going to do it beside you."

I gave a half smile. "That sounds tragically noble," I joked, trying to ease some of the shadows in her eyes. To fool myself into thinking this wasn't quite as serious as I knew it was. That it wouldn't end as I suspected. "The soldier of St. George and the dragon, killed together on the field of battle."

"Fighting on the other side of the war," Ember added. "Even though they're supposed to be mortal enemies who hate each other. Like the Montagues and Capulets."

"If Romeo didn't die from poison," I finished. "And Juliet was a fire-breathing dragon."

She chuckled, tilting her head. "That's an interesting thought," she mused. "If she was, do you think the story would've ended like it did?"

I gave a weary smile. "I think we're going to find out," I murmured, and kissed her. She leaned close, one hand gripping the front of my shirt, the other sliding into my hair. I closed my eyes and breathed her in, searing this moment into my brain, in case it really was the final one.

Ember pulled back very slightly, her gaze finding mine. "I love you, soldier boy," she whispered. "I know you've heard it before, but I'm going to keep saying it...just in case I don't get another chance. And I wish we had more time. We didn't have a lot to begin with." A shadow of anguish crossed her face before she blinked it away. "But I'll take whatever we have. And Martin is probably getting impatient. So go on." She gave my chest a little push, drawing back. "Before this gets any harder. I'll find you again, I promise." Though her eyes remained dark, she gave a tiny, wicked smile. "Don't start the fight without me."

"Wouldn't dream of it." Leaning forward, I kissed her once more. "I love you, too, Ember," I murmured. "We'll see each other soon." And, even though it was one of the hardest things I'd ever made myself do, I slid out of the booth and walked away. Out of the bar, and into the dimly lit parking lot.

Martin was waiting for me outside the door in the flickering light of a broken streetlamp. His arms were crossed, and his gaze was scrutinizing as I approached. "That took longer than I thought it would," he said as I stopped in front of him. "The Sebastian I knew once could barely hold a conversation with a civilian, let alone a girl." His eyes narrowed. "What were you and that dragon talking about that was so interesting? You know what…never mind." He held up a hand. "I don't want to know. Do you have everything you need with you?"

Everything except the girl in question. "Yes, sir," I replied simply.

"You are armed, I take it?"

"Yes, sir," I said again.

He nodded, unsurprised. "All right. Before we go, let me make one thing clear, Sebastian," he said gravely. "The only reason I'm even considering this is because the Order is so fractured, and the hierarchy within St. George is nearly non-existent. If what you say is true, then my duty is to defend my chapterhouse and the soldiers who live there at all costs.

That said, I would watch your back when we get there. I can protect you from the soldiers when we arrive, but don't think you're going to be welcomed back with open arms. You're still a traitor and a dragonlover, and everyone in St. George knows what you've done. This is a temporary truce at best. And if your dragon friends do show up, I won't order them shot on sight, but they should stay as far away from the soldiers as they can. Is that understood?"

"Yes, sir," I replied once more. It wasn't ideal; I knew my former brothers despised me just as much as the dragons they fought. I knew I was still a traitor, still the enemy in their eyes. Much like Kain, there were several soldiers I could think of who would want retribution and might try to take it out of me themselves. Those same soldiers would be enraged if a group of dragons showed up at the chapterhouse, even ones who were supposed to be allies. I would have to be careful, to protect both myself and my "scaly friends" from my former brothers. If they hurt Ember, or any hatchling in Riley's network, I would never forgive myself.

Still, though I would have to be cautious and tread very lightly, it was a huge first step. Martin had listened to us. He'd spoken to Ember without trying to kill her. And for the first time in history, a group of dragons would be allowed inside St. George. This would change everything.

If Riley decided to show, that was. And any of us were still alive after the Night of Fang and Fire.

Martin nodded and gestured to a black jeep a few spaces down. "All right," he said grimly. "Let's move out."

As I followed him into the vehicle and closed the door, I was struck by a vague sense of déjà vu. I'd been in this jeep with Martin only once before, but I remembered it as clearly as if had been yesterday. Six years ago, when he'd picked me up from the Academy of St. George, and we'd driven to attend Lucas Benedict's funeral.

Martin didn't look at me, but I wondered if he remembered, too.

As he pulled out of the parking lot, I caught a glimpse of a red-haired girl in the rearview mirror, watching us drive away, and my stomach twisted. I would see her again, I told myself. Riley detested the Order and was dangerously protective of his underground. He would be understandably appalled at the very notion of helping the people who had killed so many of his kind. The hatchlings weren't soldiers; they were teens who had been persecuted by Talon and the Order and had every right to fear and hate them both. But if anyone could convince them to come out of hiding and stand with their ancient enemies, it would be Ember. Once she put her mind to something, there was very little that could stop her. She had changed so much from the girl I'd met in Crescent Beach; she had become a true soldier who understood what was at stake and was willing to make sacrifices for what had to be done.

I just prayed that, when this was over, the sacrifices were ones we could live with.

RILEY

"Well, that's everything," Wes muttered. "All the safe houses have been evacuated. And all communications have been severed. The network is officially dead."

"Good," I said shortly. "That should make us harder to track down. And when Talon comes for the safe houses, there'll be nothing left for them to find." I stood in the small bedroom Wes and I shared, the human sitting at the desk with his open computer, myself standing behind him. A pair of twin beds sat on opposite ends of the wall behind us, but I hadn't so much as lain down since we'd arrived. Every moment of my time had been spent securing my underground, making sure the hatchlings were settled in, going over emergency escape plans with Wes should an army of soulless dragon clones appear in the middle of the night.

"Everyone accounted for?" I asked.

"As far as I can tell." Wes leaned back in the chair, rubbing his eyes. He, too, was exhausted, having worked all night tracking everyone in the underground, contacting all our people, shutting down networks and communications behind them. "We lost several this year, Riley," he muttered, shaking his head. "More than we've ever lost in the past. The Order has been bloody relentless."

I nodded wearily. Seventeen hatchlings had made it. Seventeen, out of what had been twenty-five a year ago. It made me sick. I remembered their names, their faces, their stories and backgrounds. I knew each and every death, and it ate at me like a cancer, making me furious with myself. I was supposed to keep them safe. They'd come to me for protection, and I had let them down.

No more. I couldn't let any more die. There were still seventeen dragons down there who were counting on me, who looked to me to defend them from Talon and the Order. I was still the leader of this underground, and I couldn't let past failures or personal shortcomings stop me from what I had to do.

Even though, in the darkest, blackest corners of my soul, a tiny part of me didn't care what happened next. *Let everyone die,* it whispered. *Let the world burn and everything be charred to ashes by dragonfire. What do we care, now that she's gone?*

"Cobalt."

I turned almost guiltily. Mist stood in the door frame peering in at us, long silvery hair glowing softly in the dim light. I hadn't seen the ex–Talon agent much since we'd arrived, having been distracted with Wes, the hatchlings, the underground...and Ember. Truthfully I had almost forgotten about Mist. But it occurred to me that I had no idea what she had been doing since we got here, and that was a little disconcerting. She had been a Basilisk, and she had worked for Talon. Both were reasons to treat her with caution, to watch her closely.

"I need to speak with you," she announced in her calm, pragmatic voice. "Can we talk?"

I shrugged. "I'm not stopping you."

Mist frowned. "Alone."

Wes gave a snort and hunched his shoulders, staring down at the laptop. "Oh, please, don't let me stop you," he muttered. "I'm just the other half of this bloody operation, no one special."

I rolled my eyes. "Wait here," I told Wes, stepping around the chair. "Keep doing what you're doing. I'll be right back." I gestured at Mist, and she backed silently out of the room.

The farmhouse was dark as I closed the door behind me and stepped into the hall with the other dragon. Most of the hatchlings were asleep, exhausted from travel and the stress of getting here. Though I did have to enforce a strict "lights out" rule to prevent a few of the older ones from keeping everyone else up. That, too, was part of the talk I'd had to give once everyone arrived, laying out ground rules and the things you *absolutely could not do* while on the farm, Shifting, fighting and wandering off alone being the top three. I didn't like being so strict, but with seventeen young dragons under one roof and only three helpers to manage them, including Jess, the woman who took care of this place, I had to maintain some semblance of order or things would quickly spiral out of control. Fortunately, everyone here recognized and respected Cobalt, almost to the point of reverence. Except for the one incident with Kain, there hadn't been any problems.

Mist waited for me at the end of the hall, staking out a dark corner near the bathroom. Her face was somber as I came up, and the look she gave me was a mix of annoyance and resignation. As if she would rather be anywhere else. For some reason, that bothered me and I frowned, crossing my arms as I glared down at her.

"So, what's this about, Mist? Are you disappointed?" I nodded to one of the bedrooms down the hall and smirked.

"You finally saw my underground, and you didn't even have to torture me to get to it. Is it not what you were expecting?"

She raised an eyebrow. "Actually, it's pretty much what I thought it would be," she answered coolly. "A group of rebels and runaway hatchlings. Not particularly dangerous or inspiring. But that's not what I wanted to talk about." She drew in a deep breath, a hint of uncertainty crossing her face, as if she wasn't sure what to do now. "My employer contacted me," she went on, frowning slightly. "It seems I am to stay with you and aid you however I can, until he deems otherwise."

"Huh." I gave her a scrutinizing look. "So, what you're saying is, after our escape from Talon, your employer doesn't want you anywhere near him, in case the organization sees you together and figures out he's the mastermind behind it all."

"More or less." Mist sighed. "I certainly can't go back to Talon. They would kill me on sight. And I can't risk exposing my employer. There's nowhere for me to go that will be safe." She bit her lip, and for just a moment, she wasn't a Basilisk, but a scared young woman whose future was uncertain. She looked lost, strangely vulnerable, and my heart went out to her. Then she made a face and glanced back at me. "So, it appears I'm a rogue now," she said, annoyance and defiance coloring her voice. "Just like you wanted, Cobalt. You must be proud."

"Not really," I said. Apprehension stirred. Mist was a *Basilisk*, I reminded myself. Not only that, mysterious employer or not, she had worked for Talon. "I do have a few questions for you," I went on, narrowing my eyes. "If you're going to be hanging around, I need to know a few things. You've seen my underground—that means I can't take any chances.

If I suspect that you're a danger to everyone, or that you're going to sell us out to Talon, I *will* kill you, Mist. You understand that, right?"

She gazed at me steadily. "Yes."

"All right." I nodded. "Then here's the most important question. Who's this mysterious employer who ordered you to help us escape?"

Her expression shut down instantly. "I can't tell you that."

"Why not?"

"Because if he discovers I told anyone, *he* will kill me." The girl's voice was flat and completely serious. "I simply wouldn't wake up one morning. And don't think he wouldn't find out, or that he wouldn't be able to get to me—he has eyes and ears everywhere. Gathering information is his specialty, it's literally *all* he does."

"He wouldn't be able to get to you here," I insisted. "I don't care who he is, no one is going to find you when you're with me." I narrowed my eyes, the hint of a growl creeping into my voice. "But this is my underground we're talking about. I need to know you're not a threat, Mist. I need to know I can trust you. So tell me who your employer is."

"No," Mist said calmly.

I glared at her. "You're going to make this hard, aren't you?"

"You could always interrogate me, if you want," Mist replied, the hint of a dark smile on her face. "You went through the same training I did. Though I will warn you, I'm just as resistant to pain as you are. Without drugs or some kind of truth serum, it might take a while."

"As if I'd ever do that," I said, my lip curling at the thought. "I'm not Luther. I don't interrogate people for shits and giggles."

"Then I'm afraid we're at an impasse."

I exhaled. "All right," I growled. She wasn't going to tell me, and I wasn't going to "interrogate her" to get her to talk. "But answer me this—who were you working for that night in Vegas? When you were trying to get me to reveal the locations of my safe houses?"

"That night?" Mist furrowed her brow slightly, remembering. "I was working for Talon."

"So, you understand why I'm a little confused. Who are you loyal to, Mist? Your employer, or the organization?"

Mist glanced away, staring down the hall, as if gathering her thoughts and weighing how much she wanted to reveal. "My employer is part of Talon," she finally said. "He has his own agents, his eyes and ears within the organization, though no one knows of them. Not even I know the identities of his other informants. Officially, we all work for Talon. We do our jobs and follow orders per normal, unless our employer tells us differently.

"That night in Vegas," Mist went on, "I was following Talon's orders. My mission was to separate you from your friends, discover the locations of your safe houses and then kill you. It was business. I was just doing what the organization required."

"And your employer was okay with it?"

"Yes." Mist nodded. "Back then, we didn't know Talon was going to use the vessels against the Order. We didn't know about the Night of Fang and Fire, or what the Elder Wyrm was truly planning."

"Did you know about the clones?"

"I didn't," Mist said. "But I suspect he did. After I…failed the mission in Vegas, I expected to be punished, or at least reassigned somewhere horrible. But he pulled some strings and was able to reassign me to the lab, where you ended up." Her expression shifted to a faint look of awe as she shook her head. "I think he knew, somehow, that our paths would cross. That he could use you to get the information he wanted."

"Why help us escape, though?" I asked. "You could have easily left us there, after you got what you needed. The easier plan would have been to abandon us or turn us in, instead of having Luther see you with us and blow your cover."

"Yes, it would," Mist agreed. "But that's not what my employer desired. He wanted me to help you escape, so I did. Don't ask me why—I'm not in the habit of questioning his orders. And lately…" She paused again, a brief frown crossing her face as if she were annoyed that she was revealing something else. "He's been at odds with the Elder Wyrm for a long time. Perhaps he realized that you would be more useful alive and free. That you and your little resistance will be instrumental in stopping the Elder Wyrm's plan to destroy the Order." She shrugged. "Or maybe he just wanted another way to twist the knife. You've certainly been a thorn in Talon's side. Maybe that's why he chose to help you.

"In any case," she continued, giving me a defiant look. "That's all I'm willing to reveal right now. Have I sufficiently answered your questions, Cobalt? Are you satisfied that I am not going to run off and betray you to Talon at the first opportunity?"

I crossed my arms. "For now."

"Well." Mist gave me that faint smile. "Do let me know if anything changes."

Downstairs, the front door opened and closed softly.

We both froze. To my knowledge, all the hatchlings were asleep and accounted for. Ember and the soldier had left a few hours ago, but I'd received a text from Ember earlier tonight, letting me know she was fine, that she was on her way back and that there was something we had to discuss. That was ominous, but it wasn't like her to quietly sneak into a room, and I'd heard only one pair of footsteps come in instead of two. I wouldn't put it past a couple of my hatchlings to sneak out of the house and wander off alone, and a Viper certainly wouldn't use the front door, but right now, I wasn't taking any chances.

I drew my gun and, immediately, Mist did the same, pulling a pistol from the small of her back and slipping around behind me. She made no sound as she did, moving like the trained operative she was. I jerked my head toward the staircase, and together we crept down the hall, guns held before us, careful not to make a sound.

At the top of the stairs, I gazed down into the living room. Everything was dark and shadowy, only a faint bit of moonlight coming in through the curtained windows. Carefully, I eased down the steps, keeping my pistol trained on the room, ready to shoot anything that popped out of the darkness and lunged at me. I could feel Mist behind me, doing the same, and weirdly enough, I was glad she was there to back me up.

At the back of the couch, a ripple of movement caught my attention, a shadow moving across the room. Quickly, I pointed the muzzle of my gun at it, feeling Mist do the same. "Hold it right there," I growled, and the shadow instantly stopped moving. Its features were blurred by shadow, but I was positive this wasn't a hatchling, trying to sneak back to their room. And it wasn't Ember or the soldier, so… "You have exactly three seconds to tell me who you are," I warned in a steely voice. "So if you don't want a bunch of lead between the eyes, I would start talking now."

"Barbaric and paranoid as usual, I see," said a soft, instantly familiar voice, and a lamp clicked on, illuminating the room. I relaxed, exhaling in both surprise and relief as a slender Asian woman met my gaze across the floor. "I am relieved that some things never change."

"Dammit, Jade." I sighed, lowering the gun. The Eastern dragon regarded me calmly. "What the hell are you doing here? How did you even find us?"

She blinked. "I received a message earlier from the soldier," was the cool reply. "He told me where you were and implied that you might need my help very soon. As I had already returned to the States, I came here as quickly as I could."

I holstered the pistol, never so happy to see another dragon, even this dragon. Prejudice toward our Eastern cousins aside, Jade was a powerful Adult dragon who could more than take out her share of enemies if pressed. The trick was getting her to agree to fight; she would still rather meditate on a problem than blast it to cinders with flame.

"Did St. George tell you what happened?" I asked, and Jade nodded.

"He explained the…oh, what is the word? The gist of it. That you had been captured by Talon but managed to escape. That the organization has created an army of mindless clone dragons. That they are getting ready to…sic?…them on the rest of the world." Jade's voice grew even more grave. "It seemed a good idea to return and offer assistance before Talon wipes us all off the map."

"What about your council? That seemed important, enough for you to drop everything and go back to China. What happened?"

Her smile became tight. "That is a story for another time, I'm afraid." At my annoyed look, she raised a hand. "I will explain everything soon. It *is* a tale that needs telling. But now is not the time. There are other issues to discuss."

"I take it you two know each other," Mist said, and I couldn't be certain, but there might've been the faintest thread of awe in her voice as she stared at the Eastern dragon.

"Yeah," I answered, stepping aside a little. "Mist, this is Jade. She's a friend of the soldier."

Mist offered the Eastern dragon a respectful bow, shocking me, and Jade inclined her head in return. "Speaking of which, where is the soldier?" she asked, sweeping her gaze up the stairs behind me, as if hoping to find him on the steps. "Last I heard from him, he was impatient that we speak again."

"He's gone," I said, and she looked back sharply, eyes narrowing. "But he should be back anytime now. He and Ember left this afternoon to attend a meeting with the Order."

Jade blinked. "I'm sorry, what?" she said serenely. "Did you just say he and the girl left to attend a meeting with *St. George?*"

"Yeah, I did."

"Why?"

"Because the Order needs our help," Ember said. We all jerked around to find her standing in the doorway, her eyes shining with a subtle green light as she gazed at us. "Because the Night of Fang and Fire is going to hit any night now, and I promised Garret I would return to St. George and help him fight Talon. With or without you."

GARRET

I'm home.

Angrily, I shoved that thought from my mind as the jeep pulled through the gates of the Western chapterhouse, the guard saluting briskly as we went by. The Order was not home to me any longer, I reminded myself, feeling an ache of recognition as the familiar rows of buildings came into view over the sand. The chapel, the barracks, the mess hall. Places I knew by heart, where I had sat with my brothers and talked about killing dragons.

They aren't your brothers, and this isn't your place. You don't belong here anymore.

No, I did not. But I would still fight to defend it. Regardless of the enmity between us, the fact that I was a traitor to my Order and my former brothers despised me, I would still stand with them against the slaughter I knew was coming. Because Talon could not win. Because if they truly shattered the Order of St. George, there would be no one left to stop the Elder Wyrm and Talon from sweeping over the rest of the world.

And because, despite everything, the Order still had good people within it. Tristan, Gabriel Martin, a few others I had trained with and fought beside. They were misguided—they had been indoctrinated like every other soldier—but they were not evil. They were just like I had been, before I'd met a fiery red dragon in Crescent Beach. If I could change, if I could see dragons for what they really were, surely there were others who would do the same. They just needed to be shown the truth.

The sun was a faint red smear on the horizon, the chapter-house quiet and dark, as Martin pulled up to the assembly hall and killed the engine. He paused, hands on the steering wheel, then turned to fix me with a somber glare.

"I've called ahead and told my officers to gather the soldiers," he stated. "They're waiting in the assembly hall now. Are you ready for this, Sebastian?"

"Yes, sir."

"You know what they're going to say to you, how they're going to react. No one will shoot you on my watch, but it's not going to be pretty. Everyone in St. George knows you've sided with the dragons, but you are from this chapterhouse, and these are the men you've personally betrayed. Think about what that means, Sebastian."

"I know, sir. And I don't expect any understanding or sympathy, but this has to be done."

He nodded briskly and stepped out of the jeep. I followed him around the building to the assembly hall, thankful when we stepped through a side door instead of through the main entrance. A soldier I recognized, one of the squad leaders by the name of Williams, waited for Martin beside the door to the main hall.

"Sir." He saluted sharply, and Martin returned it. "Welcome back. The soldiers are…"

He trailed off, seeing me for the first time, and his eyes went wide. "Sebastian," he whispered, his voice laced with shock. There was a single heartbeat of silence, and then his mouth curled in a snarl. "You son of a—"

"Williams!" Martin snapped, stopping him midlunge. Williams froze, still glaring at me with darkest hate, one hand halfway to his sidearm. "Stand down, soldier," Martin ordered in a low, firm voice. "I brought him here. Sebastian is with me."

"Sir." Williams turned to Martin, aghast. His mouth opened, probably to snap at his superior officer, before he seemed to remember himself and straightened. "Permission to speak freely, sir."

"If you must."

"Sir, why is the dragonlover here?"

Martin gave a wry curl of his lip. "That's more of a question, soldier. Are you questioning me?"

"No, sir! But—"

"Sebastian is here for a reason. That's all you need to know right now." Martin's dark gaze remained fixed on the other soldier. "I will not have a riot in these halls, nor will I have Sebastian come to harm while he is here. You will keep yourself under control, and you will trust that your superior officer knows what he is doing. Is that understood, soldier?"

"I…" Williams shot one last, murderous glare at me, then nodded. "Yes, sir."

"Good." Martin turned from the soldier, dismissing him, and glanced at me. "Let's go, Sebastian."

We left Williams glowering in the hall and entered the assembly room through the back door, stepping onto the stage. As Martin and I walked to the front of the platform, I looked over the floor and saw the surprised faces of my former brothers turn to outrage as they recognized me. Furtively, I scanned the room, taking stock of who was there, looking for someone in particular. It took me only a moment to spot him. On the far side of the room, leaning with his back to the wall, Tristan St. Anthony raised his head and met my gaze, dark eyes narrowing to slits.

"You all know who this is." Martin's voice wasn't a question, carrying into the tense silence.

"The fucking dragonlover!" someone in the back shouted.

"Yes," Martin agreed, though his eyes narrowed in the direction of the shout. "We all know our former brother, Garret Xavier Sebastian. And we all know what he has done. However…" His voice dropped, becoming low and commanding. "I brought Sebastian here—he is under my protection and the protection of this chapterhouse. Which means," he went on, his expression hardening, "no one under my command will do him any harm whatsoever. Sebastian is not a prisoner. He will be allowed to move about the base freely, and he will not be treated any differently than anyone else. If I hear of anyone throwing so much as a spitball in his direction, they'll be spending the rest of the day in a cell. I hope I have made myself perfectly clear on this."

A stunned, angry silence followed his announcement. Many of the soldiers were staring at Martin like he had gone insane, and the others were glaring at me with undisguised loathing. "Sebastian is here for a reason," Martin went on, taking advantage of the shock, or choosing to ignore it. "Because he has been among the enemy, he has information that you all need to hear. I suggest you listen to what he has to say and reserve judgment until you've heard the entire story. Sebastian?" He half turned to me, nodding. "It's all yours."

I stepped forward, meeting the angry glares head-on. "Talon is coming," I said over the angry murmurs of the crowd. "They have an army, and they intend to use it to destroy the Order once and for all. Their plan is to attack every St. George chapterhouse in a single night and strike a crippling blow against the Order. One that we'll never recover from."

"You're full of shit, Sebastian," called a soldier, perhaps the same one who'd shouted at us earlier. "*All* the chapterhouses in a single night? Talon doesn't have those kinds of numbers."

"Yes, they do," I insisted. "I've seen them myself. They have an army of dragons, hundreds of them, maybe thousands, enough to attack every St. George base around the world and burn it to the ground." A disbelieving, horrified silence fell as I let those words sink in. "They're coming for you," I went on quietly. "And if you're not ready for them when they get here, everyone in St. George will be slaughtered."

"Lieutenant Martin, sir!" another soldier called, and waited for Martin to acknowledge him before he went on. "Sir, how do we know Sebastian isn't lying? He's been in contact with the lizards themselves. How do we know Talon didn't send him here to set us up?"

"We don't," Martin said calmly. "I have no idea what Sebastian has been doing in the time he has been gone. But I find it hard to believe that Talon would send him to warn us of an imminent attack. Even if he is lying, is that really something you want to risk?"

"I'm not lying," I said, facing my former brothers again. "Talon *is* coming for you. There is an army of dragons on its way to massacre the Order. And with the chapterhouses so isolated and fractured right now, the rest of St. George won't be able to help. You can't survive this alone." I paused, taking a furtive breath, then added, "But I have friends who can help."

"Friends," a soldier said scornfully, his voice pulsing with hate. "You mean *dragons*, don't you, Sebastian? Lizards."

"Yes," I replied simply as the room began to erupt again. Soldiers were swearing at me, protesting, sneering at the very idea of accepting help from dragons. Tristan stood in the corner, watching all of this, but his expression was unreadable. "Listen to me," I urged the rest of them. "I know this goes against everything we've been taught, but there are dragons out there who are not affiliated with Talon. Who have broken away and are in hiding from the organization, from their own kind."

"So what?" someone demanded. "One evil soulless lizard is just like another. What does it matter if they're not part of Talon anymore?"

"It matters," I said firmly, "because they don't want Talon to succeed any more than you do. Because Talon is trying to kill *them* off, as well, and any dragon who is not part of the organization. But they can't stand against Talon alone." I looked over the sea of angry, disgusted faces and hardened my voice. "And neither can you. To have a chance at surviving this attack, we have to work together."

"Fuck that, dragonlover!" came a voice from the crowd. "I sure as hell ain't letting a bunch of lizards share space with me. I see a dragon, any dragon, I'll do what I've always done—put a bullet through its skull."

"No, you will not." Lieutenant Martin stepped forward again, his expression dangerous. "If Sebastian speaks the truth," he said into the stunned silence, "and an attack from Talon is imminent, then we must do whatever it takes to ensure we survive. Including ally with the dragons."

"Sir." A soldier stepped from the crowd, gazing up at Martin with an almost-pleading expression. "That's...that's against the Code. The Order doesn't accept help from lizards, for any reason. If the rest of St. George finds out about this, you…all of us…" He gestured to the crowd behind him. "We could be tried for treason, sir. They might execute the lot of us for consorting with the enemy."

"I know, Roberts," Martin said in a quieter voice. "And under normal circumstances, I would never question protocol. But in this, I feel we have no choice. The Order of St. George is dangerously unstable. If an army attacks and cripples the Order or, worse, shatters it entirely, think of what that will mean for the rest of the world. Talon would have no opposition. There would be no one left to stand against the dragons. Besides…" His gaze rose, sweeping over the crowd. "It is my duty to protect this base and the soldiers under my command, no matter the cost. I will not let this chapterhouse fall, even if I must consort with demons. Afterward, if the Order demands punishment, I will accept full responsibility for accepting help from dragons. But we must survive whatever is coming first.

"We will be forming a temporary truce with a group of outside dragons," Martin went on, his tone becoming hard and matter-of-fact again. "Any who cannot accept that may leave. You can pack your things right now and go, and there will be no repercussions." He paused, as if giving the soldiers a chance to take the offer, to leave the Order of St. George and not look back. Surprisingly, no one moved. "But if you choose to stay," Martin went on, "know that for the first time in history, we will be letting dragons onto the premises. These dragons will be under the full protection of St. George, and no one is allowed to harm, insult, hassle or cause them grief of any kind. You will all be the polite, well-trained soldiers I know you are capable of being, and you will represent the Order to the best of your ability."

"And if the lizards attack us, sir?" a soldier asked, almost defiantly.

"They won't," I answered. "They're not monsters. They're going to be just as scared and nervous and wary of you as you are of them. But they know what's at stake. They have just as much reason to hate Talon, and they'll want to make this alliance work." *If any of them even decide to come.*

"One more thing, sir." Another soldier stepped up, deliberately addressing Martin and not myself. "If Sebastian's dragons show up, how will we tell them apart from the dragons that will be attacking the base? I mean…" He shot a sneer at me. "One lizard is pretty much like another. How will I know what dragon I'm supposed to shoot?"

"You'll know," I replied, addressing them all. "There will be a difference. The dragons arriving to help us will look like every other dragon you've faced—bright scales, different colors, all hatchlings. Talon's dragons are metallic gray with white horns and eyes. They'll all look the same, so you should be able to tell the difference between them and the rogue dragons."

"What do you mean, they all look the same?" the soldier wanted to know. "What, like they're the same color?"

"I mean they're clones," I said flatly. "Exact replicas of each other. Talon has been cloning dragons for several years, and now they have an army of them. These dragons have no fear and no self-preservation instinct. They will keep coming at you until they're dead."

"Mother of God," someone muttered, though I couldn't tell who, and a soldier near the front of the stage crossed himself.

Martin nodded briskly, addressing the soldiers. "We only have a few hours," he said, making several of them jerk up. "Forty-eight at the most, and probably less than that. This attack is happening—we need to prepare so that when this dragon army does come for us, we'll be waiting for them. We are St. George," he added in a louder voice. "Killing dragons is our specialty. Let Talon send their army after us. The Order will not submit. We will not break. If this dragon army shows up on our doorstep, we will do what we've always done and send them back to hell where they belong."

I hoped he was right.

RILEY

I didn't have a word for what I was feeling.

Angry didn't quite cover it. *Horrified* seemed a bit too tame. *Appalled* and *incredulous* sort of fit, but even they didn't compare.

"So let me get this straight," I rasped at Ember. The five of us—me, Ember, Mist, Jade and a very disgruntled Wes— were standing in the kitchen around a long wooden table. The rest of the hatchlings had assembled in the living room and were sitting or lounging in loose groups, watching sleepily. Ember had insisted on waking up the entire house, saying that everyone needed to hear what she had to say, that it was important.

Absolutely hysterical was more like it.

"You want us—" I gestured to the dragons surrounding me "—and the hatchlings, who have never seen a battle before in their lives, to go help the *Order of St. George* fight an army of soulless killer dragons? Are you insane? That's…" I shook my head, unable to think of a proper word for it. "No, Firebrand. Absolutely not. I'm not risking this underground to go and die for the Order, that's out of the question."

"Um, yeah, I'm going to go with Riley on this one and

say that you're off your rocker," Wes added. "Completely, utterly, barking mad."

Ember's eyes flashed green, but she answered in a calm, far too reasonable voice. "We can't hide forever, Riley."

"We sure as hell can," I snapped back. "We stay here, keep our heads down and stay the fuck out of the way. That's how it has always worked. That's how we've been able to survive."

"And what happens when there are no more hiding places? What happens when Talon destroys the Order and comes after us full scale?" Ember shook her head. "If we keep running from Talon, eventually they're going to catch up."

"So your plan is to charge at them head-on."

"My plan is that we stop running," Ember said firmly. "And start fighting back."

"With what?" I snarled at her, and gestured to the group watching in the living room. "A handful of untrained hatchlings? Alone? How long do you think they're going to last against an army?"

"Not alone," Ember agreed. "None of us can stand against Talon alone. That's why we need to ally with the Order, and anyone else that we can find. Ex-Talon servants, other rogues, Eastern dragons, everyone." She glanced at Jade and Mist, on opposite ends of the table. "If we put out the call to oppose Talon, more will join us. There have to be those within the organization who don't agree with the Elder Wyrm, who would be willing to fight if they knew there were others doing the same. But we have to start this war ourselves—we have to start actively resisting, instead of running away. If we join with the Order of St. George, we have a chance."

I could sense a stunned, nervous silence coming from the living room. Most of the hatchlings were still half-asleep, but Ember's words were waking them up quick. It would probably be only a few seconds longer before some of them started to chime in.

"Join with the Order," Jade mused, and her normally placid expression twisted into an expression of anger and loathing. "Ally with the humans who destroyed my temple and slaughtered my friends. The thought is...sickening.

"But," she added, "I do see your point. Talon is not going to stop. They were the ones who gave the Order the location of my temple. They are the ones responsible for the destruction of my home and the murder of my friends. St. George might have done the killing, but Talon was the hand wielding the weapon. All because I refused to conform to their ways. They will do the same to every dragon they find, until we are all dead or enslaved to the organization." She drummed her fingers on her arm, her expression pensive. "Change must come," she mused. "That much is certain. Perhaps allying with the Order *is* the way to bring it about."

"Join the Order?" On the other side of the table, Mist shook her head. "Well, if that's your plan, I can tell you one thing—Talon certainly wouldn't expect it."

I slammed my fist on the table, making Wes and several of the hatchlings jump. "Just like that, huh?" I said as they all looked at me. "Join the Order and go fight Talon's army with them? March merrily off to war with my underground and all my hatchlings—that's what you're suggesting?"

"Not all of them," Ember said. "Only the ones who agree to come." She turned from me then, taking a step forward to face the group of hatchlings. "I'm not going to force anyone to fight," she told the room. "But you should have the choice. You should know what we're up against, and what we can try to do to fight. We can't keep running and hiding. We have to take a stand."

"Stop it, Ember." I stepped forward, as well, furious. "Why don't you tell them the truth?" I looked past her into the living room, at the sea of tense faces, and narrowed my eyes. "If you fight Talon and St. George, you're going to die," I said, and saw several of them stiffen. "This is a *war*. It's not like television or the movies. There's nothing romantic or honorable about it. It's bullets and blood and chaos and death, and neither side has any qualms about gunning you down or tearing you apart. You've all seen St. George. You know what they're like. And Talon is even worse. If we go charging into a war zone, we're going to be killed."

"We're going to be killed, anyway, Riley." Ember's voice, though remorseful, was unyielding. "Sooner or later, whether you like it or not, the war is going to catch up. Talon isn't going to stop. Whatever they're planning, it's happening now." She faced the group of hatchlings once more, raising her voice. "We can either go out and face it head-on, or we can wait for it to come and kill us. Once Talon destroys St. George, none of us will ever be safe again. We can't run from this any longer. It's time to start fighting back."

"No," I said firmly, and stepped away from her. "I'm sorry, Firebrand. But I can't. I've spent the past decade trying to protect this underground, to take the risks so they wouldn't have to. I've already lost too many, to both Talon and St. George. I can't in good conscience send them out to fight, knowing that they're probably going to die." She gazed at me, the look on her face devastatingly blank. "I'm sorry," I said again. "But there are some lines I won't cross. This is one of them. Hate me if you want, Ember, but we're not going to fight a battle we can't win. We're not going anywhere. St. George will have to get by without us."

"I'll go."

I turned in amazement as a girl rose from the back and faced us with grim determination. "I'll go," Nettle said again, stepping forward. "I'm not afraid."

"Nettle," I growled as fear and anger surged up, making my voice sharp, "you don't know what you're saying. If you try to fight this army, you're going to die."

"Maybe," Nettle replied. "Or maybe Talon will come for us tonight while we're all asleep, and I'll die, anyway." I started to argue with her, but she raised her voice. "I'm tired, Cobalt," she said. "I'm tired of constantly hiding and being afraid. Always watching my back, being scared to go anywhere alone, waking up to evacuate in the middle of the night. It never ends. It's always something, either Talon or St. George wanting to kick down our door and slaughter us all." She slumped, rubbing her arm self-consciously. "She's right. If we don't start fighting back, we'll be running away for the rest of our lives."

Raising her chin, she met Ember's gaze. "So, yeah. I'm done with this. If St. George needs us to save them from Talon, I guess we'll just have to show them what we can do. Count me in."

"Me, too," echoed Remy, standing up. "I'm coming, too."

"Yeah. Me, too."

I stood there, dazed, as one by one all my hatchlings slowly rose to their feet, announcing their consent. Only Kain and two of his friends remained seated until the very end, but when the final hatchling stood up, he muttered a curse and climbed to his feet, as well, crossing his arms.

I shook my head at them all. "You stubborn idiot hatchlings," I almost-whispered. They set their jaws or crossed their arms, staring back at me, and I hardened my voice. "You realize what this means, don't you? Take a good look around. Count how many of you are standing here right now, because some of you aren't coming back. If you do this, there are going to be casualties. Some of you are going to *die*, that's just how it is in war. How do you think that makes me feel, trying to keep the lot of you alive all this time, only to have you charging off into the middle of a war zone?" They didn't answer, and I fought back the helpless anger threatening to smother me. At my side, Ember was quiet, watching us all. She had won. She had put out the call to fight, and the hatchlings, tired of running and living in fear, had responded. I hadn't realized how much they wanted to *do* something, anything, until now.

Deep down, even though I hated it, a part of me knew she was right. But still, this was *my* underground; for the past decade, I'd fought to keep it safe. I'd watched these kids from the beginning, watched them live and struggle and grow up...but that was the problem, wasn't it? They *had* grown up. They knew the stakes, knew what they were getting into, and I couldn't protect them any longer.

I sighed and looked at the ceiling. "All right," I muttered. "Go on, then. I can't stop you. If this is your choice, I won't stand in your way. It's not like I can ground every single one of you and expect you to not go out the window the second my back is turned." That coaxed a smile from a few of them, though the rest remained unnaturally solemn. They *did* understand what was happening, I realized. They understood all too well.

Nettle stepped forward, seeking my gaze. "You'll come with us, right, Cobalt?"

"I...yeah." Slumping, I raked a hand over my scalp. "I think this is a mistake, but I'll be damned if I stay here while the rest of you go out to fight with St. George." Shaking my head, I glared at them all. "I'm probably going to get myself shot full of holes trying to save you ingrates, but... I'll be there. And I'll fight the bastards for as long as I can, I promise."

I finally looked at Ember, standing at my shoulder, and forced a smirk. "Well, you got your army, Firebrand," I said, watching her brow furrow. "We're all going merrily off to war, it seems. Helping St. George fight Talon." I shook my head in equal amounts disgust and disbelief. "I just hope that, when this is all over and the smoke clears, you'll be able to live with yourself."

Because I don't know if I can.

GARRET

"What do our defenses look like?"

I gazed at the crudely sketched map in my hand as I walked beside Tristan down the narrow road that cut through the base. It was late afternoon, and around us, the base was eerily silent, though I knew no one was idle. A tense stillness hung over the chapterhouse, and soldiers went about their duties in full combat gear, myself included. For the first time in months, I was back in uniform, the black-and-gray combat armor of the Order of St. George. I knew I had to wear it to survive, that the suit designed for fighting dragons was my best shot at coming out of this alive, but I took no pride in it. It was just another reminder of what I had done, the years I had killed without a thought. Tonight, though, I would wear it to defend my former brothers and the dragons I had once driven toward extinction.

I glanced at the map again. The scribbled drawing showed the whole of the Western chapterhouse in messy black lines, but the layout was as familiar to me as the back of my hand. None of the hastily scrawled "buildings" were labeled or numbered, but I knew each of them by heart.

"Snipers will be set up here, here and here," Tristan answered, pointing to three positions on the map. Chapel tower, headquarters and armory roof. "We won't be staying in position, though," he added. "Orders will be your standard 'shoot and scoot.' We can take two, maybe three shots at most. But then the risk of discovery becomes too great, and we'll have to fall back to avoid being swarmed."

I nodded and gazed up at the chapel as we passed beneath, at the faded white walls and pointed steeple; it wasn't hard to imagine Tristan up there, aiming his rifle at passing dragons. "We'll need more guns in the air than just snipers," I muttered, and he nodded.

"Yeah. Machine gunners will take up position at these four points," Tristan went on, tapping the map. "So all angles of attack will be covered. Hopefully we can fill the sky with so much lead it'll be like it's raining dragons."

I tried not to wince at that image, visualizing a small red dragon tumbling limply from the sky, landing on the hard ground with a thump. For a moment, my thoughts strayed. I hoped she was all right. I had tried calling her this morning only to remember that all our personal possessions had been taken away when we'd been captured by Talon, phones included, and I had no way of contacting her. I didn't know if she'd been able to convince Riley and the hatchlings to fight, but I had to assume that we were on our own—that no help would be coming.

Truthfully, part of me hoped she wouldn't come. After sending away the civilians, the true rookies and the small number of family units, there weren't very many soldiers left. Surprisingly, few actual soldiers had opted to leave, and the number had been far less than I had expected, but the loss of every dragonslayer still hurt. From what I'd learned of the Night of Fang and Fire, Talon knew the exact number of soldiers stationed here; they would know the numbers needed to take us out. If the Order fell, if I died tonight in a hail of gunshots and dragonfire, I would rather Ember be far away, safe from the madness that was to come.

"Good," I muttered, stopping in front of the large square building in the center of the base. "That takes care of the antiair support. The rest of us will bunker down in the armory." Of all the buildings in the chapterhouse, it was the most defensible, with reinforced doors, few points of entry and heavy brick walls that would hold up well to dragonfire. Pulling the door open revealed that it had already been prepared for an attack; the glass in the windowpanes had been taken out and replaced with boards and sandbags, giving soldiers a spot to fire at incoming dragons. Iron barricades had been erected, creating choke points for enemy forces and cover for the rest of us. A machine gun turret was in the process of being set up near the door, pointing straight toward the entrance, so that if the door *was* breached, the first thing the attackers would run into would be a storm of turret fire.

I walked along the back wall, taking note of everything. Ammo, firearms, grenades, combat gear, fortifications. "Looks like we're as ready as we can get," I mused, feeling time slipping away from us. Only a couple hours till sundown, and after that, the countdown began in earnest. "I'll need to report back to Martin with our progress. Is this everything?"

"Nearly," Tristan said, stopping at a long shelf covered by a tarp. "There is one more thing."

He flipped the canvas back, revealing a pair of RPGs—rocket propelled grenade launchers, designed to pierce armor and punch through tanks. Fired from the shoulder, the weapon's pointed, nearly foot-long grenade did significant damage upon impact, and could severely cripple or even kill a full grown Adult dragon. Unfortunately, they weren't that effective against agile, fast-moving targets, nor could they be deployed in public, so the Order rarely used them.

"There is one more team we haven't talked about," Tristan explained, his dark gaze roaming over the deadly weapons. "If the dragons break through the defenses and get into the armory, we're screwed. We need an ace in the hole, a crack team to hang back and hit the dragons from behind. To strike at the perfect moment and do the most damage possible."

"Basically, you need a suicide squad," I said. "Because once that attack hits, that team is out in the open, isolated from everyone. They'll have no support and no backup once the dragons turn on them. They go in and they wreak as much havoc as they can before they're wiped out."

"Yep. And, of course, the commander will have to know just when to strike. If he springs the attack early, we lose any advantage. If it's too late, we've already taken too much damage and the base could fall. We'll need someone with experience, who can be patient and wait for the perfect moment, but who isn't afraid to charge screaming at the enemy to save everyone else." Tristan gave me an unreadable look. "So how 'bout it, partner? You up for leading one more counterstrike? Probably the very last one?" He shrugged, and a faint, rueful grin crossed his face. "Lieutenant Martin said he wanted the best leading this attack. But since we're kind of short-handed, I figured I would ask you."

I gave a tired smile. That was Tristan extending the olive branch, on the last day we might be alive. I was grateful, however long it lasted.

"Yeah," I said quietly. "I'd be honored."

★ ★ ★

"Damn fools."

I stood in Gabriel Martin's office, hands clasped behind me out of habit, watching him replace the phone and shake his head. Behind him, the clock on the wall read 5:36 p.m.; I knew he'd been on the phone with various members of the Order since early this morning. Beside the clock, the red dragon hide glimmered dully, making my stomach twist. It was strange; I'd been in this office several times before, but had never really noticed the hide until now, never thought about what it truly represented. That a hatchling had been killed, murdered by the Order, and its skin had been taken for a trophy. I wondered what Ember would say if she could see it.

Martin sighed, rubbing his forehead as he glanced up at me. "I've notified everyone I can think of," he said. "I've warned the council about the impending attack, and I've sent a message to every base and chapterhouse I could get through to."

"Do you think they'll listen?"

"I don't know." Martin shook his head. "Maybe. The council, certainly not. They believe this is a ploy by Talon to get us to panic and take advantage of the confusion within the Order." He paused a moment, then sighed. "They are already calling for my resignation. The other chapterhouses might take the threat seriously—it's difficult to say. But I've done all I can." His jaw tightened. "What's it look like on our end? Are we prepared?"

"We're as ready as we can be, sir."

Martin nodded. "And what of yourself, Sebastian?" he

asked. "Have there been any problems with the rest of the men?"

"No, sir," I replied. Most of my former brothers had either accepted my presence with cool politeness, as if dealing with a squad leader we all knew was a jerk, or pretended I didn't exist. There had been a few death glares, and one incident where someone had spit in my direction before being shouted down by his squad leader, but no outright challenges or attempts to corner me. This was partially due to the respect Gabriel Martin commanded, but an imminent attack from dragons also commanded everyone's attention. The chapterhouse had been so busy preparing for the assault there had been no time for scheming or thoughts of revenge against a single soldier.

Martin nodded, his face dark. "If they do," he said, "if there is trouble, Sebastian, I want you to come to me. Don't try to handle it yourself. If this attack doesn't happen soon, tempers are going to fray, and the tension is going to drive some very foolish decisions. I don't want this base to fall into chaos, nor do I need anyone in the infirmary right now. I know most of the men will follow orders, but I can't be everywhere at once. If you think there could be trouble, I want you to tell me. Is that understood?"

"Yes, sir."

"And that goes for your dragons when they get here, as well."

"They might not show up, sir. There are only a few hours of daylight left." *And the attack is supposed to happen tonight.* I swallowed the bitterness in my throat. *Ember, it's probably for the best that you don't come. I suspect very few of us are going to live to see the next morning.*

"Even so. If they do arrive, we'll have our hands full keeping everyone in line."

"Yes, sir," I said again, and he fell silent. I knew he was thinking of the Order, his chapterhouse and all the soldiers under his command. We both knew he was asking a lot of them—accepting the word of a known traitor, not surrendering the traitor to St. George, allowing *dragons* into the chapterhouse without repercussion. Such blasphemous procedures had never been considered before. But nobody had walked. No one had challenged him or me. I'd known leaders of other chapterhouses who'd governed through fear and intimidation, who'd had the soldier's deference and obedience, but never their respect. Martin was not one of them. The soldiers of the Western chapterhouse trusted him with their lives, even if he was breaking every rule and tradition from the time the Order had been founded. I remembered the way he'd looked out for me after Lucas Benedict's death, remembered how he'd come to my defense when I had accused the Patriarch of treason, the only officer to consider my words in an assembly of hundreds. And I wondered how many other secrets this man kept close to his chest.

"Can I ask you something, sir?" I ventured. He glanced up and nodded, and I took a deep breath. This might not be a good time to bring this up, but I might never get another chance. "Sir, how long did you know my parents were part of Talon?"

He let out a long sigh, as if he knew this had been coming for a while now. "From the beginning," he replied, and gestured to the seat across from the desk. I slid into the chair, and Martin folded his hands on his desk. "Right after the raid on the compound," he began, "Lucas contacted me and told me everything. That the mission was a success, that the

target and all its servants were dead, but there was one sur-
vivor from the compound that he could not bring himself
to kill. When he told me his plan was to bring you into the
Order and raise you as a soldier, I said he was making a mistake. I told him that anything that came from dragons was
evil, and that one day, you would turn on us and sell us out
to the lizards."

"Sir…"

He held up a hand. "Regardless of what I thought, Lucas
would not hear it. He was determined to raise you as a soldier of St. George. He was adamant that there was something
from that compound that could be saved, that didn't have to
be pure evil." He paused, then said in a slow, weary voice,
"Lucas knew your mother, Garret. That's why he took you
that day. Before he became a soldier, before she married a
scientist and started working for the organization, they knew
each other. Apparently, they were very good friends, perhaps
even lovers, before life pulled them apart."

I sat there, reeling. More secrets, more truths that I had
never suspected. How much had the people I'd trusted really
kept from me? Was my entire upbringing one big lie?

"When you were born, your mother no longer wished to
be part of Talon," Martin went on. "Perhaps she didn't know
what she was really working for until later, or perhaps she
didn't want to raise you in the company of monsters. But she
knew that she could not simply take you and disappear—Talon
would track you both down. So she waited, and somehow,
she found Lucas again. She made a deal with him, that if the
Order attacked the compound, her family would be spared.
They would escape and disappear without Talon's knowledge.
And Lucas agreed that St. George would let them go." Mar-

tin sighed. "But something went wrong. Your mother was killed, caught in the crossfire when the dragon showed itself."

"And my father?" I asked numbly.

"His body was never found," Martin said. "But we believe he was shot or burned to death along with the rest of the servants. No one in that compound survived." Another heartbeat of silence, and then he added, "Lucas never forgave himself for that night. That's why he took you in. If he couldn't save your family, he would at least save something. But that is your true heritage, Sebastian. And that is why we are here. Because Lucas saw something in you that I did not—at least, not at first. He saw...not a Talon servant, not a soul tainted by dragons, but a boy. An orphan who was alone in the world, because of him. He decided then and there that he would not let the dragons have you. That he would honor your mother's last request and save you from the organization."

For a long moment, I was silent, trying to process it all. I'd thought I knew Lucas Benedict. But he'd had another life before we ever met. He'd known my mother, and that thought sent a spear of anger through me. For years when I was a boy, I had dreamed of my mom and the family I'd forgotten. I wished I could have known them, especially my mother, but it seemed Benedict knew more of my family than I did.

"Who else knew of this?" I asked, finally glancing up. "How many knew who my parents really were?"

"No one who is alive," Martin said quietly. "Myself, Benedict and the Patriarch were the only ones who knew your parents were Talon servants. But not even the Patriarch was aware of your mother's connection to Lucas. He made me promise never to reveal that to anyone."

"Was he ever going to tell me?" I rasped. "Were you? Or were you going to let me believe that Talon killed my parents my whole life?"

"No." Martin's eyes narrowed. "When you graduated basic training, Lucas was going to tell you himself, tell you everything. But after he was killed, I watched you push yourself to become that perfect soldier. I watched you in battle, watched you go after the enemy with a single-minded hatred I've only seen in veteran soldiers, and I knew that if I had told you your true heritage, it would have destroyed you. So I made the decision to let that other boy die. You became Garret Xavier Sebastian, the Perfect Soldier of St. George. The boy who was raised with dragons...we buried him and hoped he would never resurface."

"What were their names?" I asked softly. "My parents. Before I became Xavier Sebastian, what was my real name?"

Martin gazed at me for several heartbeats, then rose and walked to the filing cabinet behind him. He opened a drawer and riffled through the contents, then spun and walked back to the desk, tossing a manila folder in front of me.

I flipped it open. Inside, several photos, files and newspaper clippings peered back at me. The story of a mysterious explosion at a private lab that had apparently killed every worker there. And a sheet of paper, crinkled and yellowed with time, that read Certificate of Birth at the top and had a familiar name typed into the line below it.

"Garret David Olsen," I murmured, then scanned the rest of the sheet. "Born in Cambridge, Massachusetts. Mother's maiden name, Sarah Beckham. Father's name, John Olsen."

"I took the liberty of researching your family once you came to live with us," Martin said as I stared blankly at the sheet of paper, not knowing what to feel. "I think Lucas

wanted you to have this eventually, despite my misgivings."
He sighed. "But who you were then and who you are now...
it doesn't make any difference, Garret."

I looked up, surprised. Both at hearing my first name, and
that Martin would say something like that. Martin, a staunch
supporter of St. George and all its ideals, who believed that
a soul corrupted by demons was beyond hope. He hesitated,
as if gathering his thoughts, then continued in a grave voice.

"I once told Lucas nothing good comes from a dragon.
That even a four-year-old boy was tainted beyond hope.
That the evil within him would fester and grow, and eventually he would turn on us. And there are those in St. George
who would say that is exactly what happened." His face grew
even darker. "The Patriarch certainly thought so, and it cost
him his life.

"However," he went on, "I find it ironic that the one who
accused you of treason was himself corrupt beyond mea-
sure. And that you risked your life to expose him." Martin
shook his head, his gaze becoming intense. "I've watched you
through the years, Sebastian. I know you better than most.
Though you did make me doubt you the night you escaped
with those dragons, in this, at least, I can admit when I've
been wrong. If there is evil festering in your soul, I've yet to
see it." His smile had no humor in it whatsoever. "Though
that does throw everything the Order believes into question, doesn't it?"

I took a quiet breath. "The Order can change," I said carefully. "I've lived with some of these dragons. I've seen what
they're really like. They want nothing to do with Talon or
the war. All they want is to live freely, without the fear of
St. George coming for them in the middle of the night." I
paused; Martin was watching me intently, eyes dark, but he

wasn't openly protesting or calling me a heretic. Still, I chose my next words carefully. "Sir, if you would just talk to one of them, let them explain their side, you would see that they're not all soulless monsters. Honestly, some of them are a lot like us. At the very least, they don't deserve to be slaughtered just for existing."

Martin sighed. "Perhaps it is as you say, Sebastian," he said. "Perhaps it is time for the Order to look at things anew. Unfortunately, we cannot do anything about it now. Let us first see if we survive the night before we talk of change."

"Sir?"

Martin looked up as Tristan came into the room and saluted just inside the door. "We're ready, sir," he announced. "Everyone is in position, and the rest of the base is locked down. We're just waiting on your orders."

Martin nodded. "I guess it's nearly time, isn't it?" he mused, rising heavily from his seat. Gazing at each of us in turn, he gave a small smile. "Sebastian, St. Anthony, I can truly say it's been a pleasure serving with you. Good luck to us all."

DANTE

It's time.

I stood on the raised dais at the back of the command center, gazing at the bank of screens in front of me. Each showed satellite images of a familiar desert, a familiar cluster of buildings in the middle of the darkness. On one screen, the base was dark, save for a large square building in the very center. This structure was brightly lit, and that made me suspicious.

"Are we ready?" I asked. Around me, the team of humans were quick to respond. I knew the Elder Wyrm was listening somewhere as every Talon command center around the world prepared to go to war. The Night of Fang and Fire had finally come. Tonight, among many others, the Western chapterhouse of the Order of St. George was going to fall. By any means necessary.

Then let's begin. I took a deep, steadying breath and commanded, "Send in Alpha flight one."

"Sir." Immediately, one of the senior humans glanced at me, brow furrowed. "Just the one flight, sir?" he asked, as if I didn't know what I was doing. "We have five flights and the Omega protocol on standby. Shouldn't we send them all at once? We're sure to overwhelm the base, and we'll take fewer casualties ourselves."

"No." I narrowed my eyes at the human. "You don't know this chapterhouse or who resides there. And, lest anyone has forgotten, this is St. George. They know how to kill dragons, and how to defend themselves from dragons. Before we throw everything we have at them, I want to know what kind of firepower they've got and how to deal with it. So, this is the last time I will repeat myself—send in Alpha flight one. Hold the rest in reserve until I say otherwise."

"Yes, sir."

I crossed my arms, watching the screens, waiting for what the night would reveal.

The match has been set into motion, St. George. Let the games begin.

GARRET

Three minutes till midnight.

Outside, the air was still. A sickly white moon hung in the sky behind a few wispy clouds, unable to pierce the darkness blanketing the chapterhouse. I stood at a window on the upper floor of the barracks, watching the sky for dragons. Behind me, the rest of my team—four of St. George's best—sat or lay quietly on cots while I kept watch. Fifty yards away, the armory sat huddled in shadow, silent and dark. My gaze went to the spots where the snipers were hiding, Tristan among them. I wondered if he would survive this night...if any of us would survive. We'd prepared as best we could, but who knew what kind of numbers Talon would throw at us?

"All squads, this is Anvil Six," came Martin's voice over the radio. The lieutenant was in the armory with the rest of the squadron. "What's it look like out there?"

"Anvil, this is Longshot Six," came Tristan's voice, cool and unruffled. "Nothing on our end. The sky is clear."

"Anvil, Storm Six," said the commander of the machine gun squad. "Same here, just sitting on our asses waiting, sir." A few chuckles echoed that statement, and I smiled faintly.

"Anvil, Scorpion Six," I said into my headset. "Nothing

here, either. We've got a clear line of sight to your position and everything is quiet."

"All right," Martin replied. "You know the drill, gentlemen. Keep your eyes open and radio the second you see anything, lizard or otherwise."

"Sir," we all answered, and the line went quiet.

I glanced at my team. They seemed calm, cavalier, even, but that was to be expected. We'd all done something like this before. Never on our own turf, of course, but we all had experience in staging ambushes and waiting for the battle to start. Worrying and dwelling on the upcoming fight was useless; there was nothing we could do until go time.

Ember, I thought as my watch flipped to 11:59 and a blanket of clouds crawled across the moon. *I wish I could have seen you one more time. Wherever you are right now, stay safe.*

"We got movement!"

I jerked up. Tristan's voice crackled over the radio, tense and chillingly eager. "Hostiles inbound. About two clicks away, from the west side of the fence. Ugly gray bastards like Scorpion said. Ten targets, maybe more." A heartbeat of a pause, and Tristan added, "Damn, they really are exactly the same. Looks like the party is about to start, sir."

"Copy that, Longshot," Martin replied. "You may fire when ready."

I held my breath, waiting. Outside, the night was still. I couldn't see anything in the darkness but the armory in front of me.

Then a shot rang out, the report crystal clear in the silence. A half second later, Tristan's voice echoed smugly over the radio.

"Lima down, Anvil Six, lima down."

A cheer went up, my own team joining in. "Quiet," I

warned, glancing back at them. That was just the first casualty. We couldn't celebrate yet.

Two more shots echoed, ringing over the buildings. "Shit," hissed another sniper, one I didn't recognize. "Dodgy bastards. Anvil Six, they're coming in fast."

"Storm," Martin snapped. "Get ready. When you see the targets, light them up."

A chilling scream rang out, making my blood run cold, as several dark, winged shapes appeared through the clouds. Eyes glowing silver against the black, they dropped from the sky with shrieking battle cries and swooped toward the armory.

DANTE

"We're taking fire!"

On the screens, lights flared, illuminating the darkness. The distinctive white streaks of gunfire.

"They've got machine gunners on the roofs," someone called out, as if he hadn't expected anything like that. I considered firing him on the spot. It was St. George; how could he *not* expect they would be ready for an attack made by dragons? This was precisely why I wanted to send in the first wave, to gauge their defenses and fortifications and test what kind of surprises they had waiting. None of this was unexpected.

"Sir, we've got snipers," called another human, staring intensely at the screens. "Coming from the chapel and the headquarters roof, I believe. Alpha one-three and one-seven are down, and one-nine has been severely wounded. Should I order it to return to base?"

"No," I said calmly. "If it's going to die soon, there's no reason for it to return." I swept a hand toward the screen. "Have Alpha one-nine ram the chapel tower. Hopefully that will get rid of at least one shooter. The rest of them should take out the machine gunners and the other snipers."

There was a moment's pause. I could feel the eyes of the

rest of the team on me, wide and stunned. "Are my orders unclear?" I asked softly.

"No, sir!" The man quickly turned and spoke urgently into his radio, and the rest of the team averted their eyes. Casualties were to be expected, I told myself. The vessels were tools. Bred to fight, kill and die. And when they died, they should take out as many enemies as they could. I was commander, and victory was nonnegotiable. The life of a single vessel, a dozen vessels, didn't matter. They existed only to ensure that the battle was ours.

"Sir," said another human, "what of the armory? We've got shots coming from that building, too."

"Ah. That would be their headquarters," I mused. "Their bunker for this attack. If we destroy it, the fight is ours." I raised a hand. "Send in flight two," I ordered. "Have them concentrate fire on the armory."

GARRET

The scene outside dissolved into utter pandemonium. Metallic-gray dragons swooped through the air, breathing flame and lighting up the darkness. Turret fire roared, and the occasional bark of sniper rifles could be heard over the cacophony. Dragons tumbled from the sky, falling to the ground or crashing into the sides of buildings. We seemed to be holding our own, but I knew this couldn't be the whole strike force. Talon had to be holding something in reserve, just as we were.

Behind me, I could feel the tension in my squad, watching the screaming chaos through the windows, their hands on their RPGs. I saw several looks shot my way, wondering when they would receive the order to fire, to aid the rest of the base. *Not yet,* I thought at them. *Hold your ground, it's not time yet. We get only one shot, and we have to make it count.*

Voices crackled over the radio—Martin calling orders to his men, the other squad commanders responding in turn. I listened, helpless to do anything else, knowing our time was coming but not yet. I heard Storm commander snarling defiantly at the dragons swooping by, heard the chatter of machine gun rounds, before his voice abruptly cut out over the radio. Martin called out to him, demanding his status, but he didn't respond.

And then, Tristan's voice, oddly calm, like he was watching a head-on collision but couldn't do anything about it. "Oh, shit—"

With a streak of metallic scales, a dragon slammed full speed into the chapel tower with a boom that shook the ground. Wood and plaster flew everywhere, splinters raining to the earth as the steeple wall collapsed with a groan and a snapping of timber.

"Tristan!"

Someone behind me hissed a curse. I ignored him, putting a hand to my helmet as I snarled into the headset: "Longshot Six, come in. Longshot, this is Scorpion. What's your status?"

Nothing. The buzz of static and the echo of gunfire were the only answers to my repeated calling. Numb, I closed my eyes, fighting the helpless rage within. *Dammit, Tristan. You weren't supposed to die on the front lines. You were the one who was supposed to survive this.*

Outside, the fight continued. A gunner frantically tried shooting down three dragons at once, but another swooped in from behind and landed on his back. Narrow jaws snapped, and the soldier slumped lifelessly over the gun. As I watched, a second dragon flew straight into the hail of machine gun fire, didn't stop and crashed headfirst into the turret, crushing both the gun and the soldier operating it.

"Sir," one of my men growled. "More dragons incoming."

I looked up as another wave descended from the clouds and swarmed the armory. Jets of flames erupted from their mouths as they swooped past, strafing it again and again, and I could feel the immense heat even from here.

"Ready to fire, sir," the soldier said, hefting the weapon. "On your order."

"Hold," I snapped, and his jaw tightened. "Not yet," I told him and the rest of the team. "There are too many dragons in the air. If we move now, we'll be wasting our shots and giving away our position. Our orders are to wait until we're sure we can do the most damage possible. Until that time, we stay put."

Johnson glared at me with suspicion and defiance. "Are you sure we're holding back because of orders, *sir*?" he asked, his tone softly dangerous. "And that you're not feeling sympathy for the lizards?"

Any other time, I might have hit him. Dragons were attacking, the base was being destroyed and I'd just watched my best friend die in front of me. I was not in the mood for insubordination, and laying him flat on his back was a viciously tempting thought.

Instead, I turned and calmly pointed the muzzle of my sidearm in his face. He froze, as did the rest of the squad, and I smiled coldly.

"Not yet," I said, my voice flat and dangerous. "We hold position until I say it's time. Is that clear, soldier?"

He glared for a moment, then dropped his gaze. "Yes, sir."

I returned to watching the battle, a cold lump settling in my gut. Talon was still holding back. I didn't know how many more waves of dragons were coming, but I did know they weren't done, not by a long shot.

I had the sinking feeling that they were just getting started.

DANTE

"Losing more vessels, sir," said a human, turning to look at me with wide eyes. "Nearly all of Alpha has been killed, and Bravo is at half-strength."

"The building is holding, sir," said someone else. "It must have fire-resistant walls. Our forces can't burn it down."

I smiled coldly. *Well, St. George. You're putting up as big a fight as I thought you would. How long can you hold out? I wonder. Very well. If the rats won't be burned out, we'll go in after them.*

"Send in flight Charlie," I ordered, "and have them concentrate all physical efforts into getting into that bunker. I don't care what it takes." I narrowed my eyes at the stubborn building on the screen and clenched a fist. "Tear it down!"

GARRET

This was endless.

I watched yet another wave come in, this one even bigger than the last, dragons descending from the air in a swarm. Our forces were dwindling. The machine gunners were all dead, and I hadn't heard a sniper report in a long time. And yet, the dragons kept coming, a relentless, never-ending hoard. Maybe Talon did have an infinite supply of them, and they would continue to attack until they had slaughtered every last soldier in the chapterhouse.

"They've stopped trying to burn down the armory at least," one of the men growled beside me. "What the hell are they doing now?"

I didn't answer, watching as the new swarm of dragons dropped from the air, rushed the armory walls and began tearing at them viciously. Inside, soldiers stuck their guns through the windows and fired on their attackers, but there were too many dragons and too few places to fire from. Bricks began crumbling and falling away as the clones' relentless assault continued.

But they were on the ground now. A massive group of them, all in one spot. I looked at my team, saw the same realization in their eyes and nodded. It was time; we would never get a better shot.

Raising the RPG to my shoulder, I carefully aimed the rocket through the window, at the cluster of writhing, squirming wings and tails. Beside me, the others did the same—five lethal high-powered grenades, going right into the heart of the enemy forces.

"Ready," I muttered, curling my finger around the trigger. "Aim." I paused for a heartbeat, for that moment when my body was perfectly, absolutely still, then released the breath I was holding. "Fire!"

With a deafening, piercing hiss, five rocket powered grenades streaked from the windows of the building, flying into the mob of dragons below. Five massive explosions followed as the grenades erupted into roaring balls of smoke and fire, turning everything white for a split second. Dragons were flung in all directions, shrieking, tumbling through the air and crashing lifelessly to the ground. The smoke cleared, leaving a large section of scorched, blasted earth that was now covered in blown-apart dragons, some twitching weakly but far too wounded to stay alive.

The men beside me let out wild cheers and howls of triumph. I imagined the same was happening inside the armory, but there was no time to celebrate. The surprise attack had decimated the dragon numbers, killing half of them in one lethal blast, but there were still more out there, clawing at the armory, slowly pushing their way in. If they managed to get inside, we could lose the battle.

"Let's go!" I snapped to the team, and grabbed my M-4 from where it lay beneath the window. "Before they have a chance to regroup." When they did recover, we would likely be killed, but this was our job. This was our part in the battle: hit hard and fast, and kill as many as we could before we died.

Sprinting down the stairs, we charged into the chaos, into the heat and screams and smoke, and opened fire.

DANTE

A huge explosion rocked the screen, turning it white for a moment.

"Shit!" cried one of the humans as the rest of them gasped in horror. "Sir, we've got multiple wings down. Bravo one, two, three, seven, ten. Charlie two, six, seven, eight, ten. Delta four, five—"

"Excellent." They stopped and stared at me, stunned. *As I expected. That was their ace in the hole. I knew they were holding something back.* I smiled grimly. Victory was close. Just one final push.

"Send in the rest," I ordered. "All wings, attack. Take that base down, now."

GARRET

I'd been told that there is a point in every soldier's life when he knows he's going to die.

You expect it, of course. In every battle, every ambush or enemy engagement. You're aware that this could be it. This could be the one that ends your life.

But there's a difference between being aware that you could die and knowing, beyond a doubt, when the situation is hopeless.

New dragons dropped from the sky in a dark mass. More swooped toward me and my team, jets of fire erupting from their mouths. I dove aside, feeling the heat blast through my armor as I rolled to a knee and fired on the dragon streaking by. It shrieked and crashed through a window, shattering glass and leaving jagged shards behind.

One of my men screamed. I whirled to see a dragon swoop in from behind, grab the soldier by the armor and carry him off. He kicked and flailed for a moment before pointing the muzzle of his gun back at his captor and opening fire. The dragon jerked in the air, shuddering, then plummeted forty feet to the ground. Both bodies struck the earth with a hollow thump and didn't get up again.

"Scorpion!" Martin's voice crackled in my ear. "The hostiles are about to break through the walls. What's your status? Did the strike not work?"

"Yes, sir, it did!" I raised my weapon and fired as two dragons came swooping in, then quickly ducked as one barely missed me. I felt the tips of its claws scrape my helmet as it soared past. "But there are reinforcements. We're trying to get to the armory now."

"God, how many of these things are there?" An explosion sounded somewhere close, and Martin cursed. "All right, get to the east wall, Scorpion. The bastards are nearly through."

"On our way."

I motioned to the rest my team, of which only two were left, and we headed to the east wall. Dragons streaked through the air or bounded at us from the ground, weaving through flames, rubble and smoke. I reacted on instinct, firing at any dragon that got close while trying to stay out of range of its claws and breath. One of my teammates got caught in a line of dragonfire and reeled away, blazing like a torch.

The eastern side of the armory was crawling with dragons, tearing at the walls or digging at the roof. I fired into the swarming mass, taking several down, before a section of the hoard broke away and rushed me with piercing shrieks.

"More dragons incoming!" someone shouted, but I couldn't take my attention from the flood closing on me. I shot down three scaly bodies as they drew close, but one vessel lunged at me with a hiss, jaws gaping, and I knew I wouldn't be able to kill it in time.

And then a small crimson dragon dropped from the sky with a snarl, crushing the clone to the earth. Spreading her wings, she raised her head and roared a challenge as a swarm of brightly colored dragons soared overhead with ringing battle cries and dropped into the fray.

Whirling around, the red dragon shot me a fierce, defiant grin, eyes flashing green in the darkness. "Hey, soldier boy. The cavalry's finally here."

DANTE

"Something's happened, sir."

I frowned at the confusing shapes on screen, trying to determine what was going on. Bright shapes darted across the sky, flurries of frantic movement that could belong to only one thing. "Are those…dragons?" I asked incredulously, leaning forward. That was impossible. How could there be *that* many dragons who weren't our own? But, watching the figures dart around the screen, I knew they could be nothing else. More dragons. How? Who would…?

No. It couldn't be. She was supposed to be safely at Talon headquarters with the Elder Wyrm. She was supposed to be out of this fight, away from the slaughter. And yet, I knew it was her. She was the only dragon in the world who, after somehow escaping Talon, would turn right around and aid the Order of St. George on the night they were supposed to be destroyed.

"Ember," I whispered. The bright streaks of color darted across the screen, mingling with the darker, more subdued vessels, and I clenched my fists. "What the hell are you doing?"

"What should we do, sir?" asked a human.

I stared at the scene in growing rage. Ember was down

there…but I couldn't falter now. I couldn't turn from this path. The Elder Wyrm demanded victory; she expected me to succeed. Even if my own sister was killed, I could not forfeit the most important mission of my life. Talon's future, and my own, hung in the balance. Sacrifice, as always, was necessary.

Though someone would pay for this when it was over. Someone would be punished for my twin's death. I would see to it myself.

"Unleash Omega," I said. "We end this now."

EMBER

Oh, man, this is nuts.

I shook my head, watching what had to be the craziest battle in the world unfold in front of me. Hatchlings, clones and soldiers of St. George soared or darted through the flames and smoke, shooting or breathing fire onto their opponents. Brightly colored hatchlings flung themselves at the darker metallic clones, using group tactics to gang up on their soul-less counterparts. A vivid green hatchling and a smaller black hatchling tag-teamed a clone, each darting in and slashing at it when its attention was on the other. A vessel pounced on another hatchling and seemed ready to tear it apart, when a silvery white dragon dropped silently onto its back and sank her claws into its throat.

"Ember." Somehow, Garret's voice reached me over the screams of dragons and the howl of assault rifles. I turned to the soldier, finding him. "You made it," he said, as if he couldn't quite believe it.

"Yeah." I nodded, managing a smile. "I made it. *With* re-inforcements. Sorry we couldn't get here sooner, Garret. We came as fast as we could."

With a deafening roar and a crack of thunder, a forty-foot Eastern dragon soared overhead in the direction of the armory. Cries of awe and alarm rang out as Jade swooped in and began snatching clones from the air, crushing them in her powerful jaws and flinging them aside. The vessels tried to swarm her, raking her with teeth and claws, but they were no match for the immensely powerful Adult and were smashed out of the air one by one.

The soldier blinked, watching the Eastern dragon wreak havoc overhead, a grim smile crossing his face. "I see Jade got my message," he said in a voice of dark satisfaction. "Is Riley here, as well?"

I nodded again, following his gaze. "And Mist, too. Somewhere. It was a fight, but everyone decided to come in the end." Lowering my head, I met his gaze and bared my teeth in a savage grin. "I told you I'd come back. Though you started the battle without me, I see."

He stepped forward and briefly touched his forehead to mine. I felt the heat of his skin against my scales, and a rush of fire spread through my veins. "You're incredible, Ember," he murmured. "Thank you."

I swallowed. "I told you, soldier boy. We end this together."

"Yes." Stepping back, he raised his gun, eyes hard. "Let's go," he told me, starting forward. "While they're distracted. Let's finish this."

We sprang back into the fray. Clones and hatchlings battled each other on the ground and in the air, streaks of color and shadow all around us. Fires blazed, men shouted and gunfire chattered from all directions. Dragons, both friend and foe, swooped from the sky or bounded through the flames, dark blurs against the hellish light. I saw dragons locked in battle with other dragons, wings and tails thrashing as they clawed and tore at each other. I saw a few soldiers of St. George firing on their quick-moving targets and desperately hoped they could tell the difference between a savage clone dragon and Riley's hatchlings. A vessel leaped at us, snarling; Garret's M-4 chattered, and the thing crashed to the ground. Another streaked overhead, breathing fire into a cluster of hatchlings; I sprang into the air with a snarl, colliding with the scaly body and bringing it down with me. Claws slashed at me as we landed, tearing through scales and raking gouges of pain down my shoulder. My vision went red; with a roar, I pinned my rival to the ground, clamped my jaws around that long snaking neck and jerked up as hard as I could.

The dragon below me shuddered, wings and tail twitching, before it went limp. I dropped the neck and backed away, surprised at how quickly it had died, how easy it had been to kill it. For just a moment, I thought I might feel horror, disgust at what I'd done. But something had changed. I was a dragon, and these things were trying to kill me, my friends and everything I loved. There was no time for regret. This was a war.

I bounded to Garret's side again, blasting a cone of flame at a vessel coming in from the left. The flames didn't stop it, but they did blind the vessel for the split second it took Garret to turn and gun it down.

"Ember! St. George!"

Cobalt swooped down, landing beside us with a blast of wind, his eyes blazing golden as he swung his head around to glare at the soldier. "We're taking pretty heavy damage, but I think we're slowly driving them out, thanks to Jade." All three of us glanced at the sky, where the Eastern dragon was coiling back and forth among her smaller opponents, swatting or snapping them out of the air. Cobalt snorted and looked back at Garret. "She should be able to handle the cleanup. Where do we need to go?"

"The armory," Garret said immediately. "We have to get to Lieutenant Martin, see if any of the clones broke through."

Cobalt gave a brisk nod and bared his fangs. "Lead the way."

We fought our way across the yard, to where the large square building loomed at the edge of the walk. A group of soldiers now stood in front of it, firing their guns at any clone that got close. They were, I noted in relief, shooting specifically at the vessels and not at the rogue hatchlings. The last thirty feet to the armory was a mass of writhing bodies, and we had to claw, shoot and fight our way past several clones before the way to the building was clear.

"Lieutenant!" Garret called as we rushed up.

"Sebastian." The older man shook his head with a wry smile. "Still alive, are you? I'm glad. Looks like your dragons got here, after all." His hard black eyes shifted to me and Cobalt, standing a few feet away. "You didn't mention you were bringing an Adult."

"That a problem?" Cobalt asked with only the barest hint of a curled lip.

"Not at all." Martin spared a glance upward as Jade soared past, chasing a few stray clones. "We may actually win this fight…"

He trailed off. I felt the ripple of…*something*…go through the air, and a chill slid up my back. Maybe fifty feet overhead, Jade curled gracefully around to pursue the clones—

—and something hit her from above, bursting through the clouds to slam into her back. Huge and dark, with leathery wings and blank silver eyes, it hit the Eastern dragon like a falling airplane, driving them both to the ground. Jade didn't even have time to look back before she struck the earth with the other dragon on top of her. The crash from the two behemoths shook the ground, and a cloud of dust billowed up where they landed.

An enormous shadow rose from the swirling dust storm, its scales the metallic gray of the clones, only this dragon was much, much bigger. Pale horns framed its face and twisted back from its skull, and a line of bony ridges curved wickedly down its spine to the tip of its tail. Looming over the motionless body of the Eastern dragon, the monstrous vessel reared onto its hind legs and roared, making everything inside me cringe in fear.

Cobalt snarled, crouching down and half opening his wings in a semi-instinctive reaction. "What the hell? They have an Adult clone? Where has Talon been hiding *that*?"

Garret's commander looked pale. I didn't blame him; in one swoop, the clone had taken out our strongest ally, and with her our best chance at stopping it. From this distance, I could just make out the graceful curve of her body, lying motionless in the sand, and felt sick with grief, anger and fear. Was Jade really dead? It didn't seem possible that the Eastern dragon was gone. Without her, I didn't know what we could do against a massive Adult dragon that showed no fear and no instinct for self-preservation. Unless we killed or severely crippled it, it would keep coming, and something that huge would cause massive destruction before it was finally put down. The soldiers of St. George stared at it, too, their expressions grim. They knew, better than most, how nasty Adult dragons could be, how difficult they were to take out.

"I don't suppose you lizards have any more tricks up your sleeves?" the commander muttered, never taking his eyes away from the Adult. "Another dragon you've kept in reserve, just in case?"

"Sadly, our reserve of Adults is rather slim at the moment," Cobalt growled back. "Jade was our heavy hitter before that thing blindsided her." He shook his head at the enormous Adult vessel, his spines bristling in fear. "Shit. Any bright ideas, St. George?" he asked, turning to Garret, who stared at the huge dragon with narrowed eyes. "'Cause I'm feeling a little outgunned right now."

"Lieutenant." Instead of answering, Garret turned to Martin. His voice was surprisingly calm. "Sir, are the keys to the garage in the same spot?"

"Yes." Martin frowned, obviously as confused as we were. "I take it you have a plan, Sebastian?"

"I hope so." Garret turned to me and Riley. "Stall that thing," he told us, making Riley snort in disbelief. "Just for a few minutes." His gaze went to mine, dark with worry. "Can you do that, Ember?"

"Yeah." I gave him a savage grin. "Don't worry, we'll hold it. For as long as we can."

He nodded. "I'll be right back."

Spinning, he sprinted away into the flickering darkness.

Cobalt shook his head. "Oh, this is gonna be fun," he muttered, and gave me a look from the corner of his eye. "If I don't get eaten by a dragon, Firebrand, I'm never letting you forget this."

Before I could respond, he leaped into the air, flying straight up so that he could be seen by everyone. "All right!" he roared, jerking everyone's attention to him. "Hatchlings, fall back! Get out of sight, and *do not* engage that Adult! I don't care how much you want to help, this is nonnegotiable. Retreat to the rendezvous and stay there until you hear from me or Wes. Go!"

With a flurry of flapping wings, the hatchlings rose from the ground in a bright swarm and soared over the fence line. As the last dragon swooped out of sight, Cobalt landed beside me with a grim smile. "There. At least the only dragons that thing will be eating tonight are us."

Opening its massive wings, the Adult vessel gave a leap that propelled it into the air and then streaked like a fireball in the direction of the chapterhouse.

RILEY

Godzilla was coming.

Stall the thing, St. George had said. Easy for him to say. Shit, this was a bad idea. How were two non-Adult dragons and a handful of human soldiers supposed to stall that thing? It was an Adult. An *old* Adult, by the size of it, close to forty feet from head to tail. Maybe if it choked on us while we were sliding down its windpipe? I was just relieved the hatchlings were in full retreat and that no one had argued about staying to battle this monster.

The Adult clone landed in the center of the yard with a boom and another roar that made my eardrums throb. As soon as it touched down, every soldier of St. George left opened fire, filling the air with the roar of assault rifles. The bullets that struck the chest and belly plates sparked harmlessly off, and the ones that did get through seemed as effective as air pellets. The Adult gave a chilling, banshee-like howl and lumbered forward, plowing through the bullet storm and coming right toward the armory.

I looked at Ember. "Ready for this, Firebrand?"

"Not really," she replied, her eyes glued to the approaching giant. "But I'm right behind you."

We leaped into the air and flew straight at the monster's

jaws and eerie, glowing eyes. It hissed and reared back its neck to strike, mouth opening to show curved ivory fangs. As we drew closer, it lunged, snapping at the air as we veered aside and split up to go around it. Snarling, it whirled, huge jaws agape as it snapped and swatted at us, like we were giant scaly wasps buzzing around its head. Gunfire still echoed somewhere behind us as the soldiers of St George continued to pump rounds into the enormous dragon. Thankfully, the bastards' aim was better than their manners, though I still expected that, at any second, one of us would get caught in the crossfire. Thankfully, I was so busy trying not to be crushed by a gigantic clone dragon, I barely had time to worry about being shot by overzealous dragonslayers. I dodged a taloned forepaw nearly as big as my head, darted between two buildings and heard the clone smash through the wall as it followed, tearing out chunks of brick and mortar as it forced its way between. I landed, spun around and immediately had to leap away as those curved claws raked a two-foot gouge into the earth.

Shit. The thing was fast as well as big. I ducked, dodging the teeth that snicked shut inches from my head, saw Ember bound forward and rake both claws down the monster's back leg. It snarled and whirled, swatting at her, but stumbled a bit from being hamstrung, and she bounced back out of reach. I darted in, slashing its flank with my talons, and it hissed—whether in pain or annoyance I couldn't tell—and spun on me again.

Well, this is fun. I dodged a nasty blow to my skull and saw Ember leap at its back again while it was distracted. But it was wise to her methods now and sidled away from her talons. *Whatever you're planning, hurry up, St. George. We can't keep harassing this thing forever.*

And then it happened. The thing lunged with a roar, snapping at me. I swerved to avoid those snapping jaws of death but didn't see the claw coming until it smashed into my ribs. I heard something snap and was flung away, crumpling to the ground and rolling several feet before I came to a dazed stop.

Gritting my jaw, I tried to push myself upright, but then someone jammed an invisible knife between my ribs and I sank back with a hiss of pain. The ground rumbled beneath me, and I looked up to see the Adult looming closer, a snarling Ember clinging to its back, ripping at its shoulders. It ignored the red hatchling, its blank silver eyes fixed on me as it stalked forward to end my life.

Oh, that's great. I'm going to be eaten by a dragon. Wait till Wes hears about this.

Something streaked past me in a silvery blur. Mist flew straight into the dragon's face, sinking her claws into its eyes and muzzle. The Adult bellowed and reared back, shaking its head, trying to dislodge the dragon clawing at its face. Mist snarled and refused to relent, beating her wings for balance as the clone roared and flailed.

Finally, with a mighty fling of its head, the clone hurled the silver dragon into the air. She spun gracefully midfall, flapped her wings and flew toward the armory. From its back, Ember leaped skyward, as well, just as a black, armored truck slammed full speed into the Adult dragon, knocking it to the side. It let out a screech, the first real sound of pain I'd heard, as the truck plowed straight into a wall, crushing the dragon between several tons of metal and brick. Blood streamed from its mouth and nostrils as it gave a defiant scream and thrashed violently, tearing at the vehicle with tooth and claw before it finally freed itself. Soldiers rushed forward, firing their weapons as the huge dragon staggered, stumbling forward in an almost-drunken manner. Blood poured from its mouth in streams as it turned in a confused circle, staring blearily at the humans swarming around it.

Finally, with the last groan of a dying giant, it collapsed to the dusty earth. For a moment, it lay there, panting, still confused as to what was happening to it. Then the silvery eyes turned dark, the great jaws stopped gasping and the enormous head slumped to the side as the vessel shuddered one last time and didn't move again.

I slumped to the dust as cheers rose around me. I would have joined in the celebrating, but I didn't particularly feel like shouting, or moving, at the moment. My side throbbed; each breath sent a stab of pain through my obviously broken ribs. Lying here and breathing as shallowly as I could seemed like a pretty good idea.

With a creak, the door of the truck opened and the soldier staggered out, his face a bloody mess. Instantly, Ember launched herself over the dead clone dragon and flew to his side. Her eyes were worried as she leaned in, wings half-spread in alarm, and the human gave her a tired smile, probably assuring her he was fine.

Oh, sure. Go see if the human is all right. Don't mind me; I'll just lie here and try not to bleed on everything.

A shadow fell over me, and Mist landed a few feet away, blocking my view. "That," she stated, peering down at me with glowing blue eyes, "was probably the stupidest thing I have ever seen anyone do, dragon or otherwise. Now I know how you've avoided Talon for so long—pure dumb, crazy luck."

I chuckled, but it turned into a painful, raspy cough. "Uh, pot meet kettle," I said, not bothering to move from the dirt just yet. "If it was so crazy, why did you come and help us?"

She sniffed. "I was told by my employer to aid you in battle tonight. He made it very clear that he did not want you or Ms. Hill to die." Her chin rose defiantly. "My orders were to prevent that from happening, in whatever way possible."

"Ah. So it was just orders, then."

"Of course." Mist rolled her eyes, but she wasn't looking at me anymore. "I take my job very seriously, Cobalt. You wouldn't understand."

"Sure."

Clenching my jaw, I pushed myself to my feet, grimly observing the battlefield and taking stock of our losses. The dead vessel, outlined in moonlight, sprawled like a black mountain in the center of a war zone. Bodies, both soldier and dragon alike, lay everywhere. Most of the dragon bodies were clones, but here and there, brighter scales glinted among the dull metallics, and a cold, sickening lump settled in my stomach.

Stupid, brave hatchlings, I thought, just as my gaze settled on a small brown dragon, crumpled between two larger clones. My heart sank. *Remy.* And now he would never tell stories again.

The sick feeling turned to anger, making me want to sink my claws into something's face and char the skin beneath my talons until it melted and fell off. I suddenly wished the clone was alive again, just so I could kill it myself. *You wanted to fight*, I raged silently. *You didn't want to hide any longer. Was it worth it? Was any of this worth it?*

"You couldn't have protected them, Cobalt." At my back, Mist's voice was surprisingly gentle. "Talon would still have come for them in the end. Sooner or later, they were going to have to fight."

"I know." Suddenly tired, I sat down, feeling like I was

perched on the edge of the abyss, seconds from watching the whole world crumble into darkness. Or maybe explode in an eruption of dragonfire and burn to ash. "And it's not over yet, is it?"

"No." Mist came forward and sat beside me, and together, we stared over the battlefield, at the carnage Talon had left behind. The bodies they had wasted, and the dragons they had killed. "I'm afraid this is only the beginning."

GARRET

The infirmary smelled like blood, disinfectant and smoke.

Fourteen dead. Fourteen soldiers who had been killed in their own chapterhouse. Eleven injured, more than half of them severely, and at least a couple who wouldn't survive the morning. One stressed-looking medic scurried back and forth between rows, clearly overwhelmed by all the beds that were filled with bandaged, charred, bloody soldiers. I made my way through the room, passing the wounded, the barely conscious and the dying. I'd already been here once; after the collision with the giant Adult clone, my forehead had needed stitches. I had more than a few bruises, but my body armor had absorbed a good deal of the impact. I would ache for the next few days, but I had gotten off easy. I wished I could say the same for everyone else.

"Hey, Sebastian."

The voice was raspy, weak with pain and drugs. I paused at the bedside of the soldier, gazing down at him. Bandages covered half his face, and one of his arms was wrapped in gauze to the shoulder.

"Your lizards," he husked out, "did good."

He might've wanted to say more, but it was evident that even that bit of talking was painful. So I simply nodded and moved on, passing other cots with wounded soldiers, until I came to a corner that had been sectioned off with a curtain.

As I pushed it back, my throat tightened. Tristan St. Anthony lay on the sheets, still as death, his chest and head wrapped in bloody gauze. They'd found him buried beneath the rubble of the church tower, barely breathing but miraculously still alive. He remained unresponsive, and the medic didn't know if he would pull through. But he was still one of the lucky ones.

Pulling up a chair, I sank down beside him.

"Hey," I greeted him softly. "I just…uh…wanted to let you know how everything went. It worked, by the way. We won. Took some losses, of course, but at least some of us are still standing. Martin sustained a concussion and a broken wrist when part of the roof fell on him, but he's still up, and he's still managing the chapterhouse. Though the medic keeps pestering him to lie down. You almost shared a corner with the acting leader of the Western chapterhouse."

No response from Tristan. The machines around him beeped softly, and his chest rose and fell with each shallow breath. It was strange, seeing him like this. In all our years of fighting together, even when he'd gotten himself sent to the infirmary, Tristan was always awake and alert and rarely stayed down for more than a few hours. I kept expecting him to open his eyes and smirk at me, amused with his own prank.

I sighed. "You'll probably hear this when you wake up," I began, refusing to accept that he might *not* wake up, "and I wish there was another way to say this, but…the Order has been destroyed, Tristan. Martin has been trying to contact anyone from St. George all morning, and no one is answering. The other chapterhouses have gone dark, and the council isn't responding at all. We might...be the only ones left."

I paused as the gravity of that statement hit home. I knew it was too soon to really tell. Others might have survived the assault. There might be more of us left than I thought. But with every passing hour and no word from anyone in St. George, it was becoming more and more apparent that the Order had been decimated. That Talon had won this battle, perhaps even the war, and the Night of Fang and Fire had succeeded in striking the final blow against their ancient enemies.

That left us. Myself, a few rogue dragons and a handful of soldiers. The few remaining survivors. "I don't know what's going to happen," I admitted, mostly to myself. "I don't know if we'll ever recover from this, but if we do, the Order has to change. We can't remain alone and isolated any longer, not with the power Talon now commands. I think Martin is realizing that we need all the allies we can get, if any of us are going to survive whatever is coming."

"There you are." There was a hiss of cloth as someone came through the curtains, and a moment later Ember slipped her arms around my neck from behind. I put my hand on her arm as she leaned in, her body warm against my back. "How are you holding up, soldier boy?"

"I'm all right." I wasn't. My best friend was at death's door, the chapterhouse was in shambles and the Order I'd known all my life was gone. I was enough of a soldier to realize that things looked pretty bleak. We had survived the battle, but the war was far from over. And we didn't stand much of a chance against Talon and their army of dragon clones.

I could feel Ember's worried gaze on the back of my head and knew she saw right through my lie. "Are the others settling in okay?" I asked to distract her. Martin had given the surviving hatchlings the officers' housing for temporary quarters. The few families who lived there had already fled, and more important, the building was isolated from the rest of the soldiers. Most of them were here, in the infirmary, but Martin was taking no chances.

"Yeah." Ember nodded. "Everyone is shaken up, and there are a few who took some nasty injuries, but they're recovering. Riley has organized things pretty well."

"And Jade? How is she?"

"Hurt," Ember replied. "Cranky. She has her own private room where she insisted no hatchlings would come tripping over her, and she keeps admonishing the Order for not having any tea." Her tone, though solemn, became a little lighter. "I think she's going to be fine."

I felt a glow of relief, tiny as it was, that Jade was among the injured and not the dead. The Eastern dragon had suffered several broken ribs and a few deep lacerations where the clone had slammed into her, but it was amazing she had not been wounded more severely. I wondered if she would stick around after she healed; with things the way they were, none of our futures were certain. And Talon was just getting started.

Silence fell again, though it wasn't awkward. The machines beeped, and the murmur of voices echoed through the curtain behind us. Ember drew back, then pulled up the remaining chair and sat beside me.

"How is he?" she asked, her voice very soft.

I swallowed. "Tristan has always been a fighter," I said numbly. "If he can survive the next twenty-four hours, they think he has a good chance of pulling through." I gave her the words the medic told me that morning, but we both knew what it really meant. Ember paused, and then her hand came to rest over mine, fingers curling around my palm. I squeezed her hand as all the fear and uncertainties I'd suppressed rose up like a flood, threatening to drown me. I'd protected this chapterhouse, kept it safe as best I could, and Talon had still managed to nearly destroy it and everything I cared for.

"I don't know what's going to happen now," I admitted. "The Order is gone. There's no one left to stop Talon from doing whatever it is they're planning."

"Yes, there is," Ember said quietly. "There's us. We're still alive, Garret." She glanced down at our clasped fingers, her expression darkening. "I don't know what will happen, either," she said. "I don't know what Talon has planned, or what Dante and the Elder Wyrm are doing now. But whatever comes, we face it together. Nothing is over yet."

I met her gaze, feeling the heat rise up in my veins, letting it burn away the fear and uncertainty for now. Ember was here. I had lost a great deal—we all had—but at least the dragon I loved was still beside me. And I knew she would be there until the final battle with Talon loomed on the horizon. It was closer than ever. For better or worse, tonight the countdown had begun, and we were all rushing toward that final confrontation.

"Talon made a mistake last night," Ember murmured. "They didn't manage to kill us. And now we know what we're up against." Her eyes gleamed, fiery and determined, and for a moment, I could see the dragon, beautiful and terrible, overlaid like a second skin. "I think it's time that we took the fight to them."

EPILOGUE

DANTE

You failed, Dante.

Standing outside the doors to the Elder Wyrm's office, my hands shook as I reached for the gold handles, hearing the echo of her words in my head, making my stomach turn over.

Failure. I had failed. Talon, the Elder Wyrm herself, had entrusted me with this assignment, and I hadn't been able to complete it. It didn't matter that we had decimated St. George. It didn't matter that their numbers had been reduced to a handful. *Almost* was not success. My mission was the complete and utter destruction of the base and every living thing in it. If even one soldier survived, that was a failure in the eyes of Talon. Worse, nearly all the vessels in my command had been destroyed, including the Adult that was supposed to have ensured our victory. I didn't know what had gone wrong. But somehow, Ember and Cobalt's arrival had thrown everything into chaos, and they had snatched victory from the jaws of defeat.

Ember, I thought furiously. *I won't forgive this. Next time, you can expect no mercy from me.*

If there was a next time. With a deep breath, I turned the handle and walked into the office of the Elder Wyrm.

Like many other times, she was standing at the windows,

gazing down at the city far below, and she didn't turn when I walked into the room. Heart pounding, I crossed the floor until I was a few feet behind her and clasped my hands together, waiting for her to acknowledge me.

"The Western chapterhouse still stands, Dante."

I swallowed the dryness in my throat. "Yes, ma'am," I replied simply. "Ember and Cobalt arrived at the last minute with a group of rogues and were able to rout the attack."

The Elder Wyrm was silent for a moment, then gave a dry chuckle.

"And so you continue to defy me, daughter," she said, sounding more amused than angry. "Very well. Play your games, if you like. It will make no difference in the end."

She turned from the window then, and I cast my gaze to the floor as those piercing eyes fixed on me. "Do not worry, Dante," she said, and my legs nearly gave out in relief. "The survival of a single Order chapterhouse is a minor thing. St. George is truly broken now. They have scattered to the winds, and it will take a miracle to bring them back together." She smiled, and it held the weight of a thousand years behind it. "Our last opposition is no more. The Order of St. George was the final obstacle that needed to be removed. Now, nothing stands between us and our day of triumph. It is time to move on to the final phase."

★ ★ ★ ★ ★

Thank you for reading LEGION!
Don't miss The Talon Saga's fiery conclusion,
as dragons clash and the world burns…
INFERNO
only from Julie Kagawa and Harlequin TEEN!

EMBER

Tramping through the jungle for hours on end was not my idea of a good time.

It was hot, insanely so. Normally, heat didn't bother me, but the humidity level beneath the canopy had been cranked up to like two hundred percent. It felt as if I was walking, and breathing, through a wet, heavy blanket. My clothes—the olive drab shirt, cargo pants, even the socks in my combat boots—were damp with sweat, and tying my hair back did not prevent it from hanging in my eyes and sticking to my forehead. Insects droned in my ears, in the trees, everywhere around us—a constant, high-pitched buzz that faded into background noise unless you concentrated on it.

Behind me, Garret moved like a shadow, making virtually no sound as he glided through the undergrowth. I couldn't see him without turning, but I knew he was there. I could sense him—the steady rise and fall of his breath, the heartbeat thumping quietly beneath his jacket. Lately, I didn't even have to look at him to know where he was; his presence, both in my thoughts and in the world around me, became more prominent with every passing day. I knew he was worried. Not for us and our situation, though as always he remained hypervigilant and alert to our surroundings. But I knew his thoughts were back home, with the Order and the people we'd left behind. I couldn't blame him. Across a continent, a war was brewing. Back in the States, Talon was on the move, and though we didn't know their plans, we did know they had a massive clone army, a huge force of dragons bred for war, programmed to follow orders without fail. They had already used that army to wipe out the Order of St. George, striking a devastating blow against their greatest enemies, nearly destroying them completely. The Order, what was left of it, was in shambles. Talon stood unopposed to do whatever horrible thing they were planning. And where were we? Tromping through the deepest, darkest parts of the Amazon jungle, fighting bugs and vines and heat exhaustion, searching for something that should not exist.

Ahead of us, Riley followed our guide down a narrow, winding trail that could barely be called a path, cutting through vines and undergrowth with machete in hand. Though the rogue was putting up a good front, he was worried, too. Garret wasn't the only one to leave people behind. Riley's underground—his network of rogues and the hatchlings who'd escaped Talon—was in danger, too, as the organization was systematically eliminating every dragon who didn't conform to Talon. This trip almost hadn't happened. Riley had been extremely reluctant to leave his underground, consenting only when Wes and Jade both told him to go, that they would take care of the hatchlings and the rogues. In the end, Riley had agreed, but I could tell he wanted to get this over with as soon as possible and return to the network he'd left behind. I knew Garret felt the same about the Order.

But this was important. Whether we liked it or not, the war with Talon had come, and the organization was poised to unleash destruction upon everything we cared about. We needed all the allies we could get, and if this lead turned out to be real, then it just might give us a chance. Not a great one, but it would level the playing field a bit.

The guide, tall and rawboned and carrying a machete much like Riley's, suddenly paused. The trail ahead had been blocked by a tangle of vines and branches, so with a quick "One moment, please," he went to work hacking through the undergrowth. Riley, rather than standing back, joined him, and together they started slicing through the tangle in short order.

After stripping off my rucksack, I rummaged in the pocket and pulled out a canteen, feeling the heat and humidity pulsing from my skin. I took a few sips, then handed the container to Garret, who accepted it with a nod of thanks.

"Well…" I sighed, leaning back against a thick, gnarled tree. Above me, the trunk soared into the air until it joined the canopy far overhead. Insects flitted through the branches, and only a few patches of sunlight made their way down from the blanket of leaves above us. "This isn't the way I thought I would spend my weekend." I took a breath, and it was like breathing the air in a steam room. "Air-conditioning is a wonderful, wonderful invention, Garret," I told him. "How did we ever get by without it?"

Garret offered a faint smile as he handed the canteen back. He looked natural out here, in his boots and camo jacket, pale blond hair cut short. He looked like a soldier. "I thought dragons liked the heat," he said with a glance at the guide, still whacking vegetation with Riley. I sniffed, crouching down to stuff the canteen back in the rucksack.

"Yes, well, most people think we like sitting on piles of gold in dark, dreary caves. You don't see us doing that anymore, do you? Especially since we can track our funds from a computer, in the comfort of an air-conditioned office." A mosquito the size of my thumb landed on my arm, looking hungry, and I slapped it away. "And maybe it's made us soft, but I for one am glad that we've caught on to the conveniences of modern life. Air-conditioning and indoor plumbing beats sitting in a cave full of treasure any day."

Garret's voice turned serious. "Not all dragons think that apparently."

"No." I shivered a little as I rose and pulled the rucksack over my shoulders once more. The jungle seemed to close around us, reminding me why we were here. "I guess not."

Riley walked back to us, breathing hard. He had tied a bandanna around his head to keep his hair back, but a few dark strands had poked out and stuck to his forehead. The white tank beneath his open, long-sleeved shirt was streaked with moisture. For the briefest of moments, in the shadows of the canopy, his eyes glimmered gold.

Warmth fluttered somewhere deep inside me, like a candle dancing in the breeze. The *Sallith'tahn*, the life-mate bond, telling me that Riley—or rather Cobalt—was my Draconic other half. But it was weaker now. Barely a flicker, when before it had been a rushing, surging inferno of heat and desire. I had broken the *Sallith'tahn*. I, as a dragon, had decided to be with someone else. To choose love over instinct. I suspected the *Sallith'tahn* thing would never truly go away, and I doubted Riley would ever forgive me for rejecting him but, for now at least, the war and the threat of Talon took precedence over our petty squabbles and jealousy. We had to work together to survive. Alone, we didn't stand a chance.

"Our guide says we're almost there," Riley informed us, unscrewing the cap of his own canteen. "Another forty-five minutes to an hour, according to him." He took a few quick swallows from the container, then raked a sleeve across his face. "Man, I forgot how sucky the jungle is. Good thing Wes isn't here. He'd never stop complaining. Still have that compass, St. George?"

"Yes." Garret frowned slightly. "Why? We have a guide."

"Not anymore." Riley turned to glare at the guide, who was still hacking through vegetation and deliberately not looking at us. "There's some kind of statue marking the trail about a mile from here, and from then on, we're on our own. He says the path keeps going, but he flat-out refuses to venture beyond that point."

"He's leaving?" I scowled. "That wasn't the deal."

"Apparently, it was." Riley replaced the cap and slung the canteen over his shoulder, his own expression disgusted. "He said he would take us as far as he could. Well, that's as far as he's willing to take us."

"Why?"

"Because, in his own words, beyond the statue is the territory of a god."

A chill crept up my back, even in the suffocating heat, and I swallowed. "Then I guess we're on the right trail."

"Yep." Riley rubbed the back of his skull, looking both nervous and annoyed about being nervous. "Never did like the idea of meeting a god. Somehow, I get the feeling gods just don't like me very much."

"You?" Garret asked, the hint of a smile crossing his face. "With your complete disdain for authority figures? I don't see why that would be."

"Ha, ha, laugh now, St. George. We'll see how funny it is when we're all piles of dust being scattered by the wind."

We started off again, walking single file down the narrow path, following our guide toward the territory of a god.

If possible, the jungle got even thicker, more tangled, with branches and vines clawing at us from either side of the trail. Our guide came to a sudden stop and murmured something I couldn't understand. Ahead, sitting to one side of the tiny path, a stone statue rose out of a cluster of vines and roots, the snarling visage of some scaly, horned creature peering out at us.

Riley cocked his head at the statue. "Huh," he remarked. "Is that supposed to be a dragon? It looks like a wild pig had a baby with an alligator."

I shook my head at him. "Can you be any more irreverent? I haven't been struck by lightning on this trip yet."

The guide turned, his dark face solemn in the shadows of the undergrowth. "This is as far as I go," he said. "From this point on, you only have to follow the path. I will wait here until your business is complete."

Riley frowned. "I thought you said you served this master or god or whatever you call him."

"I do. But I am simply his voice outside of the jungle. Only those who have been invited can step into his territory unharmed. Therefore, I will wait for you here. If you do not return by sunset, I will know you are not coming back. Now, go." He nodded down the trail. "My master is not a patient god. It would be unwise to incur his wrath."

We went, slipping deeper into the jungle, venturing into the unknown. Into the territory of a god.

Almost immediately, I knew something was wrong. My dragon instincts stirred, edgy and restless, though I couldn't see anything unusual. But I could feel eyes on me. I could sense something watching us, stalking us down the trail, keeping just out of sight.

Garret moved closer, walking by my side, even down the

narrow path. His eyes were hard as he murmured, "Something is following us."

"Yeah," I whispered back. My hand twitched, wanting to reach for the Glock hidden beneath my shirt, but I didn't want to give away that we knew we were being stalked. "Should we tell Riley?"

"He knows," Garret replied, keeping his gaze straight ahead. His posture was calm, but I could sense the tension in him, ready to explode into action. "Stay alert. Be ready to move when it happens."

As he said this, we entered a clearing, and figures melted out of the undergrowth. Tall, slender, with only a strip of cloth tied around their waists, they moved like ghosts, making virtually no noise as they stepped forward. Before we could say anything, they had surrounded us, and a dozen bone-tipped spears were leveled at our hearts.

★ ★ ★ ★ ★

Turn the page for a special sneak peek at
SHADOW OF THE FOX,
the first book in a magical new series
from Julie Kagawa and Harlequin TEEN!

CHAPTER ONE:
BEGINNINGS AND
ENDINGS

It was raining the day Suki came to the Palace of the Sun, and it was raining the night that she died.

"You're the new maid, are you?" a woman with a narrow, bony face demanded, looking her up and down. Suki shivered, feeling cold rainwater sliding down her back, dripping from her hair to spatter the fine wood floor. The head housekeeper sniffed. "Well, you're no beauty, that's for sure. But, no matter—Miss Satomi's last maid was pretty as a butterfly, with half the wit." She leaned closer, narrowing her eyes. "Tell me, girl—they said you were running your father's shop before you came here. Do you have an intelligent head on your shoulders? Or is it as full of air as the last girl's?"

Suki chewed her lip and looked down at the floor. She *had* been helping to run her father's shop for the better part of a year. The only child of a celebrated flute maker, she was often responsible for dealing with the customers when her father was at work, too engrossed in his task to eat or talk to anyone until his latest piece was done. Suki could read, and do numbers as well as any boy, but being a girl, she was not allowed to inherit her father's business or learn his craft. Mura Akihito was still strong, but he was getting old, his once nimble fingers stiffening with age and hard use. Rather than marry Suki off, her father had used his meager influence to get her a job in the imperial palace, so she would be well taken care of when he passed away. Suki missed home, and she desperately wondered if her father was all right without her, but she knew this was what he wanted. "I don't know, ma'am," she whispered.

"Hmph. Well, we'll see soon enough. But I would think of something better to say to Miss Satomi. Otherwise your stay will be even shorter than your predecessor's. Now," she continued, "go to the kitchen and fetch Miss Satomi's tea. The cook will tell you where to take it."

A few minutes later, Suki walked down the veranda, carrying a full tea tray and trying to remember the directions she'd been given. The Emperor's Palace of the Sun was a miniature city in itself; the main palace, where the Emperor and his family lived, loomed over everything, but a labyrinth of walls, structures and fortifications lay between the keep and the inner wall, all designed to protect the Emperor and confuse an invading army. Nobles, courtiers and samurai paraded to and fro down the walkways, dressed in robes of brilliant color and design: white silk with delicate sakura petals, or a vivid red with golden chrysanthemum blooms. None of the nobles she passed spared her a second glance. Only the most influential families resided this close to the Emperor; the closer you lived to the main keep of the palace, the more important you were.

Suki wandered down the maze of verandas, the knots in her stomach growing tighter as she searched in vain for the right quarters. Everything looked the same. Gray-roofed buildings with bamboo and paper walls, and wooden veran-das between them so the nobles wouldn't sully their clothes in the dirt and dew. Blue-tiled turrets towered over her in regal splendor, and dozens of different songbirds trilled from the branches of the perfectly groomed trees, but the tight-ness in Suki's chest and the churning of her insides made it impossible to appreciate any of it.

A high, clear note cut through the air, rising above the rooftops, making her freeze in her tracks. It wasn't a bird, though a thrush perched in a nearby bush warbled loudly in reply. It was a sound Suki knew instantly, having memo-rized each and every note. How many times had she heard it, drifting up from her father's workshop? The sweet, haunt-ing melody of a flute.

Mesmerized, she followed the sound, momentarily for-getting her duties and that her new mistress would almost certainly be very annoyed that her tea was so late. The song drew her forward, a keening, mournful melody, like say-ing goodbye or watching autumn fade. Suki could tell that whoever was playing the instrument was skilled indeed; so much emotion lay between the notes of the song, it was as if she was hearing their soul.

So hypnotized was she by the sound of the flute, she forgot to look where she was going. Rounding a corner, Suki squeaked in dismay as a young noble in sky blue robes blocked her path, a bamboo flute held to his lips. The tea-pot rattled and the cups shook perilously as she swerved to avoid him, desperately trying not to spill the contents. The sound of the flute ceased as the samurai, much to her amaze-ment, turned and put a hand out to steady the tray before it toppled to the veranda.

"Careful there." His voice was high and clear. "Don't

want to drop anything—that would be an awful mess. Are you all right?"

Suki stared at him. He was the most handsome man she had ever seen. *No, not handsome*, she decided. *Beautiful*. His broad shoulders filled the robe he wore, but his features were graceful and delicate, like a willow tree in the spring. Instead of a samurai's topknot, his hair was long and straight, falling well past his shoulders, and was pure white, the color of mountain snow. Even more amazing, he was smiling at her— not the cold, amused smirk of most nobles and samurai, but a real smile that reached the mirthful crescents of his eyes.

"Please excuse me," the man said, releasing the tray and taking a quick step back. His expression was calm, not irritated at all. "That was my fault, planting myself in the middle of the walk, not thinking anyone could be rushing around the corner with a tea tray."

Suki opened her mouth twice before anything came out. "Please forgive me, my lord." Her voice was a whisper. Nobles did not speak like this to peasants, even she knew that. "I am Suki, and I am only a maid. Please don't trouble yourself with the likes of me."

The noble chuckled. "It is no trouble, Suki-san," he said. "I often forget where I am when I am playing." He raised the flute, making her heart leap. "Please do not think any more of it. You may return to your duties."

He stepped aside for her to pass, but Suki didn't move, unable to tear her gaze from the instrument in his slender hand. It was made of polished wood, dark and rich and straighter than an arrow, with a distinctive band of gold wood around one end. She knew she shouldn't speak to the noble, that he could order her flogged, imprisoned, even executed if he wished it, but words escaped her all the same. "You play magnificently, my lord," she whispered. "Forgive me. I know it is not my place to say anything, but my father would be proud."

He cocked his head, a flicker of surprise crossing his beautiful face. "Your father?" he asked, as understanding dawned in his eyes. "You are Mura Akihito's daughter?"

"*Hai.*"

He smiled and gave her the barest of nods. "The song is only as beautiful as the instrument," he told her. "When you see your father again, tell him that I am honored to possess such a masterpiece."

Suki's throat closed up, and her eyes grew hot and blurry. The noble politely turned away, feigning interest in a cherry blossom tree, giving her time to compose herself. "Ah, but perhaps you are lost?" he inquired after a moment, examining a chrysalis on one of the slender branches. Turning back, his slender brows rose, but Suki caught no derision in his stance or voice, only amusement, as one might have when speaking to a wandering cat. "The Emperor's palace can be dazzling indeed to the uninitiated. Who's quarters are you assigned to, Suki-san? Perhaps I can show you the way."

"L-Lady Satomi, my lord," Suki stammered, truly stunned by his kindness. She knew she should bow, but she was terrified she would spill the tea. "Please forgive me. I have come to the palace only today, and everything is very confusing."

A slight frown crossed the noble's face, making Suki's heart nearly stop in her chest, thinking she had offended him. "I see," he murmured, mostly to himself. "Yet another maid, Lady Satomi? How many do you need?"

Before Suki could wonder what that meant, he shook himself and smiled once more. "Well, fortune favors you, Suki-san. Lady Satomi's residence isn't far." He raised a billowy sleeve, pointing an elegant finger down the walkway.

"Go left around this building, then walk straight to the very end. It will be the last doorway on the right."

"Thank you, my lord," Suki whispered. Her hands trembled, making the teapot vibrate on the tray.

"Daisuke-san!" A woman's voice echoed down the veranda before Suki could even whisper her thanks, and the man turned his beautiful face away. Moments later, a trio of noblewomen in elegant green and gold robes sashayed around the building and gave him mock frowns as they hurried forward.

"There you are, Daisuke-san," one of them huffed. "Where have you been? We are going to be late for Hanoe-san's poetry recital. Oh," she said, catching sight of Suki. "What is this? Daisuke-san, don't tell me you were here all this time, talking to a maid."

"And why not?" Daisuke's tone was wry. "A maid's conversation can be as interesting as any noblewoman's."

The three women giggled as if that were the funniest thing they had ever heard. Suki didn't see what was so amusing. "Oh, Taiyo Daisuke, you say the most wicked things," one of them chided from behind a white fan painted with cherry blossoms. "Come, now. We really must go. You," she said, directing her gaze to Suki, "get back to your duties. Why are you just standing there gaping? Shoo!"

As quickly as she could without spilling the tea, Suki hurried away. But her heart still pounded, and for some reason she couldn't catch her breath. *Taiyo.* Taiyo was the name of the Imperial family. Daisuke-sama was of the Sun Clan, one of the most powerful families in Iwagoto, the blood of the Emperor himself. The funny feeling in her stomach intensified, and her thoughts became a swarm of moths, fluttering around the dazzling memory of his smile and the melody from her father's flute.

Somehow, she found her way to the correct door, at the very end of the veranda, looking over the magnificent gardens of the palace. The shoji panel was open, and Suki could smell the smoky hint of burning incense wafting from the darkened interior. Creeping inside the room, she peered around for her new mistress but saw no one. Despite the nobles' unified preference for simplicity, this apartment was lavishly cluttered. Ornamental screens turned the room into a small maze, and tatami mats lined the entire floor, thick and soft beneath her feet. Paper was everywhere; origami sheets of every style and texture lay in piles around the apartment. Folded paper monkeys, cranes, flowers and tigers peered at her from atop every flat surface, dominating the room. Suki brushed a herd of origami horses from the table so that she could set the tea down.

"Mai-chan?" A gossamer voice drifted out of the adjoining room, and the sound of silk rustled over the floor. "Is that you? Where have you been? I was getting worried that you— Oh."

A woman appeared in the doorway, and for a moment, they stared at one another, Suki's mouth hanging open in amazement.

If Taiyo Daisuke was the most handsome man she had ever met, this was the most elegantly beautiful woman in the whole palace. Her billowing robes were red with silver, gold and green butterflies swarming the front. Shimmering black hair was beautifully styled atop her head, pierced with red and gold chopsticks and ivory combs. Dark eyes in a flawless porcelain face regarded Suki curiously.

"Hello," the woman said, and Suki quickly closed her mouth. "May I inquire as to who you are?"

"I…I'm Suki," the girl stammered. "I'm your new maid."

"I see." The woman's lips curved in a faint smile. Suki was sure that if her teeth showed, they would light up the room. "Come here, if you would, little Suki-chan. Please don't step on anything."

Suki obeyed, placing her feet carefully to avoid squashing any paper creatures, and stood before Lady Satomi.

The woman struck her across the face with her open palm.

Pain exploded behind her eye, and she collapsed to the floor, too stunned to even gasp. Blinking back tears, she put her hand to her cheek and gazed blankly up at Lady Satomi, who loomed over her, smiling.

"Do you know why I did that, little Suki-chan?" she asked, and now she did show her teeth. She reminded Suki of a grinning skull.

"N-no, my lady," she murmured, as her numb cheek started to burn.

"Because, I called for Mai-chan, not you," the lady replied in a relentlessly cheerful voice. "You might be a stupid country girl, Suki-chan, but that does not excuse your complete ignorance. You must come only when called, is that understood?"

"Yes, my lady."

"Smile, Suki-chan," Satomi suggested. "If you smile, perhaps I can forget you have the accent of a sweaty country barbarian and the face of an ox. It will be dreadfully difficult not to loathe you on sight, but I will do my best. Isn't that generous of me, Suki-chan?"

Suki, not knowing what to say to this, kept her mouth shut and thought of Daisuke-sama.

"Isn't that generous of me, Suki-chan?" Satomi repeated, an edge to her voice now.

Suki swallowed hard. "*Hai*, Lady Satomi."

Satomi sighed. "You've smashed my creations." She pouted, and Suki glanced down at the origami creatures crushed by her body. The lady sniffed and turned away. "I shall be very angry if you do not replace them. There is a quaint little shop in the Wind district that sells the most delicate lavender sheets. If you run, you should catch them before they close."

Suki gazed through an open screen at the storm clouds roiling above the palace. Thunder rumbled as silver-blue strands chased each other through the sky. "Yes, Lady Satomi."

★ ★ ★

The passing days made Suki long for her father's shop, for the quiet comfort of sweeping, stitching torn clothing and cooking meals three times a day. For the customers who barely gave her a second glance, concerned only with her father and his work. She'd thought it would be easy enough to be the maid to a great lady, to help her dress and run her errands and see to the mundane little tasks that were beneath the notice of the nobility. Perhaps that was how it should have been—certainly, the other maids did not seem to share her plight. Indeed, they seemed to go out of their way to avoid her, as if associating with Lady Satomi's maid would attract the ire of her mistress. In some ways, Suki couldn't blame them.

Lady Satomi was a nightmare, a beautiful nightmare of silk, makeup and heady perfume. Nothing Suki did suited the woman. No matter how she scrubbed or cleaned, the laundry never met with Satomi's satisfaction. The tea Suki brewed was too weak, too strong, too sweet, always too something. No amount of cleaning sufficed within Lady Satomi's chambers—there was always a speck of dirt to be found, a tatami mat out of place, an origami creature in the wrong spot. And each failure brought a little smile from the lady and a shockingly powerful slap.

No one cared, of course. The other maids looked away from her bruises, and the guards did not look at her at all. Suki did not dare complain; not only was Lady Satomi a great and powerful lady, she was the favored concubine of the Emperor himself. To speak poorly of her would be insulting Taiyo no Genjiro, the great Son of Heaven, and would result in a flogging, public humiliation or worse.

The only thing that saved Suki from complete despair was the thought of running into Daisuke-sama again. He was a great noble, of course, far above her station, and would not care about the troubles of a lowly maid. But even catching a glimpse of him would be enough. She looked for him on the verandas and the paths to and from Lady Satomi's chambers, but the beautiful noble was nowhere to be seen. Later, she learned through servant gossip that Taiyo Daisuke had left the Palace of the Sun not long after she arrived, heading off on one of his mysterious pilgrimages across the country. Perhaps, Suki thought, she would catch a glimpse of him when he returned. Perhaps she would hear her father's flute again, and follow it until she found him on the verandas, his long white hair flowing behind him.

A ringing slap drew her from her daydream, knocking her to the floor. "Oh dear. You are such a *clumsy* girl." Lady Satomi stood over her, resplendent in her stunning silk robes. "Get up, Suki-chan. I have a task for you."

In her arms, the lady carried a coil of fine silken cord, bloodred in color. As Suki staggered to her feet, the rope was thrust into her arms. "You are such a feebleminded little thing, aren't you? I despair of ever making a good maid out of you. But surely even you can take care of this one small task. Take this rope to the storehouse in the eastern gardens, the one past the lake. Surely you can do that much? And *do* stop crying, girl. What will people think of me, if my maid goes around weeping everywhere?"

★ ★ ★

Suki awoke to darkness with a throbbing in her skull. Her vision swam, and there was a weird coppery taste in the back of her throat. Overhead, thunder growled, and a sharp, ozone-scented wind blew into her face. The floor beneath her felt cold, and hard, stony edges were pressing uncomfortably into her stomach and cheek. Blinking, she tried pushing herself upright, but her arms would not respond. A moment later, she realized they were tied behind her back.

Ice flooded her veins. She rolled to her side and attempted to stand, but her knees and ankles were bound as well—with the same rope she'd brought to the storehouse, she realized—and a rag was stuffed into her mouth, tied with a strip of cloth. With a muffled shriek, she thrashed wildly, writhing on the stones. Pain shot up her arms as she scraped along the ground, cutting her skin on rock edges and leaving bits of flesh behind, but the ropes held firm. Panting, exhausted, she slumped against the stones in defeat, then raised her head to gaze at her surroundings.

She lay in the center of a courtyard, but not the pristine, elegant courtyard of the Sun Palace, with its swept white stones and trimmed bushes. This one was dark, rocky, ruined. Dead leaves and broken stones were scattered throughout, and in the flickering light overhead, she could see the glint of eyes atop the walls—dozens of crows, watching her with their feathers spiked out against the wind.

"Hello, Suki-chan," said an eerily cheerful voice somewhere behind her. "Did you finally wake up?"

Suki craned her head back. Lady Satomi stood over her, looming against the night, her hair unbound and tossed by the wind, the sleeves of her red-and-black kimono fluttering like sails. Her eyes were hard, and her lips were curled in a tiny smile. Gasping, Suki flopped to a sitting position, wanting to cry for help, to ask what was happening. Was this some terrible punishment for disappointing her mistress, for not cleaning, fetching or serving to her standards? She tried pleading with her eyes, hot tears leaking down her cheeks, but the noblewoman only wrinkled her nose.

"Such a lazy girl, and so fragile. I cannot abide your constant weeping." Lady Satomi sniffed and moved a few feet away, not looking at her anymore. "Well, be happy, Suki-chan. For today your misery will come to an end. Though it will mean I must acquire yet another maid—what *is* it with all these serving girls running away like mice? Ungrateful wretches. No sense of responsibility at all." She gave a long-suffering sigh, then looked at the clouds as lightning flickered and the wind picked up. "Where is that oni?" she muttered. "After all the trouble I went through for a suitable compensation, I shall be very cross if he does not arrive before the storm."

Oni? Suki must've been hearing things. Oni were great and terrible demons that came from Jigoku, the realm of evil. There were countless stories of brave samurai slaying oni, sometimes armies of oni, but they were myths and legends. Oni were the creatures parents threatened wayward children with—*don't wander too close to the woods or an oni might get you. Listen to your elders, or an oni will reach up from beneath the floorboards and drag you down to Jigoku.* Scary warnings for children and monstrous foes for legendary samurai, but not creatures that walked Ningen-do, the mortal realm.

Thunder boomed, and in between the blinding flash of white, a great horned creature appeared at the edge of the courtyard.

Suki screamed. The gag muffled it, but she kept screaming until she was out of breath, gasping and choking into the cloth. She tried to flee, and fell hard against the stones, striking her chin on the rock, but she barely felt the pain. Lady Satomi's lips moved as she gave her a withering look, probably chastising her shrillness, but Suki's mind couldn't register anything but the huge demon, for it could only be a thing of nightmares, prowling forward into the torchlight. The monster that shouldn't exist.

It was massive, standing a good fifteen feet overhead, and just as terrible and fearsome as the legends described. Its skin was a dark crimson, the color of blood, and a wild black mane tumbled down its back and shoulders. Sharp yellow tusks curled from its jaw, and its eyes glowed like hot coals as the demon lumbered forward, making the ground shake. The tiny part of Suki's brain not frozen in terror recalled that, in the stories, oni dressed in loincloths made of great striped beasts, but this demon wore plates of lacquered armor; the red shoulder pads, thigh guards and bracers of the samurai when they rode into battle. True to the myths, however, it carried a giant iron-studded club—a tetsubo—in one hand, swinging it to a shoulder as if it weighed no more than an ink stick.

"There you are, Yaburama." Lady Satomi lifted her chin as the oni stopped in front of her. "I am aware that time in

Jigoku doesn't exist, and it is said that one day is akin to eight hundred years in the mortal realm, but punctuality is a wonderful attribute, something we can all aspire to."

The oni chuckled, a deep, guttural sound emerging between his fangs. "Not my fault," it rumbled, its terrible voice making the air shiver. "I had to wait for these worthless things to catch up."

Behind the demon, spreading around him like a colony of ants, a horde of smaller monsters appeared. Standing only a few inches above the knee, their skin different shades of blue, red and green, they looked like tiny oni themselves, except for their huge flared ears and maniacal grins. They spotted Suki and began edging forward, cackling and licking their pointed teeth. She shrieked into the gag and tried wiggling away, but got no farther than a landed fish.

The oni growled a warning, deep as distant thunder, and the horde skittered back. "Is that mine?" the demon asked, its glowing crimson gaze falling on Suki. "It looks tasty." The creature took a step toward her, and she nearly fainted on the spot.

"Patience, Yaburama." Lady Satomi held out a hand, stopping it. It narrowed its eyes and bared its teeth slightly, but the noblewoman didn't seem disturbed. "You can have your payment in a moment," she went on. "I just want to make certain you know why you were summoned. That you know what you must do."

"How could I not," the oni replied, sounding impatient. "The Dragon is rising. Another thousand years has passed in this pathetic excuse for a realm, and the night of the wish is nearly upon us. There is only one reason a mortal would summon me into Ningen-do at this time." A look of amused contempt crossed its brutish face. "Worry not, human. I'll get you the scroll." The burning red gaze slid back to Suki, and the creature smiled slowly, showing fangs. "After I collect my payment."

"Good." Lady Satomi stepped back, as the first drops of rain began to fall. "I am counting on you, Yaburama. I am sure there will be others looking for the scroll, as well. You know what to do if you meet them. Well..." She opened a pink parasol and swung it over her head. "I leave it to you. Enjoy."

As sheets of water began creeping across the courtyard, Lady Satomi turned and began walking away. Suki screamed into the gag and threw herself after the noblewoman, crying and begging, praying to the Kami and anyone else who would hear. *Please*, she thought desperately. *Please, I cannot die like this. Not like this.*

Lady Satomi paused and glanced back at her with a smile. "Oh, don't be sad, little Suki-chan," she whispered. "This is your proudest moment. You will be the catalyst to usher in a whole new era. This empire, the whole world, will change, because of your sacrifice today. See?" The lady tilted her head, observing her as if she were a whimpering puppy. "You've actually become useful. Surely that is enough for someone like you."

Behind Suki, the ground trembled, and a huge claw closed on her legs, curved talons sinking into her skin. She screamed and thrashed, yanking at the ropes, trying to writhe out of the demon's grip, but there was no escape. Lady Satomi sniffed, turned and continued on, her parasol bobbing through the rain, as Suki was pulled toward the oni, the minor demons shrieking and dancing around her.

Help me. Someone, please, help me! Daisuke-sama... Abruptly, her thoughts went to the noble, to his handsome face and gentle smile, though she knew he would not be coming. No one was coming, because no one cared about the death of a lowly servant girl. *Father*, Suki thought in numb despair, *I'm sorry. I didn't mean to leave you behind.*

Deep inside, anger flickered, momentarily snuffing the fear. It was terribly unfair, being killed by a demon before she could do anything. She was only a servant, but she had hoped to marry a good man, raise a family, leave something behind that mattered. *I'm not ready*, Suki thought in desperation. *I'm not ready to go. Please, not yet.*

Clawed fingers closed around her neck, and she was lifted up to face the oni's terrible, hungry smile. Its hot breath, smelling of smoke and rotten meat, blasted her face as the demon opened its jaws. Mercifully, the gods decided to intervene at that moment, and Suki finally fainted in terror, her consciousness leaving her body the moment before it was torn in half.

The scent of blood misted into the air, and the demons howled in glee. From Suki's mangled body, unseen by the horde and invisible to normal eyes, a small sphere of light rose slowly into the air. It hovered over the grisly scene, seeming to watch as the minor demons squabbled over scraps, Yaburama's booming roar rising into the night as he swatted them away. For a moment, it seemed torn between flying into the clouds or remaining where it was. Drifting aimlessly higher, it paused at a flash of color that gleamed through the rain, a pink parasol heading toward the gates of the castle. The sphere's blue-white glow flared into an angry red.

Zipping from the sky, the orb of light flew soundlessly over the head of the oni, dropped lower to the ground and slipped through the door to the castle just before it creaked shut, leaving the oni, the demons and the torn, murdered body of a servant girl behind.